Maisey Yates is a *New York Times* bestselling author of over one hundred romance novels. Whether she's writing stories about strong, hard-working cowboys, dissolute princes or multigenerational families, she loves getting lost in fictional worlds. An avid knitter, with a dangerous yarn addiction and an aversion to housework, Maisey lives with her husband and three kids in rural Oregon. Check out her website: maiseyyates.com.

Canadian **Dani Collins** knew in high school that she wanted to write romance for a living. Twenty-five years later, after marrying her high school sweetheart, having two kids with him, working at several generic office jobs and submitting countless manuscripts, she got The Call. Her first Mills & Boon novel won the Reviewers' Choice Award for Best First in Series from *RT Book Reviews*. She now works in her own office, writing romance.

A BRIDE FOR
THE LOST KING

MAISEY YATES

MARRIED FOR
ONE REASON ONLY

DANI COLLINS

MILLS & BOON

First Published in Great Britain 2021
by Mills & Boon, an imprint of HarperCollins*Publishers* Ltd,
1 London Bridge Street, London, SE1 9GF

www.harpercollins.co.uk

HarperCollins*Publishers*
1st Floor, Watermarque Building,
Ringsend Road, Dublin 4, Ireland

A Bride for the Lost King © 2021 Maisey Yates

Married for One Reason Only © 2021 Dani Collins

ISBN: 978-0-263-28255-9

07/21

MIX
Paper from
responsible sources
FSC™ C007454

This book is produced from independently certified FSC™ paper
to ensure responsible forest management.
For more information visit www.harpercollins.co.uk/green.

Printed and bound in Spain
by CPI, Barcelona

A BRIDE FOR
THE LOST KING

MAISEY YATES

MILLS & BOON

For Henry Cavill, in *The Witcher*,
who really made me think a lot about the virtues
of sword fighting.

CHAPTER ONE

"WHICH SWORD SHALL I take with me to meet your brother, Highness?" Agnes examined her wall of weapons critically.

She was the sworn protector of Lazarus, King of the secret kingdom at the center of the Dark Wood, in the country of Liri. A fairy tale, she would have said, something out of a picture book, until she had been brought to see it with her own eyes.

A country within a country, comprised of a village that looked as if it were part of another time, and a palace that was set deep within a mountain.

Of course, there were modern conveniences, even if hidden. Access to internet via fiber-optic cables, hot water and toaster pastries—which were her favorite.

The people in the wood were safe, kept so by the legends that surrounded it.

And outside was Liri.

Liri, ruled by King Alexius, Lazarus's brother. The brother he'd been separated from when he'd wandered into the woods as a boy and been half savaged by wolves, saved by Agamemnon, the ruler of the woods at the time.

In Lazarus he'd seen greatness. In him, he'd seen the salvation of his people, occupied and kept down by the Lirians, before they were driven to the brink of extinction.

As far as all the world knew, their kingdom did not exist.

And until a few weeks ago, the world had not known Lazarus existed.

He had traveled freely, under an assumed name, and no one had ever suspected he was the long-lost prince thought long-ago dead.

But Lazarus had been planning revenge against his family for years. In fact, he had been intent on stealing his brother's fiancée. Literally stealing her. Right from the woods, until an interaction between the two of them had stayed his hand.

He had promised the previous leader, Agamemnon, that he would avenge the people. For as she was sworn to Lazarus, so was he to the previous leader of the people. He had promised that he would return their people to their rightful place on the throne. For it was not Lazarus and Alex's family who held that right, but the people of the trees. They had been killed. They had been weakened and shunted off into the forest, but they had not diminished. No, there they had grown. She was not of them. Not by blood. But it didn't matter. Not to them. It was the outcasts that they took. Those who were left to their own devices. Those who were in need.

Like her.

"You shall not be bringing a sword, Agnes."

When Lazarus made a pronouncement, in that deep voice like velvet dipped in gold, she never argued.

She liked the way he said her name. *Ah-nes.* As if she were something exotic and not something neighboring an agate. Which was how she always thought of her name.

But she did *not* like what he'd just said.

"I cannot travel without a sword, Highness, for it is my sworn duty to protect you. A blood oath bonds us." She tilted her chin upward, meeting his gaze.

Lazarus was tall, over six-five, with the sculpted face of an avenging angel. At least in part. It was his scars—deep, lashing and cruel, covering half of that face—that gave him the manner of devil. Dark eyes, hard as obsidian, and a mouth that turned over into cruel with the slightest curve. He was not a man who looked as if he needed protection.

But in her world, in *their* world, in the wood, when a person was saved from death, they swore fealty to their savior. As she had done to Lazarus when she was just sixteen, and in the eight years since.

They were bonded by something deeper than blood. He had risked his life to save hers. Her blood, her very breath, belonged to him.

Though she needed a sword if she were to be effective.

"Bringing a sword into the palace is an act of war, Agnes," he said, as if she did not know.

"It is an act of caution. You do not know your brother well."

Agnes could not deny that she felt a slight bit of relief hearing him speak in a way that seemed to indicate he would not be waging war.

His aim had shifted since the time he had decided to leave the forest and seek his revenge on Alexius. That first day, that meeting, she had been hiding in the woods. In the darkness with her sword ready to be drawn. But no fighting had ensued. They had simply talked. And in the times since, Lazarus had been opaque. Regarding his plans to return to the kingdom of his heart, of his blood, and regarding his intent when it came to his brother, Alexius.

If she were a woman who believed she could know the mysteries of a man like Alexius, she might have taken his connecting with his brother at face value.

But she was not. So, she did not.

"Well, I suppose a dagger..."

"We do not come to make *open* war," he continued. "Revenge must be accomplished quietly."

She stopped, the hair on the back of her neck standing on end. "I thought you were through with revenge."

"Did I say so?"

"No, but you...you spoke to him. You advised him to stay on with...with Tinley. To love her. I heard you."

"It is true," he said, "I did. And it softened what I am willing to consider. But he will still have a difficult choice to make. Reconciliation. And recognition of me as King. Or..."

"King?"

"Over Liri and the wood. To give our people that which they've been denied."

"And why didn't you tell me this sooner?"

"My plans are not for you to know, little one."

"I wish you wouldn't call me that. I could cut down any man where he stands, whether he was anticipating the attack or not. Small though I may be, I am deadly."

"To be certain," he said. "But little all the same. And while your skill with a sword is greatly appreciated, Agnes, it is not what I need of you at this time."

"What is it you do need?"

"You've sworn your loyalty to me. Whatever my commandment, you shall fulfill, is that not the way?"

"Whatever your command," she confirmed. "My life is yours." And she meant it, from the deepest part of her soul.

"Good. You are not coming as my shield maiden."

She blinked, feeling off-balance. "Then what am I? If not your protector, then what am I?"

"You will be coming as my fiancée."

Agnes was stunned. She was… Well, she was *barely* a woman, in all actuality. She had been trained to follow the way of the sword. The way of battle. Her body was honed into one of ruthless athleticism, her instincts sharpened by years of training. Training that she had taken at Lazarus's own hand. She did not know feminine ways. And often felt outside of the groups of brightly dressed women in their kingdom.

But then, she was an outsider.

Saved by Lazarus. Brought here.

He had incapacitated the five men surrounding her with ruthless brutality and speed. And while she had been grateful, she had also been left standing there alone.

Except for him.

He was dressed nicely, black pants and a crisp white shirt that was still somehow clean in spite of what had occurred. His clothing was improbably civilized. The man himself had the look of a barbarian. Black hair cut to ruthless precision, broad shoulders. His sleeves were pushed up past his elbows, revealing well-muscled forearms.

He was terrifying and beautiful. A savior and a potential danger.

And her father was dead. And even though her immediate threat had been dispatched, the danger out there in the world for a sixteen-year-old girl who knew nothing of life, who knew nothing other than what her con man father had taught her... There was nothing good to be had. She had known of a great many things she could do to survive, but she was loath to do any of them.

And so, when the mighty warrior had turned to leave, she had followed.

"Where are you going?" she asked.

He didn't spare her a glance. "Back to my kingdom. At least, at some point today, I will be."

"Can I go with you?"

He had stopped. Then turned, regarding her with seriousness. And in that moment it had struck her that he was the most beautiful man she had ever seen. Beautiful and terrifying.

All at once.

"In my country there is a tradition. If one saves the life of another, that person swears that life to them. Your service. Is that the life you want?"

"Who talks like that?" she asked.

"I do." His accent was heavy, but beautiful.

"Are you a King of some kind?"

His lips curved. "Of some kind."

And she realized that she could be stepping out of one danger and into another entirely. But he had saved her life, and he didn't have to. So at the very least, he must not intend to kill her. As for the rest... Well, she could cope.

And it had turned out that Lazarus was all that he claimed to be. Especially when it came to his expectations for her. When it came to his adherence to tradition. He had helped her become a warrior, an option that she had not thought existed for a woman such as her. And so she had sworn her loyalty to him. To their country. She had changed her every thought and expectation about her future, all for him.

"Your fiancée," she said, feeling very much like she had reached the end of her loyalty in that moment. For that was... An impossibility. Something she knew was an impossibility. He was a King. She was a no one. From the streets of nowhere in particular. America originally, but then Italy, France, anywhere her father could run a scam. A girl who spoke bits and pieces of different languages but had never really owned any of them. Had never sworn allegiance to any one country, to any one leader. Until now. Until him.

And she had sworn with all of herself to protect him, because she could never be anything more.

It was foolish.

He was more than a man. He was something more

like a god. And he was untouchable. Especially for her. She didn't know his age. It had never seemed to matter. It just wasn't relevant. For he was more than she was. More than she ever could be.

Untouchable. Remote and unreachable.

"I'm sorry," she said. "I must've misunderstood."

"I think we both know you did not. Your senses are finely honed, thanks to my training."

"Yes. All glory to you," she said, barely able to keep the sarcasm from her tone. She did mean that. Typically.

"And so, you see, this is what must occur."

"No, I am afraid I do not see."

"You are my right hand, Agnes. And have been these many years. This is my sworn duty to this country. To lay claim to the throne."

Yes, she was his right hand. A tool. A weapon. A shield.

She was not a woman. Not to him.

And if Agnes had found it to be incredibly painful, it was only her problem. No one could solve it for her. And it was one she would simply have to bear. She had borne a great many disappointments in her life.

What was one more?

She loved him. With all that she was. Her soul, her heart, her sword. Her body.

She had discovered desire sparring with him, watching the play of his muscles as he moved. She had become acquainted with what it meant to be a woman.

He lit up the most womanly places in her, enflamed fantasies that she had not ever thought she'd entertained.

He did not see her as a woman, however, and she had accepted that.

She was his Agnes, and whatever she was, she was at least singular.

If she could never have him as a woman did a man, she would take that. She mattered. She was not like the endless parade of curvy beauties who had his attention for a night.

What she had was better.

She cared for him though, a great deal, even if she had accepted he would not be hers.

She had assumed then, wrongly, that Lazarus had decided on a path of forgiveness. And it occurred to her now that she didn't actually know what her King sought to do.

"It is not war. But a reckoning. A reclamation. Sad, indeed, that there may be bloodshed. Blood which I share."

Agnes thought of King Alexius's lovely bride-to-be. With her beautiful red hair. The future Queen Tinley. She was truly a lovely girl. And Agnes did not like the thought of something evil befalling her.

Agnes had only seen her once. From her position hiding in the forest. But Agnes had seen enough.

"You will spare Tinley."

"I will spare him if he will give in to what I ask. What I demand. But it is rare that a King will give up his kingdom."

"But you do not think the kingdom rightly belongs to him."

"It was stolen. By my family. By my bloodline. *Our*

bloodline. And it is up to me to make it right. I have sworn my loyalty here. Not to them. But here. To these people. It must be fulfilled. Those promises. That loyalty. If Alex wishes to make his reparation I do not see the point in taking anything by force. But if he does not…"

"I do understand," she said. "But it seems that there could be…"

"This is not a con, Agnes. There is no negotiation to be made. No side alleys that one can take." Her cheeks stung with heat.

And shame.

"I did not mean it in that way," she said.

Her father had been a con artist; she was not.

"I know you did not. I'm simply pointing out that we are made from different molds, you and I."

"I am made from the mold that you forged me in," she said, tilting her chin up. "And I do wish that you would allow me to bring a sword."

"As I said, we are not making open war."

"But we *are* making war."

The way that his mouth shifted seemed to confirm that, whether he would say it or not.

"You will be provided with a wardrobe. From Paris."

"What do I care of Paris?" she asked. "I've seen it."

"You've seen alleyways. It is not the same."

It was not like Lazarus to take pains to remind her where she had come from. He was not usually cool. But it didn't matter. It didn't matter what he said, when or how. Her loyalty was sworn. Her fate was set. Whether she agreed or not, it made no matter. Whether she wanted to or not, it had no bearing. She was Agnes, with no family name. Agnes of the Dark Wood. And nothing more.

Agnes, Shield Maiden of Lazarus.

And thus she would remain.

"Whatever you require of me," she said. "This I shall do."

"Then you shall come with me now," he said. "To Paris."

CHAPTER TWO

MONEY DIDN'T MATTER in the Dark Wood. But Lazarus himself knew how to wield it to his advantage, knew exactly how to slide into the moneyed circles that he sometimes must inhabit.

Agamemnon had taught him that a leader—even a leader who operated in secret—could not afford to be ignorant of the world. He had helped him create a background that would give him the necessary paperwork to travel. To exist. He had taught him about money, investments, which Lazarus had taken to easily. He had taken the money held by his people and increased it tenfold.

He moved seamlessly between the borders of the wood and other parts of Europe, where he slid off the mantle of guardian of the forest and put on a suit.

He did not take Agnes with him on such sojourns, not usually. Though, it was how he had found her in the first place. But it was the only time they had traveled in this manner together. She never liked it.

She didn't like to let him out of her sight.

She was dedicated, his warrior, though he knew that he didn't actually require her presence in order to keep himself safe. No, it was more to do with her. With protecting her, though he knew that she would bristle at the assertion.

Poor Agnes.

But this… This was the way in which she could prove useful. For Alexius desired the two of them to have a relationship—one like brothers. And if Lazarus had not been hardened by his years, by the early loss of his family. A family who had not even searched for him. Then he might feel guilt that he had no such intent.

They had met only twice since he had first revealed himself to Alexius, with Alexius inviting him to come and stay before his wedding to Tinley. He'd had a few weeks to consider that and decide his next move.

The presence of a fiancée on his arm would soften Lazarus's appearance.

Since his own face would not do it.

He had come to terms with his scars long ago. In the wood it was a symbol of survival. Of his strength.

Out in the world sometimes he was greeted with terrified stares.

But there were many women who worshipped those scars. Who found them dangerous and very, very appealing.

And so he had learned to use them.

As he would use Agnes. To make himself seem human.

Not that Agnes was soft. She was fierce and sharp, and much like traveling with a live possum. She was comically small but muscled from her years of training. She was fast, and she was quick in mind and movement.

And currently, she was seated on the floor of his private jet, wearing her typical uniform of baggy linen pants and an equally loose-cut top. Her knees were pulled up to her chest, her black hair pulled up into a high ponytail. Her dark eyes glittered in distaste. She was a woman with no country, she had said it often, until she had come to live in his. His hidden country at the center of another. And she was also a woman whose heritage was impossible to divine. Her eyes were cat-like and tilted upward, her mouth full, her skin a cinnamon color.

She was pretty. Though, he did not often ponder her appearance.

It was relevant now only because her beauty made her a believable choice as fiancée.

"It would not harm you to come and sit on the furniture."

She looked up at him. "I've no need."

"You are not a feral animal, and it does not benefit either of us for you to behave as such."

She frowned. "Does it benefit a warrior to grow soft?"

"You are not needed in that capacity."

"I resent it."

"Do you? What I require is someone I can trust. Absolutely. That, I assumed I could do with you. No one knows of my plans. It is not safe. Can I not trust you?"

She scrambled to her feet. "You can trust me. With your life."

"And so I thought. This is simply another kind of mission."

She wrinkled her nose, then with some reluctance came to sit at the far end of a couch with a great distance between her and the chair in which he sat.

Funny creature. Was she so thrown off by his request for her to fulfill this new role?

Well. He supposed she was so unaccustomed to this kind of softness. They enjoyed the simple life in the wood.

She seemed happy there, though she did not seem to have friends. But then, neither did he. He felt that he and Agnes were of the same mind in many ways. They kept to themselves. They cared more about their disciplines. About their responsibilities.

Neither of them was frivolous.

And yet he would have to engage in some frivolousness now. The truth was, the news of his resurrection from the dead had been internationally recognized, and he was not used to such a thing.

He was known in business circles, and had been for some time, but he did not court the spotlight. For clear reasons.

But that had changed, and it meant that this engagement needed to occur on the same stage. Otherwise, it would not look real. His brother would not believe that he took a woman without showering her in gifts. Without a trip to Paris. At least, that was not the sort of man he wished the world to believe he was.

He would have to marry, it was true. He would have to have an heir. But, in the woods, courtship rituals were much different. Vows were spoken between the lovers, the world was not involved. It seemed to him a fine way to conduct courtship. And yet, it was not the way of the outside world. Whether he agreed with it or not, he could understand it.

When the plane touched down in Paris, there was a car waiting for them. All of their items were loaded into it, and Agnes walked with her head down, her expression determined.

"Where have you acquired all these things?" she said, when they were on the road. He wondered if she was trying to act unimpressed with the city around them. Though, as she had said, she had been here before.

"Surely you must know that I have taken the riches of our kingdom and multiplied them."

"Yes," she said. "Though, I confess I did not realize it was… Riches in the sense of what exists out in this world."

Value in the wood came from what was useful, and what was beautiful. The time and effort and talent put into creating. It was different, but they could not thrive without bringing in amenities from the outside world. It was simply not possible. And so, money was necessary.

And he had made it abundant. His first step in securing a better, safer future for his adopted people.

"Of course it is," he said. "I'm a practical man above all else, Agnes."

"Well. I know. But I find the world out here to be *impractical*. You forget that I used to live in it. For longer than you did."

He looked at her for a long moment. He didn't forget much, but he supposed he did forget that on occasion.

"True. You are a woman of this world."

"I'm not," she said, shaking her head. "I have released my hold on it. There was never going to be anything for me out here."

She looked out the car window.

"You're resourceful," he said.

"It's true," she said. She turned to look at him, her dark gaze bold and direct. "Being here though, is a stark reminder of what I would have become. I was prepared to do what I had to do. But prior to your teaching me to fight, prior to your teaching me to defend myself, I had accepted that the only option would be eventually to sell my body. I did not wish to do it."

The idea of Agnes being forced to sell her warrior's body, being forced to tear pieces off her strong, proud soul stirred anger in his blood. "This world is a scourge," he said.

Lazarus's infusion of money had brought technology, had given them the means to import goods used by their small nation that numbered no more than one thousand.

But modernity brought its own vices, as well as its virtues. Their world was not perfect.

But it was a small community, and when there was an injustice it was corrected, and quickly. Taking advantage of anyone poor was not permitted. And when there were resources to be shared around, no one was left without food. They shared among themselves. Their economy existed largely as one rooted in trade. And those who were weak were cared for.

"You get no argument from me. I much prefer to wield a blade."

The car carried them directly to the department store they would be shopping from, and they were led into a private room at the very top of an exclusive elevator.

The room was all brightly lit, with dark wood and walls of mirrors. There was already a slim dress rack with several selections on it. Everything prepared for their arrival, as he had commanded.

A very slim woman dressed all in black appeared a moment later.

"This is she?" she asked.

"Yes," Lazarus said, not bothering to answer in French or English. He used Lirian, and the woman would figure it out.

Agnes, on the other hand, slipped easily into French. The woman took Agnes into the dressing room, and a moment later shrieked.

She came out, speaking English to Lazarus. "Your creature has a knife on her person."

"I could not come unarmed!" The woman walked out from the curtain, and Agnes poked her head out behind her. "I will not use it on you."

Lazarus waved a hand. "She is not a creature. She is a warrior. And my fiancée. And you will relay none of the information about the knife, but will tell whoever asks you that she is lovely, and loved beyond all women. Or there will be no payment made to you, do you understand?"

The woman's cheeks went red. "Understood, Your Highness."

She disappeared again, and there was a rustling

sound, and a moment later, Agnes was forced from behind the curtain.

Agnes felt foolish. She had never worn anything like this. Usually, when she had been with her father, she had been dressed to look younger. Or to look like a boy. Either to be pitiful, or to be discreet. But she had never worn anything like this. The dress was red, bold, clinging to her body in such a way that she felt naked. Naked, standing before Lazarus, which made her feel like she was melting, possibly like she was on fire.

"It is unseemly," she said, turning and walking back behind the curtains and closing them definitively. She could nearly feel the indignation of the woman who had helped her dress, even from the other side of the curtains.

She looked in the mirror, glad to be shielded from Lazarus's all too keen gaze.

She didn't recognize the woman that she saw standing there. Who looked surprisingly thin and shapely all at once, and whose body seemed to be firmly entrenched in this world, while her hair remained wild and part of another place and time. And then suddenly, the curtains parted, and he was there.

"This is hardly the loyalty you profess to bear, Agnes."

"I do not recall wearing gowns to be part of my training."

"Whatever my order." He looked at her, hard, and she realized she was... Defying him. Something she had never done.

Lazarus was a strong man, a strong leader, and he

had no issues with people speaking their minds to him, and Agnes often shared her thoughts. But that was not the same as direct defiance.

But maybe it was being here.

In Paris.

Where her old life had ended and her new life had begun.

It had her on edge.

He had her on edge.

She turned to him. "I do not like it."

She felt more than naked before his burning gaze. She felt something else entirely, and she did not care for it in the least.

"Agnes," he said, his words as hard as his stare. "You will do this."

"I hardly think that I need trot out in front of you like a fashion model."

"I've no use for fashion models," he said. His gaze was assessing. "It is not the fashion that I care for, but rather whether or not you play the part well."

"Am I not looking the part?"

"We will see if that is so once your hair is dealt with." He snapped his fingers. "On to the next garment."

Then the woman was back, the curtains closed again, and Agnes was peeled out of the dress, and the second was practically painted on over her body. It was green, and the fabric draped in places, and it made her look even curvier than the first, though it wasn't quite as tight. The top draped down low, exposing the sides of her breasts.

Lazarus looked at her in that, and her skin felt

scalded. Because now he was looking at her as a woman, but still not as she would like. He was seeing her as a tool, and evaluating her appearance as if that would tell him how useful a tool she was.

Far better to have him evaluate her skills with a sword than her body. For this hurt far too much.

But the indignity did not stop. After that dress, there was a gold gown, with a skirt yet more voluminous, and she didn't think she would have a hope of hiding a scabbard in the folds, and that was cheering to an extent. At least until Lazarus appraised her, with that same detached efficiency that she found exceedingly unnerving.

"We will take them all," he said. "And other supplemental pieces. You have a very fortunate figure, Agnes."

That made Agnes want to claw her scalding skin right off. "A *fortunate figure*?"

"Yes. Every style seems to suit you."

"Maybe I don't like them," she said.

"I do not care for your preferences, little one. It is mine that will be served. As I think you know."

An angry pulse beat between her thighs, and she could not reconcile it with the anger that flowed through her veins. That at least was the burden she had borne for years. This need of him. A need she had accepted could become nothing.

And yet also, beneath that was loyalty. Loyalty she could not escape or deny. She had sworn her life to him. When she had sworn her allegiance to their nation. It was the first time she had ever been part of anything. Anything other than that accident of birth. Which was nothing true or real. Her father had not been a real father to her. He had loyalty to nothing but himself. And Agnes prized her word above all else, because when she had been brought into Lazarus's life, she had been made a new creation. A woman who knew the keenest of loyalties. A woman who believed in truth. A woman who prized honesty. A woman who made it her mission, every day, to find her place in this broad world. She had made herself a woman of truth.

Her father would have turned her into the same sort of scammer con artist that he was. Seeking only her own comfort, seeking only her own pleasure.

She would have to remember that even now, that her own feelings were not what mattered. For that was a philosophy that carried you only to the depths of extreme selfishness, and then on to ruin. And she should know.

Her father had used her as a pawn, and he would've signed her death warrant if not for Lazarus.

"As you will it," she responded.

And that was how she found herself being bundled back into a car, feeling edgy and angry. But they did not go back toward the airport.

"What are we doing?" she asked.

"We are to make our debut as a couple."

"What is all this?" she asked. "Debuts and shows for the press. Lazarus, if you're on a mission of blood, how does raising your profile in the world help you at all?"

"It's not that simple. And, as I said, it is not my goal to kill my brother. Rather I would like that he willingly step aside."

"And what is this game?"

It was the deceit that truly got to her. And it was recognizing that Lazarus felt a sense of honor here, but that he was…

She respected him, so much, and knew he was a good man, but she did wonder if he could always see clearly.

How could you when your soul was shrouded in darkness?

"I must put him at ease."

She swallowed hard, conscience pricking at her eyes. She understood where Lazarus was coming from. She knew him better than she knew any other person on the planet. He was her mentor. He was… Well, he was everything.

They drove until they arrived at a lovely building, with the Eiffel Tower at its back. And just then she had a feeling that he was right, and she had not ever truly seen Paris before. He got out of the car, and opened the door for her, taking her arm and ushering her into a building that she was very truly not dressed for. But no one gave them a second glance, everyone committed to being the center of their own universe in this beautiful space filled with ancient stone, marble and gilded edges.

They went to an elevator that opened with the touch of Lazarus's hand, and it went straight to the very top of the building, the doors opening inside a brilliantly appointed penthouse.

The views of the city were sweeping, and the entire wall of windows in this unexpectedly modern space stole the attention from the rest of the interior. For it was Paris that was the true decor. The Arc de Triomphe, the Eiffel Tower, the Seine running through the lovely brick streets, and she could see artists with their canvases set up, ready to paint the world as they saw it, fashion mavens wandering the streets in long coats and large sunglasses, with brilliantly bored expressions.

It was all there, and all very French. And it took her a moment to realize that the inside was no less chic. It was modern. Cement floors and countertops, black details and chrome lines.

"Did you choose this?" she asked.

If so, it was an insight into him that she never had before. Who he was away from the wood, away from his castle made of rock and stone.

"No. I had an employee select something suitable. Others of my people will be here for you soon."

He was not wrong, as a moment later, a man and two women appeared, and she found herself being nearly bodily carried into a bathroom the size of an apartment she had once shared with her father. Lazarus was nowhere to be seen as she was stripped, reluctantly divested of her weapon and placed into a steaming tub of water.

She was scrubbed, she was combed, her hair was cut by one of the ruthlessly thin females, who took her mane from the middle of her back, up to the bottom of her shoulder blades in a blunt, asymmetrical line.

They put foils in her hair, and the scent of chemicals was strong. It made her eyes prickle, because it reminded her of dyeing her hair when she and her father had been running, or creating new identities.

Blond. Brown. Black. Red.

Her hair had spanned every color of the spectrum. This was different, though, as what they did didn't transform her entire head. No. Rather her black hair faded to a sort of caramel brown at the ends, and she looked grown-up in a way she never had before. And never really thought about.

Her nails were painted, and so was her face, with a thick liner making the already turned up corners of her eyes even more dramatic, and a pale blush staining her high cheeks, along with a gloss on her mouth.

And then there were clothes. Not the gowns that she had tried on earlier, but a knee-length, cashmere skirt in a camel color, and a pair of sky-high black shoes. A buttery soft gray sweater, and a coat that matched the skirt and nearly touched the ground.

She didn't recognize herself. But one thing she did comfort herself with was the fact that the lines of the outfit did allow for weaponry.

And just like that, the team who turned her into this entirely new being vanished, never really speaking to her, never really acting like she was anything more than a life-size doll. The stranger in the mirror was disquieting. Because though it was certainly something more than what had happened when she had changed identities when she and her father had changed locations, it still reminded her of that time.

That shape-shifting that had been born out of a necessity to… To live.

And now, even as she was being true to Lazarus, she was part of a lie.

But you are loyal to him. You are true to him.

You are still Agnes of the forest.

And not Agnes of lies.

She looked at herself again and felt a strange sense of…pride. She looked soft. She felt beautiful.

Like a woman.

She rejected that. Hard.

She took a breath, and walked over to her suitcase, where she had concealed a sword.

Is this not a lie?

She did not listen to that scathing tone in her voice. She didn't have the time for it. Nor the patience. And she took a rather substantial-size dagger out of the bag, and lifted her sweatshirt, undoing her skirt before strapping it ruthlessly beneath her clothes, and then she went out into the living area to await her orders. But she was not prepared for what awaited her there. For there was Lazarus, but as she'd not seen him. Wearing a superbly cut black suit, and a long black coat. His black hair was pushed back off of his face, showing the sharpness of his cheekbones, the extreme perfection of his features.

And for the first time, she fully appreciated who she was looking at. He was Lazarus, a prince of Liri.

A man who should've grown up in splendor, in a palace, had he not been left to his own devices in the woods. Had he not been taken in by the people of the forest.

And for the first time, she wondered that he was not more angry at them. For they had taken him from a life of luxury, and brought him into a hard, hard world.

And though it was one that she personally loved, her own destiny had not been a palace, but death at the hands of the men who had killed her father. She would have died in a French alley if not for Lazarus and the people of the wood.

But Lazarus would have been a prince. Lazarus would've had a family. A mother and father.

He would have been beautiful, not scarred.

Though his scars were beautiful to her.

They represented all he'd suffered. And her own salvation as a result.

"Come, Agnes," he said, extending his hand. "For we have dinner reservations."

CHAPTER THREE

HE HAD NOT anticipated just how beautiful he would find her. He had never looked at her and seen a woman.

She was a creature that he had rescued, and for the better, as she had been such a small, soft thing when he had first discovered her.

Not much more than sixteen and cowering in terror in an alley, about to be killed. But likely not before she endured other travesties.

Her father had already been gone, his blood spilled on the pavement.

He would not allow the same fate to befall her. And he had known that. He had also known in that moment that they were bonded.

It had been the same for him.

When he had been a boy, and he had wandered off into the woods from a palace he could now no longer remember, he had been backed into a corner by wolves. Flat against the side of a cliff, those evil beasts snarling at him.

And in a breath, they had fallen on him. His skin torn away from his flesh.

Being devoured even while he screamed.

He had waited for death. Hoped for it. Even as a small child.

But then Agamemnon had come.

Agamemnon of the Wood.

He had taken Lazarus, bleeding and broken, back to the village. Had given him rest and medical attention.

He had told him going home was not safe at first. And indeed, at first, he had lacked the strength.

Agamemnon had explained if he were to ever show his face out of the wood, their people would be destroyed. And Lazarus, young though he was, had asked why.

And what he had learned was the hideous history of how the conquerors who had come to their land had renamed it Liri. Had pushed the original inhabitants to the outskirts. Tried to snuff out their culture.

He had said Lazarus's parents would search for him.

That they would find him and then the people of the wood would be rewarded and not harmed.

They had never come.

Scouts had watched for them. No one had ever looked.

Agamemnon had become like a father to him. It was not the same soft childhood he'd had at the palace, but the memories of it had faded soon enough.

He ran around the campfires with the other children. He was fed by the women there too. He grew strong outdoors.

Eventually, Agamemnon had introduced him to his dogs. Hulking, great beasts that helped keep the people safe.

Lazarus had looked at them and seen only wolves.

Terror had streaked through him, and his memories of pain had been too much to bear. Agamemnon had not let him run. He had been firm.

You will learn to care for them.

They will be yours.

You will overcome your fears.

I saved you, and you will swear yourself to me, Lazarus. It is the way of things. I saved your life, and it is mine.

And Lazarus had done so. And his parents still had not come.

He had grown into a man without fear, a man without pain, and his parents had not come.

But Agamemnon and his adopted people had been enough.

If it had not been for Agamemnon, he would've been consumed by those beasts. Eaten, as he had found out his brother he had never met was. The brother who had replaced him.

It had been too late to save him.

Lazarus mourned that.

He mourned the loss of that boy.

He did not mourn the loss of that life he would've had at the palace, though. Though the distinction of how heirs were chosen in Liri was important. A brother could challenge his brother for the throne. And the people could choose a new leader.

It was his great-grandfather who had sidelined his people. Who had destroyed their way of life. His blood. And when he swore allegiance to his new family, he had been clear that he would see all things put to rights.

It was his duty, sworn and solemn, to avenge them. To restore balance, and well he knew it.

It was his duty to do as was his right. To challenge the heir to the throne. To seek that which could be rightfully his. Rightfully his people's.

Yes, he had known, the moment that he had rescued Agnes, that she had consequence in his life. For was it not simply—she had come to understand later—that the person you saved must swear their allegiance to you, it was only that being entrusted with that life was incredibly weighty, and binding. For both members of the blood bond.

Just as her life was his, that responsibility held meaning. There was a purpose behind it.

The purpose behind him being saved by the people of the wood was that he might restore an entire nation to its rightful place, and Agnes was a key part of that. Deeply important to the cause.

And so, it should not surprise him at all that she was perfect to play the role.

She was elegant, a quicksilver beauty who he knew to be deadly, but what surprised him the most was that she could still be soft.

For the first time since he'd first met her, Agnes looked hesitant.

Perhaps it was because they were back in Paris. He had not fully thought about it, but it made sense that she might be… That she might be frightened. Of Paris and all that it represented. Of the memories that lurked here. He could well understand.

He was not looking forward to going back to the palace of Liri, but fear did not live inside of him. Not anymore. He had banished it when he had first touched the dogs that looked so much like the beasts that had savaged him. The lesson in that had been that a man must be stronger than pain, than weakness.

Agnes was young. A warrior, yes, but she had also been sixteen when she'd left Paris. It was possible there were memories here for her she had not yet come to terms with.

"Are you well?"

"I am as ever," she said, lifting her chin. He held his hand out to her, and she took it reluctantly.

And the moment that his skin touched hers, he felt a kick of extreme arousal. It echoed that which had roared to life in him when she'd begun to try those dresses on. Showing her body in a way that was undeniably feminine.

It was unwelcome. This was Agnes. And she was not a woman that he could use in such a fashion. She was his... His ward in many ways. His responsibility on a deep level. There were many willing, round women back in the forest who could satisfy his urges as they satisfied their own. A pleasing transaction all around. It was the way of things.

His adopted culture was open about sex. But it was something that must be kept in its place.

He was a warrior.

Female warriors were to be treated as brothers-in-arms. With Agnes being even more complicated because she was his responsibility.

His.

It was the power that he wielded over her life, the power that he had, that made it unacceptable.

She was looking very serious as they walked out of the penthouse and onto the elevator. But he did not waver. They arrived down at the lobby to the building, and he moved nearer to her, and he could feel her every muscle tighten, get twitchy.

He put his arm around her and pulled her yet more closely. And felt hard steel beneath her clothing. As soon as they were out on the street he turned his head and pressed his mouth to her ear.

"Agnes," he said. "Do you have a sword beneath your clothes?"

She did not look at him. But for the first time, her expression became sanguine. "I'm committed to my duty."

"I believe I told you no swords. And already you nearly created an international incident in the dressing room of a very nice shop. Why is it that you saw to ignore my edict and arm yourself?"

"I have sworn a duty to protect you, my Lord, and I will do so. To the best of my ability and as I see fit."

"You will do as I see fit," he said.

"I believe it is within my right to judge whether or not I believe the situation calls for added protection. And in that you do not have the right to tell me what to do."

"I have every right," he said. "I have every right to tell you exactly what you should do for me."

"I have agreed to this," she said. "Do you not think that perhaps I have a fair idea of what my function is. Even if you have replaced it entirely."

"I value you, Agnes, and I do not take our bond lightly, but please drop this idea that I require you for protection. That you could do anything for me that I cannot do for myself."

He heard her gasp, but she swallowed it quickly, and the two of them carried on down the street.

The crowd parted for them, and Lazarus took it as his due. Royalty were given deference because of their position in society, because of the fear that people felt that they might face consequences should they fail to genuflect as expected. Or the hope that they might be rewarded should they behave in a certain manner. Lazarus did not need to be raised a prince to create a parting of the seas. It was not that he was royal, but that he was a man of consequence. A man of consequence did not need status in order to influence the crowd. He simply needed to breathe.

They continued on down the street to the restaurant, which was a building with a simple limestone facade. Exactly the sort of place that one might go if they wished to avoid the paparazzi. Lazarus did not wish to avoid the paparazzi, quite the opposite. He intended to court them. But the paparazzi were always where they felt they might not be wanted, and so it made the perfect location for such an endeavor.

They walked in, where they were known by sight, and were ushered to the finest table, in a corner of the restaurant that allowed them to see out over the room and place no one at their backs.

Neither he nor Agnes could ever bear sitting with their back to a door, or to a room of people. A wall it must be.

"Are there menus?" Agnes asked.

"A waste of time and paper. We will be served only their finest. And all of it."

Agnes, for all that she was trying to be casual, glittered with interest then.

That was one thing he appreciated about Agnes. She liked food. She liked it quite a bit.

There were certain little things that she seemed to enjoy, hearkening back to a time, he knew, when she had little.

For all that he had not grown up in a palace, Lazarus had always had plenty. Agnes, he knew, had experienced having nothing.

And when there was a feast, she ate her fill and then some.

"I do hope there is steak," she said.

Agnes was not disappointed on that score. There was steak. Marrow, cheese and bread. And a host of the desserts. And for a moment, he allowed the mission to fade into the background as he watched her enjoy all that was set before her.

And he felt... Self-congratulatory. For on this, he had kept his word, and his honor. Her life was his. In his care, and he had presented her with true finery. He had been much softer to her than Agamemnon had been to him. He had not had her sleep upon the rocks in order to earn her right to a bed by proving her strength.

She was better for having met him.

She looked up at him, her expression suddenly narrow. "And what is it you're thinking about?"

"Your good fortune," he said. "To be in my care."

The corner of her mouth went tight. "Oh, is that so?"

"Yes. Look at this food that you enjoy."

"I have *eaten* the food that I enjoy," she said. "I did not spend any time looking at it. Nor will I."

"A beast you are, Agnes. We must work on that." He had spent time in the world, it was why he had found her. How he had saved her.

It was, perhaps, one area of his responsibility where he had been remiss with her.

Agnes was in his care, and it must be acknowledged that her life with him had been… Narrow. And if that was so, it was a failing.

The concept of ownership, when it came to things, to land, was loose among their people. Yes, the King was steward of the riches of the people, but it was not the same as ownership.

Even his own life was not his possession, for it belonged to the people who saved him.

But a lifesaving bond, as the two of them had, was binding.

Agnes was the one thing that was truly his.

"I shall work on nothing but this cake," she said, taking a large slice of chocolate cake from the dessert platter that sat on the edge of the table.

"Careful. You do look a bit feral."

"I *am* a bit feral. It is not my fault that you elected to take me to this restaurant without any forewarning. Trussed up in finery I may be, but I am what I am."

"We both know that isn't true. You have the ability to fit in wherever you go. You were raised to do so."

"I don't like that part of my life."

"When you were in Paris did you ever go to places such as this?"

"No," she said. "I did not. And I think you know that."

"A question. For I wondered if this return to Paris was one filled with memories."

"I do remember the alleyways," she said sharply. "Particularly when I nearly died in one. Why were you in Paris then?"

"Part of my education," he said. "Agamemnon never intended to keep me in the forest, wholly uncivilized. I'm only mostly uncivilized. But I have to be able to blend in with my surroundings when it is required, and it is required soon. I'm grateful for that time."

"I had no such time. But I don't want it."

She was his. His to do right by. His to protect. And now he was having thoughts about her that were not honorable. He had kept her apart from the whole world, which was not as Agamemnon had done for him later. And he was...

He could not trust his intentions toward her entirely.

He had to think about her. And her healing. About her potential.

She would fare well out here in the world. She was beautiful and smart and capable.

And he alone possessed the power to give her the chance to be all she could.

Something in him softened. "Agnes, when this is through, I will release you."

Her eyes went wide. "What does that mean?"

"You want not to be tied to me forever. I've taken care of you. And I have done a wonderful job."

"If you say so yourself."

"Do you not have skills? Can you not defend yourself? Are you not fed and clothed?"

"I am all those things," she said tartly.

"Then I have done well by you, have I not?"

"I imagine so."

"And I find my responsibility toward you is quite deep."

She shifted. "Do you?"

"A person cannot know how they wish to spend all of their time on this earth if they have not experienced different facets of life. You must experience more."

"And if I don't wish to?"

She was being stubborn, as she often was.

"It is not a matter of what you wish. It is simply a matter of what is. But you must have your education. You must have your time in the civilized world."

"Must I?" she said.

"Yes. So in the end, I will allow you the same freedom that was given to me."

"Catch and release," she said, quite meanly as she took a bite of her cake.

"Yes. And you may not wish it, because you are attached to the familiarity of your existence. But none of the familiar will remain when we have accomplished what we set out to do. Everything will change. And your role will be fulfilled, for a time. You will go and see the world, and then return when you have done so."

"I see."

"I hope you do."

"And you do not need me to defend you."

"Indeed, I do not. Thank you for your understanding."

Once they were at the end of their meal, and they were both drinking strong coffee, Agnes having moved into stony silence, he decided it was time.

He fished into the pocket of his suit jacket, and took out a small black velvet box.

He had not seen the gem inside, but like the house, had sent someone after it, trusting that the people he hired would fulfill his requests to his standards. Could they not do that, he would not have them in his employ.

And with a curve of his mouth, he dropped down to his knee before Agnes, the ring held out before him, and he opened the box. The gem was an emerald. And he found himself pleased about that, for a diamond was far too insipid to be on Agnes's finger.

It would look wrong. And anyone who saw her wearing it would know that.

"Oh," she said.

"Agnes," he said. "Will you marry me?"

"Yes," she said, her mouth straight, her bearing stiff and regal. And then she extended her hand, and he slipped the gem on her finger. And with one fluid, decisive moment, he pulled her off her chair, down onto his knee, and pressed his mouth to hers.

CHAPTER FOUR

AGNES HAD NEVER been kissed before. Not really.

Once, when she was fifteen, a terrible man who had been doing business with her father had grabbed her and forced his mouth onto hers.

But it had not been a kiss. It had just been violence.

She had forced her knee into that part of him that intended vile things for her and run away. This was something else. Something else entirely. His lips were hot and firm, and he smelled delicious.

Like the forest.

Like smoke and wood and spice.

He was a comfort, as he had always been. Big and strong and singular.

He wanted to send her away, and it made her feel like she was breaking apart. But right now, confusingly, after that edict, she was in his arms. And she knew that it was all part of the show. The one that dictated he put an emerald on her finger, but it was miraculous all the same. Her heart was pounding, and that pulse between her thighs overrode any anger that resided in her veins.

Oh, how she wanted *him*. How she wanted this.

What shocked her most was his tongue. The briefest touch against her own, which set off and ignited flame in her belly that burned hot and fast and made her tremble with need.

Need for... For more of him. His hands, his...

She pulled away from him, breathing heavily.

"I have agreed," she whispered. "I think that is enough."

They left the restaurant then, and she had not seen him pay, but then, Lazarus seemed to wave his hand and things magically occurred. He did not participate in the world the way that others did. He did not do things the way common folk did.

And with each step they took back to the apartment, anger goaded her.

She began to tremble. For he had criticized her sword and said that he didn't need her, then told her that she could go on her way, all after she had been scrubbed and plucked in cotton, fashioned into this creature that he wished to put on display. That creature that was layered over the top of the warrior that he had sculpted from muscle and struggle.

How was she meant to find a place in the world? Apart from him? She was all that he had made her to be, and now he was making proclamations about how he did not need her. Not really.

And she was... She was enraged.

By the time they got back to the penthouse it had only grown. When they got inside, and the elevator doors closed behind them, she shifted herself next to him, her hand on the hilt of her sword. And she was determined that she would prove her point. The doors opened again, and they went inside the penthouse.

And she did not hesitate. Instead, she exploded. She drew her sword, rounding on him, curving her leg around the back of his and taking him down to the floor as she drew her blade.

But he had barely hit the ground when she found herself being pulled forward.

He disarmed her, flinging the weapon across the room. She howled in rage as he maneuvered himself onto the top of her, his large, muscular body a weapon in and of itself as he pinned her shoulders to the ground, his eyes blazing with black fire.

"What game are you playing?" he growled.

"You doubt me," she said, breathing hard, not from exertion, for she had not begun to exert herself, but from rage and adrenaline. "You think that you can best me. You think you don't need me."

"I taught you everything you know, little one. And you are but a very small thing."

She slipped from his hold, making herself boneless before tightening her muscles yet again and climbing up onto his shoulders, curving her arm around his neck, beneath his chin and holding him fast. "*Small* does not mean *inconsequential*, my Lord."

"You test me," he growled.

"I would've broken your neck were this real."

She found herself being flipped over the top of him, lying down on her back, gazing up at him upside down, as he brought his face close to hers.

"Darling, I would've broken yours the moment you

moved to draw your blade," he said, his words husky and somehow erotic.

She growled, rolling to the side and making a grab for her sword. But he was faster. He picked it up, pressing the tip of it to her chin.

"You would be no more if this were true combat," he said.

She moved away from him quickly. "I would never have stopped if this were real combat." He lunged toward her, but she moved to the side. And put her foot on the wall, climbing up above him, wrapping her legs around his neck and flinging them both to the ground with her thighs spread on either side of his shoulders. And at the same time, she reached into her jacket and took out the very small dagger that she had placed there without him realizing. She put it to his throat and grinned.

"You don't need me?" she asked. "I could destroy you." He tried to move, and she allowed the blade to prick his skin. "You do not have the measure of me."

Then his large hands moved, but they did not harm her, instead, they went to cup her rear, squeezing her gently, and he rolled beneath her, a growl rumbling in his chest that resonated in her thighs. And she faltered. In that moment, he grabbed her hand, twisted it and relieved her of her dagger, but he did not change their positions.

"Do not play games with predators who have teeth sharper than you could ever imagine, Agnes," he said. "You are an innocent."

"I don't... I've not been innocent," she said, wiggling, trying to get away from him.

"Are you speaking of the things that you have seen in the world? Perhaps not. But you are untouched by men, are you not?"

She lifted her head high. "I'm a warrior. I opt for celibacy as a way to maintain my integrity."

"I do not," he said. "In fact I find that very few things bring the appropriate release after the heat of battle." His face was stone, his eyes dark. "Here again perhaps I have been remiss in your education."

His words sent a cascade of something unfamiliar through her body.

And suddenly, he pulled her forward. And she felt... Exposed, for all that she was wearing a skirt. But then he pushed it up over her thighs, and she knew full well that he was looking at the black lace of her panties, which would barely cover her most feminine secrets. Feminine secrets that were not secrets to him, of course, for as he said, he did not engage in celibacy.

A tangle of unnatural feelings rolled through her. And then he turned his head and he bit her thigh.

She squeaked, squirmed, as arousal warred with the slight, sharp sting of pain that his teeth left behind. And then, his one arm acting like a vise grip across her thighs, he used the other to sweep her underwear aside and expose her.

And when his mouth made contact with that molten center of her body, she squeezed her legs, using all of her strength to try to close her thighs, but he was stronger. And he only used the momentum to pull her forward, more firmly against his mouth. And he lapped at her, ate at her core while she shivered and shook.

While anger turned into something much hotter. Much more forbidden.

She had wanted him. She had wanted him in ways that she didn't even have names for. But she had been certain he did not return the feeling at all. Particularly tonight when he'd said he had no need of her.

She had need of him. She always had. She had made vows in her heart to this man, and she had meant always to simply be his protector. But now this…

And then she could not deny the arousal pouring through her, not anymore. Her release was like a thunderclap.

She was accustomed to this being a quick, shameful feeling. And sometimes in the dark of her room, she did touch herself, and always, she thought of Lazarus and tried not to. Of his strength. His rough hands. Her desire to have him use them on her in a way other than sparring as they had done just now.

But this went on and on. This was something more than fantasy. This was dangerous.

This was…

She cried out and moved away from him, and he let her go.

"I…"

"Consider that a lesson," he said, looking at her with eyes more feral and beast-like than anything she'd ever seen before. "You do not have the control here. You are not more powerful than I. And if you do not learn to understand life, as I said, every facet, you will never be able to win."

He was more monster than man here, that darkness she knew lived in him on full display.

But she was more wildcat than woman just now. And she would not be bested.

And it was anger that fueled her then. Anger and a deep pride. She moved forward, pressing her hand against the front of his pants. Where she could feel that he was hard with desire.

"It seems to me as if you do not have all the power here either."

He growled and all but threw her to the side.

"We leave tomorrow for Liri."

"Is that all you have to say?" She was fractured. Broken and undone on the floor of this Parisian apartment. Disarmed and dishonored. In the moment that she had proven to him that she was not the loser, he was withdrawing.

She desired him, yes, she always had. There was no question. But this was nothing more than a bid for control to him, and she had been shattered. She would not bear it.

"There is nothing left to say," he threw out. "My point has been proven."

Anger and hurt pride spurred her on. "That you have the self-control of a rutting beast?"

"That you do not have quite the upper hand that you seem to think. You are good with a sword. But you do not know men. You do not know your own body."

"I do know my own body," she spat. "You do not get to tell me what I know. Or who I am. These are mechanical things. Any woman would have succumbed. It means nothing."

Except she was trembling inside. And it meant everything. Absolutely everything. And now she had to go and play the part of his fiancée. She still wore his ring.

In defiance, she took it off, then leaned down and dropped it into his hand.

"I do not need this now. It's only needed in public."

"You will wear it when I say."

"You are releasing me after this," she said, her pride breaking. It was one thing for him to best her in a fight. It was one thing for him to command her to be his fiancée. It was one thing for him to send her away. But to take her and manipulate her with that deep, secret attraction that she felt for him... She could not forgive it.

Because above all else she had trusted him to never use her intentionally. To never harm her or treat her callously knowingly.

And she would accept being sent away if he was going to play games with her body. For it meant nothing to him. Yes, he might have gotten hard, and she knew what that meant. Of course she did. She wasn't a child. But it was no more for her than any of this was. She was simply convenient. He would likely use her to warm his bed, in the absence of any of the usual sorts of women that he favored, and not think anything of it.

But she would.

She cared too much. And that was the problem. She cared too much, and when this was all over... Well, she could now see the kindness of his setting her free. They had been linked together for too long.

"I believe when this is through," she reiterated. "And you have already broken the bond. The only reason that I'm doing anything that you ask me now is because I want to. I will help you with this, as repayment for all that you've done for me. But my life does not belong to you. Not now."

"Agnes…"

"No," she said. "I'm not a child. Nor am I a chess piece for you to move around at will. I swore my life to you because it was my honor to do so. I changed everything that I was because when you saved me you gave me a chance at something new. I never did it because I was being manipulated. I never did it because I was forced. I will not be toyed with now. I offer this to you as my final act of service. And then I will go. Off to make my life, as you have suggested."

"So be it. No more swords when I bid you not carry them."

"If it pleases the King."

And with a defiance that she didn't quite feel, she looked down at the front of his pants again. "For I will not engage in what else might please the King."

Then she turned on her heel and walked from the room, waiting until she was back in the bedroom before her legs collapsed beneath her.

Had it only been a day?

He had whisked her to Paris, given her a makeover, forced her to wear skimpy clothing, engaged her in a sword fight, gotten engaged to her and given her the first orgasm she'd ever received from a man.

She could scarcely cope with it all.

And then Agnes did something she had not done since she was a girl. Because it was a weakness, and people use your weaknesses against you. Because there was no point to it. Because she knew better.

It didn't matter. Still, big fat tears slid down her cheeks. Still, she dissolved into misery.

She got into bed and pulled the covers up over her head. And she wept like she couldn't remember weeping.

She wept like her soul might fracture. Perhaps it already had.

For the first time in eight years she had no idea what would become of her. And she felt very much like that sixteen-year-old in an alley, following after a warrior and hoping that she might find a safe place.

Your safe place is gone.

Shattered like she had been only moments earlier. Shattered along with any illusions about her singularity.

She knew Lazarus to be a man with a healthy sexual appetite. He took lovers. She had seen him do it. And it had taken strips off of her heart to watch it, but she had comforted herself with the fact that she was special. She might not be his lover, but she was his. He could not manage without her. She was his protector. And he was hers.

They occupied a singular position in each other's lives, and she had told herself it made her matter. But with a flick of his tongue over the most sensitized part of her body, he had turned her into another of his women. He would've taken her and never thought of it again.

And so, Agnes of the Dark Wood had become common, and in that way, nothing. Nothing to him, at least.

And of all the things, that hurt the worst.

CHAPTER FIVE

LAZARUS HADN'T SLEPT. He had spent the entire night going over strategies in his head.

And he cursed Agnes mentally, repeatedly, for her behavior, which had necessitated he teach her a lesson. She was barely more than a girl. She didn't know anything of the world, which was why he needed to give her some time there, why he needed to let her be harder, savvier.

And still, she would not ever be allowed to defeat him.

That lesson had been unavoidable.

She'd overestimated herself.

But it was the lingering desire he felt for her that was what he cursed most of all.

She had been so epically responsive to his touch and he had taken things much further than he'd intended.

In his effort to exert control, he'd shown he had none.

And in the end she had looked so upset that he'd wanted to take her in his arms and hold her...

No. She was not for him. But there was something about the way she fought. Furious and feral and ferocious, and she was a worthy opponent. He did not train her to be indulgent—he never had. That could have easily spelled disaster for her. He had trained her to draw blood, and he had trained her to be lethal.

What he had not expected was for her abilities to appeal to him in this way.

She was strong. Strong enough to withstand the beast inside of him. The beast that he never let out.

He liked the soft, round women that he made bed partners of back home, but they were delicate. He treated them with softness. With deference, as one should.

But the lean muscle of Agnes's body demanded to be tested.

Tested her he had, but he had not imagined he might find himself tested as well. That strong body begging him to give it his worst—pleasure and pain alike.

But it would not be borne, not again.

And he was impatient. The meeting between himself and Alexius was sure to be… Tense. He would have to evaluate just what Alexius was thinking, what he wanted.

He would be staying in the palace. That place that was little more than an echo in his memory. And Agnes was nowhere to be seen.

"Agnes," he roared.

And she did not appear. He stormed across the room, as if her bad mood was her fault, and he flung open the doors to her bedroom.

She sat up, and he saw the rosy crests of her breasts. She was not wearing any clothes.

And his control suffered another mighty blow. It would not be endured.

She gasped and covered herself. "What are you doing?"

"You overslept," he growled.

"I have not overslept," she said. "You didn't tell me when to wake up."

"You never sleep past one."

"I am never in Paris."

Another truth sizzled between them.

"Indeed not."

"I have no patience for you today," she said.

Agnes did not usually snipe at him.

Nor did she usually wear his ring.

Or shatter beneath his mouth.

Or display her breasts.

"What happened to *my Lord*? What happened to *Your Highness*?"

"What happened to sanity?"

He stormed out of her room, and she appeared a moment later, looking freshly scrubbed and angry, back in the clothing that she had arrived in yesterday.

"We depart for Liri in an hour."

"It is a private plane, so you and I both know that you just decided that right this moment, and you had no preexisting plan, and you are now making it my problem that you didn't tell me."

"Quiet yourself," he said.

"I would rather contend with a toothless bulldog than you right at the moment."

He smiled and made sure to show all of his teeth. "Not toothless. And you cannot wear that."

"Why not?"

"We will get off the plane and have an immediate audience with my brother."

"You have arranged this?"

"It will be so."

"You cannot just make demands of him. He doesn't care that you're the King of the kingdom he does not recognize."

"Perhaps not. But we will show that I am not to be trifled with. Eventually, that is what he will learn."

"What do you intend to do to him?"

"All we're doing is fact-finding at the moment. We need his trust. We need to learn everything we can about Liri. About the kingdom as it is structured. About the weaknesses in the palace. About those who may not be loyal to him."

"I know how to run a con, Lazarus," she said, using his first name aloud, which she never did. "I only never imagined running one with you."

"This is not a con, Agnes. This is not about lining my pockets with money. It is not about benefiting myself. It is returning to my people what is rightfully theirs."

"Have you forgotten that you're Lirian. You might have grown up in the wood, but you are not one of them."

The words were like that dagger she carried sheathed at her beautiful thigh. He had not forgotten, of course he hadn't. That it was the blood of the disloyal—those who had sacrificed their child to a forest. The blood of the murderous traitor—the ancestor who had crushed a people beneath his fist in the name of power. That was the blood that ran through his veins.

He could never hope to have as much honor as the people he'd adopted.

"And neither are you," he said.

A dangerous thing thrashed about in his chest.

"I'm aware. But I'm not the one who is intent on deposing their own brother."

"Perhaps not," he said. "But you know how it is. My life belongs to Agamemnon. My life belongs to the people. I survived that I might complete this task. Whatever else happens doesn't matter."

"Nothing?"

He shook his head, the blank, dark black hole in his soul feeling particularly cavernous at the moment. "No. Nothing. There is nothing else for me but this vengeance. But it is more than vengeance—it is a restoration of justice."

"What am I to wear?"

Unbidden, his mind went back to the sight of her breasts. They were beautiful. Just as she was. All that well-honed muscle. He would've said that was not his particular type for a bed partner. But there was a roughness that he fantasized about...

She was suited to that. She would hold up against the pounding that he wished to unleash...

Never.

Agnes was his the way another person might own a rare artifact. It was the way of their tradition. She was to be valued, cared for and honored. He was her master, but if she fell into disrepair, he and he alone would bear the shame of it.

"Yes," he said. "The red dress."

As if the devil was in him, suggesting that.

"Isn't that a bit much for meeting with your brother."

"I should like you to wear the red dress. With red lipstick. Go. See that it is done."

She vanished and returned very quickly, her hair down, nothing but the barest hint of mascara on her lashes, along with the bright red lipstick he had commanded. She was stunning like that. It was only truly beautiful women who could play such games with makeup and win. "Have I met with your approval, my Lord?"

"You please me," he said.

He approached her, and he heard her breath catch in her throat, saw her pulse quicken in her neck. "Now you must only put on a convincing performance as a woman who is madly in love with me."

"I would like to eviscerate you with my teeth presently, so it will be a challenge."

And in spite of himself, he felt a kick of lust hit hard right in his stomach. He would like very much to have her use her teeth on him. And he would use his own on her in return.

He didn't know where these thoughts were coming from. These aberrations. He was not a man who was controlled by his appetites. They were an appetite like any other, and when he felt the need, he indulged them. But that was it. Right now, his desire for her was intruding. In ways he did not appreciate or accept.

"Come," he said.

"What about all of my things?"

"They will be gathered and brought. No need to fret."

"I am not fretting."

Almost as soon as they were down in the lobby, a pair of men dressed all in black went back up to the penthouse.

"They will bring all of your things to the plane."

"Well, why bother to leave without our things?"

"I thought you might like a pastry. Perhaps some coffee."

"In a gown? At ten in the morning?"

"We are in France, and we are newly engaged. We may do whatever we like."

And it was difficult for her to be angry once she was settled with a strong coffee and a pastry, and he could see that it enraged her on a new level. That she could not deny his hospitality.

She never could deny food.

She nibbled at the pastry in a rather delicate manner, which he found amusing, as he knew she was not delicate at all.

"Satisfied?"

"Not by half," she said, stiffly.

"Now you're just being spiteful."

"Perhaps I'm enjoying being spiteful. I've had to be nothing but eminently grateful to you for the past eight years, and do you know, it gets very tiring."

"Yes. I imagine it so much more tiring than the life that you led before."

"You don't know anything about the life I led before."

"I certainly do. Your father was a con man."

"Yes. Who tangled with the wrong men in France

nearly a decade ago. But what else do you know? Where else that I lived? Where I'm from?"

He took a sip of his coffee and stared at her. "Clearly you're American."

"Am I?"

"Yes. Originally. Though you do speak a great many languages."

"With great proficiency," she snapped. "But yes, I was born in America."

"And where?"

"Ohio."

He laughed. "Where is Ohio?"

"1997." She answered it with a straight face, and he did not understand what she meant by that. "It's in the Midwest," she said.

"Yes. Flyover states, I hear."

"A lot of snobbery for a man who was raised in a forest by people who are little better than wolves."

"They are a lot better than the wolves, darling," he said, yet again making certain to flash his teeth, hoping she took note of his scars. "The wolves would've simply eaten me. And were I a wolf, I would've simply eaten you." But the truth that he in fact had eaten her settled between them heavily.

And desire roared in his gut.

"My mother died when I was four," she said. "I don't think we were normal even then. I think my mother helped my father with his scams. But I don't know for sure. I… My first memory of my father is him telling me to pretend to be lost and crying. He taught me how to pick pockets. He taught me to take advantage of little old ladies. And they never suspected. Because I was small and cute. He taught me to use every asset that I had. To hurt other people."

Oh, Agnes. He might have been savaged by wolves. She had been raised by them.

And he wondered if he had not given her enough credit for that. If he had not given enough space to her wounds.

"A sad life."

"The only life I knew. Until this one."

It reinforced the fact that he had to send her off on her own.

"You will enjoy a life on your own terms, I think."

"I don't know that I will. But I suppose I have to try."

When the car stopped, he leaned in and pressed his thumb to her lips, then rubbed her lipstick gently. Most of it coming off on his thumb.

"What are you doing?"

"I would like my brother to have to imagine where on my body that lipstick ended up."

"What does it matter?" she said, her cheeks turning pink.

"It matters a great deal. If I'm to present myself as a man in love, it must be believable. He must believe that this is real. That I am changed. Soft."

"He never knew you were hard to begin with."

He had hurt Agnes last night. Not her body, her heart, and he'd seen it. She had already lived with those who had been callous with her.

And it made him want to give her this. So she was not alone in her sharing.

"Do you know what I remember of my life?"

"What?"

"Him. I remember my brother. And how I looked up to him. We played out on the palace lawn all the time. But the forest always fascinated me. I couldn't turn away from it. Even though I knew it was supposed to be dangerous. Part of me didn't believe it. I had to wonder why the stories were in place the way that they were. It was as if it was to… Deter people for some reason. And yes, I know. Wolves."

"Your youngest brother…"

He shrugged. "I never knew him. I don't mean to be cruel, but I don't grieve him."

"Of course not," she said. But she didn't sound convinced.

"I understand now. Why they didn't want us to go in there. They didn't want us to know. They didn't want anyone in Liri to know. Those people were almost snuffed out. By a power-mad King who wanted all of the land. By a man who didn't respect the old ways. The old traditions. That man was my great-grandfather. And it is up to me to make right what was done wrong. Because no one else will. These people are owed their land. They are owed freedom."

He waited to feel something in connection with that. But he did not.

Instead, he could simply feel the burn of her mouth against his thumb. Feel the red against his skin like a flame.

"And you wish to do that. You feel that strongly about it."

He felt nothing. But that was a sad state of affairs for most of his life.

It was as if he had left emotion behind along with his title. As if he had left it behind along with his mother and father.

They had left him behind quickly enough. They had been quick to announce his death. He had been informed by Agamemnon when it had happened, and he'd looked it up for himself his first time in Paris. He was not necessary. He was the spare, after all, and there was a reason that those in line for leadership in land ownership were referred to in such a fashion. He had done research on his own disappearance when he had gone off into the world. They had not, it seemed, mourned for long, and why would they. One child could be replaced easily with the next. And so they had done.

It was fate. He had accepted it. He was not mortally wounded by it. In a sense, it was how it must be.

For he had a goal to accomplish, a purpose higher than himself. And it was what mattered.

Not feelings. Those unreliable, unwieldy things that could be counted on for nothing. "It is what I must do," he repeated.

When the plane landed in Liri, he took her arm. "No sword?"

She looked down at the gown, which fitted to her form perfectly. "Where would I put one?"

"You and I both know that you are resourceful."

They began to disembark from the plane, moving slowly down the steps. He was aware that there were photographers. He paid them no mind.

"There is one," she said, tilting her face up toward him. And if he didn't know any better, he would say that she was madly in love with him. For her face was radiant, her smile wide, and her lipstick smudged just so, as he had designed it. "Strapped just to my inner thigh. If you were to put your hand up my gown and feel me there, you would find it. But you might get more than you bargained for."

He ground his teeth as her words had what he could only imagine was the desired effect on him. He studied her profile, her flat, curved nose and upturned upper lip, which gave her a regal bearing, her dark, unknowable eyes. She was a con woman, as she had reminded him only yesterday. Raised to lie, to fit in wherever she had to, to accomplish whatever she must by whatever means necessary. And what an actress. It was impossible to say what she wished him to glean from her words. Perhaps it was a threat. Perhaps she intended to take control as she had tried to do last night, by ensuring that he was aroused.

Sadly for her he did not exist in shame or regret. He only lived for the next moment.

"Let us both hope you've no need of it."

"But if there is need, I will use it. Remember, I am free now." She looked at him, her eyes liquid.

"As you wish, Agnes. For if one tightens their hand with too much force around a fragile thing, it shall shatter, and then what good does it do anyone? Except ensuring that no one else can have it."

"I'm not fragile," she whispered.

"I think you are more fragile than you believe."

"You're wrong."

"You shattered beneath my mouth easily enough."

Heat smoldered between them, burned in his veins. The memory pulsed between them and made a liar of him. For he was not living in the present moment, but in the moment when he'd touched her not like a teacher, but like a lover.

"I cannot wait to be free of you."

But she only smiled for all to see, and only he knew that she was venomous with him.

They got into a car, which drove them along the winding road that led to the palace. That led close to their home. The edge of the Dark Wood. They did not come and go from the country through this way. Rather they left out the other side of the forest, and used airports of the neighboring nation, typically.

A habit. For Lazarus had been in hiding from Liri for a very long time, and moreover, there was such an animosity between his people and the Lirians… An animosity the Lirians did not even know existed.

At least, as far as he could remember. He had been such a small boy when he had wandered away from home. Then he had not known that it would be the last time he would see the palace. That it would be the last time he would see his brother.

His mother and father…

The castle.

The memories that washed over him were strange and stretched. Not something that a person could make sense of. Not easily. For they were lost somewhere in the mists of childhood, twisted by that lens, and once again warped by the reality that was now before him.

The way that he saw the place as a man well into his thirties.

More than thirty years he'd been away from home.

No. It was not home. The wood was home. Those were his people.

By blood, he might be a Lirian, and for that he would have to atone. But in his soul, he knew who he was. These soft things were not his. These people were not his.

This palace was not his home.

Just as this land was not theirs.

"Are you well?" she asked.

She asked the question stiffly, and he could tell that she resented feeling anything about his mental state at all.

"I am as I ever am," he responded.

"A nonanswer," she said, her words clipped. "As ever."

"We are not friends, Agnes."

He could feel that land much harder than he'd intended. Or perhaps not. Perhaps he'd wanted to distance her.

"I am aware of that, my Lord."

But there was no difference in her tone, and there was no affection either. He had broken something last night. But he was not the sort of man who had the capacity to regret it.

The car pulled up to the front of the palace, and they got out.

"Announce us," he said to the man who had driven them. He wasted no time in obeying Lazarus's command. And then the palace doors were open to them, wide, and the procession of staff came out, standing sentry along the lines of the high-gloss corridors.

There was no army, no suspicion.

The staff allowed him in simply because he had a genetic link to Alexius. Who believed that they were brothers, in spite of the years that stood between them.

His own fault.

He had advised him.

Played the part of… Well, he had played the part of brother when Alexius and his Tinley had separated, and had told him to reconcile with her.

Lazarus still felt what he'd told him then was true. He'd found a woman who loved him—something Lazarus himself never thought to have—and he should keep her.

But it remained to be seen if they would have a long life together.

Something was uncomfortable, pinching at his chest, and if he had been another man, he might've called it guilt. But he was not another man. And he could not be.

He moved himself closer to Agnes, holding her arm in his, and Agnes, to her credit, remained serene. That warrior's posture became something softer, more elegant. And yet, he could see in every line of her being that she was a fighter. He could only hope that his brother did not perceive the same thing he did.

A man dressed all in black came to stand alongside them. "Allow me to announce you to His Highness," he said.

"Please do," Lazarus responded.

"And how shall I announce you?"

"King Lazarus of the Wood," he responded. "And Agnes."

The man went ahead of them, and Agnes's shoulders wiggled. "And Agnes," she repeated, in a poor imitation of his voice and accent, in his opinion.

"I'm sorry, do you have an issue?"

"I've no title," she responded. "I am Agnes, warrior of the wood, sworn protector of the King."

"You are not," he said. "Not here. And anyway, I was given the impression that you had abdicated your position."

"Yes. Though I will still be fulfilling it here."

"Agnes, my fiancée, and nothing more."

She looked flattened by that, and he tried not to care.

A moment later, the two of them were ushered into the throne room. Alexius did not sit on a throne, and neither did Tinley, his fiancée. Rather, they were sitting in what looked to be a regular, casual receiving area, plush and welcoming. There were trays of sweets, and he stole a glance at Agnes, who was looking pleased by this development.

"Brother," Alexius said, standing. His older brother was nearly his height, possessing more of a lean strength than Lazarus's own. Tinley was petite, with massive amounts of red hair. She was soft. She had a cat sitting on her lap.

Agnes saw the creature, a line pleating between her brows, as her mouth turned down into a frown. It was exceedingly Agnes to be confused by the cat.

"I'm glad that you came," Alexius said. "We have so much to discuss."

"Thank you for the invitation," Lazarus said. "I'm newly engaged, and it is good for Agnes and I to spend time here. Good that she gets to know you as well."

"I saw that," Alexius said. "Very newly engaged. As it was in the news this morning."

"A resurrection and an engagement. A big month for me."

Alexius chuckled. "Indeed. Come, brother, we have much to discuss. We can leave Tinley and Agnes to get to know one another."

CHAPTER SIX

AGNES HAD A feeling that was her cue to sit, but she found she did not want to. She was fractured still from last night, and the plane ride with Lazarus had done nothing to make it better. The way that he had touched her mouth… And the way that he insisted on continuing to bring up her… Shattering. And now she was here, talking to this woman they were intent on betraying. This woman who had a… A cat.

That she kept as a pet.

"You can sit," Tinley said, smiling brightly.

"Thank you," Agnes said.

She took a seat as far away from the cat as possible.

"Are you allergic to cats?" Tinley asked. "Because I can send him out."

"Oh, there's no need. It's only that… It is strange to me. That there should be an animal indoors."

And cats frightened her. They were disconcerting. And this one, called Algie, had large yellow eyes that made her feel seen.

But she would not say that.

"Oh, yes. Alexius finds it strange also, but I do not give him a choice."

She wrinkled her nose. "You tell him what to do?"

Tinley smiled happily. "Yes. Occasionally. I have many animals inside the palace. He does not like it. They had their own room. They were not allowed in ours. Though, there are often exceptions made. When I wish them to be made."

"Lazarus is not quite so malleable."

"I wouldn't call Alex malleable," Tinley said. "Only that he is more so now than he was when I first came to live at the palace. By which I mean when I was a child."

"You are much younger than him," Agnes said.

"Yes. I was engaged to his brother. His... His younger brother... Younger than Lazarus."

"Yes," Agnes said. "I know of him. The one who was killed."

"Yes," Tinley said.

She looked sad, though it was not heartbroken sort of grief.

"Are you in love with Alex?" Agnes asked.

She wondered, because Lazarus had been moved by their connection. She wondered, because Alexius shared blood with Lazarus.

And in spite of herself, Agnes loved him.

"Yes," Tinley said. "It became clear to me later that I always was. Always. It was only that... I did have a great deal of affection for his brother. I still feel badly about what happened. Very sad. But I recognize now that I did not love him like that, and never would have. We would not have... We would not have worked."

"You can be certain about that?"

"A certain as I can be about anything. Alex was the

one I was always meant for. I don't think Dionysus had to die in order for that to be so. I fear rather we would've collapsed a monarchy with our need to be together eventually. But fortunately, that did not have to be. I mean... Unfortunately... You know."

"Yes," she said. She thought of the many fortunate unfortunate things that had to occur in order for her to be in Lazarus's life.

Though, she was not certain now how fortunate she was. No. She only felt mean toward him at the moment.

And this woman... In spite of her cat... She was very nice, and she found that disconcerting. All things considered.

"How long will you be staying with us? Of course you are welcome to stay as long as you like. There are other houses on the grounds. You could stay in the palace, or you could stay at some of the estates."

"Whatever it is Lazarus wishes."

Tinley tilted her head to the side. "How do you know my brother-in-law?"

Agnes figured that in situations such as this the answer that was closest to the truth was likely the best.

"He saved my life," she said. "And I... I have loved him ever since."

The words sat in the room and seemed to fill the space. She had never admitted this out loud before. She had no one to admit it to.

But they were true.

And they resonated in her soul as they did from the walls around her.

She loved him, and she felt no shame in it. Not here. It was part of her, as was her loyalty to him.

"You are younger than he is," she said, turning that question that Agnes had asked back around on her.

"Yes," Agnes confirmed. "I am. But he has long been my protector, and he is... He is a man of honor."

"And you love him," Tinley said.

"More than anything in the world."

And the thing she hated most of all was that it seemed very close to the truth of the matter.

Even as she was angry. Even if she was sitting here next to a cat.

It was soon that Alexius and Lazarus returned. "You may stay as long as you like," Alex said. "I have offered Lazarus the east wing of the palace. It is both of yours, if you wish."

"My thanks," Lazarus said. "I look forward to our getting to know one another. To this restoration."

And Agnes knew that there was truth beneath those words. But the restoration that Lazarus had a vision of was hardly what Alexius would be expecting.

"I would join you for dinner tonight, but I have an engagement in England I cannot escape. Instead, I will have something special laid out for you and your fiancée."

Agnes's stomach tightened. How many more special dinners could she possibly endure with Lazarus? Particularly if they ended in sword fights. Which ended in...

"Much appreciated."

Lazarus paused. "Make sure that the spread is heavy on sweets. My fiancée has a fondness for cake."

He took her arm and led her from the sitting room, moving toward what she assumed was the east wing. She had never seen any place this grand. It was a palace that seemed to be built from foundational stones of the earth. Old and filled with history, layered over the top with precious gems. It was true there were riches in the forest, but it was different than this.

"Here it is," he said. "My inheritance, as it were."

"It is a beautiful palace."

"Exactly as I remember it," he said, his voice taking a dark turn. "Shining and glittering. I thought that perhaps it was a trick of my imagination. For no place could... No place could be quite this grand."

"Is that so?"

"It is so," he said. "And yet... It is also real. This place. I was happy here."

She stopped walking. She had never heard him speak of his family in that way. He didn't speak of them at all. He spoke of it in matter-of-fact terms. How he had once been a prince of Liri, but then had gone into the wood.

But he did not speak of it with softness. And even now, she wouldn't call it... She wouldn't exactly call it softness. It was something more. But there was emotion to this, and that was something he did not typically demonstrate. The corridors were long, and suddenly the glitter seemed to take on a sinister aspect.

"Yes," he said. "My rooms were here."

That statement hit her full in the chest. It wasn't the place that was darker, it was his mood.

Deeply so.

And of course. For this had been the place that he...

That he'd started his life, the place that he had lost forever after he had wandered away.

And suddenly, she felt a deep kinship to him, and she had never experienced that before at all. And she didn't know why she should. Because she hadn't started life in a palace, but it was simply… Perhaps it was simply knowing that there was something you should have that you did not. A loyalty from your parents that you should have that didn't exist. A sense of home that you were denied.

They might be from very different backgrounds; they might be from very different places, but that was the same.

It was the same.

The bedchambers that had been appointed to them were definitely not children's rooms, and the splendor of them stole her breath, took her focus away from the sadness that had lodged itself in her chest at least.

It was so opulent. But the large bed at the center of the space was what made her heart freeze.

"Do not worry," he said, his voice dripping with humor. Very dark humor. "I am accustomed to sleeping on rocks, Agnes. The bed is yours."

"I am also strong enough to withstand a few nights on the floor."

"Excellent. Perhaps we might both curl up on the floor as animals, both to prove the point to one another, and the bed can sit there unused, soft and utterly wasted."

"I shall do what I please, in the end. I shall do as pleases myself from here on out."

"Yes. The emancipation of Agnes has been quite proclaimed."

"It is as you commanded."

"I did not command you to leave entirely. Of course, I will not stop you from doing so, but I am very aware that you dishonor the pact which we have made."

"I dishonor nothing," she said.

"So be it. You will also continue to fulfill this role as I see fit. My brother has said that we are allowed use of this entire facility. Indeed, he has suggested that you and I make use of the baths prior to our dinner. Apparently, it is to be an exquisite affair. One set up on the terrace, well lit and brilliant. A reminder, I'm certain, of all the opulence that I missed growing up."

"He likes you. Don't you feel any guilt about that?"

She might feel some pity for Lazarus, but it was just impossible. To be here and be around Alexius and Tinley and not feel a certain measure of guilt. How was this not a con? Tricking people. Fooling them. Gaining their trust and breaking it.

She had done it countless times as a child with her father.

Stealing people's money. But worse, stealing their trust. Stealing their hope.

Creating a world where people would not be as generous, because she had been part of taking advantage of it.

She had made the world a worse place in the first sixteen years of her life, and she might not have been in charge of the scenarios, but it was all the same in the end. The outcome was the same. In this...

What if he did kill Alexius?

What if he broke all these people who simply had the misfortune of descending from a people that had committed gross acts. What if there was another way?

And they weren't looking for it because the easiest way was the path of the sword?

The easiest way was the path of lies?

And here they were, taking advantage of this hospitality and pretending to mean things to each other that they did not.

"What?"

"He trusts you," she said. "He trusts you, and he wishes to be a brother to you. I do not approve of this."

She loved her home in the wood. She loved the people there. She felt loyalty to him, but first her loyalty was to Lazarus, and his very soul.

And to honor.

She could not find the honor here.

"This is our moment," he said. "Our chance to take hold of that which has been denied us all this time. Is it not worthy, Agnes? Are you too good? Perhaps that is because it is not truly your right."

"That isn't it. It's not what I think. I just think… You are not your great-grandfather, any more than Alexius is. Maybe there's a way to restore what our people are owed without bloodshed. Maybe there's a way where you can still be brothers."

"I do not believe that such a thing is possible."

"Only because you were not given a path to that way. But perhaps you have to make your own."

"What makes you an expert? You, Agnes, who have no family name, because you have no family."

She gritted her teeth. "I am an expert because anytime I am emulating a behavior that my father would have engaged in, then I can be most certain that it is wrong. My father was always a coward. He always took the route of least resistance. The least amount of work. He wanted nothing more than his own comfort, and he cared nothing for the needs of others. Do you know why? Because it is hard. It is hard to try to get what you deserve, and be concerned with your own morality. And my father never did anything that was hard. Ever. Perhaps I believe that you are strong enough to do hard things. The more I find myself feeling as if I am engaging in another low-level con as my father would've done, the more I am certain that this cannot be the answer."

The look he gave her was filled with iron. And she had the sense that had she been anyone but Agnes he would not have allowed her to speak in such a fashion. In fact he would not allow her to speak at all.

"You speak of things you don't understand," he said. "You live because I rescued you. You exist because of the help that I have given. Help that your father did not give you. You dare compare me to him? You dare compare me to him when you know full well that he died and left you alone, while I thought nothing of risking myself to elevate you. What I do is not for my own personal enrichment, but for honor. But for the restoration of the people. But to heal the scars of the nation. That is why I do what I do. If you cannot understand that, so be it. And if you must leave now, then leave."

Fear slammed into her chest. "I will not leave," she said.

The small note of terror in her voice seemed to call her a liar. All of the stances that she had taken since last night, her proclamations that she would strike out on her own... What did they mean? They might as well have been notes written on paper and cast into the wind for all that they mattered. For she had proven now that she feared—deeply—that future without him.

She did. Oh, how she did. And that wounded her to confess it.

"If you have no honor, then leave."

And she could not allow him that. Would not.

"I will finish what I have sworn to finish. But I will not go along quietly. I will not. They are good people. And I've spoken my piece."

"Good. Have yourself a rest, and then, we will make use of the baths."

Her skin prickled. "Why?"

"It is not yours to question me."

And with that, he left her there in the bedchamber, disappearing into another part of the wing.

And she did not know what would happen next. For the first time in a very long time, she did not know.

Lazarus was still angry about the confrontation he had with Agnes a couple of hours earlier. But he was intent on doing exactly as his brother had bade him. He was not here, so he would not see whether or not Lazarus and Agnes used the baths, but he had offered it. And it was entirely possible that news of whether or not they had would filter back to Alexius. And he must do nothing that would cause him to question Lazarus's motives.

He went into the bathroom and stripped naked, putting on one of the robes that had been provided for them. And then he took the other one that was hanging in there and brought it out to the bedchamber, where he found Agnes, sitting on the bed, looking angry. She was still wearing the red dress that she had had on since that morning.

And the idea of being alone with her in the baths made his blood hot.

"Put this on," he said.

She looked up at him. "Now?"

"Agnes," he said. "I haven't time for you to develop a sense of maidenly modesty. We are fighting a battle. Take your dress off, put the robe on."

And perhaps it was more for him than for her that he issued this challenge. Perhaps it was about proving that he was a man in control.

A man who could still keep Agnes in her proper place. As he must.

Her expression was scathing as she stood from the bed and reached around behind her back. Then she turned away from him, lowering the zipper, and it took him a moment to realize that he was standing there staring, his gaze fixed on her body. And even when he realized, he did not alter course.

Rather he clenched his jaw, tightening his hands into fists as the scarlet fabric dropped from her golden skin and slithered down onto the floor. She unhooked her bra with deft ease, and then pushed her panties down her thighs. Stepping out of them when they reached the floor. He had a good sense of the shape of Agnes's body. They had trained together, after all, engaging in intense physical hand-to-hand combat. But seeing all that ripe golden skin was different than simply having an understanding of it. Her rear was round and well muscled like the rest of her, but still looked as if it would make a pleasing handful. Too quickly, she slid the robe on, covering her body, and then she turned to face him. And he managed to will his body into absolute submission. Managed to keep himself from getting hard. He was a man of eminent control, and so it would be the same with her.

"Ready," she said, giving him an evil look.

"I'll lead the way."

One good thing about testing himself with Agnes's body and her beauty was that it gave him a chance to focus on something other than the hauntingly familiar halls of the palace. He did not wish to have memories. Not of this place. He did not wish to think of his childhood here.

That boy that had been born in this palace was dead. He had been dead to his family from the moment he had set foot in the forest, and he must be dead to Lazarus himself. It was the only way. The only real thing. And so those memories were nothing. This was nothing.

They went down to the lowest part of the palace, as Alexius had instructed, but this room was not a typical bath.

It was… An indoor river that seemed to flow beneath the palace, lined with gems, which glittered on the walls.

He looked at Agnes, whose eyes were wide, her mouth dropped open into a perfect circle.

"You like it," he said.

"Yes," she responded.

"I do not remember this," he said.

And he detested the words as soon as they were out of his mouth, because he was not giving any credence to his memory at all. Whether it was there or not.

"I imagine this was not a place for children."

It was true. This was a place of very adult luxury, and he knew well enough to know that it existed in part for debauchery.

For no place so lavish could avoid being the site of many a sexual adventure.

He dropped his robe without preamble or warning, and Agnes's cheeks went scarlet. She looked away from him quickly, not even bothering to pretend that she was not shocked and horrified by the sight of his bare body.

And it restored a sense of power to him, which he appreciated. He stepped away from her, and toward the water, so immersing himself and covering anything she might not have seen before.

He looked back at her, but she was still not looking at him. Her hands were at the belt of her robe. And he could see the moment she decided to meet his challenge.

And then his control was badly shaken. For her hands began to work at the knot on her robe, and in that moment, there was nothing. No vengeance. No palace. Nothing but this.

Agnes.

His strong, brave Agnes, removing her robe from

her shoulders and exposing her entire body to his view. Those high, round breasts, her strong, lean body, and yet gently curved hips. And that dark thatch of curls between her legs, that place where he had tasted, and suddenly his mouth watered for more. He was hard as an iron bar beneath the surface of the water, and he was only grateful that she could not see. Because she would see this as exactly what it was. A weakness.

He was not doing well in fighting against his desire for this woman.

And how could that be so?

For they were bonded in a way that made that impossible.

And yet.

Did she not break the bond?

She had. She was leaving.

Leaving.

And suddenly, suddenly, he saw his world for what it was. Dark and devoid. But there was something about her that made it feel like it might be more. Something about her that made his life seem more... More like a life. And she would remove herself from it. Entirely. And he no longer had any say in the matter. For he could not... He could not keep her in a cage.

Could you not?

And for what purpose?

But if she was no longer his and she was no longer under his protection? Not in the way that he had always seen himself as her protector. And if that was the case, did it not just make them a man and a woman in this moment?

A man and a woman in this space.

And she was… She was glorious.

Brave and strong, a goddess as she began to step into the water.

And she did it all because she was angry with him. She did it all filled with spite. But it made no real matter to him.

For she was here.

The one and only thing that had ever truly been his. Agnes.

She got into the water, up to her waist, covering that delectable space between her legs, but leaving her breasts bare to his view.

"Why do you look at me like that?"

"You're beautiful," he said. "And I am a man."

"I thought you were rock."

"I am rather hard at the moment."

She blinked. "I've not ever known you to make jokes. Particularly not of that nature."

"I've not ever known myself to make them either," he said, not certain as to what was happening now.

He took a step toward her.

"Don't," she said.

And he stopped.

"Don't want?"

"Do not… Do not play games with me. I'm not a plaything. You used my body against me last night. Used a feeling that I'm not familiar with to make a mockery of me, and I hate it. I would beg you not to do that. Not ever again."

He looked at her, and he felt all the need contained in the universe echo inside him. "And if I said I simply wanted you?"

She looked away. "Why?"

A good question. And suddenly the answer seemed clear.

"Because you're going to go out into the world after this, a free woman, you say. And I want… I want to be part of teaching you what it means to be a woman. Have I not always been there for you? Have I not always been your teacher?"

She looked away from him. "I hardly think…"

"Let us not think."

He was angry all of a sudden, that he should want this, want her, here in this place, and feel denied. This palace…

How he wanted her. And he didn't want to be denied. Not anymore. Not her, not anything.

No, he did not wish to exhibit restraint. There were hard lessons that she needed to learn. The world was unforgiving, and she would have to be strong. She was strong in many ways. In the ways of battle. But she did not understand this sort of fight, and she had no tolerance for it.

She would have to learn or find herself harmed in the world.

And was that not the function of a mentor?

He had been made to face a pack of dogs after nearly being consumed by wolves.

She would face him.

Reckon with the need she had created in him.

Her eyes went wide and she backed away from him, against the wall, the gems glittering behind her, the reflection of the water casting glowing waves over her skin.

She was beautiful. And he didn't believe her showing of fear. Not for one moment. For she could attack him if she saw fit. Best him in any sort of battle that she so chose. So why play the uncertain maiden? It made no sense.

"Where has your fire gone?"

"Don't," she said. "You've already proven that my defenses against you are not where they should be. You've already proven that you could take advantage of me if you had a mind."

"What makes you think I require this display of you?"

Her eyes sharpened. "What makes you think it's for you? Am I not allowed to have my own feelings? You're right. I've never been touched by a man. Not like that. Not before yesterday. Not… I had one man, once, attempt to have his way with me. But he was rough and violent. And I fought him off. But this? You made me desire you. And you are supposed to be… You are supposed to be safe. But you've gone and changed the rules."

"I have," he said. "You attacked me with a sword, Agnes. And you act like my giving you an orgasm is somehow worse? More of a betrayal?"

"Well, yes. Surely that wasn't the first time you've ever been attacked by a sword."

"Why don't you show me what you're made of."

"Why?"

"I like your spirit."

She laughed, the sound hollow. "You don't like my spirit. You only like it when you can bend me to your will. When you can be amused at it. A waste of my spirit."

He braced his hands on the wall, on either side of her shoulders, and her breasts came very close to brushing against his chest. "What is it that scares you the most? That this is unknown? Or that you desire me."

"What does desire have to do with anything? I am a woman, after all. For all that I have attempted to fashion myself into a warrior, and only that, you have not done the same. I have watched you satisfy your urges with many women. They come and go from your chamber in an alarming pattern. No, it is only women who must become strong by denying their desire. By denying their gender. And so this… This is only the same. The same as you and all those other women. I have a desire, and you are here. You've taken your clothes off." She looked over him. "It is natural that I might think of how things could be between us. But you…"

He grabbed hold of her hands and quickly wrapped his fingers around her wrists, drawing them up over her head. Pinning her against the wall. And then he did press his chest flush with hers, feel the excited tips of her breasts against his chest. "And yet you do not desire another man, do you?"

She was breathing hard, her eyes wide, but she did not fight him, and he knew that she could. That she could make him very uncomfortable, very quickly.

"I don't know any other men."

But she would. Someday she would give all this strength and softness to someone else. It was part of allowing her into the world. A part of allowing her to experience time away from him. He had taught her to fight. He had taught her to protect herself. Why shouldn't he teach her this? Why shouldn't he be the one to teach her all that her body could do?

She was the one intent on breaking their bond for good. The one intent on shifting the power balance. And why then should he keep her at arm's length?

And why... Why should she get to dictate what happened between them? So many pronouncements from this woman he had cared for. From this woman he had...

There was no deeper bond than the one that they shared. It did not exist. Not in the whole of the universe.

And she wanted to walk away from him completely.

"What are you afraid of, little one?"

She lifted her chin. "Not you."

"Are you strong enough then, to have me this way."

She squared her shoulders, her chest pressing forward. "And what will I get for it? In the end, I will go on my way. And what will I have gotten? For becoming one of the many women who have paraded through your bedroom. One of the many women to satisfy your baser animal urges. I would be better, I think, for having turned you away. For who is strong enough to do that?"

"But you want me? So what does it matter?"

"Because I have been inconsequential. I have been nothing. And in you, in the wood, I found a home. It matters. And if you just wish to use me as you do your other women, to combat the fact that I have defied you, to make me into something that you forget... Well then, I want nothing to do with it. Nothing at all."

He looked at this woman, this woman whose life had

been so linked to his own. Who was so different from every woman he had ever desired.

"You are Agnes," he said, for it was all he could say. He was never at a loss. Not ever. And yet, she put him there. "I would never confuse you with another."

And he looked at her, really looked at her, and he saw that her fear was real. But with it, she was strong. With it, she was exhibiting great strength.

And it occurred to him then, he didn't know why he had not thought of this before. But he had to keep her. He would have to keep her with him forever.

He had wanted to give her distance from him because he had not accepted the truly honorable thing to do.

To bind her to him forever. In every way.

The truth was, he could not have Agnes in halves. Once he wanted her, he had to let her go...

Or make her his bride.

For she was his in a profound sort of way that he could not give voice to. His in a way that went beyond logic. And she would need... Not this.

Shows of strength, battle, it was what Agnes knew. And she had been used. Many times. Used by her father in order to accomplish his ends.

But had anyone ever worked to gain her trust. Really and truly. Had anyone ever done anything for her. It was clear now what she wanted. Agnes wanted to feel special. And as for himself, Lazarus knew nothing about feelings. What he knew was strength. What he knew was power. A sense of duty and honor. And a sense of ownership.

He knew care, because it was what one did when

they had a responsibility to another person. Yes, he knew about those things.

But he had to figure out just how to show those things to her. To find a way to reach her so that this time when he pleasured her she was not hurt or upset.

He had to try something new.

And he took a step away from her.

"Enjoy your bath."

"What?"

"This should be for you. You have been without comfort for so long."

"Why?"

"You're right. I have no right to make demands of you. You… Agnes, you must be cared for. I have no wish to frighten you or take advantage of you in any way. And here we are, in this place of luxury. Are you not to enjoy that?"

"Why?"

"Because you should. Because you do matter. Because you are not like other women, not to me. Not like any woman. I am… I am sorry."

He turned away from her and waded out of the bath, walking up out of the tub and grabbing his robe again.

And then he left Agnes sitting there in the water.

CHAPTER SEVEN

AGNES COULD NOT understand what had happened. One moment she had been engaged in... She didn't even know. Some form of seduction at his hands, and the next... Well, the next.

The next he had walked away. She had no idea what her body was doing; her heart felt like it was about to hammer straight out of her chest.

And she was... She was disappointed. She was angry. She couldn't countenance why. Except that she had wanted his mouth on hers again. And on other places. And she felt restless and unsettled for having not gotten it. She should not feel this way.

She didn't know what was happening with Lazarus. A man who was usually... He was usually so easy to read. He was a man of great integrity. And therefore his actions tended to be deliberate. Never random, never...

But he had been like a wild beast these last few days and she... Her heart couldn't take it. She loved him. And she had tried very hard to put that love in its proper place. But now the things that he'd done... It indicated that he desired her. But did he? She couldn't read him and she had no idea what he was playing at. If she was the one who mattered or not. And how would she ever know?

She knew Lazarus. When they traveled, she slept at his feet in the woods, making sure to be the one who kept guard over his body. She had pledged herself. Her heart, her life, to him. And he took care of her. Something that she knew he took great pride in, but that was not the same as feelings.

She had never actually seen an indication that Lazarus had feelings. Loving him was like loving rock. And she had resigned herself to that. Maybe that was sad.

It was why in the end she had said she needed to leave. Because if he didn't care, if he did not feel bonded to her, if he did not feel like he needed her, then what was there?

But then he had... The way that he had looked coming toward her in the bath.

Her treacherous body betrayed her even now. Her nipples were tight, and the place between her legs was wet and sore.

She would never forget the sight of him. Naked and well muscled. She had never seen a naked man in person before. And of course it should be him. Lazarus.

The very first man she'd ever seen naked.

The muscles on his body were like art. The lines and ridges there a testament to his perfection.

And his... His masculinity.

Thick and large and hard for her.

For you?

Because he had walked away, and if he could walk

away... Did it really matter? Did she? She swam farther into the bath, trying to get away from the site of her own weakness.

What would become of her if she wasn't with him?

She couldn't imagine a life, she couldn't imagine herself without him, and that was terrifying. She didn't know what manner of creature she was if she was not in Lazarus's care. And there had been a time when she had been... When she had been alone in the world and she'd had to make her own way. She had tried so hard to forget that. But maybe by doing that she had made herself far too dependent. Because he could break her. He could break her and he was on the verge of it, and she did not know what to do about that.

She lay there in the water, floating. And she wondered about herself. Then she submerged herself beneath the water and tried not to think anymore. It didn't help. Certainly wouldn't fix the gnawing ache in her soul.

A few things had become clear to Lazarus while he had set about making sure that the dinner would be to Agnes's standards. The first was that he must seduce her. However he could. The second was that once he did so, he would make her his wife in truth, not just in a showy way for his brother. No. He did not have time to be thinking of this now, and he knew it, but Agnes was forcing things to a crisis point, as was his newfound desire for her.

And perhaps it was because she had threatened to leave. Perhaps it was because she was abandoning him.

You said you did not need her.

He didn't. He could protect himself just as well. He had no actual need of Agnes. And that was the strangest thing of all. He was not a man that clung to the things that were superfluous. But Agnes did not feel superfluous. Not in any manner. Rather she felt significant.

But then...

He felt a bond to Agamemnon, long dead though he was, and a responsibility to him, because he had saved his life. And while he would not consider himself a spiritualist in the sense that the people of the wood were, while he did not necessarily literally believe in spirits and fae inhabiting the trees, he could not deny that there did seem to be a spiritual connection inherent in the saving of a life. Lazarus had few connections in his life.

Agnes was the one who remained.

And so perhaps it was not wholly without merit to keep her with him.

He needed a wife eventually. Particularly if he were going to rule Liri in the fashion that monarchs did. The idea made him extremely uncomfortable. He was not a man who craved power. He was not a man who wanted it. But in order to do what needed to be done, he would have to take it. And that meant he would need a Queen. And she would need to bear him heirs.

He had thought of finding himself a soft, lovely princess who had been raised to expect such a fate.

But a woman such as that wouldn't be able to handle all that he was, and in many ways Agnes had been in training to be by his side for the last eight years. She could share his bed as well. Get round with his child.

The idea made heat run through his veins.

He stood for a long moment, at the beautifully appointed table on the balcony where Agnes would meet him soon. And he tried to think of when exactly his feelings for her had changed.

Perhaps it was just basic male need.

The desire for a bedmate that could match him.

He had not yet found one.

Agnes was his match in battle, and maybe on some level he had always known he was training her for his bed.

No. He had not.

He thought back to her, scared and wide-eyed in the alley in Paris.

He had not felt those things for her then, but one thing he had known was that she would be in his life forever. And he had turned to walk away. He had tried then to break that bond that Agamemnon had told him existed between two people when a life was saved.

"Where are you going?"

"Back to my kingdom."

"Can I go with you?"

And he could remember regarding her then. And wondering what on earth he was going to do with a girl such as her. She was so small. Frail almost.

Her black hair was dull, her expression one of a near permanent frown.

What could be done with her? What could be done with such a creature?

He had taken her back against his better judgment, and they had begun to train. And that sense of confusion as to why she was with him faded as he saw her improve. As her hair became glossy and her petite frame became strengthened by muscle. As her coordination grew and her speed and sense of timing became unerring.

She was a glory. This girl.

And then she had become... Inevitable.

She was with him when he needed to make decisions. She was a constant. As though she were part of him in a way that no one and nothing had ever been.

And only a few weeks ago, she had been tending the fire at the camp, and the flame had caught her expression, lit up her smile, her skin a golden glow in the light.

And he had known then that he could use her for this. To be the woman by his side when he came into Liri. And truly, he had realized there could be no other.

So why did he think there could be another in truth? There couldn't be. It would have to be her. And so, he would give her what she needed. For had she not told him exactly what it was? To be special. To be in an exalted position, while he could give her that. And why not? It made sense.

She had come from a gutter, from such an unstable life. It was understandable in the extreme that she should want something better for herself as she made a life going forward. And perhaps he would not have to let her go at all. Perhaps she did not need an education outside of him if he were to expand her knowledge.

It was then that she appeared out on the balcony. Wrapped in that gold gown that had been chosen back at the store in Paris. She was an exquisite thing. And he wished to devour her.

She looked at him, with deep suspicion on her beautiful face. "This is for show?"

"It is for you," he said.

"For me?"

"Yes. It was set up for show, yes. So that my brother would think that we are together. But it is more than that." He pulled her chair out, and she crossed the space, pausing in front of it. "Will you not sit?"

She did so, looking up at him with wonder on her face.

"A second fine dining experience in only a week, it is very strange."

"You want to have these things. Don't you think?"

"I don't think there's anything I ought to have. I have a great deal more than I ever expected to. Stability and home and… I suppose that will change when all of this is over. You will be here."

"Perhaps. Or perhaps I will move the seat of power into the wood."

"How will you rule if the people cannot see you?"

He laughed. "I don't know. But I never feel uncertain for long. Eventually it becomes clear."

"You're very confident."

"Of course. Have I not always been right?"

"Were you right down in the baths?"

She was baiting him. He should've expected nothing less from Agnes. "Yes," he said. "I was right to leave you because you were uncertain. If there is to be sex between us, Agnes, then you must want it."

Her face turned red. Like a beet. It was not delicate, and it was... Surprisingly female. In a way that he found appealing.

"I never said I wish there to be. Or that I didn't. I... I found it overwhelming."

"And then you are not sure. Sex should not be something you are uncertain about. It should be something you cannot go without. Something you cannot deny. The decision should be made with your body. And once your body is in the space of being able to make that decision for you... Then it is clear. There is no place for uncertainty, not then."

It became clear to him then what he wanted from Agnes. The next surrender. She had sworn her life to him out of obligation. Now he wanted her to beg for him in desperation. And he could make her do that. Of this he was sure. And it was what he desired above all else. Seduction.

That would make her his. He had her with him all this time, and he had failed to see what it was she actually desired. He would not fail there again.

"And now we eat."

The food was exactly as he had instructed. Perfectly made and exquisitely presented. Heavy on the sweets.

There was an array of cakes for dessert, in addition to rich chocolate truffles and lovely cream pies. Anything, essentially, that his Agnes could desire.

"Tell me about Ohio," he said.

Agnes laughed. "That is something that... No one has ever said to me."

"Will you tell me?"

"I will. What little I remember." Her lips turned down. "You know, I don't remember anything. I remember the house. Two story, but not fine. It was drafty in the winter. Sometimes the power was turned off. I remember my mother, but never smiling. And then... Well, and then I remember her funeral. Not many people came. I think her parents were there, what would be my grandparents. But they didn't stay, and they didn't talk to my father. They didn't seem to want to know me.

"I remember my father said they came from Hawaii. So they were cold. It was Ohio and it was winter. I don't know. That's all I remember. And then we started to move. My father said that he had a business opportunity and we were going to fly on a plane. And I had never done that before. After that we got on a very long flight. And I had one bag. From there on out we spent my childhood moving around Europe. We started in Germany. Then went to England. Luxembourg. Belgium. We were in Switzerland for a while. Then Norway. I loved it there. It was beautiful and wild. We spent time in Iceland, which I also loved. And along the way I picked up bits of all those languages. I forgot everything about my life before. At least, as much as I could. And I just sort of lived. Whatever reality, whatever moment we were in. It was easier. Easier to forget that I had ever gone to a real school. Easier to forget that I had a mother. That I had grandparents somewhere. It was all just easier. My father ran cons wherever we were. Sometimes with the aid of other people, which was why we would move. Or sometimes the law would close in on us and we would have to leave. I had no less than six passports before I was ten."

So strong. So brave. He had been too late. Would that he'd been there to save her then.

"That is no kind of life," he said, his voice rough.

"It was the only one I knew. Then we went to Paris. Which… At fifteen felt very exciting. But it began to wear on me quickly. It's a beautiful city. But like any place… There's an underside, and it is often bleak. Grim. All of the glamour and glitter on the top is just that. You take too deep of a breath and you blow it all away, and you just have the grime beneath. But I still loved walking to the Eiffel Tower. Gazing up at it. And I would take what little money I had, then buy myself bread and sit there. And imagine what it would be like if there was someone… Anyone who could take me away from that life. And then you came. And you rescued me when everything seemed lost. I'm grateful to you for that forever."

He could not help himself. He reached out and pressed his thumb to her cheek, only for a moment. Agnes, warm and alive and his.

She had sworn loyalty to him from the first, but this was different.

Entirely different.

"I don't know that I deserve gratitude for doing what anyone should have."

"Many people would have had to call the police. There would've been no other choice. They could not have single-handedly destroyed all those men and protected me."

"Well, that is down to my upbringing. In the end, we are all that we are created," he said.

"Until we are shown a different way. You took me away from the life that I knew. And you made me something different. Like I told you, I used to think about nothing. Just a moment. And every so often I would dream. But that was it. I didn't dwell on the things that were around me because they were… I knew that I didn't want to steal people's money, but I didn't know what else to do. I knew that I didn't want to be a con man, and I knew that I didn't think what my father did was right. But finding a way out was hard, and I couldn't see it. So I took my thoughts away, and I just did my best to not have them. It is not the best way to live. It is not. I think we are all what we are shown until someone gives us the strength, the insight, into something new. Until we are safe enough to want more. That's what you gave to me."

"Do you remember your last name?"

She shook her head. "No. I don't like to go that deep. I'm sure it's there, somewhere. I must've written it on assignments at school. But it's just been so long."

"And it's part of a person you wish to forget."

"Yes."

She looked around. "I cannot imagine being back at my childhood home. What is it like for you?"

He looked around at the expansive, beautiful terrace.

His childhood home. Such an odd thing to call a palace, and yet it was true.

But he had been four years old when he'd left, and Agnes had been more like six. So perhaps that two years carried with it more memories than the previous four could have.

And yet... And yet.

He let his mind go to the watercolor past, which was blurred and beautifully colored, but nothing distinct. But it carried with it feelings, like a painting by a master. The meaning could be unclear, but the emotion was not.

And for the first time he let himself stay in it. Stare at it. Marvel at it.

"What I have are vague pictures. Vague impressions of a time when I was here, more than... More than real memories."

"Do you remember your room?"

"I carry a picture of it. In my head. And I remember lying beneath the covers of the bed, and a woman reading to me. Perhaps it was my mother. Perhaps it was a nanny. I'm not sure."

Except he knew it was his mother. Not because he could see her in his mind, but because he could remember the feeling that he had in his chest. Of happiness and contentedness, a sense of well-being that he knew could only, and had only, come from her. He knew this to be true. As sure as he knew anything.

"I remember sitting at the table and having my favorite dinner. It was... Chicken nuggets."

Agnes laughed. "I would never have thought that I might have something in common with a prince. But that was my favorite too. I didn't know they would've made it for you at the palace."

"If I recall correctly I would sit with my brother at

a corner of the table opposite my parents, and we were served a different meal."

"Right. Your brother. I didn't have any siblings."

"I didn't either. After I was four."

"Tell me about that day. You have spoken of it, but it's different than telling the story, I think."

"I… I was playing with my brother on the lawn. I remember that. How our ball rolled into the woods and I remember… I remember going after it. And after that I remember it was dark all around me, and I could not see. I thought for sure that the palace was just behind me, but I kept on walking and it wasn't there. I didn't find the ball. I couldn't find my way back home. What seemed dark at first became overwhelmingly pitch-black. And then I began to hear the wolves howl. I knew about the Big Bad Wolf. Always wolves, wolves coming to eat children. Yes, I knew. I knew and I tried to hide. But I could not see. My eyes refused to adjust to that sort of darkness. I wedged myself as far as I could beneath the rock outcropping and slept for a time. And when I woke the sky was gray. I came out, and there they were. A pack of them. And they began to close in on me, and I tried to get back into my safe spot, but it was blocked. They are hunters, and they know how to track their prey.

"And then Agamemnon came. He beat them back with a large stick and set them on their way. He did not kill them. He told me later it was because the people of the wood had learned to exist with the animals. They did not take more than their share—the wolves did not take from the camp. I didn't believe him for a long time, but in all my years there, no one was ever taken by a wolf. But the minute my youngest brother wandered in…"

"Yes," she said. "He was eaten."

Lazarus nodded. "So perhaps there is truth to it. Agamemnon said I was branded as one of them from that moment on. That I was to swear my loyalty to him, and I did. It was easy enough. Easy enough to do. He told me I would have to forget my family. That they could not get me in the wood, and wouldn't. Because my father was afraid to go into it. And then he told me. He told me the story of how my great-grandfather had decided that the native faction of the country was too dangerous. How he had driven them from their homes. How he had demanded they not have their own government anymore. And eventually… They sought solace in the woods, because it was the only way they could escape. But many of them were killed. This was their land. Before explorers came from Greece and established their own hold here. And over the years the cultures mingled, but those that did not…

"Those that did not were always viewed with suspicion. But it was my great-grandfather who decided that it could be no more. That he would stamp out all that made them… Them.

"I was a gift sent to them, Agamemnon said. To right the wrongs that had been done. And it is as you said… You only know what you were raised with until you are shown something else. It is injustice that was done to the people of the forest. And I am the one that was sent to make it right."

"Did Agamemnon never read you stories?"

"No. Not as such. Not tucked into my bed. But he told me tales around the fire. He taught me to hunt and take my own food. Taught me to cook. Taught me to fight. He made me hard, and he made me a man. I went from being a prince who knew how to do nothing but sit at his own corner of the table and eat…chicken nuggets that had been prepared for him. Who spent his days playing ball with his brother… I became a man very quickly. But in the wood there is nothing else."

"Did you ever miss it? Did you miss being a boy?"

"I forgot about it," he said. "Because as you say… It is easier."

And he had not realized that he had quite so much in common with Agnes until that moment. But he hadn't even realized he'd felt that. Hadn't realized it was what he was going to say until just then. But it was true.

"I became something new."

"And you like what you have become?" she asked.

"The man I became is the man that saved you in Paris. The Prince of Liri would not have done that. I'm sure you heard how debauched my brother Dionysus was. What would've stopped me from becoming such a man?"

"Alex is not that man," Agnes said. "Read anything about him, and you'll see that he is upright, moral. He is very like you, I think."

"So you think. But I'm not convinced."

"And what would it take to convince you?"

"There is nothing," he said. "But it does not matter. We are of one goal, Agnes. And that is justice, yes?"

"I suppose."

"What about… What about in life?"

She tilted her head, looking at him from the corner of her eye, as though she were suspicious. "I have thought little about my life since coming to you. I have not had to. All needs have been met. And like you… I became stronger. I learned to hunt. I learned to fight. If I have to survive, then I can, and I will. And beyond that…"

"You will go off in the world to have experience."

"You're the one who said I should."

"And you are the one who decided it should be permanent. So what is it you dream of?"

CHAPTER EIGHT

AGNES DIDN'T KNOW how to answer that question. Nor did she know what to do with… All of this. For she had never sat and had a conversation with Lazarus as though they were… As though they were friends.

"I once dreamed of safety," she said. "And I found it. I dreamed of always being fed, and you have given me that as well. I'm not certain I know how to dream bigger than that."

"Come now. The girl that went and ate bread at the Eiffel Tower, she did not only dream of bread. What did you dream of?"

"What all people do, I suppose. Yes, I know a great many people dream of jobs. Work and what they will be when they grow up. But those things shift with time, and change. You might want to be an astronaut when you're a child because you don't know how difficult it is to get to the moon. I didn't dream of those things. I did wonder what it would be like, though, to be loved. Not used. But loved. When I dreamed of someone coming to rescue me, I often thought of my grandparents. The ones I never really got to know. Yes, I often thought of them. I just dreamed of what it could be if I… If I found a safe place with people who might open their arms to me. I dreamed of friends."

"A lover?" he pressed.

Her skin flushed, and she remembered, all too well, the heat that Lazarus generated in her body. The truth was she had never dreamed about a lover, not before she met him. Men had always represented something rather frightening. Something foreign and potentially dangerous. And then… Then she had dreamed of a man's touch. Especially when they had begun their training. When he had held her tight and invited her to try to escape him, her whole body had been flushed with heat. And she had not wanted to escape him, not at all, no… She had wanted to lean into him.

She had wanted his hold to change, had wanted his touch to become tender. She… She was so strangely aroused by the man, and then had begun to fall in love with him. Her loyalty had become something different, something deep. But the way that he observed the separation between them had provided safety.

Her hormones had been out of control, he had spent his own with women closer to his age. Women who were not sad teenagers with terrible crushes.

But still, his calloused hands always made her shiver. And sparring exercises became the most erotic experience in her life.

Until the sword fight in his Parisian penthouse. Until he had…

And then in the baths.

Where she had seen his body. Really.

"Of course I should like one," she said. "I am a warrior, but I am not made of stone. Yes, it has been the easiest thing to devote myself to my training and cast off the idea of having a lover. But... But that is not... is not all I want."

"And so you should leave me and find a man to take as a lover?"

"Perhaps I will," she said, feeling angry now. "Perhaps I shall go off and find myself countless lovers. How many have you had?"

He chuckled. "I do not know the number. Is that what you truly want?"

She wanted him. But it terrified her. She wanted him, and she did not know what to do about that.

She wanted him, but something about it terrified her. Perhaps it was that he was... All things to her. A man of great beauty and consequence. The one who had given her shelter, who had given her purpose. The one who had changed her life.

Perhaps that was why.

He leaned close to her. "I could teach you."

His words were dark and rich like the coffee that she had just drunk with her cake. And the temptation in them was... It was so deep. So real.

"I could show you all the things your body can do, Agnes. But you deserve more than that. More than a simple training."

And now it had gone from temptation into something much, much more dangerous.

"You deserve to have a man take his time with you. To give to you. Has anyone given to you, darling?"

"I… You have given me much."

"I would like to lay you on a soft bed and spend an hour tasting your skin. Every inch of it. I would like to make love to you. Slowly, the first time. But then… You are a warrior. You always were. A woman and a warrior. And I see that. You would not be content only with slow and sweet, would you? You want to sword fight. And I would give it to you. I would test your strength while I held you in my arms. And you would test mine. I want that. Do you know… All of my lovers have been so very soft. I have never had a woman quite like you. And the idea intrigues me. More than intrigues. I want to know what it would be like to take all of your strength and have it pressed against me. Naked. So, this is why it can never be just a training. Because I need you to show me what your body can do. I need you to show me what mine could do. What it could do only with you. The pleasure I think we might find…"

He was looking at her, and he did not break focus. His words were slow and true, and achingly deliberate. Each one felt like a touch, like that promised caress. Each one felt something like magic. And she wanted it. So very desperately.

She wanted those words to turn into touch. Wanted this moment to turned into more. The pulse at the base of her thighs throbbed, and she could scarcely think past it. Was this why women made whole fools of themselves after men? She had seen women do it at the camp. Giggling after Lazarus. Wanting so badly for him to turn his attentions to them. But he did not have time for the giggly ones. He preferred experienced women, at least he always had. An observation she had made. And one that made her feel even more like she was in her own category.

But he had said… He had said that he had never wanted a woman like her before. That he had never been with one.

And that was the greatest temptation of all. He leaned across the space, and he touched her lips to his.

And her body caught fire.

His kiss was achingly slow, deliberate. But not for show, not like the one in the restaurant. He parted her lips with his tongue and tasted her deep, and she became lost in the slick rhythm. Lost in the feel of his mouth on hers like so.

His kisses made her feel drugged. And she slowly began to lose all resistance. All worries. Because there was nothing but this. Nothing but that large calloused hand on her face, stroking her rather than holding her for a fight. His mouth was not issuing commands, but rather demanding response with each pass of his lips over hers.

This was more dangerous than any battle she had ever engaged in, and she was going into it willingly. With all that she had in her. She was so desperate and wet between her legs, needy for something she knew only he could give.

Hadn't he given it to her once? The touch of his tongue on her most intimate flesh.

The kiss he had given her there would reverberate inside of her for the rest of her life.

And how much more so if he took possession of her? With that thick, glorious male member of his that she had seen for the first time in the baths.

She had been afraid then.

Because she had felt like he wanted her… Well, she didn't know why. He had been angry. She could see that. Angry, and his touch had been a demand in a way that had frightened and confused her.

But this was different.

This was different.

She found herself pressing as near to him as she could without falling off of her chair, and then he wrapped his arms around her waist and pulled her directly to his chair, bringing her legs on either side of his, placing the heart of her directly in contact with that hardest part of him. And she gasped. And found herself moving her hips in a sensuous rhythm that she somehow simply knew, even though she had never done anything like this before.

She just knew.

Her body knew exactly what it was required to do. And she was chasing pleasure. Chasing the desire that he aroused in her with all the intensity that she possessed in her soul. An intensity created by her time with Lazarus. For before she had been soft. Before she had been nothing more than a leaf drifting on the wind. And now she created the wind. All because of him.

And together… Together they were making a storm.

She cupped his face, kissing him back, deep and hard and with all of the longing inside of her. She rocked her hips against his arousal, gasping as he hit that spot that was so aroused with desire for him.

Oh, how she wanted to feel him there. Hard and thick, surging within her, and even though the idea frightened her, those virginal nerves that few could ever outrun, she also needed it. Craved it. Desired it above all else.

"Lazarus," she whispered.

"Yes?"

"Lazarus, I…"

"You can still speak," he said, dragging his thumb down her face. "That means I have not done a good enough job."

She wanted to protest. He had done a fine job. She was gasping with her need for him. Desperate.

"Tonight, I think you shall sleep, Agnes. And you will not be bothered by me."

Bothered. She was not bothered. Well, she was bothered. Rather warm with it.

But she wanted…

"I want you desperate, darling."

"Darling?"

He had called her that about twice.

"Agnes," he said, in that way only he did. "Darling Agnes."

And she did not know what to do now, for he set her back in her chair, and she felt unsatisfied and confused. He had said that when it came to sex you had to be mindless and not in control, but he still was. Or he would not have stopped it. She would not have stopped. She would have let him take her there on the terrace. She would not have been able to control herself.

And why did he want her now?

That thought pounded in her head while she sat there and finished the last slice of her cake. And again as they made their way to their bedchamber.

"Lazarus? What do you want with me?"

"I have been giving it a great deal of thought, Agnes," he said. "And I think… Yes, I said that I wanted you to see the world. I stand by that. You should have some experience away from me. But… When you return I want you to be my wife."

CHAPTER NINE

AGNES COULD NOT believe what she was hearing. He wanted her to be his wife?

"What do you need a wife for?"

"I'm to be King. I will need a wife. And I will need heirs. You are… You are bound to me in a way that I cannot explain. And now I think I understand it. This is what was always meant to be. I could never have a soft princess by my side. I need a warrior. It is built into my blood. On the deepest level of who I am. That is what I require."

And then he disappeared into the bath chamber, and she heard the water running for the shower a moment later.

She sat on the edge of the bed, her pulse pounding heavily. He wanted her to be his wife. He wanted her to be his wife because she made sense.

But with that she would have… She would have a permanent place by his side, and there would be no other women. And for Agnes, who had never done much dreaming, it was…

But it was not about love.

And she had dreamed of love once.

But you know how the world works. It is not so simple. Neither was it half so wonderful as she'd once dreamed.

It was true. How could one woman ever hope to have all of those things? A place in Lazarus's heart and by his side. Ample food and shelter.

But he's bent on revenge...

He was. And he would say it wasn't revenge, he would say that it was...

But there was more. He spoke of his family, and they were not bad memories. And yet something in him was twisted in regard to them, and it wasn't just the stories that Agamemnon had told him. She could sense that.

Inside of him was a frightened boy whose father had not found him. It was another man who had saved him from the jaws of the wolves.

It wasn't true that they had never really looked for him? Was it true they had not done so because of what had happened generations before with the people of the forest?

She wondered. And if she wondered, then he certainly did. He certainly did.

She sat, and she waited. And decided what she was going to do.

And there was only one conclusion she could come to.

That his seduction at the table was more calculated than he would have her think. And she had to test it. If this was a battle, then she would have to pick up her sword. If this was a battle, then she would have to test herself in truth. And test him.

And there was only one way to do so.

You should be mindless.

You should be unable to stop.

Agnes stood slowly from the edge of the bed and crossed the space to the wardrobe where her things had been put. Everything that she had tried on at the Parisian fashion boutique, and many things she had not.

And she was gratified by what she found.

There was an outfit—it could be called that—made entirely of gold lace. Open up the front, with a belt at the waist, and a pair of the tiniest undergarments she had ever seen. Just for the lower half.

She stripped all of her clothing off and put it on. And examined herself in the mirror. She could see the shadow of dark hair between her thighs through the underwear. Could see the dusky hint of her nipples beneath the lace of the dress.

And he would see them as well. But he had seen her naked already, so why not this?

Why not?

And she waited. Waited for him to emerge again.

And when he did, he had nothing but a towel wrapped around his waist, his glorious torso gleaming in the golden light, water droplets rolling down his chest, rippling over his ab muscles. He was a truly beautiful man. The most beautiful that she had ever seen.

And will you regret this?

No. The answer came, swift and simple. Whatever happened after this, she would not regret it.

Because there were only two possible outcomes. He would pass her test, and she would agree to be his wife.

She would. It was that simple. Or he would fail and…
Well then, she would remain a virgin. And she would
go on into her new life and find another lover. One who
was mindless for her.

"Agnes," he said, his voice rough.

He was not unaffected.

"As we have discussed," she said. "You are not my
King any longer. I do not have to follow your every
order."

"Do you not?" His voice was deceptively calm. But
she knew him well enough to know that a person could
not have any sort of false sense of security when it came
to Lazarus.

"You stopped things before I was ready."

"You don't know what you're ready for."

"You cannot help it. You say that you do not wish to
be my teacher, but you cannot help it. But sex, Lazarus,
requires two people to be desperate. To be mindless.
And you think far too much."

She walked toward him, and she tried to remember
the way those other women moved. Slow and sensuous,
with a rock in their hips, their breasts thrust out into
prominence. Yes, she tried to think of that and keep her
gaze on his. And a surge of power went through her
when she realized he could not take his eyes off her. He
was waiting to see what she would do next, and he did
not know. She did not know what she would do either,
but she was gratified that she was able to surprise him.

Even if she would have to surprise herself, and make
decisions very quickly.

And when she reached him, it seemed obvious. She

did exactly what she wanted to. She wanted to touch that great and glorious chest, for she always had. For he was incredible and beautiful in all ways, and she had lusted after his body since before she understood exactly what it was she was feeling.

She could remember clearly the first night she had understood that she desired him the way that a woman desired a man. It had been when a woman had approached him at the campfire, all curves and heavy-lidded smiles.

She had put her hand on his chest, and Lazarus had responded, taking her hand and going off with her into the darkness.

And that was when she had realized exactly what they did in the darkness. And when she had imagined putting her hand on his chest. When she had imagined what might happen if she were to touch him that way. And what it would be like if he led her off into the darkness. What then? She felt sick with jealousy but things had made sense then. In a way they had not before, and in some ways she was grateful for it. Because it had given her clarity. And so there was that. But it had eaten at her as well.

And so she did it now.

Touched his chest.

She had wanted to then. As she had wanted to do since she was just seventeen and falling desperately in love with him, while understanding slowly what that meant. How impossible it was.

In some ways, though, she had been happy. Because at least she had felt love. Even if it wasn't returned. She had loyalty. But now… Now she could touch him, as a woman touched a man. Now she could reach down into those hidden parts of herself. The woman, not the warrior. The woman who had sworn so much more to him than fealty, but had sworn her heart.

And now she would swear her body to him, if he would have it.

And you will extract all the desire in his whole being from him.

She knew it then. For perhaps what he'd said was true. And he had really never had a woman like her.

And yes, it was to be her first time.

But she did not want gentle. She wanted them. What they were.

Not what someone else might be. Not how he would handle a virgin, but how he would handle Agnes.

Hand flat, splayed over his chest, she moved it down his body boldly, taking in the sensation of his muscles, of the crisp hair there that was so different from anything on her own body. He was a man. And there was no denying it. And she was a woman.

Often with them those lines blurred, because they were warriors, but here in this space it was undeniable. Here in this space, they were one. And, too, such very different entities all at the same time.

"I want you," she said. "Do you know how much? How unfair it was when you put your mouth on me when I was not prepared after spending years working to banish the fantasies that I had of you? It was nearly impossible to endure. And then you… Then you changed everything. You changed everything when you put your mouth on mine, and when you put your mouth…there. On that secret place where I've… I've tried not to want you. And you think of me as innocent, I know you do, but my fantasies of you have not been innocent. Not for a very long time."

And then she pushed her hand down beneath the edge of the towel, which loosened the knot, and she saw it falling to the floor. And his body was exposed to her. Oh, his body. It was so beautiful. So incredibly beautiful.

"I want you," she repeated, and she wrapped her fingers around his thick length, around the evidence that he was just as desperate for her as she was for him.

He groaned, harsh and short, his breath hissing through his teeth. His eyes closed and his head fell back, and she had never seen him… She had never seen him like this. There was a resignation in the action that was nothing like the Lazarus she had known these last eight years.

She felt powerful. Holding him like this. And breathless with desire. It was the strangest thing. To feel both strong and weak all at once. Like she could do anything, and like he could defeat her were he to place his lips on hers and kiss her until she was mindless.

But they were locked in a battle where both would emerge victorious in the end.

A thrill of excitement raced through her.

"Do I please you?" she asked, lifting her eyes to his, and then following some instinct she hadn't known she possessed, drawing her tongue across her upper lip.

And that was when he moved. He gripped her wrists,

propelling her backward, and taking her down onto the bed, his naked body looming over hers.

"Little witch," he said.

"Perhaps," she said. "This feels a bit like magic." And then she arched herself upward, and she could feel him respond. Could feel his powerlessness to do anything but meet her there. His desire as intense and terrifying as her own. And then, with all the strength she possessed, she wrapped her leg around his waist and reversed their positions, so that she was on top of him, looking down at his glorious naked form. She put her hands to the belt on the dress, letting the fabric fall loose, and then shrugging the gold film from her shoulders, letting it fall so that she was bare breasted above him.

"Is this a fight for dominance then?" he asked, his voice silky. "Because I warn you. I will win."

She thought of how strong he was. The glory she would feel in such a defeat. "I think we would both win in that case."

He growled again, and she found herself flat on her back, her panties being ripped from her body. "Do not play with me."

"This is not a game," she said. "You were treating me as if I were game. A quarry. Something to be snared and caught, and you were so controlled. You had me begging for you, and you would not give me what I wanted. This is no place for games. Not you and me. Either we need to have each other, or we don't have each other at all."

The growl intensified, and he gripped her hands, lacing his fingers through hers as he pressed them down into the mattress. "Can you handle the manner of my need?"

"I know nothing else," she said. "Are we not a product of the environment wherein we were shaped and created? Because I was shaped in your world, Lazarus. Honed into the thing you see before you by your own hand. Were you not always making yourself a bedmate?"

Something flashed through his eyes, and she knew that she had bested him. Yet again.

He said nothing, instead he lowered his head and kissed her, the gesture a punishment that she was more than willing to take.

She could feel his heart raging in his chest, raging out of control.

And then she knew, yet again, exactly what she would do next. She pulled away from him, scattering kisses down his chest, and then she wiggled out from beneath him, and he moved so as to catch her, and she took that opportunity to bring herself back to him, kissing his stomach, the hard ridges of his ab muscles, all the way down to where he was hard and thick for her.

Because why should he be the only one who could undo her?

She put her mouth on him, then opened her lips around the thick head of him, drawing him in as deeply as she could.

His hand went to her hair, gripping her tightly as he swore violently and she didn't stop. He didn't make her. And he could have.

Just as she could've made him stop when he had

eaten into her in the Parisian penthouse. And she had not. Because the desire was too strong. Because the need for release was greater than the need for sanity.

Mindless.

Desperate.

How they knew it well. She pleasured him like that, until he was shaking, until his hands in her hair were nearly beyond pain. And then he wrenched her away from him, brought her back up his body and kissed her. Then those rough, large hands were between her thighs, stroking her, taking her to the brink, before bringing her back again.

"Please," she whimpered. "Lazarus, please."

"Beg me," he growled.

"Lazarus…"

"Beg me for your release."

"Please," she said again.

"Please what?"

"My Lord," she said. "Please."

And then he moved his hand just so and gave her exactly what she had needed. Exactly what she had been longing for. Desire broke over her like so many scattered stars, her release of fractured glass pane cracking all around her.

And when she came back to herself, he was there, over her, the thick blunt tip of him pressed against the entrance to her body.

"This may hurt," he growled, and then in the next moment he thrust home, swallowing her gasp of pain with a kiss.

And it was only pain.

Pain existed only to the degree that you allowed it, something she had learned in her training. And she let it fall away. She made it so that it did not matter. Pain was immaterial. What mattered was that he was inside of her. Connected to her. Closer than she had ever been to another person.

Lazarus. Him.

And then he began to move, taking those pieces of pain and replacing them, thrust by thrust, with pleasure that ran deep.

Until she was sobbing, gasping with it.

Until she was begging him for more. For everything.

Until she was poised on that brink once again, that shattering place that only he had ever really brought her to.

And when it burst, it was all glitter. And there was nothing dark or insidious beneath. It was bright all the way down, the kind of glory that she had only ever dreamed existed in this world.

And when he shattered right along with her, it was like dying and being made new again.

Mindless. Desperate.

No different than her. It was not a game, or a manipulation. Or a means to an end. Not for her either. It was just beyond her. Beyond them.

And then Agnes, who had not shed a single tear even when her father had been killed in an alley in Paris, began to cry.

CHAPTER TEN

LAZARUS LOOKED DOWN at the trembling woman in his arms. His Agnes.

And he… He could not recall the last time he had completely lost the plot like that. He never had. That was why he could not remember it. Because the moment did not exist. She had taken his plans and twisted them, made it so he could not even remember the aim of his seduction. And she had turned it into her seduction. And he had… He had succumbed. Quickly. Willingly.

Were you not always making yourself a bedmate?

And now she was weeping. This woman who had come toward him with such strength and power was shattered in his arms, crying like a child. And he did not know what to do.

He was comfortable dealing with battle. Comfortable dealing with a fight. But this… This moment was out of his reach. He did not know what to do. He did not know what it made him. There had been a time in his life when someone had tucked him in and read him bedtime stories. But it was not now. And it had not been for a very long time. There had been softness in his life, but he could not remember it. And yet he held her up against his chest, because it seemed the right thing to do, whether he fully understood or not. He felt like there was a large space between them, and he did not know how he might cross it. He did not know if it were possible.

"Why...why are you crying?" he asked.

She pressed her cheek against him, wet from her tears getting on his skin. "I don't know."

"Have I hurt you?"

"No," she said on a jagged sigh. "I'm not injured."

"Then I do not understand."

"I don't either." She looked up at him, her eyes shining bright. "It is okay to not understand, Lazarus."

No. It wasn't. He was a man who did not traffic in unknowns. But rather in the things that he could see and touch. And he had been proud of this. For much of this time. He had... It made sense. The things that were tangible. That he could see and touch and taste. And beyond that... Beyond that none of it mattered. At least, he had thought so. Until he lay there with this woman, holding her, trying to make sense of what she was feeling. And of why he wanted so badly to protect her when there was no threat.

"You don't like this," she said. "Because it was not your timing."

"God laughed at my timing," he said wryly.

And it was true. He had sought to control her with desire, and she had turned it around on him, as a blade wielded sloppily by an enemy who had underestimated his foe.

He had underestimated her. And he had underestimated his desire for her. But perhaps… Perhaps because she had desired him this whole time, perhaps because she had known… Perhaps that was why she had managed to best him so effectively.

She was acquainted with this desire between them while he… It was new to him. Or at least, the understanding of it. But he had not known.

"You have wanted me?" he asked.

She nodded. "You are the only honorable man I have ever known. I honestly wasn't sure if I had any use for men until I met you. And you… You are so brave and steady. And you put your life at risk to save mine. So yes, I wanted you. But in every way. To wish to keep me in your life, to approve of me. To hold on to me. And I knew… I knew when I saw the way those women touched you that I wished I could touch you the same. But I… I also knew that I would never do anything that would make you want to send me away. That I would never do anything that would make me any less to you than I was. And so I determined that I would be Agnes. The most and best, the one who swore everything to you. And if that meant being chased, that I would be. For my desire was tied to you anyway."

"Agnes," he said, feeling unequal to the declaration in the moment. "There is no other one like you."

And then she settled her head against his chest. "And there is none like you."

There was something in that statement. Something in that declaration that soothed a beast inside of him he had not known was roaring there.

He wanted to keep her, but not in the same way he'd felt compelled to do so before. This was not about holding hard, but gentle. Keeping her in contact with him, his skin, but not holding so tight as to trap her, to crush her.

He just wanted to hold her.

And so he did. And whatever happened next, he would meet at the head then. But for now, Agnes was soothed, she had stopped crying and she was in his arms. Everything else would take care of itself.

The next morning Agnes was invited to tea with Tinley. It was a very frightening request, all things considered. She had just been with Lazarus for the first time, the way women and men were, and they were lying to Tinley and Alexius. She felt a jumble of nerves as she walked into the future Queen's personal sitting area, which was lovely and well-appointed.

"Good afternoon," she said.

"Agnes," Tinley said, smiling broadly. "You look… well."

But she could tell the way that Tinley said that meant she did not. Agnes blinked.

"Is there something wrong with me?"

"No," Tinley said. "There's nothing wrong with you. Why would you think that?"

"You look very disconcerted."

"It's only that you look sort of pale."

Great. So everything that had happened with Lazarus was written all over her.

"I'm fine. I'm very much looking forward to tea. You know I really like desserts."

"Lazarus has said. You don't suppose there's a chance you could be pregnant."

She felt her eyes go wide. And the truth of the matter was... She and Lazarus had done nothing to prevent such a thing. They hadn't even thought of it. Or discussed it. It hadn't crossed her mind even once. But technically, she would not be pregnant yet. "I... Likely not. It's fine."

"And is everything well with you and Lazarus?"

"I... Yes," she said. "We are well. Lazarus is a hard man, but he is good," Agnes said.

"And you love him," Tinley said. "Please sit down. I'll pour you some tea."

This was that female heart-to-heart sort of thing that Tinley wanted to have. And Agnes had never engaged in. She had always been hiding things about herself. And right now it was no different. She was hiding.

"Lazarus saved my life," Agnes said. "Literally. I was a girl on the streets of Paris, and he... He undoubtedly saved me from a very grim fate. I have loved him since I was sixteen years old."

"Sometimes that isn't love," Tinley said. "And I don't say that to be discouraging. It's only that... Agnes, I have some experience with that. I thought I loved Dionysus very much. I couldn't sort out the feelings that I had for Alexius. Until... Until much later. What I felt for Dionysus was not love. It was just a childish sort of infatuation."

"I'm not infatuated with Lazarus," Agnes said, laughing. As if that word could be applied to the two of them. The sword fights and sparring. The way that he talked to her. The way that he touched her. It was nothing half so simple as infatuation. If only it could be. "I love him," Agnes said. "But there is... An intensity to that."

Tinley laughed then, a high, pleasant-sounding sound. "Well, if you had a late night, you should've simply said that."

"Yes," Agnes said. "A very late night. Thank you for the romantic meal, and the time at the baths. I... I very much think that it... Enhanced that."

She felt uncomfortable sharing so much, even though she was only sort of playing a part. But was she? And now Lazarus wanted her to be his wife in truth. So what did that mean. What did any of it mean.

"He and Alexius are going riding today," Tinley said. "Brotherly bonding. You have no idea how much Alexius has felt... Lazarus's loss weighed heavily on him. For all of his life."

Guilt started to chew at Agnes.

"The loss of both of his brothers... It's been a shadow over him. Over his life. It took a lot to get him to where he is now. And he... He really is wonderful."

"Lazarus is not an easy man. Because he didn't have an easy time. Life in the wood is not easy. It's very difficult, and he had to figure out a way to survive. As a young boy who lost his family the way that he did. And in his mind, he did lose them. As soon as he was in the wood, he was beyond their reach. He... He doesn't know softness."

And neither did Agnes. Not really.

"And you? He saved you and brought you into the forest? How has that been for you?"

"Good. As long as I've been with him."

And it was true. She was happy when she was with him. So why couldn't they be together. Really be together. He had proposed marriage, and she knew that it had nothing to do with love. Not for him. But she did love him. It was the true thing that bonded her to him, not honor, not anything else. Perhaps that was enough. Perhaps it could be enough.

One thing she knew, the sooner they finished here the better. She did not like lying to Tinley. And she did not know how to reconcile her feelings for Lazarus with the growing discomfort over what it was he planned for their hosts.

For there was more to that man she loved than revenge. She knew it.

But she did not know if she could ever make him believe it.

CHAPTER ELEVEN

"A GOOD DAY to ride," Alexius said, as they reached the top of the mountain and looked down over the castle, over the wood, over everything.

"Yes," Lazarus agreed. For while he might have to be guarded around his brother, he would not lie about something so obvious. It was a good day for a ride.

"What do you see when you look at it?"

Lazarus glanced at his brother. "I'm sorry, I don't understand."

"The kingdom. What do you see when you look down upon it. Do you see your home? Or is the wood your home?"

"That is a complicated question," Lazarus said.

"I had a sense that it was. I'm trying to understand, from you, Lazarus, what it is you wish."

"Why do you think I wish anything?"

"Because you're not a man of inaction. And yet you have been sitting in the palace enjoying my hospitality and… And that's all. Your fiancée is lovely, and I heard that you greatly enjoyed the dinner that was set out for you, and I'm pleased to hear that. But I wonder… I do wonder if there is more. More that you want. More that you need."

And this was the moment then. To speak. To state his intent. And above all else, Lazarus was a man of honor. And so while it was one thing to sit and engage in some manner of subterfuge without speaking of what it was he wanted, he would not lie. Not directly. He would give his brother a chance to face him head-on. And he would do so now.

"What do you know the history of Liri?"

"As much as any schoolchild. But undoubtedly more. Our father made certain that I knew everything."

"And yet you did not know there was a kingdom in the woods."

"No," Alexius said, his voice faltering. "I did not."

"And have you asked yourself why that is? Why he would want to keep it a secret. Why it would not be spoken of widely. Why is it that none of you living in this kingdom know that there was another kingdom within it?"

"I don't know," he said.

"They stole this land. You know that this place was settled broadly by Greeks, Italians, others from that region of Europe."

"Yes. There was a lot of land and ample opportunity here."

"Yes. A great and vast wilderness. And what became of that? It was tamed. And what happened to the people who lived here first?"

"I confess that I don't know."

"They went into the woods, Alexius. And there they have waited. For something. For justice of some kind.

And I have been charged with ensuring that justice is done."

"And what, to you, is justice?"

"My people were driven from their homes. They were driven from this land. They have no say in this government. They do not have the ruling body they once had. For our great-grandfather... He was threatened by it."

"Tell me everything. Show me everything. Lazarus, I will not stand by and let injustice be done. If there's one thing I've always been certain of, it's that our family was cursed. Two brothers going to the woods and neither come out? There's a reason for that. There has to be. There has always had to be. It's a punishment. And I'm certain of it.

"This history is a blight on our family," Alex said. "I want... I want to do something to fix it."

"Do you?" And Lazarus could not pinpoint quite why he had imagined his brother would be a villain in this. Except... Except. He had not wanted to think that anyone in his family could be anything more than that. On some level he had wanted to believe that the only way to be true, the only way to be good, was to stick to that Spartan life he'd been led into. That there was nothing more beyond the wood, and there could not be. Not and also have goodness. Not and also be right.

He had wanted to believe...

He had wanted to believe that the only answer was to destroy his family.

The only answer.

Why?

This was the only time in his life he'd ever had the chance to ask someone—outside the wood—who had been there. Who knew.

Alexius might have been a young child, but he'd been there the day Lazarus had gone. He had been a witness to it.

But the words stuck in his throat. Part of him preferred the legend.

Didn't legends exist for a reason?

But he was no coward. And he knew Agnes, honest, forthright and bold, would never sit in a lie when she could be certain of the truth.

It shamed him, that he had been tempted to cloak himself in a story.

And so he spoke.

"What happened?" Lazarus asked. "The day that I disappeared?"

Alexius's face became shaded. "Our mother... Our mother changed after that. She blamed me. As she blamed me for the loss of Dionysus. Our father too. They were never the same."

"And you?"

Alexius lowered his head, and the raw emotion Lazarus could feel coming from his brother in waves was a shock. He had not expected him to have feelings—especially not so deep—about something that had happened so long ago. "I was supposed to protect you. I was supposed to protect you and... We were children. We were children and you were lost. And I felt deeply that it was my fault, and also... That I could not have stopped it. I didn't know. But losing two brothers the way that I did, I was afraid... You know it felt like it must be my fault. It did. I was devastated to lose you," Alex said. "And I know that we can never have that time back. But in many ways I lost my family that day too. I'm so glad that you were cared for. I am. But I have missed you, Lazarus. And these things are not easy for me to talk about. I was not a man raised to feel my emotions. I couldn't. And my history with family is very complicated. I... Tinley was originally engaged to Dionysus. I was intent on seducing her away from him. The night he was killed. I have struggled with my own purity of intent for much of my life for that reason. Also for the loss of you. But Tinley has made me... She's made me different. She's made me understand things about myself that I didn't before. And she's brought me peace. Peace I didn't think I could ever have. Not a man like me. She has made me... She has made me into the King that I need to be. I hope the man as well. I wish to be a brother to you. I wish to be a brother to you in ways that I have not been. And I wish to... I wish to bring restoration to your people. The people who cared for you. You shall rule by my side."

The words were as a bullet, straight to his chest. They might have knocked him off his horse had he not found a way to steady himself.

He had not come here for this. For *restoration*.

He had not known such a thing was possible.

He had come for destruction. For in his mind the only option was conquer or be conquered.

Perhaps that was the blood of his great-grandfather. A man who had not seen how people could exist side by side.

And it shamed him.

He could see that it wasn't as simple as his brother being ignorant, or uncaring. And Lazarus himself was not more enlightened than Alexius. He simply knew different angles.

Lazarus knew some of the dark, hard things in their family history.

Alexius knew the humanity.

And if you put all of those things together, they created a whole that was quite different than either of them had previously thought or believed.

"You would rule with me?"

"It's the only way I can see forward. We must have unity, Lazarus. We must have our family together. Life without you, life after your loss, it was dark. And there is nothing I can do about the loss of Dionysus. There is nothing I can do to put Mother and Father at peace. There is nothing I can do to change what our ancestors did to the people of the wood. I cannot go back. But we can go forward, and we can do things differently. And that is something I think we are honor bound to do."

"You do not wish for bloodshed?" Lazarus asked.

Alexius looked at him, one dark brow arched. "I do not. Were you prepared for it?"

He nodded slowly. "I was prepared for anything."

"And how does this sit with you? A truce?"

"It sits better with me than I would've thought."

He thought back to when he had nearly taken Tinley. Something to hurt his brother. Something to get revenge.

An act of open war. And he had told himself that the reasons he had given his brother for his not taking Tinley were all emotional, and he had told himself it was not true. That for him it had been about maintaining peace where he could, and giving himself time to plan things out a bit more strategically.

But the truth was, seeing the way his brother loved Tinley had done something to him. It was something he could not understand.

"Come," Alexius said. "We will talk about logistics. And I will race you back."

And so they did. Going as fast as their horses could take them, all the way back down to the palace. And Lazarus felt something like joy. Something like freedom. Like fun. Like a childhood that had slipped through his grasp when he was four years old, never to be reclaimed. Until now. Until this moment.

And when they arrived, Tinley met them, coming out of the palace. And she was… Radiant. Her face glowed with joy as she ran toward Alexius. He dismounted his horse and picked her up from the ground, holding her gently for a kiss. And there was something… Something. Something between them that he couldn't even understand. Love, he knew that it was. But it was that same feeling he had looking at his brother from the wood when Tinley had vanished. Mystified. Furious. And it had to do with the limitations in his own soul. Even the confusion that he felt when Alexius proposed a merger. When he proposed peace. All of it was so foreign to him. Mercy. Compassion. Softness.

His mother…

He had learned to build a wall over his fear, his hurt. It was how Agamemnon had told him to survive. But he had lost so many things. So many pieces of himself.

And there was Agnes. Agnes who had wept after they'd made love. Who he held in his arms while she shook, but felt like a mountain trying to find ways to soften for a weary traveler. He did not know how. He did not know if such a thing were possible. Stone could not be made soft. And he still felt like a boy, standing in the woods, separate from this bright and brilliant world. Separate from this reality. From this truth. He was not the same as his brother. And he didn't know how to be.

Perhaps he was too shaped by those years away.

But then... Didn't the answer lie here? As to being a leader... Alexius understood softness more. Alexius understood many things he didn't, he could see it. And yes, he would have to go back to his people and say it would not be the grand coup that they had all imagined. But it would be something. And it would be better in the end.

And maybe this was the softness. Maybe it was all he had.

Tinley took hold of Alex's arm and looked up at him, the look on her face brilliant. "Did you have fun?"

"Yes," Alex said.

And Lazarus found that he would've said the same. Which was a strange realization indeed.

"Where's Agnes?"

"She's gone to the baths. We had a very nice tea, but she was tired." Tinley's eyes glowed with humor, and he could not quite say why.

"I will need to journey back into the wood tonight. I will return. But... I will need Agnes."

"Are you sure Agnes should make that journey?"

He laughed. "You forget, you have seen Agnes in quite her finest clothing. But she is the same as I am. Agnes is a warrior."

And the woman he was going to marry. It was no longer a lie. Perhaps nothing here was.

Perhaps it was… Perhaps there was a way.

"We may return tonight, but late. I will… I will see you."

By the time he found Agnes she was in their bed-chamber, fully dressed.

"Put your walking clothes on," he said.

"Why?"

"We're journeying back home tonight."

"Lazarus…"

"I will explain on the way."

Lazarus was grim and silent on the journey, his disquiet nearly a physical thing. The darkness began to get oppressive, and Agnes knew that they wouldn't make it back to the encampment tonight.

"Are we to sleep out here?"

She did not fear the wolves of the wood, nor any of the other dangers. Lazarus was the most dangerous thing in this forest.

"Sure, yes, we shall stop here."

He put their bags down, and then began the work of making a fire. It didn't take him long before the flames were high and hot. He was so experienced in survival. He was just the sort of man who could keep her safe. Who could take care of her, who could take care of a nation.

"Do you know why we have to go back?" he asked.

"No. Because you didn't tell me."

"And you didn't ask," he said, looking at her intently.

"All right. Why?"

"I don't think… I don't think there's going to be a revolution. I spoke to Alex, and he… He was regretful to hear about the history of the country. He wants to make it right. He wants me to rule with him, and to represent the interests of the people of the forest. We will talk more later about the particulars, but he… He wants to restore what was taken. He wants to find a way. For us all to coexist peacefully. For us to be a family."

"And that is…what you want?"

He didn't have words for what he wished. It was a tangle of hard frustration in his chest, and he had no idea how to say one way or the other whether this was good or bad. Whether it was within his expectations or not. It was nothing like he had imagined. But none of this was. Lazarus had always known firmly who he was and what he was for. An instrument of vengeance if nothing else. And now… Now it was not to be so. But perhaps it was better. Perhaps this was better. But what would it mean to their people?

What would it mean to their way of life? Would they want this compromise.

"I began compromising the moment that I saw Tinley standing in that clearing. I was going to take her. I was going to make her my war bride. But then… I saw the way he went after her. I saw what he did. I do not understand those feelings. Alexius seems to have ripped himself open and carved out space for this woman in-

side of him and I do not understand. I can't understand.
I was made to be something else entirely, and this…
This road to compromise is painful like the breaking
of a limb."

"Lazarus…"

"You were part of a family once. Even if you can't
remember."

"So were you."

"Can you show me, Agnes? I need to understand.
I need to understand why she looks at him like that
when he comes back to the palace. I need to understand
why he changed. That's what he told me. That Tinley
changed him. That she made him see himself differently. I… I do not understand this. And I… I need to.
Agnes, I need you."

Agnes felt at a loss. There was a hard edge to his
voice, desperation to his words, and she did not know
how she was supposed to call the answers up to these
questions.

"I don't know," she said. "No one has ever cared for
me, Lazarus, not really. The closest thing has been you
in your obligation to me. I only know the same things
you do."

"When we touch it is fire," he said. "And I can see
that between them. It is that the core of what they are.
At the core of their connection. Can we not find that?"

"I don't know," she said.

"Teach me," he said. "Teach me to be like him. Teach
me the way to make you look at me in such a fashion."

"I don't know what you mean."

"She looks at him as if he is the sun, the moon and

the stars, and I… I don't know how to be anything but the mountain."

She put her hand on his face. "The mountain has sheltered me."

"But cannot hold you," he said. "I am to be a leader to my people, and I don't know how to be a leader that is something more than blood oaths and promises of war. I have to go back there, I have to tell them. That everything has changed. I have to be different."

"Lazarus."

And then he was kissing her. And it was fierce and hard, and everything that was always between them. But there was a desperation now, a lack of control that superseded even what had occurred between them last night. Because this wasn't the snapping of self-control at the end of a seduction. It wasn't that build of desire. This was an explosion. He was angry. And he was seeking. Taking the kiss deeper and deeper, as if he could find the answers he was looking for at her very center. As if he could taste her deep enough, hold her hard enough and find what he was after.

"I want to…" But he couldn't finish the sentence. His eyes were wild, and full of black fire, and they searched hers, and she knew that she did not have the answers.

"I am no more civilized human than you."

"More fool me," he ground out. "Because I created you. In the same fashion that I was created. And it is broken. I was here deceiving my brother, with the full intent of killing him by my own hand if I had to. I would've taken his bride. I do not know compassion. I do not know mercy."

"We are showing it," she whispered. "You do know it. You rescued me from the alley…"

"With blood."

"Sometimes blood is needed. I don't know, Lazarus, maybe some people come together in glitter and fairy tales, and you and I are deadly vows and sword fights. Maybe that isn't wrong. Maybe it just is."

"Show me," he said.

His mouth was on hers again, his kisses punishing, bruising. And she gave back everything she got, trying to find the more that he was looking for, trying to call it out from inside of herself and give it to him, because he needed it so desperately, and she did not want to deny him anything she had in her that might be good. Anything that she had that he might need.

You love him.

She did. But what would he understand of those words?

He saw love between Alex and Tinley, and he could not understand it. What would the words mean if he could not understand the feeling?

"It is not fair what happened to you," she whispered against his mouth. "You were turned into a weapon, not treated as a boy."

He growled, pushing her down to the earth, his large body over the top of hers. "No talking," he said. "Show me. Show me with your body. Show me how to feel."

And that she knew she could do. That she understood. Because she had never been emotionless, however much she wanted to be. Because she had always been with him out of more than loyalty. Because she had always been with him out of love.

"Yes, my Lord."

And of her own free will she stripped the clothes from her body, bare to the soft earth, bare to him. And he stripped off his own clothing, kissing her hard and long before lifting her buttocks up off the ground and pulling her onto his body, impaling her in one swift stroke. He gripped her hips hard, guiding the movements, putting one thumb roughly between her legs and rolling it over the source of her pleasure as he continued to move her body up and down. And she let him. Let him find the rhythm that would quiet the demons in his soul. Because what he didn't realize was she didn't have to do anything. She felt. She loved him. And that was it. It made no sense. And he was right. They were two people twisted by their upbringings. And then shaped imperfectly into something that could survive.

But no one had modeled these things, these feelings for them. No one had shown them what it meant to love and be loved. And yet, she felt that way. And somehow knew that there was nothing deeper or more true than what she felt for him. Because if it wasn't love, if it wasn't the deepest, purest of loves, how could she want him in this way. Inside of her. Astride him, or him over her. How could she wish to swear her entire life to him. Possibly commit herself to an existence where she did not ever see the outside world.

You've seen the outside world.

And you've told him.

It was true. Lazarus was the first truly honorable man she had ever known. And she might've disagreed with what he was planning on doing, but she had never questioned his motivations. He was not selfish. And he was good. When given the chance to make a better choice, he was doing so. Even though it tore him to pieces. And she didn't quite know why, but she sensed that there were reasons deeper than the political.

Lazarus had never craved power. What he craved was honor and righteousness. He was a leader, through and through. And all he ever wanted to do was the right thing by his people. But there was something raw here. Something raw and wounded. And it was more than simply being raised in a Spartan environment.

Because he's afraid that no one loved him. He's afraid he doesn't know love because he's never had it.

And that was when she found her courage. That was when she whispered against his mouth, "I love you."

And he growled, pushing her down into the earth, his thrusts becoming hard and wild. And she lost her thoughts. Lost her sense of anything but this war between them. For it was always a war. A battle for pleasure. But a battle for more than that. For connection.

And perhaps that was what they were always engaged in. Whether it was a sword fight or sex. A deep need to be as close to each other as possible. To be with someone who understood. Who else understood but him? Really. And who else could understand him but her?

They had been taken from the life they had known and brought into the wood. They had lived lives where they had felt a lack of love. They had lost people who had cared for them.

And all of these things might've happened at different times, but they knew each other's feelings. Real and true.

And he might not realize that, but it was so.

"I love you," she whispered again, and then the desire inside of her boiled to overflowing. She gasped, pleasure rolling over her in a wave, and then he shuddered in her arms, kissing her as he found his own release. As he spilled himself inside of her.

And then he reached into their supplies and unrolled a large sheepskin blanket, folding it over the top of them and laying them by the fire. He said nothing. And when she awoke, the dawn was gray, and he was standing with all of their things prepared, her clothing folded next to the blanket. "We must be going," he said.

He said nothing more about what had occurred last night. And when they arrived at the village there at the center of the forest, all multilevel houses built into the sides of the hills, she waited for the lift of homecoming to bolster her spirits. But it didn't. Because there was a heaviness to Lazarus, and she could feel it echoing inside of him. And she did not think that she could feel any sort of real happiness so long as he felt this deep and terrible weight.

It was as if his own heart had been placed inside of her chest. And she could feel everything he did keenly.

"It will be well," she said.

"You don't know that," he said.

She shook her head. "No," she said. "I don't. But I know you needed to hear it." And that, she decided, would be her lesson for the day in feelings.

That sometimes you just said the thing to soothe the person you cared for because they already knew the truth, and that gesture was more important in that moment than truth could ever be.

"I'm sure the people will hear whatever you have to say."

People came out of their houses and made their way toward the main fire pit, which was roaring, early morning breakfast prepared for those who wished to eat all together. Many people ate their family meals privately, but there was always a meal prepared at the fire for anyone who might be without. For anyone who might be alone.

But they knew that Lazarus was back. They knew their King was back. And so they all came.

"I have been with my brother," he said. "King Alexius of Liri. We have decided on peace."

There was a ripple in the crowd. "Bloodshed will only bring more bloodshed. I do not want to lose any people here. Any more than my brother wants to lose his. We will be planning a way for us to have our independence. A way for me to rule alongside him. A way that will open up opportunities for everyone here, while preserving our way of life. It is about choice. Everyone here should have it."

And very much to the surprise of Lazarus and Agnes, the response was not angry. There were questions, many of them, and they passed all three meals there by the fire, talking about what would be. And when the light began to fade, people still stayed. And talked.

"I went with a single purpose. But I realized, I did not see things fully. It was only when I met my brother that I was able to see. These ideas are new, I know. But I believe *new* is the only way forward. No matter how much wisdom I could see in the old way…it will only take us back. I don't want anyone here to lose a son or daughter," Lazarus said. "A wife, a husband. A brother. That is why peace is the best path. But we shouldn't have to hide anymore. And he has promised me that isn't the case."

"It's so different from the way that Agamemnon spoke," one of the women said. "It is foreign, this thing you propose."

"Peace and mercy? I know. But I wonder if it might be the only way. The only real path. To life. It will not right every wrong. But I wonder if sometimes… If sometimes there is no avenging wrongs too deeply wrought. Because what will it gain us? We will lose. In the end. We will all lose something. And for what? To satisfy a grudge that is not even ours? I will not scar us in that way."

"And if he's lying?"

"He isn't. I'm confident in that. But you have my word that my role will always be to represent our best interests."

"But you're one of them," a man said.

"I'm not," Lazarus said. "I am, and always will be, the King of the Dark Wood. This is my home. This is where I was raised. This is where I was given shelter and safety."

"A man cannot serve two masters," someone else shouted from the back.

"And I do not," he said. "I serve you. Trust me as you always have."

And all the while, Agnes stood by his side, her hand on her sword. For in the end, her loyalty was to him. And if there was a battle, she would fight for him.

In the end, they voted, they agreed. They agreed that

this was the path. At least to try. And Lazarus swore to take a small band of men to the palace to be part of the discussion process.

To be part of this new world. They spoke of all the technology in education that would be open to them if they chose to take it. They spoke of opportunities. For them, for their children. Of choice.

And when they were exhausted, they went back to the palace. Lazarus's palace. The glittering, black castle deep in the rocks of the largest mountain at the back of the forest.

Spiraling turrets merged with the mountainside, all onyx and obsidian. The door was inset with gems, also made of rock, and it opened upon Lazarus's approach. The integration of technology into the wood had begun to happen before Agnes had arrived, and she was not shocked by it now. But she remembered being in awe of it at first.

Automatic doors and fingerprint sensors seemed more like magic here in this place that lacked so many of the markings of time.

It retained its medieval air while possessing a shocking amount of creature comforts within its glittering black depths.

Agnes had always found it to be home. And she did not wait to be invited. Rather instead she followed him to his chamber.

"That went well," she said.

"Yes." There was a large tub at the back of the room, black and iron. The water came straight from the heart of the mountain spring and was heated quickly by a sophisticated system. Lazarus turned it on, and began to take his clothes off. And Agnes began to slip off her own. Without waiting to be invited. He cast a glance at her, his gaze hooded. "Would you join me?"

"I was not going to wait to be asked."

"My appreciation for you not attempting to bring a dagger into the bathtub."

"Don't give me a reason to use it and I don't feel the need to be armed."

When the tub was full, he shut the water off, stepping into it, and she followed suit, letting the hot water roll up over her skin. She pressed herself against his large body, her back against his bare chest, her bottom nestled firmly against his manhood. And they were quiet, there, in that moment. His hands comforting on her body, the warm water creating a cocoon around them. She rested her head against him. This was the first time they had been here. In this place where they had lived together for many years, not like this at all, in this changed state.

"What bothers you so much?" she asked.

He kissed her temple, and she shivered. "You, at the moment. I should like to be inside of you."

"I would like that," she said. "But that isn't what I meant."

"I know," he said. "I made my family into an enemy, Agnes, because I could not have them. Because it was easier than grief. My mother is dead. My father is dead. My youngest brother is dead. All that I will have, ever…is Alexius. And it was easier to tell myself that there could be no reconciliation. But they were… That they were everything Agamemnon said they were. Because I cannot have those years back. I cannot become the man that I would've been. I cannot... My mother used to read to me. She loved me. I know she did. I remember feeling secure. I remember feeling... Happy. I can remember playing ball with Alexius and it was fun. And when he and I rode horses yesterday, I felt that again. That's real. It has been so many long years since I felt anything like it. I was never a child here. A grim sense of duty is all I have known. And I forgot what it was to be part of the family. Having to try to remember now and realizing that those parts of myself have grown dark and weak from disuse is... I am alone," he said.

She understood. It was what he'd been chasing last night. That connection. That sense of being part of something and someone. She did understand. She understood it deeply. Because she felt the same way.

She had been with Lazarus for years, but felt like she was always holding pieces of herself back. She lived with her father, and had felt utterly outside of herself the entire time.

"Remember what I said to you about choices my father would make? About how I felt that if we were doing the same thing he would do, taking the easy way, it couldn't be right?"

"I do. It was a stinging rebuke, Agnes."

"Being who you are is not easy. Having the bravery to face these complicated things... It is not. Not in the least. This is honesty. And it forces you to be true to pieces of yourself you would rather not. I know. I understand. But isn't this better? I think this is where you might find the connection you seek."

"It hurts," he said. "Like reopening a wound to clean it."

And she did not find the analogy off-putting, because she herself was a warrior, and she understood those terms. "I know," she said. And in this moment, she felt like she might be his teacher. Much in the same way he had been hers. It made her want to laugh, but there was nothing funny about this moment. It was heavy. She felt that same heaviness that had descended upon them the moment they had come into the forest. That heaviness he was carrying with him.

"I can share your burden," she said. "I'm here. You're not alone, and neither am I. The truth is, neither of us have been, not these last eight years—it's just that you and I are so used to being an island we didn't realize when we were not."

"Do you really love me?"

He asked that question in the same tone of voice as he had said everything else during this conversation, but there was an edge to it. Just underneath the surface.

"Yes," she said. "With my heart. My body. My life. I love you."

"But you cannot mean it. Not really."

"Why not?"

"Because I am…"

And he couldn't finish that sentence either.

"I spent a great deal of time in my own thoughts, Lazarus. Trust that I know them now. That is the benefit of this kind of lonely life."

"And yet I feel as if I know nothing."

"Good for you," she said. "You're otherwise always so certain. Perhaps a bit of uncertainty will do you well." Then he lifted her up from the tub, kissing her, but different than he had done by the fire. This was gentle.

This was something she didn't know. A tender touch, his rough palms skimming her bare skin as he brought her down onto the bed. Both of them were still wet, but she didn't mind, and he didn't seem to either. His kisses were sweet, but not in the way they had been that night he had been attempting a seduction. This was an attempt at nothing. It simply was.

And she knew they were both mindless. Desperate with need for each other. Desperate for things that only the other could provide.

He kissed every inch of her skin, and she felt right, incandescent with her need for him. Then he positioned himself over her, entered her slowly. This coupling didn't have the wildness of last night, didn't have the violence of their first time. Didn't have the calculation of their first kisses. This was simply Lazarus and Agnes. As they were, as they might've been. As everything. And in that moment, she had to wonder if each sharp and broken rock on the paths that they had walked had been left there for this specific purpose.

And she felt nearly ashamed. To think that perhaps his fate had never been what he had imagined, and that her fate had never been simply to swear loyalty to him. But that their fate was now. In this slow, deep build of intimacy that was teaching her things with each and every stroke of his hardness inside of her. It was more than pleasure. More than simple connection. This wasn't the blind fumbling of two people simply in the throes of lust. They touched here at their souls. This was stripping layers off them both. Layers of protectiveness. Layers of damage done by the world. Done by the people who were supposed to care for them. Or in Lazarus's case, by the loss of the people who had loved him very much.

This was something real.

She began to tremble with pleasure, and she felt an answering quiver in his muscles. And when he found his release, she found hers at the same moment, and he cradled her face, pressing his forehead against hers, growling with the intensity of it. And her cries mingled with his, echoing off of the stone walls. And she knew that this was always meant to be. These walls were always meant to house their mixed cries of release. And she snuggled against him, beneath the covers. Her hand on his chest.

"We go back to Liri in the morning," he said. "We will try to make the journey in one day. Are you prepared for that?"

"Yes," she said.

"I should not have dragged you here."

"You need me," she said.

And she looked up at him. "It's okay to admit that."

"I need you," he said.

A rush of relief washed over her. For it was all she had wanted to hear from him. All she had wanted to hear from him that night in Paris when she had ambushed him with the sword. And she had been told that he did not. She needed him. It was only fair that he needed her right back.

"Good. Then there should be no more talk of sending me away."

CHAPTER TWELVE

THE ENTIRE JOURNEY back to the palace, Lazarus felt a strange sort of frustration. He wanted to do something for Agnes. And he did not know what. He wanted to give her something. In truth, he wanted to give her everything, but he certainly didn't know how to accomplish that. And he had to focus on the task at hand. Joining these two people together, working out the details of it with his brother and figuring out how a joint leadership situation worked. He did not need to be obsessing about a woman who had been his shield maiden up until a couple of weeks ago.

Still, they stopped and took a break, and Agnes seemed like she was filled with some sort of forest magic as she hopped from rock to rock, until she was up at the top of a very tall one, sitting with one knee pulled up and the other leg dangling over the edge of the moss-covered stone. She looked like a fairy. And she was to be his fairy princess, he supposed.

While Agnes sat and drank in the rays of the sun, he went into a thicket and found vines and flowers. He had learned to make things out of vines very early, a practical technique when you lived in a place with so many. He quickly fashioned together a crown, placing flowers all around, feeling especially silly as his large hands moved over the delicate material. And when Agnes came down, he placed it upon her head. "If I am to be a King," he said.

Her dark eyes shone bright, and she smiled, bigger than any of the smiles she had given when he had brought her designer dresses. No, she had looked more annoyed about those than anything else. But this... This thing fashioned from the forest she was alight with joy over.

It did something to ease the knowing feeling in his chest, but not everything because he still felt...

Agnes had lived such a difficult life. Didn't she deserve a man who had not? He had asked her to show him what feeling looked like, he had desperately begged her to, and based on what?

He knew full well that what he was asking of Agnes was... It was unfair. Asking her to fix these things inside of him when he had no reasonable method of fixing anything in her. Nor did he have any expectation of being able to do so. It was not fair.

And yet, when he looked at her, with her crown of flowers on her face full of sunshine, he could do nothing but continue to walk with her. For he was losing his grip on all that he was supposed to be, and Agnes felt like an anchor. She felt like the path forward. Like the thing that might make all of this possible.

Things had gone well in the wood. And not only that, she felt the bond between herself and Lazarus grow stronger.

It was not about things that they owed each other, not anymore. And now that he was firmly set on joining forces with his brother, she could breathe. She didn't have that horrible knot in her chest when she looked at Tinley. In fact, she and Tinley were becoming friends, and it was a wonderful thing. Agnes could not remember the last time she had a friend. She wasn't sure she ever really had. Growing up, she had moved around so often, and she had never wanted to lie to the girls that she had come into contact with, as usually, her father was swindling their parents. Consequently, she had been very lonely. Always. And she loved Lazarus, with all of her heart. Her days with him here at the palace were not as intense as the time they'd once spent together. He had other duties. He was currently entrenched in meetings with Alexius, and the other men of the wood, trying to figure out a reasonable system of government. Trying to figure out how to... Rewrite a nation. It wasn't easy. But they were good men, and they were doing their best, and whatever they didn't get perfectly, Agnes had absolute certainty they would sort out when the problems were identified.

The nights though... They were a great deal more intense than the nights they had spent together before.

He took her in his arms every night at bedtime, and turned to her multiple times between fits of sleep. He was insatiable, and so was she. Reaching for that connection they had found with each other, and only each other. And she knew it to be true. With him as well as with her.

That he felt exactly the same thing she did. It was a glorious thing, this.

They had spoken no more about marriage, though, and she realized that she had never formally accepted him. She had simply… Not refused him. And she found that she wanted him to ask again. Even if that was silly. And after they had been at the palace for two weeks, it filtered down to Tinley that Lazarus was planning something.

"All I know is he has asked for there to be many cakes," Tinley said, grinning.

"Then it is certainly for me," Agnes said, feeling jittery.

"Do you care to tell me the whole story of your relationship with Lazarus?"

There was no reason not to tell Tinley, not now.

"Well," Agnes said. "It is just that we were not engaged when we came. He was… He thought that it would soften his image. If he pretended that we were in love."

"I see," Tinley said. "But you… You were in love with him."

Agnes nodded. "I am. I have been. That much was true. I have been in love with him since I was sixteen. I love him with all that I am. And now, as things have changed between us I can only hope that he loves me too. But I don't know. I don't know, and I don't know that I shall. I don't know that he'll ever speak of his feelings. It's okay. He has said that he wants to marry me. In truth."

Tinley nodded slowly. "I know a whole lot about men who have difficulties opening up their hearts. The Alexius that you have met is very different than the one that I knew for most of my life. He was a stone wall. And I was so convinced that I loved his brother that I could not understand the overwhelming feelings that took me over completely when I was in his presence. He was and is the best of men, though. And it was true even before he could figure out how to tell me what he felt. Things between us were not easy. Not in the beginning. Not when he was… Not when he was trying to figure everything out. That was very difficult for him. As I mentioned before, he was so scarred by the loss of Lazarus, by the loss of Dionysus…"

"I fear that Lazarus has begun to address his scars," Agnes said.

"So the question is, what are you willing to do for him? Do you require that he be able to tell you he loves you? Do you require that he be able to show it in exactly the same way you show him?"

She thought back to when she had been a girl, taken in from the streets of Paris. She thought back to how he had rescued her. And taught her to fight, slowly and painstakingly. How her muscles had been soft at first before becoming honed, her instincts finely tuned. You were what you were made. But you could become something different. But it did not happen overnight. And it took someone who was willing to come alongside you and help with the reshaping. He had done it for her. Could she do any less for him?

"I am willing to meet him where he is. Because whether it's tomorrow or thirty years, when he finally says the words, when he's finally able to… I will feel the same. Whether I'm here or somewhere else. Whether I am off in Paris pretending to laugh while I drink champagne, or sitting in the palace and the wood with him. And I would rather be with him."

"I knew the moment I met you that you were as good a woman as there was, Agnes. The exact woman strong enough to love my brother-in-law. I have known the two of you for the exact same amount of time. But I see so much of Alexius in him. And I feel a great deal for him based on Alexius's feelings. You are exactly what he needs."

Agnes nodded, but then Tinley continued, "Is he able to be what you need?"

"Did you care? When you were having to decide about Alexius?"

Tinley offered her a rueful smile, and then shook her head. "No. I confess I didn't much care as long as I was with him."

"It is the same for me. There are many things out there in the world, and my father spent his entire life chasing them. Fortune, esteem. He was always after something that he could not grasp. And he had a child right beside him who would've loved him, if only he would have spared one single moment to look my way. But he saw me only as a tool, and nothing more. He saw me as something to be used. I have been out in the world. I have been to most countries in Europe. I have learned languages. I have been rich off of the money of other people, and very poor. But never have I been happier than when I was by Lazarus's side. No matter the nature of our relationship. It is the people in our lives that make it worth living. Circumstances change. But if you can never look to who is beside you, who would stay beside you no matter what, then you will never truly find happiness. My father died unhappy, in front of his child, who only ever wanted his love."

"You are young, Agnes," Tinley said. "But your soul isn't."

"I don't think Lazarus or I ever had the luxury of young souls."

"I hope tonight brings you what you want."

Lazarus was planning on proposing to her. Really proposing to her. He had visions of her as his bride, a crown of flowers in her hair, like the one he had made her in the wood. Yes, he could adorn her in gold, and might even like to sometimes, but mostly, he wanted her as his forest fairy. His little earthen warrior. For anyone could gleam in gold, but it took someone truly special to glow with vines and leaves.

And his Agnes was special.

Alexius had suggested a picnic on the lawn, as it was a gesture he had used with Tinley, and one that she had liked very much. Lazarus didn't quite know what to do with this new brotherly relationship. This new input that he received from him. It was a strange thing indeed. And yet, he could not say he was opposed to it.

When she came out onto the balcony, his heart caught in his chest. She was wearing a bright orange dress he had not seen before. The fabric flowed over her curves like liquid. The deep gold of her skin made the color catch fire, and her hair, glossy and dark, was arranged in a beautiful style high on her head. There were little orange flowers placed throughout, and she was exactly as he had just been thinking. A forest fairy.

A forest fairy who could cut him.

His body responded with intense pleasure.

He cared for this woman. Would fight armies to ensure her safety. She smiled when she saw him, and that was when he noticed she had gold makeup on her cheeks, her eyes.

"Did Tinley have a hand in this?"

She blushed.

"Yes. Do you like it?"

He wrapped his arms around her waist. And he kissed her, with all of the hunger inside of him. "It is a good thing we are in a semipublic space."

"Is it?" she asked, lifting a brow.

It was strange how they could know each other as they did, and still find new ways to speak. New ways to be. Their relationship had been marked by seriousness for a great number of years, but now they could laugh. And he could touch her. However he wished. And she seemed to enjoy it. She also returned the favor, with frequency.

That was one thing he liked very much about Agnes. She returned his enthusiasm for making love with passion and intensity. Gave as good as she got.

His physical equal in all things, as he had suspected.

She walked out to the center of the lawn, where there was a table and chairs set out for them, lights strung overhead.

"It's beautiful." She looked toward the wood, a strange smile touching her lips. "Isn't it odd, how it feels like were in an entirely different world and we're only about two hundred feet away from where we came from?"

She looked abashed. "Well, I guess you started out here."

His chest went tight of a sudden. Because of course he had come from here. It had been this very lawn where they had been playing before he had wandered into the woods.

"I know what you mean," he said.

"Good," she said.

He looked at her as she sat at the table, with the wood behind her. And he realized… It was so. He had not really gone anywhere. And neither had she.

Hadn't he promised her something more? Hadn't he promised her experiences?

And he supposed it was only a man with a very big ego who would consider his body the experience that she required.

And no one could ever accuse him of having a small ego, it was true. But that was not all he wanted for her.

And there was something… There was something stifling about sitting here like this. On the lawn. He should've thought more critically about this. Should've thought more deeply about how it would feel to sit here with her.

But he had told her he wanted to marry her, and it was true.

It was true. In his pocket, he had a ring. Alexius had brought in tray upon tray from a jeweler down in Liri's largest city. And he had selected the grandest for Agnes.

He knew that it was something a lot more ostentatious than her typical style, but it had to do with what he wanted to give her. Which was simply everything.

Everything he could. And it was in his pocket now. Ready for him to propose to her, because he felt that she deserved that at least. Not these demands that he had been making of her before.

And yet, all of this was beginning to get tangled up. In the promise he made to her before. How had things changed?

And she had declared that she wanted to be free, had she not?

But then, he had dismissed that as injured pride, since she had clearly been furious with him when he'd said he didn't need her.

And the fact was, he did need her. He needed her more than he could ever say. He needed her in a deep, profound sense, and there was a strange twisting and burning in his chest, and suddenly, Agnes rose from her seat.

"It's funny, this, how it hit everybody for so long, how these woods tore so many lives apart out here, but you and I simply saw home."

Had he? Had he really seen it as his home?

"Have a seat," he said. "Dinner will be coming soon."

And of course, he wasn't afraid of the wood. But for some reason he didn't like the image of her standing there at the edge of it. He could remember when he had been the dangerous thing lying in the deep waiting for Tinley. He didn't like… He didn't like seeing Agnes in that position. And it clotted another memory too. One that he simply didn't want to have.

"It's funny," she said. "How we never see the wolves."

"They're real," he said. "I've seen them."

"Yes. I just mean… I was only commenting that it's funny how…"

"Yes," he said, a leaden weight in his stomach.

Their meal came, and he did his best to brush off the strange feelings coursing through him. There was steak and bread, cursory vegetables, though he knew that Agnes didn't really want them. And afterward, trays of cakes, which he knew for certain she did want.

They ate, and all the while, he was planning on issuing his proposal as soon as they were through. But then they finished, and Agnes got up from her chair again, wandering to the edge of the wood.

He could follow her. Ask her.

He stood from the chair, and overwhelmingly, abruptly, the images in front of him were not the images of now. He began to have flashes of memory. His ball, bouncing to the edge of the wood. And he stopped, looking inside. And he could see something. Something moving. And then he saw a hand scoop the ball and take it farther into the trees. He remembered being afraid. But he was a prince. There was nothing he should be afraid of, not in his kingdom. He and his brother played with wooden swords, and they were heroes. He knew exactly what to do if there was a foe. Prince Lazarus did not run. And he wanted his ball.

So he went forward into the darkness. And that was when he realized his first mistake. It was impossible to see. But then he could see his ball, somewhere deeper, and in he went. And just for one moment, he saw a man's face, hiding in the bushes, right behind the ball.

Agamemnon.

Agamemnon.

It had not been an accident that he had been in the woods. He had been lured there.

It had been the plan. All along.

The wolves...

There were wolves. But Agnes was right. Why did they hear from them not at all now? And why...

A sour feeling turned in the pit of his stomach.

Dogs.

The dogs that Lazarus had cared for, until the pack had eventually reached old age and died. The same dogs that had torn his face to shreds.

At the behest of their master.

Agamemnon was the one who wanted to stage a bloody rebellion, and he had been intent on using Lazarus to do so. He had also not intended to die, Lazarus was certain of that. But he had.

Everything... Everything had been a lie. He hadn't been saved. He had been brought in and manipulated. Trained. He knew that what Agamemnon had told him about the land being stolen from their people was true. He had done his research outside of Liri. Agamemnon's anger had come from a real place, but what he had done...

And he must be responsible for the death of Lazarus's brother, the one he had never met. Of Dionysus. For it could only be Agamemnon's dogs. Of course. This idea that the wolves never touch those who lived in the wood… They were kept contained. And he had listened to folk tales and fairy stories and taken them on as real because he had been wounded that his family had not come for him.

And he had nearly… He would've killed his own brother in the name of Agamemnon's vengeance, a bloody vengeance that would serve no one. Because he had been the only father he'd ever known and remembered and he would have…

He'd have done anything for him.

Nearly had.

His family was not cursed. They were targeted. And those things were not the same.

Targeted for the sins of a great-grandfather that they had never met. Something they had never known about.

Their entire life had been twisted, his own uprooted.

He didn't know anything about himself. And the raw horror that was bleeding through his chest made it impossible for him to think. He was nothing that he thought he was. Nothing. And here he was, trying to bind Agnes to him, and for what? As a Band-Aid to all the shortcomings inside of his own soul? It could not be endured. Not for Agnes.

He could not do this to her. The anger that was inside of his veins was a crushing, suffocating thing. And it would destroy him. It would destroy her along with it.

He wanted… He had been desperate for her. Desperate for her to teach him to love. Desperate to feel some kind of connection with another human, and he did. But he didn't know how to give it back. His veins were full of poison. He had spent his life being conned. And he hated it. He hated all of this. He could not in good conscience keep her with him. Everything he was, was a lie. And everything he had believed in…

He had believed that Agamemnon had saved his life, that he must follow this arcane practice of being bound to him because of that. He had thought that Agamemnon had taught him all those things out of care, but it had never been that. The only father figure that he could remember had simply been manipulating him. Using him. He had not gotten lost in the wood; he had been stolen from the palace. His life had not been saved; he had been put in danger by the very man who professed to rescue him.

And from that had come Agnes. And his bonding her to him. And she was so grateful. The same way that he was to Agamemnon.

How could he ask her to form any feelings for him based on that?

All of it was a sick life. All of it.

How could he propose to her now? How could he promise her anything?

The simple truth was he could not.

He had to let her go. He had to tell her to leave.

To go to Paris or back to Ohio or wherever she wanted to be. He had to set her free. Because her feelings were born from an arcane practice that put too much weight on the person who was saved.

She had to have a chance. The chance he had never been given. To unlearn what he had been taught. To decide what manner of person he was for himself.

He could not use Agnes as a surrogate for a heart

that he had never been able to develop because of the way that he had been shaped.

It was not fair.

For inside of him was anger, and it was nothing like the connection between Alexius and Tinley. Nothing at all.

Nothing at all.

And when he did not propose, he could see the disappointment on her face. But she didn't know.

He was standing there going over the scorched, destroyed remains of his soul. And she didn't know.

They went back to their room, and she began to undress. He stopped her. "Agnes, there is something I must say."

She turned to face him, her expression full of hope. And it was his job to kill it, and she would not understand that it was a mercy. But he had to separate her from him. He owed her that. He could not keep her under the weight of this terrible responsibility.

"Agnes, I am going to get you an apartment. Wherever you would like. Anywhere in the entire world. And have you enroll at a university there."

"What?"

"We talked about this. That you wished to be free."

"That was before," she said. "Surely you must realize that was before."

"No. It must be now. It was easy for me to keep you. Because you would make a lovely Queen for me, and you must know that. You are beautiful. And you are strong. And as I said to you... The only woman that has ever been able to withstand all that I wish to give her. And giving that up is a very difficult thing."

"Is that all?"

He nodded slowly, the lie pushing against the back of his throat. "That is all. I realized some things, and I…"

"What?"

"What I wanted from you, what I demanded of you with the fire that night… I don't understand love, Agnes. I am what I was made."

"Agamemnon cared for you…"

"Agamemnon lied to me," he said. "I did not realize it until… Until we were standing there at the edge of the wood. And then I remembered. I remembered that he was there. I remembered that he lured me there to the wood. Yes, I remembered. And once I remembered… I realize that none of it was true. None of it. Down to you being bonded to me. Because it is a chain. A chain of lies, is it not? He stole me from my family. And he told me they didn't care about me. And that was the man that I was raised by. No one loved me, Agnes."

"I do," she said.

"Because you were bound to me. And I know what that does to you. I know. Because it was what I had. It was what I had with him and…"

"It is not the same," Agnes said. "If you really think I'm strong, if you really think that I know my mind, then how can you dismiss me like this?"

"I do it for your own good," he growled.

"You do it for yours," Agnes said. "Don't you think that I see the fear in you?"

Her words were like a sword. Pointed, as they were in reality. "This has frightened you. And I know you're sending me away because I frighten you too."

"No," he said.

"It is grief, Lazarus. It's grief that you're feeling. Because whether or not he deserved that, you did care for him. You did. And it causes you pain that he lied to you. That is normal."

"No," he said. "It isn't so simple."

"Then tell me. Explain it to me so that I can understand. It might not be simple, but neither am I," Agnes said. "I can understand you. Maybe better than you realize."

"Nobody…"

"No one can understand you? Have you ever tried? Who knows you, Lazarus? Who knows you apart from me? Don't tell me that I can't understand. I am probably the person who can understand you the most. The best. Because we've talked. We have spent time together. And I care about you. I care about you beyond your connection to the royal family, beyond these missions. I care about you. So tell me. Tell me what frightens you, and I will… I will pick up my sword."

"I'm not frightened of anything. I'm simply facing the reality of what is. If Agamemnon lied to me, he did not save me. If he did not save me, we were never bonded. And you deserve the chance to find out who you are for yourself."

"I know. I already know. Lazarus, I have played a great many parts in my life. At the behest of my father. I have done what he has asked me to. I know when I'm longing. I know when I'm being lied to. This, what we have, what I feel, it's real. It's real and I know it. You do not need to teach me. Not in this. Perhaps I need to teach you."

"No. That is not your job. You do not…"

"Stop telling me how strong you think I'm not. If you have one downfall with me, that is it. I am not the girl you found in that alley." And then suddenly, she stopped. "Maybe I am. Maybe I am the girl that you found in that alley. And I was stronger then too. Because I survived. I survived that day, and yes I had you. But I had survived every day up until that point. And I may not have done so with a sword, but I did survive. And you keep telling me you don't need me. You keep telling me that you can fight without me. But what if you can't. What if I am a strength you didn't know you had. What if I am more than your shield maiden. What if I'm your heart?"

"You must go," he said. "There can be no discussion. I am not cutting you out of my life, Agnes. I am going to continue to take care of you…"

"I would love to tell you no. I would love to not accept. But the fact of the matter is, I cannot afford that. I cannot afford to live without your protection. And those things are physical, so I can't deny them. I must have shelter. I must be able to learn a trade if I'm to be on my own. So I must take what you have offered. Maybe you need me in ways that you cannot see."

He turned away from her, his heart a slow, dull thud in his ears. "I will have you sent wherever you wish."

"So that's it? I don't get to choose?"

"You get to choose. Wherever you wish to go."

"Paris then," she said. "Send me to Paris."

With a wave of his hand he dismissed her. "It is done."

CHAPTER THIRTEEN

IT HAD BEEN a week since he had sent Agnes away. A week since he had seen her. A week since he had held her in his arms.

For good reason.

He had hardly been able to sort through that dread that had filled his chest when he'd realized the truth of his background. Since then he had spoken to Alexius about it at length. But they had not talked at all of Agnes.

Tinley had taken to giving him long looks that spoke of her deep disapproval. But he could not please Tinley. In truth, he could not please himself. It was possible he could not please anyone.

He was okay with that. Everyone else would have to learn to be.

It wasn't until dinner on the night that marked exactly a week since Agnes left, that his brother finally addressed the situation.

"And is Agnes returning to us?"

"No," he said.

He had set her up with a lovely apartment in Paris, and had hired someone to guide her in enrollment in a university there. Last he heard she had not chosen what she was to study. But then, she was angry at him, so it was entirely possible she wasn't telling anyone what she was thinking because she didn't want it to filter back to him. But she… She loved him. And there was nothing he could do with that.

"I see. And why is that?"

"Agnes needs to go and experience life on her own. There are things about our relationship that you don't know…"

"Not true," Tinley said. "I told him everything Agnes told me. We have no secrets, my husband and I."

"Great," he said, his tone dry.

"I have told you what I learned about my past. That I was taken. Our family is not cursed. We were targeted. It is a very different thing. And I…"

The words that had been about to come out of his mouth were foreign to his mind. He had not ever thought them before. And he hadn't known he was about to speak them.

"The one person that I spent my life trusting lied to me," he said. "Not about what happened in our history. But about the part that I was to play. He had already set about exacting revenge on our family. He is the reason that Dionysus was killed."

"I know," Alexius said, his voice rough. "And I know that this may make no sense to you, but there is something of a comfort in that for me, because I was sure that… That it was something in me. Something that I had done."

"Aren't you both a pair," Tinley said. "Look at you. Sitting there and comparing the darkness inside of you. It wasn't your fault," she said. "Any more than it's yours." She directed the last part to Lazarus. "It isn't your fault, and Agnes knows that. Agnes loves you."

"That isn't it," he said. "I don't blame myself for the things that were set in motion before I was born. But what I do blame myself for is... I trusted the wrong person. How can I ever trust anything inside of myself ever again?"

And that was the truth of it. How could he ever trust his heart? How could he ever trust his feelings? Agnes said that she loved him, and he was... There was something in him that was desperate for that. That clawed rapidly at his chest, wanting to get free. Wanting to touch her. Wanting to be near her, to be consumed by it. But his feelings were not trustworthy. They told lies. And what could that mean for her? He did not worry about his own pain.

Do you not?

He thought of Agnes, beautiful and bright. And he thought of how he had sent her away. On his request. At his choice. In his timing. What if she decided to leave one day? What if he began to believe that love between them, and it turned out that it was not so? It was simply her own inexperience. It was simply...

"There are many people in this world who lie," Tinley said. "My own mother long acted as if there was something irrevocably broken in me. I understand what it is to not be certain of your place in the world because of what the people around you have said. But when someone comes along who says they love you, who has shown you they love you... Has she not shown you,

Lazarus? Has she not been there for you? Agnes has been loyal and brave and true. It is more than words. It's more than feelings. It's eight years of action. She loves you."

"But…"

"And you're afraid. You're afraid of that pain you felt when you lost your family. But ask yourself this, do you feel any better now?"

He looked at his soon-to-be sister-in-law. "I don't know what I feel. I don't know how to feel anything beyond… I fear I don't understand love."

"If Agnes's life were in danger, would you risk yours to help her?"

"Every time," he said.

"If she was cold and she needed something to keep warm, would you take the cloak off your back for her?"

"I would," he said.

"If another woman wanted to share your bed, but you knew that it would hurt her…"

"I want no one else."

"What do you think love is?"

"I've seen the two of you together. There is a softness there, a sweetness that I cannot understand."

"We've grown into that," Alex said.

"It's true," Tinley said. "At first it was all very frightening. Very painful and sharp. And sometimes the sharpness is still there. But we have grown to trust in this love. And at first it's hard to do that. Love is not comfortable when it's breaking through the barriers that you've put up around your heart. In fact, then love can be very, very painful."

Well, he had the pain.

"But what do you do? How do you guarantee that everything will be okay?"

"You can't," Alex said. "It's impossible to guarantee that anything will be okay. The Dark Wood is still there, and there are still monsters. That is the way of the world. But being in love, having someone to walk alongside you, it makes it not half so terrifying. When you can find the person who makes the sharp things worth it, then you hang on to them."

"You may not trust your own heart, Lazarus," Alex said slowly. "But do you trust Agnes?"

Agnes. Who was everything bright and brilliant and good. How could he not trust her? It was fear causing him to hide like this. Fear and he knew it. And as Agnes had said before she had gone, a deep underestimating of her strength. Which was simply not fair. Not when she had done nothing but swear loyalty to him. Unending and true.

And then love.

And what had he sworn to her? Nothing. If he felt like he wasn't known, it was because he had never let his guard down.

And what was it that Alex had said? That love, when breaking through those walls, was nothing but extremely painful. He believed it. He believed it because he felt it. It was not her. It was not her that lacked strength.

It was him. Because there was more to strength than being hard. More to strength than being a mountain. It was the softness, the vulnerability that Agnes possessed, that was where the real strength lay.

Hadn't she said just that? What if she was his heart? What if she was his heart.

And he had torn his heart out, had torn his heart out and sent it to Paris. And for what? To try to keep himself safe. Safe from more pain. Safe from betrayal. For hadn't it been that betrayal that had caused him to change course?

That... That slap in the face of realizing that he'd been wrong.

Are you so weak? She stood there and said she accepted you regardless. She always has. And you turned away because of fear.

"And what if I went to get her?" Lazarus asked.

"Go," Tinley said, at the same time as Alexius said, "You should."

"I want to get to her as quickly as possible."

"I have a private jet," Alexius said. "You should take that."

"I won't argue."

CHAPTER FOURTEEN

AGNES WAS ALL out of tears. That was what she told herself, every day when she got up in the morning and pored over the catalog for the university she was supposed to start soon. Every afternoon when she went for a walk around the park and then the museums. Every evening when she went and got some bread or crepes and sat by the Eiffel Tower as she had done when she'd been sixteen.

Then she got into bed at night and wept again.

Because she wasn't out of tears for Lazarus. She feared she never would be. Behold, she was Agnes, unto herself. Free and unable to be anything more than a puddle of tears.

She sat in front of the tower and pulled a chunk of bread from a wax paper bag and stared straight ahead. At least she had bread now, and weeping to look forward to later.

Then, down in front of her, she saw a pair of black, shiny shoes. And there was no reason at all that shiny black shoes should trigger anything in her, except everything went still.

Then she looked up. And up yet still.

And it was him.

Lazarus.

Here.

In Paris.

At the tower.

"A girl once told me," he said, coming to sit on the cement curb beside her, "that she came here and dreamed of finding someone to love her."

Agnes's heart was beating hard in her head. "Did she? A foolish girl."

"I'm sorry to hear that," he said. "Because I had hoped to sit here. And dream awhile."

Her heart twisted painfully. "You don't need to dream. You had someone who loved you."

He sighed, the sound heavy. Deep and from his soul, and not part of this game he was playing at all. "I was afraid of that." He looked at her. "Agnes, I am so sorry. I was afraid. As you accused me of being, I was a coward. I thought…the grief that I feel over realizing I put my trust in the wrong person is… I wasn't prepared for that. My life is a lie and in that moment I decided everything must be, but Agnes, that was me being foolish. You have never been a lie. You have always been all that is true and just and faithful. And you showed me in a hundred ways what love was, what loyalty was. And I… Everything in my chest was this great and terrible sharpness and I thought that could not be love. But a wise man told me that love is very painful when it is knocking down the walls you've built around your heart."

"Oh… Lazarus." Tears pushed against her eyes. "It is that."

"I am here, even if I am late. I am here in Paris to say that I love you. That whatever the truth about Agamemnon, my path led me to you. And that was not a mistake. It was not a lie. We are true. This is true."

She threw her arms around his neck and started to weep, and he held her. This softness, this closeness, so different to where they had started. And so deeply, wonderfully true.

"I want you to marry me. Not for show. Not because I need a wife." They parted and he wiped the tears from her cheeks. "Because I need you."

And in that moment she thought about the past, the present and the future all at once, and feared none of it.

She was that girl that had sat here and dreamed. She was the woman in his arms, now and forever.

Then he took her hand and drew her up so they were standing.

And he turned and began to walk away.

"Where are you going?"

He paused and looked at her. "We are going home."

She laughed, the echo of that first day they'd met, when he'd saved her life, clear. "And where is that?"

He took two steps back to her, then cupped her chin in his hands. "For me? Home is wherever you are. It can be here while you do school, or back in Liri. Either way, all will be well. I trust Alexius."

"You would let me stay here?"

"If you wanted."

She laughed. "You know, I think we should go back to the Dark Wood."

"You just like the bathtub."

"That is true."

He leaned in and kissed her mouth. "Wherever we go, Agnes of My Heart, one thing is true. You have saved my life. And I swear my fealty to you. For all of my days."

* * * * *

MARRIED FOR
ONE REASON ONLY

DANI COLLINS

MILLS & BOON

In this trying time, I'm so grateful I've been able to continue writing stories that lift my own spirits and hopefully lift yours. I couldn't have done it without the wonderful teams at Harlequin and Mills & Boon, particularly my editor, Megan Haslam. My heartfelt thanks go out to all of them for their support and their dedication to delivering hope and happiness to readers everywhere.

CHAPTER ONE

ORIEL CUVIER OPENED her hotel room door anticipating birthday roses and confronted a cleaning gent with a mop.

Mon Dieu, even the maintenance men were exceedingly attractive in Italy. Her startled gaze had gone straight to the yellow bucket, but as she dragged her attention upward, she arrived at eyes that were so dark they were nearly black. Much like the cup of espresso had awakened her senses an hour ago, she felt as though she was yanked from dull, mundane thoughts to a readiness to experience everything her day had to offer.

"*Mi scusi*. I heard you were out." His Italian was stilted, his smile a tense, flat stretch of his lips that apologized for his butchering of the language. "I was told to clean a wet." His voice was as deeply seductive as Italians were purported to be while his accent and dark coloring suggested he was South Asian.

Oriel had always felt an inexplicable kinship with people from that corner of the world, even though her parentage was supposedly a mixed couple from Eastern Europe.

"*En Français?*" she suggested. "Or English?"

"English. Thank you." His speech became as crisp and flawless as a graduate from a British boarding school. "I was told you were out for the day and I should clean a spill."

Honestly, he could be employed in her line of work with those sharp cheekbones, sensual mouth, mussed high-top haircut and devil-may-care stubble. He was substantially taller than her five-eleven, and his broad shoulders strained the seams on his blue boiler suit.

"I didn't request anyone," she said in bemusement.

"Who is it?" Her agent, Payton, spoke in her ear.

"Oh, one minute." She had forgotten her call and pointed at her wireless earbud so the hotel worker would know she wasn't speaking to him. "There's a man at the door, but there seems to be a mistake. I didn't call anyone."

"The maid texted me." The cleaner brought his phone from his deep pocket.

"The maids haven't been in yet," she said.

How was this godlike, educated man pushing a string mop? With that build, he could be laying bricks or bouncing clubs at the very least—which would also be a complete waste of a startlingly magnificent presence. The camera would love him.

She loved him. Oriel saw beautiful men all day every day, but none had ever emanated this sort of powerful energy that almost had her taking a step back in awe while wanting to bask in his presence at the same time. It was like an electric current that made her nerve endings tingle.

And even though handsome men rarely affected her, she had a nearly unbearable urge to twirl her hair and cock her head and wait breathlessly for him to speak.

"Send him away," Payton said in her ear.

She probably should have. Her career was her entire focus these days, providing the sense of achievement that otherwise eluded her. She would never admit to anyone the profound sense of inadequacy that stalked her, or that she had a hole inside her that craved approval and attention. It didn't even make sense. She had everything anyone could want—health, wealth, intelligence, and independence along with looks that ticked all the boxes for modern ideals of beauty.

She would be mocked to death if she revealed her feeling of being "less than," so she pushed her angst into climbing toward the very top of her field, allowing nothing to distract her, including men.

Suddenly she had nothing but time for watching how this stranger swiped his thumb across a screen, though. He studied it with an air of concentration. The strength of her fascination was embarrassing, but she couldn't help it.

He flicked his gaze up to meet hers, catching her giving him moon eyes like a love-struck adolescent. It caused a swoop in her stomach as though she'd crested a wave.

"My mistake. Wrong floor. And my colleague has dealt with the issue." He pocketed the phone while his penetrating stare kept hold of hers.

Her skin tightened and her bones grew soft. She knew when a man was interested in her. She rarely reciprocated such things, but here she stood. Involuntarily reciprocating with every fiber of her being.

It was disconcerting to be so overcome. To feel so helpless to do anything but stand there while he took in her snug, high-waisted corduroy trousers with matching suspenders over a low-cut floral top.

His mouth relaxed, and the angle of his shoulders eased. It wasn't all sexual interest, though. There was something else in his study. Not calculation, precisely.

Investigation? He liked what he saw, but he was delving into her eyes as though looking for answers to unasked questions.

She wasn't sure what that cooler side of his appraisal was about, but it was far more unsettling than if he'd worn a wolfish grin and said something suggestive. She could have handled that with flirt or frost. Whatever *this* was made her neck prickle with premonition. This man was going to change her life.

How silly, she scolded herself, trying to pretend she wasn't flushing with her reaction. But she was filled with anticipation and something else—her own curiosity. A far-reaching sense of possibility. Excitement.

"Was there anything else I could do for you while I'm here?" he asked in a bland tone.

The tension left the air with a withering dissipation.

She was reading him wrong, she realized with chagrin. He was an employee of the hotel waiting for her to dismiss him. That's all the lengthy, charged silence had been about. Could he tell she was drooling over him, wanting him to feel the same way she did? How mortifying.

"Yes, actually." As a hot, self-conscious blush stung her cheeks, she latched on to the first excuse she could think of to cover why she had kept him lingering. "The ceiling fan in my bedroom is rattling." It had driven her crazy all night. "I haven't had time to report it. I wondered if that was something you could fix?"

In the pause, she could have sworn she heard the gears in his head give a whir of computation. Then, "I can have a look."

Oriel's heart was pounding with nerves, but she pressed her back to the wall, allowing him to enter the small passageway.

He left the mop and bucket outside the door and briefly crowded her, seeming to steal all the oxygen from this tiny foyer.

Her instincts prickled another warning, not because she thought he posed a physical danger, but from awareness of the power that radiated from him. He could seduce her without even trying. Her blood was turning to molasses in the seconds that he loomed close and allowed one corner of his mouth to dent. Those dark eyes of his promised long, sensual nights.

She had never felt this way on meeting a man. It was pure magic, holding his gaze and feeling connected at a level that went far beyond what happened between strangers.

Then his expression hardened with refusal. He snapped his gaze forward and stepped into the room.

He knows. And had decided he didn't want to make a play for her.

Her whole body went into free fall, and her self-worth crumpled on impact. Oriel felt rejection *very* deeply. She had her theories as to why—being adopted and an only child. In her observations, people who had spats with siblings and were still loved afterward had more resilience to the small scuffs of life.

She hated that she allowed small rebuffs to strike such a deep place inside her, but they always did. The tiniest slights landed directly on that achingly tender center of her soul.

It was such a perverse reaction, because coming on to a guest could cost this man his job. She had no room in her life for romance, anyway. What did she care if a man she would never see again thought she was worth his time or not?

Nevertheless, she was so stung she thought about

asking him to come back later, but he was already trying the switch on the wall and looking at the fan over
the coffee table. He wasn't wearing a ring and didn't
have a tan line where one was missing, she noted. She
was annoyed with herself for looking.

"The one in the bedroom," she murmured, waving
across the small lounge.

"You didn't let him in." Payton's voice startled her
again.

She seriously had to get her head on straight. "I did.
It's fine."

"This is how scandals are created!"

"With me doing what? I live like a nun." She did
more scandalous things in public, parading down run-
ways in her underwear, than she did in private. She
didn't travel with any jewelry worth stealing or have
any secret predilections worth exposing, either.

She lowered onto the sofa, deliberately turning her
back on the man flipping the switch inside her bedroom door. Trying not to think about how his shoes had
looked far pricier than the kind she expected a man in
his profession to be able to afford.

Perhaps they'd been left by a guest and happened to
fit him. She occasionally left wine or clothing behind
when she traveled. Most hotels had an arrangement in
which the housekeeping staff could divvy up abandoned
items as a small job perk.

"If someone saw you letting him in, it could ruin the
interest from Duke Rhodes," Payton said.

Ugh. Right. The reason for his call. Oriel had been
introduced to the aging action star at a cocktail party
a few nights ago.

"Do you really think I should go to Cannes with him?
He's twice my age."

"He likes you."

"We spoke for five minutes." He had tried to kiss her on the lips. "I honestly couldn't say whether I liked him or not." She hadn't. "Have *you* spoken to him? Caught a whiff of his breath?" she added with a wince of recollection.

"It's part of his image that he always has a cigarette in his hand."

"And a drink in the other? He smelled like scotch." The sour, lingering stench of heavy drinking had emanated from his pores.

"It's *good* scotch, angel. He smashes box offices. The cameras follow him everywhere. Do you want to take your career to the next level or not?"

"Of course, but that's my only week of vacation this year." And her parents were celebrating their thirtieth anniversary. "It will chop into the first two days of it."

"You can fly straight from Cannes to Tours. His people will pay for all of it."

Payton was the best in the business. One didn't move from runway to international ad campaigns without a man like him paving the way. Thanks to him, she no longer shared a room with other models and was given first-class suites like this one, with gorgeous views of the Milan skyline.

Even so, she found his strategy disheartening. What about working hard? What about advancing on merit? Why resort to timeworn gimmicks? Who would respect her if she couldn't respect herself?

"I'm concerned about what a man like Duke Rhodes would expect if—"

A dull thump and a sharp curse had her sitting up and twisting to see into the bedroom.

The maintenance man had draped a spare blanket

over the bed and was flat in the middle of it, pushing the fan off his chest while blood welled on his forehead.

"I have to go." She pulled out her earbuds and leaped to her feet.

"Be careful. Stay on the bed," Oriel Cuvier rushed in to say. "I'll call down for help."

Vijay Sahir sat up to set the contraption on the floor. "I'm fine."

He was rattled and bruised, but it was his own fault. He'd been scanning the room for clues about her, eavesdropping on her conversation while thinking less than honorable thoughts about her and the bed he was standing on.

He'd been paying no attention to the fan he'd been pretending to fix, giving the housing an absent wiggle. The damned thing had come down on top of him, ringing his bell hard enough to leave him angry with himself for being so careless.

"That could have come down on *me* last night." She eyed the wires dangling from the ceiling. "Your head is bleeding. You need first aid, and I need to make a proper complaint."

She stepped around the broken fan and reached for the cordless phone in its bedside charger.

"No!" He threw himself across the bed to catch her wrist. "They'll fire me."

They wouldn't. Couldn't. He didn't work here. Which would be even trickier to explain.

"Well…" Even wearing a frown of consternation, she was the most beautiful woman he'd ever seen.

Her profile said she was of mixed Romanian and Turkish blood, adopted at birth by a French couple. Vijay would be damned if she didn't look Indian with that natural golden tone in her skin and those strong brows. Hell, in person she looked even more like Bollywood legend Lakshmi Dalal with her big brown eyes, her delicate bone structure in an oval face, her near-black hair in an untamed disarray of wavy curls. Her mouth was naked, but still made a bold, full-lipped statement when she pursed it stubbornly.

"I won't let them fire you." She stood tall and wore the confidence of wealth.

Don't be a hypocrite, Vijay. You're wealthy, too.

Even more so very soon, but he had a well-earned aversion to spoiled heiresses.

"I'm still new here." Whether she took that as new to this hotel or this country didn't matter. Both were very weak versions of the truth. He unconsciously stroked his thumb against her incredibly soft skin in persuasion.

Her breath caught, and a confused spark flashed into her eyes, one that arced across to stab an answering heat into the pit of his belly.

Everything about her was slicing his brain into sections, making it difficult to remember she was the subject of an inquiry. Or possibly an innocent bystander chosen for her resemblance to a Bollywood icon. Either way, she was the key to ensuring Vijay's sister wasn't conned out of her fortune.

Vijay made himself release Oriel's wrist and rolled to his feet on the far side of the bed. "If you give me an hour, I'll have all of this sorted," he promised. "I need to fetch a few tools."

He wasn't a certified electrician, but he could re-wire a fan.

"I actually have an appointment." She glanced at the clock.

"I can let myself in." That's what he'd been planning

to do with his ill-gotten, all-access housekeeping card. He had taken a chance, hoping she would already be out for the day. The mop had been a prop, the knock a precaution.

"I suppose." Her doubtful gaze dropped to the name tag on his borrowed coveralls, then came back to his eyebrow. "You're still bleeding. Did you realize that? Please sit down." She nodded at the edge of the bed and disappeared into the bathroom.

He touched the wet trickle that was winding its way down his temple. When he saw the blood, he swiped the sleeve of the coveralls across it, leaving a dark streak on the heavy blue cotton.

"I'll survive. Don't worry about it," he called.

"No, let me." She came back with a small bag marked with a red cross. "I asked you to fix the fan. This is my fault."

He hesitated, then sat on the bed and closed his eyes, trying not to picture the way the suspenders framed her breasts and cleavage so enticingly. He briefly thought about coming clean and saying, *Look, I need your DNA*.

A container ship of worms would open at that point, and for what? The chance that Oriel was related to Lakshmi Dalal was near zero. As far as Vijay could discern, a con man was leaping on Oriel's resemblance to Lakshmi to get his hands on the money Vijay and his sister would make as they merged ViKay Security Solutions with a bigger, global enterprise.

On the very slim chance that their "client" was telling the truth and Lakshmi did have a lost child out there, Vijay owed the man his utmost discretion. The mystery seemed too coincidental to be believed, though. When Vijay had booked this trip to Europe, he had seen an opportunity to get to the bottom of things. He'd tacked on this side trip to Milan so he could intercept Oriel. All he had to do was pretend to be a hotel worker for another few minutes, steal her toothbrush, and get on with his life.

There was a tearing sound, the pungent scent of alcohol, then a cool swipe on his brow that left a sting in its wake.

He couldn't help his small wince.

"Sorry." She blew on it, making his eyes snap open.

Her blouse gaped, and he was staring straight down the shadowed valley between her lace-cupped breasts. Lovely, abundant breasts that his palms itched to gather and massage.

He deliberately set his hands onto the blankets next to his hips, but he could still smell the fragrance of tropical body wash clinging to her skin and wanted to rub his face into her throat. He wanted to keep going, dislodging the edges of her shirt so he could find her nipples—

"There." She set a bandage over the cut, cupped his face in her cool hands, and *kissed* the injury.

He was so shocked, he snapped his head back.

"I'm sorry." Her hands fell away, but she was frozen, still leaning over him, as shocked as he was. "I didn't mean to— I have a little cousin who—Obviously, you're not a child. I'm so embar—"

"Do it again." The words shouldn't have left his chest, but there they were, rumbling up into the space between their lips. He didn't lower his attention back to her breasts. He kept his face tilted up and his gaze on her mouth.

For endless seconds, they were held in that state while she made up her mind. Then slowly, slowly she lowered her head. Her mouth pressed to his, delicate as a butterfly landing on a rose. He lost his sight. Impressions came to him in flashes as her lips slid against his—the softness of flower petals and the crushed scent of them filling his head. Velvety heat in her breath and the dark, sweetly sensual flavor of her as they both opened their mouths wider to deepen the kiss.

He skimmed his touch along her forearms, catching lightly at her elbows, inviting her closer. She braced her hands on his shoulders and leaned against him, slanted her head and sank into their kiss, stealing every thought in his head.

It was the most frustratingly delectable kiss of his life. He wanted to drag her in and take control, but he was too enthralled by letting her have her way. She sipped and experimented and decided what she liked before she pressed deeper. Tasted him more boldly.

He groaned and signaled more firmly on her arms, urging her to be more aggressive.

Her knees dug into the mattress on either side of his hips. The warm weight of her settled on his thighs. Gratification rumbled in his throat. He swept his palms to her shoulders and roamed his touch over the warmth of her body through silk. He followed the straps of the suspenders, enjoying the lithe flex of her back and the furrowed texture of her trousers where he made circles on the flare of her hips.

She sighed and inched her knees on the mattress, settling more deeply into his lap. She switched the slant of her head to the other side with barely a breath for either of them.

This boiler suit was a size too small. It pulled tautly across his back and shoulders and against his knees as he splayed his legs and looped his arms around her, trying to drag her even tighter into his lap. Her hair tangled in his fingers as he cupped the back of her head and gave in to the craving taking over him. He swept his tongue into her mouth and sucked on her lips, wanting to absorb her into himself.

She made a noise that was a helpless pang of pleasure, pure seduction, and shivered. Her arms folded behind his neck and she pressed even closer, so all he could think was how badly he wanted the heat of her sex scorching where he had hardened to titanium.

His hands cupped under her bottom and, purely on instinct, his arms hardened around her. He rolled, setting her beneath him on the bed. Now he could kiss her throat the way he'd been dying to, tasting the small hollow at the base. Her hands went into his hair and—

"Mon Dieu. Stop."

He lifted his head. Her horrified gaze was pinned to the ceiling. When she met his own, she pressed her head more deeply into the mattress, expression appalled.

Bloody hell. He wasn't a hotel employee, which would be bad enough. He had lied his way in here.

Vijay pushed himself off her, feeling as though he left a layer of his skin adhered to her. It *hurt*. He didn't dare look down to see whether these damned coveralls were disguising his arousal.

She was sitting up and smoothing her hair, ensuring her blouse buttons were secure. "That shouldn't have happened."

"No," he agreed. "It shouldn't. I'll leave." He did.

CHAPTER TWO

IT WAS A good thing Oriel's appointment this morning had only been a fitting. The main requirement of her had been to stand still and be quiet. She would have been useless at anything else. Her mind had been completely occupied by the most salacious kiss of her life.

Apparently, she harbored fantasies of making love to strange men who appeared at the door like the mythical pizza delivery hookup. What else could explain the way she'd crawled into his lap and practically offered herself? If she hadn't blinked open her eyes to see the bare wires in the ceiling, and been reminded where she was and that he was a complete stranger, she might have gone all the way with him!

Maybe it had been a dream, she tried telling herself as she looked around. The fan was back in place, the spare blanket gone, the bed made and the pillows fluffed. The suite wore the tidy polish of an efficient housekeeping visit.

When she tried the switch, the fan was perfectly silent, not rattling the way it had last night.

Should she call down and leave a message to thank him? Leave a tip with a note? What would she say? *You left me rattled. Can you fix* that?

The part that was torturing her most was, why? Why

had she lost any sense of decorum? Was she that starved for affection?

She did have yearnings for a serious relationship, but she also knew she had to love herself. She couldn't expect someone else to *make* her feel loved.

Maybe she should start dating herself, she thought, smirking around the mouth of the bottle of water she was drinking. Rather than seek outside validation, she could take herself out for dinner. It was her birthday, after all.

Actually, maybe she would do that, she decided, and started to search for a restaurant to make a reservation. She was distracted by an email from her agent. Payton had sent through a confirmation on her trip to Cannes in May. *Magnifique*, she thought dourly.

Her mother had also left a message about Oriel's gown for the anniversary party. Madame Estelle would be annoyed when Oriel told her she wouldn't arrive until the morning of, thanks to her red carpet appearance with Duke Rhodes.

She bit back a sigh and threw her phone down while she began to change, still irritated by this Cannes idea. She was trying to make her mark without riding her mother's famous coattails, but she would be riding the coattails of a one-time heartthrob who wanted to look as though he could still get off-camera action in the form of a twenty-five-year-old model. Payton would say it was how the game was played, but Oriel felt like a sellout.

She didn't have time to stand around brooding, though. She had a casting call for a luxury eyewear brand in an hour. Such things ran notoriously late, but she was always five minutes early. It was mid-March and the breeze still sharp, but she changed into a filmy summer dress that showed lots of her long, tanned legs.

She moved into the bathroom to brush out her hair and fix her makeup and found a note where her toothbrush ought to have been.

The scrawled handwriting took her a moment to work out.

Apologies. I dropped your toothbrush while washing the dust from my hands. The fan is in order now. Call me if you have further concerns.

There was a phone number in place of a signature.

Hmm. Was he offering his number in a professional capacity or giving her his number?

She tucked the note in her bag while she applied a bold red to her speculative smile, pondering whether she would text him and what she might say.

After a quick check that she had a pair of heels, and a romance novel to read while she waited, she threw on her overcoat and hurried out.

Vijay ordered a beer while he waited for a table at an upscale restaurant a few blocks from the hotel. When he checked his phone, he saw a text from his sister, Kiran, asking how the merger discussions had gone and why he wasn't home yet. He replied,

Good. I was delayed. Will fly home tomorrow.

He didn't mention that the offer they'd received was so generous, he was more concerned than ever that she was being targeted for her fortune. He also skipped telling her that he'd stolen a toothbrush to prove it.

Vijay had sent the toothbrush overnight to a DNA lab. When he returned to Mumbai, he fully expected their client, Jalil Dalal, to refuse to give up his own sample to determine whether he was Oriel's uncle. Vijay was calling the man's bluff, dismantling the excuse Jalil was using to spend so much time with Kiran.

Jalil had seen Kiran speak in Delhi at a symposium about women in business where she had relayed how she and Vijay had grown their security company from a scrappy start-up to acquisition offers. Jalil had followed her to Mumbai, where he had asked her to help him with a "highly confidential, very personal assignment."

Kiran was beautiful and intelligent and successful enough for any man to want her on her own merit, but Jalil's request was not in their wheelhouse. Vijay and Kiran had started ViKay Security Solutions to protect themselves after taking a difficult stand that had destroyed the life they'd grown up in. A few years ago, they had accidentally developed a facial recognition system that accounted for skin tone, scars and makeup.

Their system was so accurate, global powerhouse TecSec wanted to acquire it. The owner was prepared to make Vijay the VP of his Asia division, and Kiran would have an executive role overseeing programming and development for the entire organization. They could finally put their past behind them and redeem their reputations.

This was *not* the time to run private investigations searching for imaginary children of deceased Bollywood stars.

That's what Kiran had been asked to do, though. Jalil Dalal had seen a model who resembled his dead sister and claimed Oriel must be his secret niece. Jalil didn't have proof Lakshmi had been pregnant. She had gone to Europe around the time of Oriel's birth and made a few remarks before she died—of a broken heart, according to Jalil—but that was all he knew.

It was the kind of tale that appealed directly to Kiran's soft heart, though. She had swallowed it hook, line and sinker.

Vijay sipped his beer, almost wishing the story was true. It would give him an excuse to see Oriel Cuvier again. He'd been in a state of low-key arousal all day thinking about their kiss. It shouldn't have happened, but he was not nearly as remorseful as he ought to be.

Oriel definitely possessed the same sensual allure as Lakshmi Dalal, he acknowledged sardonically, but it was beyond outlandish that she could be the screen queen's secret child.

For starters, the beloved actress wouldn't have such a scandal in her past. Lakshmi Dalal was India's *didi*, first charming her way into hearts with a portrayal of an older sister who was determined to give her kidney to her ailing younger brother. In a later film, she disguised herself as a young man, both becoming a symbol of feminism to girls and indelibly imprinting herself into adolescent male fantasies when she put on a sari and danced in the rain. From there, she became a mainstay in romantic musicals, a seal of wholesomeness that reassured all parents it was safe to allow their children to watch.

Jalil claimed that's why this had to be handled so delicately. He didn't want his sister's memory tainted, but Jalil lived off what remained of Lakshmi's earnings. That had to be running low by now. He was looking for fresh income, and Kiran was a convenient target.

That might be a cynical view, but Vijay didn't trust anyone except Kiran. And after his failed engagement, he would do anything to protect Kiran from similar disillusionment.

He flicked to the next email and saw his presentation to the hotel had resulted in an agreement in principle to move forward with the security package he had pitched to them.

Vijay was the king of multitasking. He'd detoured here on his way home from the merger meeting, booked himself into Oriel's hotel and wrangled a tour of the security system by pitching his own. That had given him the knowledge to break into a maintenance area undetected. He'd finagled himself a housekeeping card, talked his way into the room of a hotel guest, and retrieved what he needed to expose his sister's paramour as the fraud he was.

A man in his position should behave more honorably, he supposed. By misleading his sister and going behind Oriel's back, he was perpetuating the sorts of lies and betrayals he'd suffered.

As if karma wished to offer him a chance to make better choices, he absently lifted his gaze to the door and watched Oriel walk in. A jolt of electrical thrill went through him.

Dusk was closing in, but she looked as though she'd just left a beach with her hair windswept and her skin glowing. She wore makeup that emphasized her wide eyes and lush mouth. As she stood in the doorway, she unbelted her coat to reveal an airy dress with a ruffle across her chest. He leaned down slightly and caught a glimpse of her slender calves.

He was definitely in the throes of a sexual crush, but she had *climbed into his lap* this morning as though it was where she was meant to belong.

Heiress, his brain reminded him starkly, but his lap twitched with lascivious memory.

He watched her glance around uncertainly. Meeting someone? *Who?* The most intense aggression punched him in the gut, but he already knew that jealousy was a pointless emotion. If the person you were committed to wanted someone else, they were already gone.

Oriel smiled as the maître d' greeted her. She must have been informed the restaurant was full, because her smile fell away. Like him, she seemed to be invited to wait at the bar until a table became free. She sent a considering look his direction, and her eyes widened as she met his gaze.

Don't, he told himself, even as he stepped off his stool and nodded at it, inviting her to join him. Hot tension invaded his belly as he waited for her to decide.

Her dark red lipstick briefly disappeared as she rolled her lips together.

Oh, those lips. So soft. So hungry. How would they feel traveling other places?

With another faltering smile, she pointed and told the maître d' she would join him. She moved like a ballerina as she approached, hair bouncing as she seemed to float on air. Her coat fell open, and her dress seemed to be made of something delicate like gossamer. It clung subtly to her breasts, and he had to exert all his control not to ogle her.

"Hello again." Her cheeks might have stained with color, but it was difficult to tell in this light. "I should apologize for this morning."

"No, I was out of line." Way, way out of line. "It was excellent taste on my part, but poor judgment."

Her mouth twitched with reluctant humor. Her gaze

flickered over his collared shirt and tailored pants, then widened with startled comprehension.

"Are you on a date?"

"I had a meeting." He debated how much to tell her. "I pitched my security company. I'm Vijay." He offered his hand, deliberately withholding his surname.

"Oriel." Her wariness dissolved into a bright smile as she put her hand in his. "You didn't sign your note. Did you think I would get you in trouble if I knew your name?"

He practically fell into the dark, sensual pools of her eyes. The soft feel of her hand in his was the only thing keeping him from drowning.

"I'm quite sure you'll get me into trouble." It was supposed to be a joke, but the truth sent a skip through his chest. "Oriel."

She laughed, and of course it was the sparkling kind that was heady as champagne bubbles. "I'll try not to. Vijay."

Spending more time with her was a terrible idea, but as he held her hand, the noise around them dimmed, and all he saw was her. It was like taking a hit of a potent drug.

The bartender broke the spell, asking for her order. Oriel requested white wine and slid onto the stool Vijay had vacated.

"Thank you for fixing my fan. It seems perfect now."

He'd had to sneak around the maid's schedule, but as he subtly drank in her scent, he had no regrets about being inconvenienced.

"You didn't want to eat at the hotel?" Ironically, he had avoided the restaurant there out of concern he would run into her. He set his elbow on the bar, pleased that the crowded space meant he had to stand so close that her knee brushed his thigh.

"It caters to tourists. I wanted to treat myself to something more inspiring. It's my birthday. Are you also celebrating? Did your meeting go well?"

"It did, but I'm just having a beer." He would find somewhere else to eat. This was madness, even talking to her again. "Happy birthday," he said as her wine arrived.

They saluted with their drinks, and her spine softened as she sipped.

"Long day? What do you do?" He already knew, but he liked that she had to lean close to him to be heard over the din.

"Model. I've been at a casting call for hours. They were whittling it down, so I had to keep doing my thing as more higher-ups were called in." She lowered a pair of invisible sunglasses and made an O of her mouth.

He didn't care what the sunglasses looked like. He'd buy them and the car that went with it. "Did you get it?"

"Who knows, but it went well enough that it's another reason to celebrate. Only one, though." She tilted her glass. "I have an early call for a photo shoot tomorrow. Then I'm on a plane back to New York."

"You live there?"

"Paris, but I spend a lot of time in New York. Actually, I spend a lot of time on airplanes." She sipped again. "You? I assume your maintenance work is a side gig while you get your company off the ground? Why Milan?"

Damn. He had implied that he had moved here.

"It's a temporary thing." He considered how to stick as close to the truth as possible. "We're based in Mumbai, but hoping to expand. I came to Milan because my sister is involved with a man I believe is trying to take advantage of her."

"Oh?" Her expression cooled.

"I can see you judging me." He pointed the mouth of his bottle at her. "Brothers are allowed to be protective, especially when I raised her and she's all I have."

He hadn't meant to reveal that, only to keep her from labeling him as some sort of patriarchal, honor-obsessed throwback.

"You lost your parents?" Her expression softened. "I'm sorry."

"When I was fourteen, yes. She was ten." He drank the last of his beer, trying to rinse away the pall of anguish, old and more recent, that their deaths still left in his throat. "Our grandmother lived with us, but she was quite frail and passed a year later."

"That must have been a very difficult time." Her brow wrinkled with compassion. "No wonder you're so close and protective of her. Does your sister live here?"

"Mumbai. What about you?" He quickly flipped it so he wouldn't have to dissemble any more than he already had. "Do you have siblings?" Everything online said she was an only child, but he might as well have it straight from her.

"No. I always wished for a brother or sister, but my mother—" She hesitated. "Maman is very wrapped up in her career. She has every right to be. She's a famous soprano. Estelle Fabron?"

He shrugged, feigning unfamiliarity with the name. He only knew it from the mention in Oriel's profile anyway.

"Madame Estelle is beloved in the opera world. Especially here." She kept leaning in to speak against his ear. Her breath tickled, and he was damned close to turning his head and capturing her mouth with his own. "She casts a *long* shadow. It's refreshing to speak to someone who has never heard of her."

Her lips were right there, ripe and tempting. He looked into her eyes, and she was staring at his mouth. *Are we doing this, my beautiful goddess?*

The hostess appeared to say their table was ready. He was not ready to let her go, but his beer was finished.

"Join me," Oriel invited.

It was the moment when Vijay should have insisted he was only here for the one drink, but he couldn't make himself say good-night. Once he used the DNA test to vanquish Jalil, he would continue his life as programmed. It was highly unlikely he would ever see Oriel again. Surely there was no harm in buying her dinner and spending another hour in her company?

Now he was lying to himself as well as her. Or at least feeding himself weak rationalizations, but he waved her to follow the hostess and held Oriel's chair before he took the one opposite.

Oriel opened her menu, but glanced over it at him. "I'd like to buy you dinner. As I said, I'm celebrating, and you did suffer that injury from fixing my fan."

Her glance touched the nick above his brow, which was visible because he'd removed the bandage as soon as it stopped bleeding.

When her gaze dropped to the menu, she bit her lips again.

The prices were on the high side even for Italy. It struck him that she thought he might struggle to afford one meal, let alone two.

Wasn't this an awkward position to be in? Very few women he dined with had ever paid for themselves, let alone bought him a meal. Irrationally, he was insulted by her offer. There was a snobbery to the move that got under his skin—which was his personal baggage coming around on the carousel. He doubted she was *trying* to offend him.

"If one of us pays for the other, it makes this a date," he pointed out. "If this *was* a date, especially our first date, *I* would pay. Yes," he replied in answer to the way her brows lifted. "I'm that sort of man."

Her mouth pursed to hide a smile. "Split it down the middle then? Since we're sharing a table out of convenience? How do you feel about sharing dishes?"

"Depends what you like."

"I like everything." The look she sent him had to be from her stock of smoldering expressions for a camera. Even so, it went into him like a spear, straight to the tightening flesh between his thighs.

He was definitely paying for dinner.

Once they ordered, he said, "You seem to be traveling alone, but I should have asked. Is there anyone you usually dine with?" He had overheard her conversation about appearing with that action star. It had sounded like an innocuous photo op, and his research said she was single.

"I travel too much to date seriously. You?" She subtly braced herself.

"I would not have allowed you to kiss this mouth if it belonged to someone else. Yes," he said as her jaw went slack. "I'm also *that* sort of man." Blunt. Possessive in a reciprocal way. He offered monogamy because he expected it.

Her chin came up. "Did *I* kiss *you*?"

"You absolutely did."

"I didn't hear you objecting. Perhaps speak more clearly next time."

"Will there be a next time? I'm delighted to hear it."

She hid her smile with her wineglass, indignant but also amused. "Do all the hotel guests receive such personal treatment?"

"Definitely not. You're an exception."

"Hmm." She relaxed and recrossed her legs, bumping his shin beneath the table.

He reflexively caught her ankle between his calves, just long enough to have her startled gaze flash into his so he could watch that haze of sensual awareness come into it.

He released her as quickly as he'd caught her, leaving Oriel breathless.

She didn't believe in fate or destiny, but she was astonished to have bumped into him this way. She had glanced at the menu on the way to her audition, but hadn't had time to make a reservation. For a moment after she arrived, she had thought she would have to settle for room service after all.

Now she was enjoying an Indian-Italian fusion of tandoori duck, curried gnocchi, and tikka masala ravioli with a man she'd been thinking about all day.

He was an intriguing man. Educated and confident and quick-witted, but difficult to read. She wanted to ask him more about how he had come to be working at the hotel, but it sounded as though he was only doing it to make ends meet while he pursued bigger things, maybe paying for his expenses while he was here.

"Tell me about your security business," she invited.

"Most of the credit goes to my sister. She wrote specialty software, and I matched it to the right components. We literally began with one customer at a time, tailoring it to each client's needs. It's grown to the point that we're close to partnering with a bigger company. Those talks are highly confidential, so I can't say more."

"Sounds like a big break. Good luck. I hope it goes well."

"Thanks. How did you get into modeling? What was your big break?"

"Nepotism," she said wryly. "My mother hoped I would have more vocal talent, but she's a once-in-a-generation unicorn, and I'm adopted, so..."

His brows went up. Most people reacted with curiosity when she offered that information.

"It's public knowledge." She brushed away having revealed such a personal detail. "Maman's career was taking off. She didn't want to interrupt it with a pregnancy, but they wanted a family. Adoption was their perfect solution."

Perhaps *perfect* wasn't the best word. They had approached parenting wholeheartedly, but babies were demanding, and they never found the right time to adopt a second one. They claimed to be fulfilled by the single daughter they had, but Oriel had a twisted, illogical sense that if she'd been different, more winsome maybe, they would have wanted another.

"While I was growing up, Maman hired teachers for me in every type of classical instruction, but I was no prodigy. The closest I came was being scouted for a pop band."

"That suggests you have musical talent." He was looking at her the way he had when he'd stood outside her hotel room door. Penetrating. Collecting hidden data. "Have you tried acting?"

It was nice to have a man look beyond her face and want to know more about *her*, but this level of attention was disconcerting. She wasn't sure why.

"I can do many things reasonably well—dancing and singing and playing piano. I don't have Maman's level of talent, though, so I couldn't bring myself to go into performance arts. I would always be compared to her. Papa is an academic, very intelligent, but I'll never win prizes for literature or physics. I thought I was destined for mediocrity, but the summer I turned fifteen, one of Maman's costume designers asked if I wanted to model some of his designs at his show. It was the first thing I'd found where the bar wasn't already set impossibly high by someone in my family. With modeling, I've been able to grow into my own version of success."

That sense of carving out her own space and rising through the ranks soothed the part of her that struggled to feel good enough. She knew her angst stemmed from her adoption, and it wasn't entirely fair of her to harbor that sense of rejection. From what she knew of her birth mother, the young woman had been in a very difficult position. She'd had an affair with a married man of a different race and didn't feel she could keep the baby that resulted, not without losing all the other pieces of her life.

Oriel didn't resent her for giving her up. Her birth mother had chosen carefully, and Oriel lived an extremely privileged life, but it didn't seem to matter how often she reminded herself of that. She still suffered this bereft sense of having been cast off simply because she was mixed race.

They went on to talk about things. As they finished dessert, she asked the server to split the bill, but Vijay had taken care of it while she had visited the powder room.

"I thought—"

"It's your birthday," he said dismissively. "And you barely ate."

Oriel ran miles every day to keep her figure trim, largely because she had a healthy appetite. Even so, "That was a lot of carbs for a woman who is going to be in a bikini tomorrow."

"You'll be fine," he assured her with smoky admiration.

The potency of this man! She sold seduction for a living and had never experienced anything like his ability to make her swoon with a softly spoken word or a half-lidded glance.

"I...um—" *Control yourself, Oriel.* "I wouldn't have been able to sample all of these dishes if I'd dined alone, so thank you. This was a nice surprise." Beneath the table, she was aware of the toe of her shoe resting next to his. "I guess this is a date now?"

"I guess it is." His smile was only a tiny bit smug.

They finished their drinks and made their way outside.

"Do you dare be seen walking me to the hotel?" she asked.

"I dare anything." His mouth twisted with irony.

"Oh, you're *that* sort of man," she teased.

"And this." He offered his crooked elbow.

She tucked her hand through it as they ambled the few blocks that were bustling with tourists heading out to dine or enjoy the theater.

As they passed a recessed stoop, Oriel spun herself into it, tugging him in with her.

"Would you like to know what sort of woman I am?"

"If you tell me you're the sort who makes love in public, I may have to adjust what kind of man I am." He set his forearms on the door on either side of her head, caging her into the shadowed space created by his wide shoulders.

"Ha. Sorry to disappoint. I'm only the kind who doesn't like that awkward moment wondering if a man will kiss her. I'd rather make it happen. If it's going to."

"I noticed that about you already." He let the tip of his nose playfully brush hers.

"Are you still banging on about how I took advantage of you?" She let her hands rest on his rib cage. "Cry for help. See if someone will rescue you."

"Help," he said faintly, flashing his teeth. "I'm helpless to resist this woman." His lips touched a corner of hers.

She shivered and slid her hands to the backs of his shoulders. She tried to chase his lips, but he switched to kissing the other side of her mouth.

"I don't usually kiss strangers," she whispered.

"Nor I."

"You don't feel like a stranger, though," she admitted, perplexed by how true that was. "It feels like we're..." *Lovers*.

That's what she was thinking. Maybe she said it aloud, because he groaned and covered her mouth with his.

She had been waiting throughout their meal for him to kiss her again. Waiting and waiting.

She sighed with relief and stroked her touch across the landscape of his back, encouraging him to press her into the door, delighting in the way he devastated her with his kiss.

Had she thought she was in control this morning? He had been toying with her, letting her think so. This man knew how to ravage in the most tender way possible, claiming and plundering and pulling her very soul from her body.

At the same time, he gave. Oh, he generously venerated her mouth, silently telling her she was the most precious thing he'd ever tasted. The most exquisite.

Their lips made soft, wet noises while an ache panged in her throat. A sob of surrender. She softened under the press of his heavy body, wanting his weight. Wanting his hard, flat chest compressing her swollen breasts. She wanted to feel his steely thighs naked against hers, bracing hers open. She wanted the unforgiving ridge that was bulging behind his fly to fill her...

"Vijay..." Her hands went down his back, urging him to press into her mound. "Come to my room."

With the same attitude of superhuman strength he'd exhibited this morning, he dragged his head up and sucked in a breath. He straightened so he wasn't touching her at all.

"You have an early morning," he recalled with a ragged edge to his otherwise stern voice. "We should end this here." He looked away into the street.

"Should? Or is that what you want?" she asked through a tight throat.

He muttered something under his breath. "Believe me, Oriel. I want to come to your room. But it's not a good idea."

"Why not?" She hooked her finger in the waistband of his jeans to keep him from retreating further. "We're single. I don't know when I would have another evening free like this."

"And it's your birthday?" He spoke lightly, but there was a note of cynicism in his tone that made her drop her hand away from his jeans.

"What is that supposed to mean?"

"Nothing." He caught her hand. "Except you're flying to New York tomorrow. I won't be here by the time you come back. I have my own work commitments." His thumb stroked across the back of her knuckles. "I don't have one-night stands. I don't think you do, either."

"That's not what this would be, though, would it? I mean, you're right. I'm married to my career right now, but this isn't a hookup. It's... I've met someone I really like. I want to hang on to what little time we have together."

He swore again and gathered her up, swooping his mouth down to crash across hers. She tasted the conflict in him and poured herself into the kiss, enticing. Pleading, maybe.

When he lifted his head, they were both panting. His heart was pounding so hard in his chest, her fingertips felt as though they bounced where they rested on his pec.

She started to take his hand and lead him back onto the sidewalk, but hesitated.

"Would it be bad for you to be seen going into a room? I'll walk through the lobby and you can use the service elevator. You have a card, don't you? You don't have to knock when you come to my room."

His arms hardened to keep her in the shadowed stoop with him. "I'll knock. If you change your mind, no hard feelings."

"I won't change my mind." She slid her arms around him long enough to kiss under his chin. "But you're right. I never do this. I don't have anything. Protection, I mean. Can you?"

His breath left him in a jagged gust. "Yes. I'll take care of it."

"Thank you. I'll see you soon."

CHAPTER THREE

DON'T GO, VIJAY told himself.

That advice might have been easier to obey if he hadn't been staying in the same damned hotel. If he hadn't had to pass her floor to get to his own.

I want to hang on to what little time we have together.

Him too, for more reasons than the fact he was randy as hell after hours of flirting and footsie, then a kiss that had set his blood alight. He *liked* her. Enough that he felt like a heel for keeping secrets from her.

She wasn't looking for a relationship, though. Many things about their lives would remain a mystery from each other. Some people made this sort of relationship a habit, preferring to know as little as possible about their sex partners.

And some people waited until a few days before a wedding before revealing how shallow and faithless they truly were, he thought dourly.

Oriel was offering refreshing honesty, a night without the false promises that kept a person dangling on a string. If they were both law-abiding, consenting adults, did it matter why he'd knocked on her door in the first place?

Vijay collected the box of condoms from his luggage and, moments later, knocked on her door again.

"Your concierge request," he said dryly when she let him in.

She blushed, chuckling as she took it, and set it aside. She sobered as she noted he wasn't laughing. "Am I being too presumptuous?"

"Not at all. I want to use one. More than one, if we are so blessed."

That made her laugh throatily, and somehow they were close enough that he snagged his arm around her without thinking. She pressed into him.

He was lost. Any better thoughts went out the covered windows as he folded his arms around her and pressed her curves into his long-term memory. She was all softness and spice, hair spilling around her shoulders as she tipped her head back and showed him the glow of exhilaration in her eyes.

She had taken off her shoes, but was still tall enough that her nose was even with his mouth. Her long, dark throat was more than he could resist. He dipped his head and tasted her skin.

She gasped and shivered, and he automatically closed his arms tighter around her, holding her still for the swirl of his tongue against her skin. How had he thought he could resist her when she responded so immediately? So wantonly. She ran her hands into his hair and arched to rub against the erection straining against his fly.

Slow down, he ordered himself, but they only had tonight, and he wanted every inch of her. She seemed equally urgent, plucking at his shirt until he lifted his mouth and fused his lips to hers.

As they kissed deeply, his pulse throbbed so hard his entire body shook under the reverberations. His hands gathered and roamed over the filmy fabric of her dress, filling his palms with her heat, her lithe waist and her round, firm ass. He had never wanted to rip a woman's clothes off, but the impulse was there tonight. It took everything in him to seek the zipper against the indention of her spine.

"There's a hook," she said as he lowered the tab.

Maybe there was, but he had enough room in the opening to caress the smooth skin above and below the band of her lacy bra.

She flexed and her hand bumped into his, trying to finish opening the dress. She moaned with frustration. "Oh, just break it."

"Thank you," he said fervently, clutching the edge of the zipper and popping the hook. The delicate dress tore in a burst of barbaric satisfaction. He swept the ruined garment forward, peeling it off her front and brushing it down her hips so it landed as a puddle of blue around her feet.

"Mon Dieu," she said on a pang of helpless laughter. "I've never felt like this."

"Me neither." When she began to untuck his shirt, he yanked it open, tearing the cuffs as he roughly pulled it free of his arms, all the while keeping his gaze fixated on the ice-blue lace of her bra and panties.

He may have spent a little too long studying her online photos in skimpy lingerie exactly like that, but reality was even more potent. As he freed his hands from his sleeves, he ran his touch from beneath her arms to her waist and down to her hips before coming back. The soft abrasion of lace against the downy warmth of her skin was a delightful contrast, as was the hint of pink rising beneath her golden skin. He wanted to bite at the dark circles of her areolas, barely visible through the lace in the cups, and *devour* the shadow behind the triangle at the top of her thighs.

"Kiss me." She ran her hands across his bare shoulders and cupped his head, drawing his mouth to hers.

He groaned as he covered her lips and gloried in how her mouth softened in surrender beneath his. He caught her hair and dragged her head back, kissing across her jaw and down to her throat. "I'm going to kiss every part of you," he promised.

Her collarbone, her shoulder where he brushed aside the strap of her bra, the place where her scent gathered between the swells of her breasts.

She opened her bra, and he nearly lost his mind as her breasts spilled into his hands. Her beautiful dark nipples were already pebble-hard as he circled his thumbs across them. He kept swirling his thumb on one while pulling the other deep into his mouth and stabbing at the little bead with his tongue.

A small cry left her, and her hands clutched at him while her weight sagged. His blood throbbed in the tip of his erection, hammering imperatives into his brain.

He ignored his own need and shifted his grip on her, bending her across his arm so he could consume her other nipple. She squirmed, and her helpless pants made him smile with dark satisfaction. When he slid a hand down to silk and discovered it was soaked with her response, he nearly lost it.

"Vijay." Her eyelids were fluttering, and she covered his hand, urging him to press harder.

"Are you going to come?"

"I don't know."

"Let's see, hmm?" He slid a finger under the lace and caressed between her slippery folds, so hot and welcoming. As he dipped his head and found her nipple again, he discovered the hard nub of her clitoris. She stiffened and trembled as he stroked, digging her nails into his scalp. He sucked harder and rolled his touch rhythmically across that little pearl, feeling her quiver and shake.

Her tension gathered until he thought she would break. Suddenly she cried out, shattering so completely, it was like holding a charge of lightning. She electrified him.

Then she went trustingly limp in his embrace, moaning with gratification.

"That was incredible." Vijay swung her up in the cradle of his arms.

"It was," she murmured, curling a heavy arm around his neck and nuzzling his throat. That orgasm had destroyed her in the most exquisite way. "I can walk," she claimed, even though she wasn't entirely confident in that statement.

"I could carry you to a cave on the top of a mountain right now. Somewhere that no other man will ever find you, so you would be mine forever. All mine. *Only* mine."

She didn't normally find possessiveness sexy, but ooh. She sought his mouth and sucked on his bottom lip. She would be his if he would be hers.

He wouldn't. They only had tonight, she recalled with a catching sensation in her chest.

She might have descended into a fog of despondency then, but he stopped walking to give her a long, luxurious kiss, playing his tongue against hers. When he released her, his dark eyes held a feral glitter.

"Do you mind?"

It took her a moment to realize he wanted her to pick up the box of condoms.

More than one, if we are so blessed.

Oui. Si'l vous plaît. She did, and seconds later, he set her on the bed.

Her gaze snagged on the ceiling fan. She had a brief moment of unease as she recalled they had only met this morning. He had been correct in saying she didn't do one-night stands. Her first sexual experience had been a seduction at the hands of a young man trying to get close to her mother for career reasons. All the rest of her relationships had died of neglect.

Her last attempt at dating had made the complaint, *You're not a virtuoso like your mother. Why does your career mean so much to you?*

In this moment, as Vijay peeled her panties down her thighs as though savoring the opening of a Christmas gift, she realized the reason her career always took precedence was that no man had made her feel like this—cherished and wanted and *necessary*. She was both helpless and powerful, sated yet aroused. Self-conscious, but losing inhibitions by the heartbeat.

"Come here." He dragged her bottom to the edge of the mattress as he lowered to his knees on the floor beside the bed.

"You—I—" She lost her ability to speak as he set her legs on his shoulders and tasted her. No inhibition on his part, either. She groaned in tortured joy as he brought her replete flesh back to searing life.

He drew her to a height of tension, then slowed and soothed, then intensified his ministrations so her need for more became acute again.

"Vijay, please," she begged, and tangled her hands in his hair. "I need you inside me."

"The problem is, my beautiful goddess…" He stood and opened his belt, dropping pants and briefs in one swift skim. "I don't know how long I will last once I'm there."

Oh, he was beautifully made. From the tree of life that decorated his torso to the root of hair that gathered in a nest at the tops of his thighs to the thick spear of flesh dark with arousal. He reached for the condoms, and she watched as he rolled one on and squeezed himself in his fist.

Her body clenched internally with anticipation.

"Yes?" He touched her knee in a request that she open her legs for him.

"Oh, yes." She was dying and scooted herself into the center of the mattress.

He settled over her, bracing on an elbow as he traced the swollen, sheathed head of his penis around her wet entrance.

"Quit teasing." She nipped at his earlobe.

His crown nudged for admittance. He had girth to him. Her body instinctively tensed as his thickness began to invade. She made herself relax, and he pressed into her. All her sensations intensified as he slowly filled her.

"You're so hot," he breathed, backing off slightly before letting his weight settle so he sank to the limits of their flesh.

She had never felt anything like this. Perfectly full. She was so aroused and swollen and sensitized, she could feel his heartbeat in the steeliness lodged within her.

"Your heart is racing," he murmured as he cupped her breast and played with her nipple.

The small caress sent a tight jolt down into the place where they were joined, and she clenched in reaction. Sensations glittered through her, making her catch her breath.

"Like that?" He continued to roll his thumb around her nipple as he kissed her. Long, lazy kisses that drove her mad because her sex was growing wetter and needier, and he used his weight to keep their hips completely still.

She stroked her hands over the curve of his hard buttocks, then twined her legs up around his waist and dug her heels into his hard globes, inviting him to thrust with muted pulses of her hips. She blatantly thrust her tongue into his mouth and arched to encourage him.

He groaned as he rocked back and thrust in, seeming to pull sensations from her like the strings of a harp, then releasing them to send glorious vibrations shivering through her.

She couldn't help the strangled noise that left her. She twisted beneath him, almost overcome by the intensity of the sensations.

"Almost too good to bear, isn't it?" He worked his hand under her tailbone, tilting her hips so he could thrust with more power. As he invaded, he touched places inside her that made her vision go white.

Sharp spears of joy pierced her. It was inescapable, so she embraced it, clinging to him and moving with him, moaning unreservedly. His hand fisted in the sheet beneath her shoulder, and the slap of their hips was a primitive drumbeat beneath the song of their sobs and groans.

Climax licked and teased and tantalized.

"Not yet," he growled. "Wait."

She had never been held like this on the precipice of exaltation. It was exquisite torture. She clutched at him and said filthy things. "Deeper. Harder. Don't stop. I need more."

He kept to that rhythm that was driving her mad,

held them in that place of utter abandonment that was too sharp to be withstood, but oh, she wanted to be right here forever.

"Now," he commanded through gritted teeth. *"Come."*

He unleashed himself, pushing her toward the high, wide ledge with unconstrained thrusts. A viscously sweet sensation clenched within her, then released her into the universe, scattering her into pieces.

From a distance, she heard him roar with the force of his own orgasm. He fused his hips to hers and pulsed hotly within her. They stayed locked like that for long, euphoric moments, holding tight to that state of utter perfection before he collapsed upon her, sweaty and heavy and replete.

She sighed, drenched and drugged by a kind of pleasure she had never experienced in her life.

And never would again, she acknowledged with a pang of melancholy.

"Who was the thief?" the photographer asked as Oriel prepared for her photo shoot the next day.

"What do you mean?" She turned from hanging the robe she'd been wearing over her first bikini.

"The one who left fingerprints on your bottom. We'll have to call the constable to dust them." The photographer winked at his own joke and waved at the makeup artist.

The woman was grinning with amusement as she brought forward a tray of pots in an array of flesh tones from ivory to intense brown and began to mix them like a painter.

Mon Dieu. Oriel wanted to die. The poor woman had already spent an hour trying to disguise the dark circles under her eyes. Now Oriel had to stand here in all her ignominious glory while the sable hairs of a brush tickled the curves of her derriere.

"Don't be embarrassed," the woman said when she rose from her squat and saw Oriel's expression. "Unless he wasn't worth it?"

"Oh, he was," Oriel said ruefully. She had absolutely no regrets. That's what she'd been telling herself as she rose from the bed and had a quick shower a couple of hours ago.

Vijay had been gone when she emerged, but he'd left a note on hotel stationery.

Thank you for an amazing night.

She had his number from the previous note still tucked in a pocket of her bag. She'd been trying to decide if she should text something similar or let last night be a wonderful, stand-alone memory for both of them. Coming on as clingy was the last thing she wanted, but the yearning to keep him in her life was nearly overwhelming. It wasn't that she had felt "complete" with him, but for those hours from dinner through waking beside him, she had stopped feeling so deeply alone.

After several hours of shooting, when she was physically drained and about to change into her own clothes, she took a selfie in the full-length mirror. She was wearing a neon-pink bikini that was almost entirely made of loosely woven strings with a few tiny patches of solid nylon over the important bits.

At the last second, she cut her head out of the photo. Wasn't that the first rule of sexting? Keep it from being too incriminating?

She sent it with a message.

Miss me yet?

Almost immediately, she saw the three dots of a reply.

Niiiice. Who dis?

She texted back.

Not funny.

Then, as it occurred to her that she might have sent it to a wrong number, she asked with growing horror:

Who is this?

Erlich. Send more.

Non, non, non. With a whimper, she turned off her phone, resolving to get a new number the second she arrived back in Paris.

Oriel didn't text him. Which was *fine*. This wasn't his first rodeo, as they said in America. They had agreed their affair would only be the one night, and he'd crossed some ethical boundaries by accepting her invitation.

Vijay had struggled as he lay in her bed listening to the shower come on. He'd considered leaving his card, but decided that slipping away with only a thank-you note had been the most prudent course. If she wanted to reach out to him, she had his number from his earlier note. Leaving it had been a way to explain his stealing her toothbrush and to forestall any awkward involvement of hotel management, but at least she had it.

Three days later, he was still fading into lusty memories of their being all over each other, dozing off their sexual gratification before greedily demanding more. The third time, Oriel had instigated it, reaching for him in the predawn light.

"My alarm will go off soon," she had murmured. "Do you want to…?"

Her caress on the inside of his thigh had been all he needed to recover and harden despite the fact he should have been drained dry. He'd pulled her warm, silky body atop him and filled his hands with her smooth skin while their legs braided together. He'd done his best to memorize her with his touch, letting her set the pace since he imagined she was tender after so much lovemaking.

Her damp mouth and cool hair had drifted a tickling sweep across his chest all the way down to his stomach and lower, anointing him in a way that had him forgetting why breathing was a thing anyone bothered to do.

When she had risen to straddle him and guided herself onto his hardness, he hadn't had a condom on yet, but after that much lovemaking, he had known he wouldn't come right away. He had let her lazily ride him and enjoyed the way she crested with a broken gasp and shivers of ecstasy. Her rippling pleasure on his supremely aroused, sensitized flesh had nearly taken him over the edge, but he'd managed to hold back.

After she calmed, he had slipped out of her, put on a condom and taken control. He'd aroused her with his mouth, making her squirm and writhe. He'd tried to be gentle because they'd been at it for hours, but by the time he was moving inside her, the beast had been gripping him with insatiable talons.

He had known it would be their last time. Each stroke

had been bittersweet. Powerful. They had completely abandoned propriety, both moaning and encouraging the other until the people in the next room had banged on the wall and yelled, "Give it a rest!"

He couldn't. He had wanted to meld them into one being for all time. Parting from her was going to leave a piece of himself behind. When the culmination arrived, he'd nearly blacked out from the force—

"Vijay!"

His sister's voice snapped him back to his office. He shifted in his chair, arousal dying a quick death as he leaned to see her across the small courtyard they shared. They left their doors open for exactly this, so they could call across whenever they had a question.

Kiran was glaring at him.

"Are you worried about the language around the patent? Me too." They'd both been studying the offer from TecSec. At least, that's what he was supposed to be doing.

"Why is Jalil texting from the coffee shop, asking me if I want a chai latte and whether I'll be sitting in on his meeting with *you*?" Kiran demanded.

"Is he here? We can do it in your office if you like."

He rose and walked through the courtyard. It was really just a short hallway with a skylight and a water feature against the back wall to provide some cooling and atmospheric noise.

The rest of their company offices were on this same ground floor of a four-story, glass-fronted commercial building. It looked onto an abstract sculpture and a collection of taller buildings. At the far end was the café where Jalil bought Kiran coffee. Above them was an architecture firm, a publishing agency, and a call center for a company in America.

They hoped to take over all of that once the acquisition went through because this was such a good space for Kiran's wheelchair, but they would also open a center in Delhi before looking to Singapore, Hong Kong and Shanghai over the next few years.

"What is this about?" She watched him close the courtyard doors with a glower of suspicion.

"Just a quick hand of poker."

"Is this why you disappeared for a few days on your way home from Europe?" She narrowed her eyes. "Look, just because I haven't found proof that Lakshmi visited a clinic while she was away, doesn't mean anything. A clinic like that would be very discrete about how they handled their records. Twenty-five years ago, they might have still been using paper."

Vijay didn't have to respond. There was a knock, and Jalil was shown in. He was a healthy widower of fiftysomething with strands of silver in his otherwise thick black hair. He held a cardboard tray of three disposable cups.

As he and Kiran saw one another, the pair lit up and smiled and shared a look of tangled emotions that was so intimate, Vijay had to look away.

He had thought he had that once, the feeling of someone else's emotions being his own. It had been a lie, and he was not looking forward to picking up the pieces when Kiran realized Jalil was toying with her.

Actually, he had thought he might have something like it with Oriel, too, but her silence spoke volumes. Sexual connection was simply that, a trick of biology, and he wouldn't allow Jalil to use it on his sister.

He couldn't wait to expose the man and kick him out of their lives once and for all.

"Vijay, Kiran said you like black coffee." Jalil's

warm smile turned stiff. He set the tray on the corner of her desk and pulled out each cup.

Kiran and Vijay provided a well-stocked break room full of coffee, tea and soft drinks for their staff, but Jalil liked to impress Kiran by overpaying for takeaway.

This was what annoyed Vijay about the man. He could have kept his pursuit of his "niece" entirely professional, but he hadn't.

Did you?

Oh, shut up, Vijay told the irritating voice in his head.

"It was kind of you to think of me," Vijay said as politely as he could. "And thank you for coming in." He waved at a chair in invitation, waiting until Jalil had seated himself before saying, "I have good news." Jalil wouldn't see it that way, but Vijay certainly did. "While I was in Europe, I was able to intercept Oriel Cuvier and get a DNA sample—"

"You *told* her?" Kiran cried.

"No. I stole her toothbrush and sent it to the lab we use. I didn't put her name on the paperwork. It's Sample X, but Jalil can offer his own sample, and we can put an end to speculation." Vijay leaned on Kiran's desk, facing Jalil. He crossed his arms and ankles and conveyed a silent and ruthless *checkmate*.

"I can't believe you would jeopardize Jalil's confidentiality." Kiran rolled out from behind the desk to move next to Jalil. "I am *so* sorry I told him what you had asked me to do."

"Don't be," Jalil said, patting Kiran's arm in a placating way. "Your brother has gone to a lot of trouble on my behalf."

Vijay had absolutely not done it for Jalil's benefit,

and they all knew it. He was trying to get rid of a man who was playing his sister.

"I know it must seem as though I'm grasping at straws," he said to Vijay. "You have every right to be skeptical of my motives, but this is something I've wondered every day since Lakshmi returned from Europe. When I saw those photos of Ms. Cuvier and read up on her details, I couldn't stop thinking about this possibility, but I didn't know how to ask her without tipping my hand. I would be devastated if Lakshmi's reputation was tarnished by false rumors. This is perfect. Thank you. How do I proceed?"

"You want to give a sample?" Vijay tried not to let his jaw hit the floor.

"Of course."

Vijay had just had his own bluff called.

CHAPTER FOUR

WORST. IDEA. EVER.

Duke Rhodes hadn't booked her into a hotel. He'd added Oriel to the roster of guests on a yacht. Granted, it was a billionaire's superyacht and was full to the gunwales with entertainment industry movers and shakers as well as artists and designers. Oriel even knew a handful of them *and* she'd been given her own stateroom—not that she was in it.

Payton had instructed her to use this to her advantage. *See and be seen.* Easier said than done when Duke wanted her by his side like a security blanket.

At least he wasn't being a creep about it. He had looped his arm around her as they walked the red carpet, keeping it colleague-friendly, not pervy, but she had still hated it.

She was so burnt out, she felt like charred bacon. She had been working nonstop for weeks, putting in long days and getting most of her sleep on airplanes crisscrossing the Atlantic. She was beyond ready for vacation, but she had to paste a smile on her face and pretend to be thrilled with Duke's latest film—which struck her as a paint-by-numbers rehash of every action flick ever made. The audience's tepid response seemed to agree.

By the time they arrived back on the yacht, the after-party was in full swing.

Oriel wished she had confessed to the headache that was intensifying behind her brow. It was growing bad enough to make her nauseous.

Duke was holding court, though, drinking and smoking and making off-color jokes. He wasn't a terrible person so much as a man in denial of his age. He wanted to be twenty, so that's how he was acting. He loved his cigarettes, which he lit with a shaking hand, making her suspect he had social anxiety, but the smell was turning her stomach.

Either way, all her years of practicing aloof, unbothered looks were being severely tested as Duke blathered on about his glory days.

"I need the powder room," she murmured and excused herself.

She needed to find a tender to run her to shore. She was flying home to her parents' in the morning and had overheard someone say the yacht was hauling anchor at first light. Why had she agreed to this wretched stunt?

She texted Payton as she moved into the crush of the saloon, telling him she was done with this pageantry, and asked if he knew of any rooms she could book at this late hour.

What happened? I told his people this was only for publicity. If he's crossed a line, tell me. I don't put my clients in harm's way.

Oriel didn't feel like explaining that pretending to be with Duke made her feel cheap. It made her think about everything he wasn't. About *who* he wasn't and who she really wanted to spend her time with.

Not that the man she *did* want had reached out in the nearly two months since they'd spent their rapturous night in Milan. Granted, she'd been on the move, but she wasn't hard to reach. She could be contacted online fairly easily.

Maybe he'd given her the wrong number on purpose. That's what she kept thinking. He could have given her his number again with that second note, but he hadn't. She was the ultimate feminine stooge who had fallen for a player's game, and it made her feel like an absolute neophyte.

She caught up to a steward, who told her she only needed to go down to the lower deck in the stern where she had come aboard. A tender was making regular trips to shore all night.

She moved down a staircase to the passageway that led to her room and halted. A man in a dark suit stood outside the door to her room.

Mon Dieu, he looked just like Vijay.

Her heart screeched to a stop in her chest while such a rush of joy exploded in her, she had to reach back and grasp the rail to stay upright. At the same time, her mind blared an alarm at how *not normal* it was that he would be here.

It had been nearly two months to the day since she'd met him. Slept with him. He'd been on her mind every day, but when the number he'd given her turned out to be wrong, she'd decided they weren't meant to be.

Or that he had never really wanted them to be. How had he known where to find her? Bumping into him in a restaurant a few blocks from her hotel had been unexpected, but a reasonable happenstance. Of all the yachts in the south of France right now, however, he was on this one? Standing outside her door?

No, he must have come to find her, but how had he gotten on board? Given all the celebrities in attendance, security was very tight. He had some sort of security company, she recalled vaguely, but it still seemed very odd.

As she stood there trying to assimilate his presence, he turned his head.

"Oriel." His voice pierced as sharply as his flaring gaze.

His innate energy leaped down the long passageway to catch at her, threatening to overwhelm her the way he had the first time. It was so visceral, it alarmed her. She hadn't properly gotten over him, and here he was about to make it worse.

Acting purely on instinct, she whirled around and fled up the stairs like Cinderella from the ball. She didn't know why she needed to get away. She just did.

She tried to, anyway.

"Sweetheart. Where you going?" Duke lurched in front of her, swaying, eyes barely open.

Oriel tugged Duke out a door so they stood at the rail and dredged up a lame smile.

"This has been so much fun." *Lie.* "But I have an early flight tomorrow. I'm going to get a room on shore."

"What's the problem, sugar? Feeling neglected?" Duke splayed a hand on her waist. "I can't help it if I'm popular. C'mon. We'll go to my room."

"What? Ew. *No.*" She tried to brush his hand off her, but he caught hers and wouldn't let her shake him off. *"Duke."*

People further along the rail turned their heads.

He crowded into her, cajoling, "Don't make me look bad, sweetheart."

Good heavens, was he begging? What a poor, desperate man.

She looked him straight in the eye and said, "You need rehab. Do you want me to ask my agent to arrange it if yours won't?"

He dismissed that with a tired curse, hissing, "I need good press, darling. Come to my room. Let people think what they think. That's all I want. Swear."

"No." She pressed his chest, but he kept her trapped against the rail. "Seriously, Duke. Back off. Let me go."

"Come *on*. I got you a room so you'd at least *pretend* we're having sex."

"I'll see that you're given a full refund," she muttered and pushed harder. *"Let me go."*

Duke was suddenly yanked back a few steps.

"I will cut you up and throw you to the sharks," Vijay said in the most frightening tone Oriel had ever heard.

"Vijay!" She shot out a protesting hand.

Before she could react further, security guards emerged from the shadows and closed in on all of them. They clapped their hands on Vijay, forcing him to release Duke.

"I know him," she blurted, still holding up her hand as if she had some kind of magical powers to stop men from acting like barbarians. *"Tout va bien."* Was it fine? Maybe Vijay was some sort of stalker who had followed her here. She didn't know.

"I'm Vijay Sahir. I work for TecSec. Let me go." Vijay tried to shrug off the men holding him. "I'll show you my card. You can call in for my credentials."

Confusion ensued. Duke spat venom in her direction about bitches being crazy, and staggered off. Oriel and Vijay were invited to quit ruining the party and wait in her stateroom until Vijay's identity was confirmed.

Oriel could have balked at being left alone with him. His presence here was growing more bizarre by the second. Her parents used TecSec. Were they okay?

He was the only one with answers, so she led him into her stateroom. It was a midrange one with built-in shelves, recessed lighting, and a double bed. The shades were pulled over the windows, and she hadn't bothered to unpack, so her suitcase was open on the rack.

Somehow, she had wound up with one of Vijay's cards in her hand.

"This says Vice President of TecSec Asia Division." At least one mystery was explained. She had mistaken a five for an eight when she had texted him her bikini photo. "You made it sound as though you were barely scraping by." Why else would he have been working in maintenance at the hotel?

"I told you we had a deal in the works that I couldn't talk about. Are you all right? Did he hurt you?" He noted she was massaging her wrist and carefully took her forearm in his two hands.

His touch. It was as beguiling as ever, sending little tingles of awareness all through her.

She made herself pull away and step back. It took everything in her not to let him see how thrown she was by his turning up this way. How defenseless he made her feel. Her whole body felt electrified. *Awake.* Which undermined her confidence, because she didn't want to be this sensitive and reliant on anyone, least of all a man who had stripped her down to her most elemental self and seemed like he could effortlessly do it again.

"I'm fine." She might bruise later, but only because when Duke had released her, she had snapped her hand back so hard she'd bumped her wrist on the rail. "Why are you here?"

"They wouldn't let me near you at the premiere, but fans of Rhodes tipped me off to the fact you were staying on board with him here. I swear, the best security system in the world is no match for autograph seekers," he said ironically. "This yacht is leaving for Italy in the morning, though. I didn't want to miss you."

He was different than she recollected. His hair was a little shorter, his tailored suit on par with those of the movie stars and producers continuing their gaiety beyond these walls. His expression was forbidding, though. Nothing like the easygoing man she'd taken him for.

Or the humble maintenance man he had pretended to be.

"How did you know I was in Cannes? Are *you* some kind of super fan?" Worse? "Have you been spying on me? Tracking my phone?" She glanced around for it as if it would be glowing with a beacon.

"Nothing that high-tech." He was still using that dry tone. "I overheard your conversation in Milan. You said this trip would cut into your vacation. I thought it would be a good idea for you to have personal time after we talk."

"That's very arrogant."

"Which part? Assuming how you'll react to what I have to say?" His voice hardened. "Or that you would speak to me at all?"

That took her aback until she recalled that she had run the minute she'd seen him.

All this time, she had been telling herself she was fine with not hearing from him. It was what they had agreed on, but deep down, she'd taken it as a rejection, one that stuck like a thorn in her heart.

As sophisticated as she'd tried to be about their night

together, she'd also been more uninhibited with him than she'd ever been in her life. That knowledge kept hitting her in ever stronger waves as she remained in his presence, like a tide coming in. Her self-consciousness was deepening by the minute, and her feet were stuck in the sand. She wanted to get away, but couldn't.

Meanwhile, he stood there with his Just The Facts Ma'am attitude, suggesting he barely remembered they'd clung to each other while moaning with abject passion.

"I was surprised to see you," she said with as much dignity as she could scrape together. "Why didn't you reach out through my website or my social profiles?"

"You had my number but didn't reach out," he said with a negligent shrug. "I wasn't sure you would take my call, and this is important."

She wanted to say, *You gave me the wrong number*, but if this card was anything to go by, he'd given her the wrong everything.

"Why were you working for that hotel in Milan? Were you actually in their security department?"

He licked his lips, the first sign of him not feeling completely in control of this moment. "We hope that hotel will join our roster of clients. I presented to them while I was there, but no. I was not working for them in any capacity when I met you."

"Then why…?" She was growing deeply uneasy, pinching his card so hard her thumbnail went white.

"I told you the truth when I said I was trying to prove something to my sister." His detached air cracked enough that his cheek ticked. "As it turns out, she was right and I was wrong."

How much did it cost him to admit that? she wondered with a twinge of grim amusement.

"What is that supposed to mean? What are you doing here? What were you doing there?" She could feel hysteria edging into her psyche. It made her sick that he'd had some sort of ulterior motive when they'd made love. It sullied her memory of a night that was otherwise pure and wonderful. It made her feel used. Not desired for herself.

Unwanted.

He flicked open his jacket as if he was overheating.

Despite how fractious this moment was, she became acutely aware of his flat stomach and had a flashing vision of kissing across his muscled abdomen while her breasts nestled his erection. He'd tangled his hands in her hair and groaned as if she was torturing him in the most exquisite way possible.

A searing mix of arousal and embarrassment poured through her. She had been utterly shameless with him. It had felt right at the time, as if they were both revealing something no one else had ever reached, but now her gaze pinned itself to the floor, mortified.

A sudden knock rapped before the door swung open, making her gaze fly up in a panicked *What now?* One of the ship's security guards strode in and handed Vijay the passport he'd taken from him a few minutes ago.

"Thank you for your patience, sir. You're free to go anytime. Please let me know if I can assist in any way."

"Thank you." Vijay pocketed his passport and nodded at the door in arrogant dismissal. The man left, closing the door behind him.

Oriel stared at the closed door, wondering if she should be reassured by the deference that man had shown or intimidated. She clung to her elbows.

"Are my parents okay? Does this have something to do with them?"

"Not in the way you think. To the best of my knowledge, your mother and father are completely fine. But you should sit down." Vijay pulled out the chair tucked beneath the built-in desk. "What I'm going to tell you will shock you. It's about your birth family."

Oriel instinctively backed away. She was already against a wall, though. Some kind of knob was trying to puncture her kidney. She barely felt it. Her hair scraped against the wood as she shook her head.

"I know all I need to about them."

His face blanked with shock. "You do?"

"Yes." Oriel repeated what she had always known. "They were a mixed race couple, and that was a problem for my birth mother's family, so she gave me up." Which cut Oriel to the bone, obviously, but not everyone enjoyed the advantages she and her parents had. She tried not to judge her biological mother too harshly, not when she didn't have all the facts. "I've never wanted to cause problems to resurface for them, so I've never tried to find them. Plus, it would hurt my parents if they thought I was looking for my birth family. So, no thank you. Keep whatever you know to yourself."

Despite her dignified refusal, her heart pounded so hard she thought her ribs would crack. Her stomach was seriously trying to turn itself inside out.

Vijay set his hands on his hips. He started to speak a few times before finally saying, "I've been thinking about this from every angle, trying to work out how to phrase things. It never once occurred to me you wouldn't want to hear it. But okay." He nodded with bewilderment. "That's your choice." He rubbed his jaw, casting about the room as though completely at sea. "You have my card if you change your mind."

He looked at the card she held. In her agitation, she

had twisted it beyond recognition. He removed a fresh one from his pocket and set it on the folded clothes inside her suitcase.

He stood there a long moment, staring at her.

A million images flashed into her mind, from his first sexy side-eye when he had entered her suite to his quick smile at the bar. The way the touch of his leg against her own had filled her with melting heat, and with a cocky brow, he declared they were on a date. His kisses and caresses and deeply generous lovemaking and his note that had claimed it had been an amazing night.

She waited for him to acknowledge any of that, but he only nodded once and said, "Good night." He started for the door.

"That's it?" she cried, panic-stricken that he would walk away so easily. *Again.* "You can't just stroll back into my life with a baited hook and dangle it like that! What were you trying to prove?"

"To my sister? You just said you don't want to know."

She pressed back into the wall again. "If you tell me you and I are related…"

"No," he choked out. His mouth twitched, but he added firmly, "Absolutely not."

She hugged herself, searching his eyes for clues. Until this moment, she would have sworn that she had no interest in learning about her birth parents. She had long ago made peace with the fact she would never know more about where she came from than she'd always known.

She suddenly discovered she did have questions, though. Thousands of them, each one making her burn with curiosity. There was a scorch of guilt that came with it. This desire to hear more felt disloyal to the people who had always treated her as though they'd made her themselves.

"I love my parents," she blurted.

"I'm sure you do." His voice gentled. "This is my mistake, Oriel. It's been a busy few weeks for my company. I got it into my head that I had to have all of that wrapped up so I could catch you here in Cannes before you went on vacation, but you're right. This is something you should learn in your own way on your own timeline. It's just..." His gaze flickered down her silver gown, which was covered in sequins that caught the light. "Well, it was good to see you again. Call if you want to talk to me."

"Why didn't they just write to me? What about an email?" She threw up a flailing arm. "Have they *always* known where I was?" The thought of that nearly broke her into pieces. Who kept something like that from someone? "Why didn't you warn me that you were planning to come back into my life with news like this? Why are *you* the one delivering this news? *Mon Dieu*, is that why you sought me out in Milan?"

It was. She knew it as she said it. Her heart hardened into a stony lump in her chest. She had thought she was special, that they had shared something extraordinary. But she had never been special. Not special enough. Not good enough to keep.

"The situation is delicate." His cheeks hollowed. "Best handled personally so things can be managed on both ends. I don't want to say more than that because you've just said you don't want to know."

"Who do you think you are?" she cried, charging forward a few steps. "You've come all this way. I'm not going to let you torture me with it. *Tell me.*"

He stiffened as though bracing for a physical attack.

His head went back and he looked down his nose, but otherwise he was very still.

"Are you sure, Oriel? There's no going back—"

"Vijay." A pulsing charge was running through her, burning painfully in her arteries, throbbing and stinging and making her stomach swish around and around. She thought she might throw up, but fought it back, glaring at him. Daring him to speak or walk out. She didn't even know what was worse right now, looking into his eyes knowing he didn't care about her, or letting him walk away with her deepest secrets still unlocked.

He seemed to hold every part of her in his wide hand. Did he realize that?

After an interminable silence, he nodded at the chair. "You look like you're going to snap in half."

Sitting down felt like lowering herself onto a bed of nails. Her whole body was prickling with confusion, wanting to react to something big without knowing what it was. She clutched her hands together and pressed them to her trembling lips, probably most infuriated by the fact he was witnessing her react this nakedly.

"My adoption is supposed to be *my* information," she told him resentfully. "*I* should decide who I share it with and how much is known. You're not supposed to come here and tell me things I don't know about myself. Not things that are so…" the word *intimate* wasn't strong enough "…*integral* to who I am."

"You're right."

She instantly hated him for that ultra-reasonable tone. It told her how badly she was betraying herself if he thought she was in danger of a breakdown and had to neutralize her emotions by sounding all calm and agreeable.

Bitter tears stood in her eyes as she watched him

lower to the corner of the bed. He set his elbows on his knees and linked his hands loosely. His expression was very grave.

"It's not much of a defense, but I didn't believe this theory would prove true. It seemed too outrageous. I went to Milan thinking I would prove to my sister she was being fed a fabrication."

"Kiran," she recollected. "You thought someone was trying to take advantage of her."

"Yes. Because reuniting lost families isn't something we even do, but this man had seen your photo and thought you looked like his sister. The timing of your birth matched a trip she'd taken to Europe a few years before she passed away."

"She's dead." A cold wind buffeted her, pushing her back into her chair. She had to take a measured breath to absorb what a blow that news was. She really had been carrying a lot of unacknowledged maybes and somedays. Tears of grief and loss gathered in her throat.

Vijay waited until she lifted her gaze.

"I'm sorry." He offered his hand. "Do you want me to give you a few minutes?"

"No," she choked and tucked her cold, bloodless hands between her knees.

"I'll tell you up front that I have no idea who your birth father is. He remains a mystery, but our client saw your photos and recalled some remarks his sister had made. He became convinced you were his biological niece. I thought he was using the mystery to spend time with Kiran, and the sooner I proved him wrong, the sooner he would leave her alone." He paused as though giving her a chance to brace herself. "I went to your room in Milan so I could steal your toothbrush. I sent it to a DNA lab."

"You're not allowed to do that," she hissed, sitting up straighter. "You're supposed to get a person's consent."

"It was expensive," he allowed with a tilt of his head. "I didn't attach your name to it. I thought the man was a fraud, Oriel. I thought I would force him to admit he was blowing smoke and make him disappear. Or he'd go through with the test, it wouldn't match, and I could tell him to go to hell for sending us on a wild goose chase. I didn't expect it would lead back to you. And I never once took for granted what I was doing was crossing a line. I am sorry."

"It matches?" Of course it did, or he wouldn't be here.

Her stomach tightened, and she pushed herself deeper into the chair. On some higher plane she was appalled that Vijay had gone behind her back. She would never forgive him for interfering in her life in such an underhanded way, but her eyes were fixated on his mouth, her ears straining for every word.

"He's...my uncle?"

"It came back with a high statistical likelihood that you're related, yes. You look a *lot* like his sister, Lakshmi Dalal. She was a very famous Bollywood star around the time you were born."

"No." Oriel dismissed it on reflex. "My birth parents were from Romania and Turkey. I was born at a private clinic in Luxembourg."

"Lakshmi went to Europe with her manager about four months before you were born, supposedly to record some songs at a private studio. When she came back, she was different. Her brother could tell she was grieving. He believes her manager pressured her to give up her baby for the sake of her career."

"Is he still alive? The manager? Has anyone *asked* him?"

"Jalil is being very careful. He's afraid the manager, Gouresh Bakshi, will attack you and smear Lakshmi's memory. Or he'll lie or line his own pockets by selling some version of the story. Jalil would love more answers, but he doesn't believe he would get the truth from that man. He hoped you or your parents might have some piece of the story. Would you be willing to speak to him?"

"Go to India?"

"Or video chat. Take as much time as you need to think about that."

"I don't need to think." She shook her head and rose. Adrenaline was pouring into her system, and her mind fixated on one thing. "I need to go home. I need to see my parents."

She needed to go to ground like a wounded animal. Her mind was too shocked to form any other thought. She began to gather her few items scattered around the room as though she could outrun the crazed hurt and anguish breathing on her neck and sending trickles of apprehension down her spine.

She couldn't make sense of what this might mean and wouldn't even try. Better to carry on with her original plan.

"Oriel." Vijay tried to catch her by the hands. "You're in shock."

"Oh, don't pretend you care!" She shook him off. "Really, Vijay? Really? This is the reason you slept with me? To steal a toothbrush and ruin my life? Go to hell!"

CHAPTER FIVE

SHE SWEPT AROUND him with a rustle of her sparkling gown. The graze of her sequined skirt against his leg was an absent caress that wafted a tortuous sensuality through him.

How had he forgotten how truly beautiful she was? He'd let his memory of her harden and dull, telling himself he was better off because she hadn't tried to stay in contact. They were too far apart in more ways than geography. If she was the kind who resorted to publicity stunts to advance her career, she wasn't that different from Wisa. He definitely didn't need anyone like that in his life again.

Despite that very sensible conclusion, from the second he had confirmed Jalil was her blood uncle, Vijay had been anticipating seeing Oriel again. Jalil had still been speechless and pale when Vijay had urged him not to make any moves without discussing it with him. He'd confessed to having dinner with Oriel, not the rest, but insisted on being the one to inform her.

He had told himself he simply wanted to come clean about his part in this discovery, that it was the decent thing to do, but he'd been impatient to see her again. His heart had leaped into his throat when he'd seen her at the end of the passageway. The animal within him had finally scented his mate.

He didn't know what he had expected, but not that she would turn and *run*.

His gut tightened at that memory of her dress swirling and disappearing up the stairs. It had stung, damn it. But had he really thought she would be happy to see him? She was probably mortified she had slept with a commoner.

Moments later, when he'd found Duke cornering her, he'd been overcome with rage. The actor was lucky he hadn't been thrown into the sea.

That sharp swing of emotions had been so unsettling, he had steeled himself to stick to the facts once they were alone.

Then she had astonished him by refusing to hear him out. It hadn't computed when he'd spent weeks thinking, *I have to get to her. I have to explain.*

He had expected her to be shocked. Anyone would be, but as someone whose beliefs about his own parents had been shattered when he had least expected it, he should have realized she would be shaken to her core.

The way she was trembling and seemed greenish-gray beneath her natural tan alarmed him.

"Will you sit down and give yourself a minute?"

"No." She clapped her case closed and thumped it onto the floor, then yanked up the retractable handle with a snap. She scooped up her shoulder bag, checked its contents, then slung it across her body before snagging her case and starting through the door.

Vijay caught the door and followed her through it.

"You're really leaving?" He set his hand on the handle of her suitcase.

She held on and crashed her furious gaze into his.

As their knuckles sat against one another's, a deeply

vulnerable glint edged into her eyes. It slid like a knife between his ribs, parting his lips on a sharp inhale. He had made a grave error. She was more than shaken. She was devastated.

"Oriel." He didn't know what else to say.

Her brow flinched, and she snatched her hand away, saying caustically, "Fine. Be my valet. Saves me the trouble of carrying it." She swished ahead of him. "But then you can go to hell."

"So you already suggested."

The throng of party guests in a small bar turned their heads as he and Oriel strode through, trading barbs. Vijay paused to get his bearings, then redirected her down some steps to water level.

"Transport to shore, please," Oriel said to the deck-hand when they arrived.

"The tender just left." The young man nodded at the running lights disappearing toward the glow of the city. "It will be back in thirty or forty minutes."

"My boat is right here." Vijay moved to where his rented speedboat was tied and set her suitcase inside it.

Oriel was a Victorian queen in that stunning dress with her hair teased up in loops. Earrings like chande-liers dangled, while she was nude from her chin down her long neck to that plunging point between her breasts. She stood with her arms straight at her sides, likely hiding clenched fists in the folds of her skirt while she glared at him in a way that declared, *Off with his head*.

Waves were hitting the yacht from all sides, causing sucking and slurping noises. The deck lifted and fell. He saw her swallow uncertainly.

"Wait for the tender if you want. I'll wait with you." It wasn't a warning, more of a promise.

"Oh—" She strung together some very un-regal

words and gathered her skirts. "I'm only going with you because it's the quickest way to get to shore and away from you."

He helped her into his tender and handed her a PFD.

"You can't get me to dry land without drowning me along the way?"

"You're wearing chain mail. If you fall overboard, you're sinking straight to the bottom. It's dark out." He didn't even want to contemplate trying to make such a rescue. "Is the gown rented?" He would have to make arrangements to return it.

"It was a gift."

"From Duke?"

She shoved her arms into the vest and closed the tabs, then lowered herself onto the seat nearest her suitcase, chin high, nose turned to the water.

Very well, then. Vijay shrugged into his own vest and started the engine, nodding at the deckhand to cast him off while he sent a quick text to ensure his car would be waiting.

Was he jealous of her wearing something another man had given her? He was so green he was septic with it. He had been from the moment he had learned she wasn't staying in a hotel but was on this yacht with the dissolute actor. At least there'd been no evidence of Duke sharing that stateroom with her, but what did he know?

What right did he have to care? None. Oriel had made clear she had no further interest in him when she hadn't reached out to him after their night. *Which was fine*. They had agreed it was a one-time thing. She didn't belong to him.

Oriel made a noise behind him, and he glanced back to see her grasp at the side of the boat as they hit a patch of wash that made for a bumpy ride. He eased off the throttle.

A metaphor for how he ought to handle her?

What was left to handle? He'd gone behind her back, and she was furious with him. The fact that he was still sexually enthralled by her meant nothing.

They arrived at the marina, and he helped her onto the dock once the boat was secured. He could feel how her hand was shaking. Her expression looked anguished.

"Are you all right?"

"Fine." She spat the word like it was poison.

He returned the keys for the boat, and she paused next to him to ask the man in the rental shack if there was a shuttle service to a hotel.

"I have a car waiting," Vijay told her.

"Good for you. I'll make my own way." She wrested the handle of her suitcase from him and rolled it toward the bottom of the ramp that led up to the parking lot.

"Do you have a room booked? Because the entire world has checked into the city for the film festival." He was staying in a middling three-star place well back from the bay where the only window looked onto the pool.

"Do you know what's funny?" She whirled to face him. "The day we met, when I let you into my room, my agent said that was how lives were ruined. I should have listened to him."

She spun away and started up the ramp. Her suitcase caught on the lip. She turned and roughly gave it a yank, trying to make it come with her, but it was well hooked. She released a noise of helpless fury and shook it harder.

Vijay moved to help, but she released it so abruptly, it tumbled back onto his legs. He barely managed to keep from losing his footing and falling into the water.

"Look," he said shortly. "We need a reset before one of us—"

Oriel grasped the rail on the ramp and leaned over it, moaning with pain.

"Oriel!" He left the suitcase on the dock and hurried up the ramp to set his arms on either side of her. "Are you going to faint? What's wrong?"

She lost her stomach over the rail into the shallow water below.

Ah, hell. He smoothed a few tendrils of her hair away from her face and neck and rubbed her back until she finished retching.

"Mon Dieu," she moaned, sagging against the rail. "How is this night getting worse?"

He offered the black silk of his pocket square. "You get seasick." Or was this a visceral reaction to him and his news?

Vijay had a pigheaded view that ignorance was not bliss. Once he'd learned about his father's crimes, he'd been eaten up by guilt that he hadn't at least made enquiries sooner.

He had twisted his contempt for himself and his own willful blindness into thinking Oriel not only had a right to know about Lakshmi, but that she *needed* to know. If Lakshmi's manager forced Oriel's adoption, he couldn't be allowed to get away with it!

He was conveniently forgetting the hours of ruminating and soul-searching he'd done getting to the decisions he'd made and the actions he'd taken.

Oriel wiped her mouth and straightened, still trembling.

"Let me take you to my hotel," he said gently. "If they don't have a room, we'll ask them to phone around. Either way, you'll be comfortable while we sort things out." He went back for her case, then set his arm around her to guide her up the ramp. "I didn't mean to cause you this much distress."

"What did you think would happen?" she asked with disbelief.

"That it would go slightly less poorly than this."

"You lied to get me into bed."

"No—" As they arrived in the parking lot, his car slid to a stop at the curb. He opened the door. She sank into the back seat, still pale and subdued.

He closed the privacy screen as the limo worked its way into the knot of bumper-to-bumper traffic.

"Oriel." He squeezed his thighs so he wouldn't reach for her. "I honestly thought it wouldn't be true. Everything we said about not having another opportunity to be together was real. I never expected to see you again."

"So you took advantage of the one chance you had to nail me? That makes it all better, then." She helped herself to a miniature bottle of water.

"I didn't seduce you."

"You *lied*."

"I kept one detail from you because I wasn't at liberty to reveal it." He held up a finger, aware this angry defensiveness was the diametric opposite from the way he'd planned to handle this. He was supposed to be giving her the sincere apology she rightfully deserved, but clipped excuses were spewing out of him instead. "If you hadn't been Lakshmi's daughter, I couldn't risk starting rumors that she potentially had one. I didn't know you would come to that restaurant. You invited me to eat with you. You invited me to your room after. Remember? *Bring condoms*, you said."

"Well, I regret that now, don't I?"

"Only now?" he asked with more bitterness than he meant to reveal.

She snapped her head around. "What is that supposed to mean?"

"The second you saw me tonight, you turned and ran."

"Because I was *embarrassed*. You ghosted me."

"No, I didn't." He frowned. "You had my number."

"You have terrible handwriting," she spat, then looked toward the window. "I sent a bikini pic to a stranger because of you, thanks very much. I had to change my number."

She was speaking contemptuously, blaming him, but he was grimly thrilled to hear she had made an effort to reach out.

"I was completely sincere with my second note." He spoke more calmly. "The attraction I felt was real. I enjoyed being with you that night."

"I hate to break it to you, Vijay, but a lot of men are attracted to me. That doesn't mean they get to sleep with me under false pretenses."

His temperature skyrocketed, but he bit his tongue because the car was arriving at his hotel. There was no doorman, so the chauffeur slipped around to open her door while Vijay climbed out his own. As he came around to her side, he saw Oriel grasp at the edge of the door. She had gone white and looked like she was going to throw up again.

He hurried to get his arm around her.

She pressed a weak hand against his chest, obviously resenting that she had to lean on him, but she needed his support.

He managed to tip the driver and take charge of her

case, but as the car drove away, he kept her in the fresh night air.

"Is this something more serious? Bad shellfish? A bug?"

"I don't know," she said plaintively. "I thought it was Duke's cigarette smoke and being on the boat that was making me feel so awful. I haven't eaten much today."

"I'll order room service." He guided her into one of the pockets of the revolving door, saying facetiously, "You're not pregnant, are you?"

They both halted.

The door bumped them from behind, nudging them into the bustling noise of the lobby.

He looked down at her sallow face. Her eyes were swallowing up her features.

A dry lump formed in his throat. A nest of cobras arrived in his stomach.

"Are you?" His lips felt numb. A vivid memory came to him of the exquisite sensation when she'd been riding his naked flesh. He hadn't come, though. Even if he had, surely he'd have been shooting blanks by then!

"No. That's—no, of course not." She didn't sound sure. She looked aghast, but who wouldn't after the last few hours? "No. That would be ridiculous."

I hate to break it to you, Oriel, but "ridiculous" was left behind long ago.

He didn't say it. He led her to the elevator and walked her to his room, experiencing a twinge of embarrassment when he let her in. The room was clean and secure, but it was no superyacht or even the classy place they'd stayed at in Milan.

"It's all I could get at the last minute." And he'd thought it would be only him.

"It's fine." She dropped her shoulder bag on the bed

and moved to the window, where she hugged herself while staring down at the guests partying alongside the pool.

"Do you…" He pushed his hands into his pockets. "Do you want me to go to a pharmacy?"

"No." Her fingernails were digging into her upper arm. "But I think you should." Her gaze flashed over to his, swiping through him like a blade when he saw the deeply apprehensive shadows lurking there. "Just to be sure."

He tried again to swallow the lump in his throat. His lungs felt tight. He nodded, glad to have an excuse to catch a breath of air and organize his thoughts.

"Order something," he said, nodding at the card on the nightstand. "Maybe you just need to settle your stomach."

Her eyes widened with persecution, as if food was one decision too many.

"I'll ask downstairs, have something sent up," he offered.

"Thank you." She was staring at the pool again.

The fact she was not throwing sarcasm and defiant looks at him said a lot. She was worried. Which worried him.

Did it? He didn't know what to think or feel.

He moved like a robot, asked for directions at the registration desk, and almost forgot to request two bowls of soup be sent to his room.

What if Oriel was pregnant? Was it even his? If it was, what would he do?

At one time he had assumed without question that he would eventually marry and become a father. His parents had been indulgent, his broader family of aunts, uncles and cousins a warm network of affection, endless food and constant laughter. The expectation of a similar life had been very natural—if intimidating when his grandmother had dubbed him "man of the house" after his parents' death. Vijay had had her and Kiran to look after, though, and his father's business to take over. He had focused on growing into the role and had been determined to do it well.

When the foundations of the business proved to be rotten and his fiancée's fidelity was revealed to be equally compromised, Vijay had put aside aspirations of marriage and parenting. Staying clothed and fed had become his priority.

Over time, as his fortunes improved, he'd become aware that women looked on him as a prize worth winning. His ability to trust was so eroded, however, he hadn't been willing to commit to anything serious. He didn't want to set himself up for another gross betrayal. Besides, he hadn't met anyone he couldn't stop thinking about.

Until Oriel.

It had been two months since he'd seen her, and he'd thought of her constantly, checking his phone like an adolescent hoping for a "like."

Surely she would have had a sign by now if the baby was his? He cautioned himself not to get caught up in a sense of duty toward her, but uneasily recognized he wouldn't cut all ties if it wasn't his. He had delivered the shock of her life. She was in a vulnerable state and could be even more so, depending on what this test told them. He couldn't wish her a nice life and go back to his own.

Damn it, why were there so many brands? He scanned the array of boxes, brain nearly exploding at the advertising flashing that promised "results in one minute" and "estimated weeks." He grabbed the two priciest ones and half expected her to be gone when he returned.

She had changed into plaid pajama pants and a T-shirt, washed off her makeup, removed her earrings, and gathered her hair into a low ponytail. She was as fresh-faced as when he'd met her that morning in Milan, except far more somber.

The soup had arrived. It sat untouched and covered on the tray on the small table.

She eyed the bag choked by his fist.

"Listen." He was too restless to sit. "Whether it's mine or not—"

"Of course it would be yours," she snapped. "Don't be rude!"

A sharp wave hit him at that declaration, one that winded him so thoroughly, it took him a second to find his voice again. A smart man would be cautious about taking her word for it, but a very primitive part of him was already aligning with this news, accepting it as truth.

He made himself say, "I thought you would have had some sign by now if that was a possibility?"

"I have really low body fat. I never have regular periods," she said stiffly, then pinched the bridge of her nose. "I've been feeling run-down, though. I threw up a few times. I thought it was a bug from travel. I've been exhausted for weeks, but I've been working nonstop. I thought it was burnout."

"I see." That sounded plausible. "Well, I'm here. No matter what." He spoke before he'd fully contemplated all that might entail, but he couldn't turn his back on her, not if he was responsible for what she was going through.

He held out the bag.

"I don't have to go yet," she said sullenly and looked out the window.

"Oh." He set the bag on the bed. "Should we watch TV while we eat?"

"Do whatever you want."

He lifted the cover off the soup, hoping the aroma of leeks and potatoes and fresh rolls would tempt her, but she didn't even look at him.

He replaced the cover. "Do you want an apology?"

"For what? Producing, single-handedly, the absolute most stressful hours of my life? For completely over-turning everything I thought I knew about myself while potentially wreaking havoc on my future?"

Vijay had had a few weeks to digest the news of her parentage and it was purely incidental to his own life, not rooted in his foundation. He was reeling under the idea that he might become a father, but he wouldn't let that sink in until he knew for sure she was pregnant and intended to keep it. For her, this meant her *body* would be taken over. He couldn't make assumptions about how she would proceed.

What remained constant through all of this, however, was his fascination with this woman. He was trying to keep his head and think about facts and next steps, but learning about her birth family had only meant some-thing to him because it was about *her*. He was angry with himself that he hadn't handled this better.

"You have every right to be angry. And scared."

The corners of her mouth went down. "I have to go *so bad*." She looked to the bathroom. "But I'm afraid of what I'll find out. Then it will be real."

He couldn't stand it. He closed in on her, moving slowly so she had plenty of time to rebuff him, but he didn't know how else to express the conflicting emotions gripping him, the remorse and concern.

When he gathered her in, she shuddered and slid her arms around his waist, tucking her nose into the nook of his neck.

It was surprisingly powerful to hold her again, to feel this sense of interlocking his life with hers. Her scent filled his head and her breasts pressed his chest and her hair tickled his chin. He wanted to press his lips to her skin, but made himself speak against her hair.

"What *we* find out," he managed to say. He was taking her word for it that he was the only possible father, but he wanted to believe it, which was its own sort of terrifying. It wasn't just a latent desire to be a father, either. He wanted to be the father of *her* child.

And no matter what was going on in his head, it must be a thousand times worse for her. He knew that because she was trembling.

"You're not alone." He rubbed her back reassuringly. "I'm here."

She nodded and withdrew, biting her lip as she picked up the bag and moved to the bathroom.

Her silver gown was hanging on the door. She unhooked the hanger from the edge and threw the whole thing toward the bed, where it slithered to the floor. She didn't seem to care and closed the door behind her.

Vijay hung the gown on the curtain rod, then took her place staring at all those mindless people going on with their mindless lives around the pool. Didn't they know that life-altering discoveries were being made right now?

He reminded himself to breathe.

This was too much.

Oriel shakily did her thing, then set the test on the

empty box on the back of the toilet without looking at the result. She stared into her ghoulish reflection as she washed her hands, fighting back a hysterical cackle. Her birth mother was a Bollywood icon? Her one-night lover was an undercover DNA thief? Her career was about to be derailed by an unplanned pregnancy?

Non. She might have been able to handle one or two of those things, but not all of them. Not all at once. It was too much. Way too much. Her vision was fading at the edges, she was working so hard to keep from breaking down.

Especially because, deep inside herself, she knew what she wanted that test to say, and it went against everything she had ever told herself. She had long ago decided that when she was ready for children, she would adopt. She understood how important it was to offer a good home to a child who needed one, and she had a lot of love to give as well as many advantages.

A man had not been a necessary part of that picture, deliberately. Of course, she had always hoped to find someone who would make a life and family with her, but her mother was an icon who had molded the life she wanted rather than waiting around hoping for it to manifest on its own. Seeing how Estelle had managed to have it all—career, marriage, family—had made Oriel open to the idea of having children on her own time-line, by herself, without waiting for a committed relationship if that was what felt right when the time came.

Pinning her future on a man was very last century, yet here she was, secretly hoping that test would tie her to Vijay forever. He didn't even want her! Not the way she longed to be wanted and loved. He might be nice enough to give her a hug when she was falling apart, but he'd also gone behind her back and *he hadn't called.*

As she turned off the taps, she heard a knock at the door. "Can I come in?"

"I haven't looked at it," she said flatly.

He came in uninvited.

She really should learn to lock him out of rooms she was in.

She ought to bash him in the chest and make him leave her alone, but that was the problem. She was feeling very, very alone right now. Who could she explain this to? Her agent? Her parents? She had cousins and friends, but they were scattered all over, and no one had any shared perspective. They would say the wrong things. You found your birth mother? Wonderful! But it wasn't. Her birth mother was already gone. You're pregnant? Exciting! But no. It meant the career that was finally taking off would fizzle.

You were treated badly by a man? Tell him to go to hell.

She couldn't. Because rather than lean around her to see the result, rather than take her by the shoulders and babble some unhelpful platitude, Vijay stood before her, quiet and calm, as though whatever happened next couldn't shake him. He was solid and demanded nothing. He was here for her, and that meant the world.

"Why didn't you want Jalil to date your sister?" she asked.

His brows went up at what must have sounded like a random question, but she'd been wondering ever since he'd mentioned it in Milan. Plus, she was putting off facing whatever that test was going to tell her.

What if she *wasn't* pregnant? Would she announce she hated him and send him on his way? She doubted she could do that, and that was the most disturbing discovery of all.

"Jalil is much older than Kiran. I thought he must be showing interest in her because of her youth or the money we stood to make in the acquisition."

"A nurse or a purse," Oriel murmured. "That's what one of my mother's friends says older men are looking for when they date younger women. I kept thinking of that when I was with Duke. That I was resuscitating his career for him. Administering oxygen so I could gain something for myself. I felt like a fame whore."

"Oof. Is this where the self-bashers meet? Because I feel like an ass for not believing my sister possesses sound judgment and knows her own heart. I interfered in her life and have overturned yours, all out of an arrogant belief that I know best."

She gave him a chiding look, but appreciated his acknowledging how much he had tripped her up. She appreciated his humor, too. She had liked that about him from the first.

"I can't tell Jalil anything about my birth mother," she pointed out. "The information I had was wrong."

"I think he just wants to know that a part of his sister lives on. I wouldn't want to be in his shoes, but if I was, I can imagine how much it would comfort me to discover Kiran had a child."

Oriel felt her mouth twisting at his sharing such a personal detail. She looked at her reflection—that remnant of a woman who was gone.

She noted the anxiety around her eyes, the lack of color in her lips. She had always known she was the result of an unplanned pregnancy, but she suddenly felt deep affinity for that mysterious person who had given birth to her. This was how Lakshmi must have felt. Overwhelmed. Frightened. Head pounding with the question, *What do I do?*

She couldn't imagine how much more difficult this would be if Vijay or someone else were pushing her around, telling her what to do. The way it was sounding, Lakshmi might have had to fight just to give birth to her.

A ferocity rose in her, an instinctual, angry determination that arrived in her like a gleaming light of truth.

"If I'm pregnant, I'm keeping the baby." Her eyes grew damp. It felt good to acknowledge that, even though it turned her crystal-clear future into a blurred vision through a fogged glass.

She looked straight at Vijay, letting him see that she would never be swayed on this.

He nodded thoughtfully, while his eyes narrowed with intensity.

"And if you're pregnant…it's definitely mine."

The way he said it made her heart lurch unsteadily in her chest. She wanted to set her chin with indignation, but it didn't sound as though he was questioning her. At the same time, she realized this was her chance to firmly eject him from her life if she wanted to.

She couldn't.

She swallowed the hot constriction in her throat. "Today I learned that everything I thought I knew about my birth parents was a lie. I wouldn't do that to my own child. You are definitely the father."

"Then, if you're pregnant—" he spoke with steady resolve "—I'll propose."

The impact of that was so monumental, her ears rang. Her chest felt as though it was pierced by a stinging arrow.

"You don't owe me anything." *Us.*

"I owe any child I make everything I am capable of providing."

Not about her, then. She realized how intently they'd been staring into each other's eyes when she dropped her gaze. A giant brick seemed to settle between her lungs.

"I'll refuse," she warned through her tight throat. "I'm still angry with you. I don't trust you."

"Trust is difficult for me, too." His mouth twisted. "But this isn't about us, is it?"

"I don't know," she said, voice nearly nonexistent. "Maybe we're arguing over nothing." They weren't. Her intuition told her exactly what that test would say.

"Shall we see?"

Biting her lip, she nodded jerkily.

When she didn't turn to retrieve it, he crowded close. One of his arms went around her waist to steady her as he leaned past her.

She tensed, ears straining. She felt the jolt that went through him. He sucked in a breath and his chest expanded.

A shower of sparkling lights filled her vision. She closed her fists into his shirt, afraid she was going to faint.

He made a small space between them and showed her the stick. She had to blink and blink to see its bright blue, unmistakable cross that indicated a positive. In a voice husked with reverence, Vijay said, "We're having a baby."

CHAPTER SIX

ORIEL'S PHONE BEGAN emanating soft harp strings that gradually increased in volume.

As Vijay reached across her to turn it off, she reached for it herself.

She must have still been mostly asleep, because as their hands bumped and their bodies shifted against one another's, a startled gasp tore out of her throat. She sat up in a tangle of blankets, hair spilling across her face. She impatiently shoved it out of her eyes.

As she stared at him, recognition arrived with comprehension and memory. She sagged and pulled her knees up to hug them, giving a little choke of helplessness.

The angels in her phone grew more insistent. She grabbed it and stabbed to silence it.

"What's the alarm for?" His voice sounded like a garbage disposal. He cleared his throat.

"I'm flying home to spend the rest of the week with my parents. I told you that."

"That's your vacation? Do you have a flight booked?" He rolled toward the nightstand on his side, picking up his own phone, but ignored the notifications.

"Yes." She fell back onto her pillow and flicked through her messages.

His eyes were so gritty with lack of sleep, he could barely see his screen.

Last night, they'd eaten and she'd gone to bed while he had stood at the window, trying to assimilate the fact he was becoming a father. He might not trust easily, but after her indignant declaration about learning her birth history was a lie, he believed her about that much.

Family was an extremely complex knot of emotions for him. He had grieved the loss of his parents and grandmother with the support of his extended family. Then he lost his parents again when he realized what they'd been covering up. The people he had thought he knew had never existed. When he exposed that, he was called an ungrateful traitor and worse. The loving safety net he'd believed would always be there for him had been yanked like a rug. None of those relations would take his calls, and he was still angry and hurt enough that he wouldn't pick up the phone, either.

Only Kiran had stood by him, and he would give his life to protect her. He'd gotten used to thinking she was all he would ever have.

Now he had this nascent, fragile idea of a person beginning to take up space in his heart. There was no question in him that he would claim his child with every part of himself and ensure his child's life was intrinsically interwoven with his own.

So that meant doing the same with Oriel.

She was a far more complicated person to weave into his life. He still wanted her physically. Desire for her was simmering beneath all his best efforts to ignore it. He recalled her as an amusing, interesting companion over dinner, but real life was not a few hours of casual conversation. Real life was *real*. He knew very little about the real Oriel Cuvier.

He had thought he did. When she hadn't called, he had convinced himself she was too stuck-up to reach out to a blue-collar boy toy.

Beneath her animosity and shock about her birth parents and the baby news, she was angry with him, though. Hurt. Because she thought he'd deliberately given her the wrong number. Because she thought he had only come to her room for a toothbrush, not *her*.

As he'd stood at the window wondering if it was time for him to quit being so damned suspicious of everyone around him, he'd heard her sniffle and realized she was giving in to the volume of emotions drowning her. He had crawled into bed fully dressed and curled himself around her.

She'd cried herself to sleep, and maybe he had dozed. Mostly he'd stared into the darkness, working through the thousand paths forward, trying to find the best one. His entire life needed to be reshaped around her and their child. They had a lot of decisions to make.

"Are you flying into Tours?" he asked her, recalling where her parents' home was located. "What time does your flight leave?"

"Nine thirty."

"Nine thirty-eight?" It was the only one aside from another in the late afternoon. "It's not giving me a seat selection. I don't think we'll be able to sit together." He booked it anyway.

"I can't take you home with me." She sat up. "What do expect? That you'll just sleep with me in my old bedroom?" She gave their shared blankets a disdainful look.

"If there's no room in your parents' *chateau*…" He wondered how she would react when he told her where *he* came from. "Then I'm sure I'll be able to find something online."

"I'm not being a snob," she said impatiently. "I'm saying I don't know what to tell them. Who am I supposed to say you are?"

"Your fiancé?" he suggested pleasantly.

"Oh, was I asleep when you proposed? I didn't hear it."

"Because you told me you would refuse." He sat up and swung his legs off his side of the bed, not wanting her to see that her rebuff had landed and left a bruise. "I'm saving my breath until I've answered a few questions for myself."

"Such as?" She dropped her feet off her side of the mattress, but twisted to look at him.

He looked over his shoulder at her. "You travel for work and I'm president of the Asia division. How will we address that? Where would we call home?"

She held his gaze. Swallowed. Then she gave him her back again. "You're right. I don't want to talk about it. I'm planning to tell my parents about..." Her voice grew muffled as she looked down and spoke to her lap. "About my birth mother. But that's all. For now."

Did it sting that she didn't want to tell her parents she was pregnant with his baby? Yes, but he accepted that the news about her birth family was delicate enough.

"I haven't told Jalil that I've spoken to you." They were still sitting back to back with the width of the mattress between them. "If you're not ready to speak to him, I'll tell him you need time to break it to your parents. He'll understand. I can say your work schedule is very demanding, and you'll be in touch when you have a break."

She gave a humorless choke of laughter. "I'll have

to tell my agent that I'm pregnant. Once I do that, I anticipate my work schedule will become much less demanding *very* quickly."

"Oriel." He twisted to set his hand in the middle of the mattress. "I—"

"Don't say you're sorry." She rose abruptly. "I know I'm sounding bitchy. I'm not blaming you. The timing could definitely be better, but I'm not sorry I'm pregnant."

Nor was he, which was a very strange realization to absorb.

He rose and opened the curtains, letting in a blast of morning sunlight that made him wince.

When he turned to look at her, she was staring at him. She stood in bare feet and rumpled pajamas with unbrushed hair. Her face was naked, her brow crinkled.

He decided this was how he liked her best, even though she was so lacking in defenses, it made his chest tighten.

"Were you planning to have kids at some point?"

She gave a confused shrug. "My career hasn't left a lot of room for thinking about starting a family. When I did, I didn't worry too much about whether my fertile years were passing me by. I've always assumed I would adopt because I was adopted."

She chewed her lip, and her brow wrinkled even harder as she continued. "I've always felt loved by all my family, but there's no ignoring the fact that everyone looks and sounds like at least one other person. They have odd quirks that mark them as related. I tried not to let it bother me that I didn't have that because it couldn't be changed, but I've always had this sense of…missing out. Or…missing someone?" Her mouth trembled, and she firmed her lips.

The sun caught on the dampness in her lashes, making his lungs burn.

"I'm so sorry I'll never meet Lakshmi. That's what I was crying about last night. I do want to meet Jalil, sooner than later. And I want to meet this baby." She set her hand on her belly. "I'm really excited to see..." Her smile wavered with emotion. "A little bit of myself?"

His heart caved in. He moved around the bed, reaching for her.

She threw her hand up to hold him off. "I'm still angry with you."

"Fair." He caught her hand and used it to reel her closer. "But know that I feel the same. That baby is a part of me, and I can't imagine not being in our child's life every day."

Her gaze searched his, and the question was on his lips. *Will you marry me?* Even the bright sunshine and dancing dust motes became too much to have between them. He drew her closer, softly crashing her curves into his hardening body.

He wanted to kiss her. Hell, he wanted to take her to bed and reestablish the connection they had shared in Milan. Her lashes fluttered, and her mouth trembled. Her grip tightened on his fingers where their hands were clasped.

He had been waiting for this, the warmth of her, the scent in her hair, the feel of her as he drew her closer. He tipped his head and started to lower his mouth across her parted lips—

"I don't think that's a good idea." She jerked back and pulled herself free of him.

The chill of her absence was an abrupt bucket of ice water splashing over him. He pushed his hands into his pockets, hoping to disguise that he was aroused.

"I did try to text." She was hugging herself again. "But you didn't. You've only ever sought me out for… investigative purposes."

"That's not true." If she only knew how obsessed he'd been all these weeks. "I had dinner with you because I wanted to. I shouldn't have come to your room without telling you everything, but I couldn't stay away. That's the truth, Oriel." He ran his hand through his hair, agitated at being forced to reveal himself this way. "When you didn't get in touch after, I accepted that you didn't want to pursue anything beyond what we'd agreed to. But once Jalil's theory panned out, I had to see you again. I wanted to see if we still react to each other like this. And we do."

Lust was a churning furnace within him, waiting to explode at the first breath of oxygen she blew across it.

She hugged herself and eyed him warily.

"Wanting to kiss you and make love to you isn't an *idea*," he said. "It's attraction. I wanted to see you again. Jalil's news gave me the excuse. Now we've learned we're having a baby, and our lives are going to be linked forever. I can understand if you're worried sex will cloud things or you simply don't feel up to it, but seducing you isn't some master plan on my part. I'm reacting to being near you, same as you are to me."

"That's exactly what I'm doing—reacting! I can't keep a lucid thought in my head or figure out what comes next. My hormones are saying, 'Have sex. Then you don't have to think at all.' That's not going to solve anything."

"I don't know," he drawled. "My hormones would love a sidebar with yours. Maybe we should give it to them, see what they accomplish."

"Pfft." She dissolved into the prettiest laughter he'd ever heard. "Nice try."

He shrugged. "Worth a shot."

The air crackled with awareness and possibility and the panting breath of a wolf circling his mate. Her eyes widened, and she licked her lips. He started to close in on her, but her phone released a more aggressive sound of church bells.

"I always set two, in case I sleep through one," she said, moving to silence it. "And I can't miss this flight. My parents are expecting me." She glanced warily at him.

"I'm coming with you," he reminded her. "We have a lot to talk about."

She started to say something, but her gaze focused with annoyance over his shoulder, and she tsked. "I forgot the garment bag for this on the yacht."

She circled around him to ruffle the gown he'd left hanging from the curtain rod.

Vijay ran his tongue over his teeth.

"I'll call the concierge. I'm sure they can send something up." He moved to pick up the hotel phone, then paused. He had to know. "*Was* it a gift from Duke?"

"Maman." She splayed the skirt to look for flaws. "For their anniversary party. She'll be annoyed that I haven't been caring for it properly. It will have to be cleaned and steamed. Repaired." She touched a loose thread at the hem. "You can have my bed at the chateau, because I'll be in the doghouse."

He snorted, but her smile faded. She seemed to remember that a less than perfect gown was the least of the things that could potentially upset her mother.

He wanted to tell her it would be okay, but he didn't

know that. All he knew was that she'd just conceded to his going to Tours with her. That was enough for now.

He called down for a garment bag and ordered breakfast at the same time.

Oriel didn't protest Vijay coming home with her. He was the father of her unborn baby. Whether she married him or not, he ought to meet her parents.

They arrived to chaos. Caterers and decorators and workmen were overrunning the place, erecting marquee tents and unloading tables, chairs, linens and dishes.

Her mother would be in her element. It was the sort of orchestration she loved best. She was not only the center of attention—her rightful place—but she was director, producer, and critic, providing a swift review if a flower head sagged or a bulb on a string failed to light.

"When you said the gown was for your parents' anniversary party…" Vijay said as they climbed from the car at the bottom of the steps.

"Um, yes. It's tonight." She grimaced as she realized she hadn't exactly prepared him. "It's just an intimate affair with three hundred of Maman's closest friends and colleagues. I did mention that she is beloved? The spare room in my suite please, Tauseef," Oriel directed as her mother's chauffeur retrieved their luggage.

Vijay lifted a brow at her. She lifted a shoulder at him. She was angry and wary of trusting him again, but she kept thinking about him saying, *I shouldn't have come to your room without telling you everything, but I couldn't stay away.*

She was equally compelled to keep him near. The way he'd held her last night had been deeply comforting. He was right that they had a lot to talk about, and she couldn't help wondering if they might have something beyond what looked on the surface to be a complete disaster.

Maybe she was kidding herself, but there was only one way to find out.

She led him into the house, where it was easy enough to locate her mother. She was nearly always in the music salon even when she wasn't singing.

They went through the oval-shaped foyer with its curved staircase and domed ceiling, then passed the large sitting room with its grand fireplace and row of arched windows that looked onto the grounds. Abundant furniture was arranged in pockets for her parents' frequent houseguests and evening soirees. On their other side, they passed the formal dining room with its long table and westward-facing windows that caught the sunset on the pond, and finally arrived at the octagonal-shaped room where her mother spent most of her time.

The music salon was no less exquisitely built than the rest of the modern chateau, but it was kept free of carpets and pollen and other dust-producers so as to preserve Madame's voice. Like her bedroom, the windows were triple-paned and the humidity carefully monitored and controlled. The grand piano was played every day while she exercised her vocal cords.

Today Estelle was surrounded by her entourage of assistants, agents, and designers along with some of Oriel's favorite aunties and cousins.

"Chou. At last." Estelle came forward to embrace Oriel, kissing each of her cheeks.

Madame Estelle was only five and a half feet tall, but she was such an imposing presence she seemed to be at least six and a half. Her hair was wrapped in a silk turban unless she was performing or making an appearance. Today, she wore one of her colorful caftans in bright yellow and magenta. It made her dark brown skin glow. She had been born with an assertive personality and tremendous operatic talent. As her voice had developed and her status rose, she had become a powerhouse in the entertainment business and a diva everywhere else.

Introductions were made, and Oriel gave and accepted all the kisses. Her mother eyed Vijay with curiosity. "A fellow model?"

"No," he dismissed with a self-conscious twitch of his mouth. "It's flattering you think I could be, but I'm in security technology."

"Vijay is the President of TecSec's Asia division," Oriel provided.

"Oh? We use them ourselves. I imagine you have many secrets about your private clients that you will refuse to let me worm out of you, but I shall enjoy the challenge of trying. I'm so glad you brought someone interesting." Estelle tapped Oriel's arm. "I feared you would bring that tired actor. I didn't know much about him, but what I did know made me certain I didn't need to know more."

Madame Estelle could get away with speaking her mind like that. Oriel would have chuckled along with everyone else, but she was too anxious over what she had to reveal.

"Where is Papa?" she asked.

"In his citadel, taking refuge from the chaos. Go along and say hello. Come down to visit after you've settled in."

"Will you come with me, please? There's something I need to discuss with you both."

"Cherie, I have so much to do, and our darling family

is here." She waved at all the faces that had grown avid with curiosity. "You'll be here all week. Can it wait?"

"It can't." Oriel smiled an apology, but let her mother see her firmness.

Estelle gave Vijay another sidelong look. "Are you here in a professional capacity, Monsieur Sahir?"

"I'll lct Oriel explain," he said with equanimity as he fell into step alongside her down the hall.

Moments later, they entered the library where Oriel's father, Arnaud, wrote his papers and studied his historical research.

Arnaud was the perfect foil for Estelle. He was a quiet, patient man who could sit for hours in dressing rooms and concert halls or amid the babble of creative people who were his wife's constant companions. If he wasn't actively reading, he held a book with his finger notched between the pages. He had absolutely no desire for a spotlight, but was sincere and effusive in his praise of his wife for earning her place in hers.

Oriel had always felt completely loved and supported by him, but also as though she was a creature he didn't quite understand. Today, her sense of being an alien was stronger than ever. She worried they would both feel slighted by what she was about to tell them.

Her hands were so clammy, her father frowned with concern when he took them. He kissed both her cheeks, then shook Vijay's hand, studying him enquiringly as Oriel nervously closed the doors.

"Are we to have an engagement announcement at our anniversary?" Estelle asked with obvious delight as she perched herself on the arm of her husband's chair. "There would be some lovely symmetry to that."

"No, Maman." Oriel glanced at Vijay, silently begging him to say nothing about the baby.

He lowered himself to sit beside her on the sofa, and she took strength from his unflinching gaze and supportive silence.

"Vijay is an envoy from my birth family."

Estelle was rarely taken aback. Her breath went in as though she was doing her most aggressive breathing exercises. She rose with quiet grace and moved to her husband's sideboard, where she poured brandy with heavy liquid gurgles.

Oriel waited until her mother had handed out all the glasses and had perched on the chair again, taking Arnaud's hand in her own.

Oriel set her own drink aside and kept to the facts, skipping over absconded toothbrushes and a dinner-turned-dalliance. She simply relayed what Vijay had told her about Lakshmi, and that Jalil wished to meet her.

"I don't understand," Estelle said. "The clinic told us Oriel's birth parents were from Romania."

"I can only presume that was a red herring meant to protect Lakshmi's identity," Vijay said. "We've been trying to learn more about the clinic itself, but it closed two decades ago."

"Are you concerned there was impropriety? They came highly recommended. The lawyer who handled our side of the paperwork will be here tonight. He's above reproach," her mother insisted. "We had our name registered with several organizations at the time. This clinic was the first to contact us. They said the young woman liked our profile. We weren't attempting anything shady."

"I'm not suggesting you were. We may never know the complete truth about how Lakshmi came to give Oriel up. The important thing is that nothing we do learn could change the fact that you and Oriel are a family." Vijay looked at Oriel as he spoke, reinforcing that he wasn't here to take anything away from anyone. "Jalil has concerns the manager may have behaved unethically, though. If he did, he would like to see justice served."

"Of course." Estelle touched her throat. "Oriel isn't in any danger, is she?"

"Not to my knowledge, but if and when this news becomes public, you should expect a great deal of attention." Vijay sent Oriel a grimace of apology. "There is one other detail I haven't made clear to you. Jalil regards Lakshmi's estate as rightfully belonging to her child. In euros, it's worth over a hundred million."

"What? Non!" Oriel would have leaped to her feet, but her bones dissolved. "Please stop giving me these shocks. I'll need defibrillator paddles!"

He chuckled and reached across to squeeze her hand. "Whether you accept it or not is between you and Jalil. I'm telling you so you can plan security. You'll need it." He glanced at her parents. "I suggest you keep this news to yourselves until you have a full contingent of bodyguards in place, especially for the initial excitement. If you don't mind, I'll introduce myself to your security team while I'm here, purely as a courtesy."

"Of course." Arnaud nodded.

"Très bien." Estelle rose from the arm of the chair in her take-charge way. "We will discuss details tomorrow, but tonight the show goes on." Her glance bounced off where Vijay still had his hand over Oriel's. "We don't want you to *look* like a bodyguard, Monsieur Sahir. Did you bring a tuxedo? Our party is white tie. Oriel, Max is in the pool house if you need assistance." She clapped her hands. "Four hours to curtain, my dears."

* * *

"Max" was Madame Estelle's personal designer. He tailored the entire family and had a full team offering an array of spa services from the cabanas around the pool.

Vijay was led there by the head of security after he and Oriel had made their rounds together.

Oriel had retired to her room by then, and Vijay hoped she was resting. He had thought her parents had taken the news as well as possible, but she'd seemed very withdrawn after.

He was concerned about her, but after walking the estate and getting a true sense of her family's net worth, he was concerned about *them*.

Back when he'd proposed to Wisa, he'd thought they were on the same level of wealth and privilege. As it turned out, his family's wealth had been ill-gotten. The fallout of discovering that had contributed to their extremely ugly breakup.

Vijay had had to start over. He was extremely comfortable now, but even though he was evolved enough not to feel threatened by the idea of a woman making more money than he did, he couldn't help being aware he would never catch up to Oriel if she stood to inherit all of this *and* all of Lakshmi's wealth. It shouldn't matter in a relationship, but it would always have the potential to.

Despite that, he kept coming around to their marriage being inevitable. He wasn't so rich in family that he could afford to let his own child be raised away from him. Oriel seemed equally devoted to being a full-time parent. That meant at least living together.

He wanted marriage, though, and not for entirely logical reasons. Wisa had proved to him that a ring didn't ensure fidelity, but the vows and formality of marriage were something *he* would take seriously. He wanted that stability for their child, but he wanted it for himself, too. And he couldn't help thinking that making those promises to each other would go a lot further in earning each other's trust than keeping their options open.

Could they make a marriage work, though? The differences in their backgrounds became even more obvious as Max asked him to remove the tuxedo he'd just tried on so it could be altered on the spot.

While he waited, Vijay's beard was sculpted and his hair trimmed. He was given a manicure for the first time in his life, even though he was also given gloves to wear. His shirt required cuff links, and gold ones appeared. The points of his white vest were a precise quarter-inch beneath the edge of his split-tailed jacket. The jacket's lapels matched the satin stripe down his trouser seams. New shoes in his size fit perfectly over his fresh silk socks. His bow tie was snow white.

Vijay might have felt overdressed and pretentious, maybe even resentful of being forced to fit in, if he hadn't looked so damned good.

He was directed to join the flock of penguins in the drawing room, where he noted that not all of the tuxedo-wearers were men. Vijay wasn't sure what they were waiting for, but they were all offered a signature cocktail with cognac lemon from sugar-rimmed glasses. Arnaud introduced Vijay to everyone and explained how each person was related to Oriel.

Vijay wasn't intimidated by titles or political power, but this level of society underscored even more how different he and Oriel were. They could negotiate how and where they would live, but at some point he would have to tell her about his father. How would she react to that?

"Monsieur," the butler said to Arnaud. "If you would

like to assemble your guests in the front hall, the rest of the family will descend."

Vijay moved with the group into the entranceway.

Madame Estelle certainly enjoyed her pageantry. A trio of strings began to play as a name was announced. A woman floated down in an evening gown of peacock blue. She was met at the bottom by a man who brought her to a spot near the door, where they would form the head of the procession out to the marquee.

Cars were bumper to bumper on the drive. Guests had been queuing up on the red carpet for nearly an hour.

Vijay politely added his glove-muted applause for each person who came down in their glamorous and sophisticated evening wear, enjoying the drama of it.

"Mademoiselle Oriel Cuvier," the butler called.

His heart unexpectedly rose into his throat as he waited for her to appear.

He'd already seen her in the gown. The sight of her shouldn't have affected him, but she was entirely too beautiful for him not to feel his breath punched right out of him as she moved into the light at the top of the stairs.

Her hair was up again, but she wore a tiara that cast sparks of light between her piles of curls. Her earrings were matched by a stunning necklace that dripped ice down her cleavage. Her elbow-length gloves were silver to match her gown, and she wore a cuff of diamonds over her left wrist.

He had not appreciated her ability to command attention purely by the way she moved, but the gown and jewels all became secondary to the enigmatic mystique she projected as she descended, seemingly oblivious to everyone watching her.

Her eyes found him, though. Her gaze beckoned him

to the bottom of the stairs. The smoldering sensuality in her expression stoked a fire in him. When he offered his arm, she bestowed a smile on him that sent a rush of pride through him. Pride that she found him pleasing. Pride that he was the escort for this stunning woman whose touch on his arm became a hot ember in his chest.

They moved into their place in the procession and turned as her mother was announced.

"Thirtieth anniversary is pearl," Oriel whispered.

Madame appeared in a gown covered in luminescent seed pearls. It rustled softly as she came to a halt at the top of the stairs and waited for the clapping to subside.

The music changed, and she began to sing. Her voice climbed and fell with deep emotion, filling the high-ceilinged space with every octave of love imaginable as she slowly made her way down.

Vijay didn't understand a word, but he felt his own heart rising and wrenching. The way Estelle never removed her eyes from her husband told him she meant every syllable. It was magnificent.

After his broken engagement, Vijay had convinced himself love was a sentiment sold by greeting cards and Bollywood musicals, but as he watched Arnaud cross to the bottom of the stairs and hold up his hand for his wife, with his face flushed and his eyes aglow, there was no denying the pair shared something beautiful and precious. It made Vijay feel small to be so cynical when, for some, love was absolutely real.

As the song ended and the final notes faded, Arnaud said, *"Mon coeur."*

The pair kissed, and everyone applauded once more.

Oriel's expression was gleaming with fierce love for them, but Vijay thought he glimpsed envy there, too.

When her naked gaze lifted to his, his heart lurched. He read her question plain as day.

She wanted what her parents had.

He needed to be completely honest with her from here on out. He'd been burned deeply by love, not just by his fiancée's infidelity, but also by his own father's betrayal. He didn't trust lightly anymore and wouldn't give up his heart easily to anyone.

When she looked at him like that, however, he wanted to promise her the world.

CHAPTER SEVEN

"WOULD YOU LIKE to dance?"

Oriel was spellbound by the romance of the evening. The marquee was strung with fairy lights, the air laden with the scent of roses and jasmine. A twenty-piece orchestra played between courses and speeches. Several songs and recitations had been performed by close friends of the celebrating couple. She herself had given a final, heartfelt toast to her parents, and her mother had left everyone in tears with one more song that had earned her a standing ovation.

Now Estelle and Arnaud, had started the dancing and Vijay was standing over her, offering his gloved hand.

She was losing her mind over how sexy he was, and it had nothing to do with the tuxedo. It was all him. His sensual mouth and half-lidded eyes were pure seduction, his air of alert watchfulness and quiet command delicious.

She almost wished things had gone worse with her parents. Then she could hate him and use her resentment to hold him off. As it was, she was falling under his spell as easily as she had that night in Milan. Had she learned nothing? He was a destroyer of worlds.

"You waltz?" Her heart tripped as she placed her hand in his and he helped her rise.

Of course he waltzed. He was a man of infinite capabilities, hidden depths and fascinating angles.

"I know the basics. Don't expect…that," he said with a wry look at her cousin, who had married her fellow champion and partner from the professional ballroom circuit. They were swirling around the floor with airy grace.

"We're a family of overachievers." Oriel swooned as he took her in steady arms and confidently led her into the steps. "That's why it was so hard to find my niche and why I still feel only moderately successful." She was babbling out of nerves and felt like she had said too much when he frowned with perplexity.

"You seem pretty successful to me."

"Well, yes. I am. I mean, most women would kill for the opportunities I enjoy, but my work is based on genetic luck and tricks like attending high-profile premieres with attention-starved actors. It's not the same as rising through practice and mastering of craft."

"Your work is still a performance. You have to distill a mood down to a single snapshot. I saw you do it tonight when you came down the stairs. I was captivated."

"You don't have to build me up," she said with discomfort. "Maman and I made our peace with our differences a long time ago. I'm just saying…this is a lot to live up to," she ended on a mumble.

"I was being sincere, but okay. How are things between you and your mother now? Is she upset by the news?"

"Unsettled. She came to my room earlier. We had a heart-to-heart." And enough tears they had had to use cool compresses after or risk looking like puffy-eyed newts at the ball. "She said she always knew this could happen, and she only wants whatever I want. She asked about you. She wanted to know if you were more than my sort of bodyguard."

"And you said?"

She didn't know! She had first been drawn to him because he had sparked a more intense attraction within her than she'd ever experienced before. Since then, he'd made her feel *all* the emotions in the most intense ways. She couldn't help but be wary of what more could come.

"I told her I'm trying to keep my distance since I have enough to worry about."

"Trying," he mused, mouth curving. "That sounds like you're having to work at it."

My hormones would love a sidebar with yours.

If her presence here for her parents' celebration hadn't been so important to her, she might have allowed them to fall into bed at the hotel. Vijay was an incredibly compelling man, confident and handsome and still capable of waking her senses with a glance. The fact he knew what she was going through and was actually facing her unplanned pregnancy *with* her made her gravitate to him even more.

She'd been starkly honest when she'd told him she was tempted to lose herself in the same wild excitement they'd shared in Milan so she didn't have to think about the more mundane and difficult details of how they would proceed. Maybe there was something very basic to her desire, too. Her body recognized he was the father of her child and yearned to pair-bond with him as a way of reinforcing their connection, ensuring he would look after both of them.

No matter what it was, she was breathless and dizzy as he steered her from the cloying scent of cigar smoke and gave her a small twirl as the song ended.

He caught her close. "How are you feeling? It's been a long day."

"I had a nap before I dressed." She was giddy from being in his arms, smiling even after he eased his hold and started to lead her off the floor. "I'm glad for the distraction of this party. Thank you for being my date. I know this is a lot."

"What I find most fascinating is that I have the feeling this sort of evening is not unusual for you." He nodded at the mime performing for a table.

"Not at all. Maman adores setting a stage and creating an experience. She began planning this two years ago, after Papa's sixtieth birthday."

"When I tell Kiran that tumblers served dessert *while it was on fire*, she will die."

Oriel laughed. "I can't wait to meet her. Will she be on the call with Jalil tomorrow?" They had agreed they would call in the morning for a brief introduction.

Vijay's expression froze.

Her heart stopped. "No? You don't want me to meet her?"

"No, of course. I hadn't considered how much I have to tell her. I won't say anything about—" He dropped his gaze to her middle. "Not yet. But..."

"I know. It keeps hitting me at odd times, too." Aside from avoiding more than a sip of champagne when she toasted her parents, Oriel hadn't been letting herself think too much about the fact she was carrying his baby.

His hand came to her upper arm in a small caress. "Tell me if you need anything."

She nodded. He stood close enough that she could feel the warmth of his body. Her shoulder was still tingling from his touch, and his mouth was right there.

Seducing you isn't some master plan on my part.

Wasn't it, though?

His gaze touched her mouth, and his lips twitched. "Bodyguard, you said?"

"*You* said it. We all went along with it even though you were holding my hand."

"I was, wasn't I? I'm thinking about doing it again."

"Holding my hand?" She tried to suppress her grin, but her heart was soaring with excitement. Why? It was only hand-holding, for heaven's sake! Even so, she gave him a coquettish bat of her lashes. "Perhaps while I accompany you on a patrol of the grounds?"

"I'm sure I'm overdue for that." As he let his knuckles brush against hers, he dipped his head to speak in her ear. "I know you dislike that awkward moment of wondering whether a man will kiss you, so I'll warn you now. I intend to."

Her skin tightened with anticipation, and she opened her fingers for the weave of his.

It was a chilly night, something she felt as soon as they were away from the marquee. The music faded and the stars opened above them.

They weren't the only ones seeking a moment of privacy. They passed two other couples tucked into shadows before they found a pocket among the hedges where the cool scent of cedar closed around them.

Oriel slid her arms over his hard shoulders and curled her hands behind his head, expecting the crash of his mouth onto hers.

He barely grazed her mouth with his own, running his lips across her jaw and blowing softly against her ear, making shivers rise up her arms and into her nape before he came back to lightly nibble on her bottom lip.

With a frustrated sob, she pressed herself tighter

to him and slanted her mouth with invitation. He reacted by sealing them into the swirling darkness of a deep, passionate kiss, one that made them both groan in gratification.

His hands roamed her back and hips, pulling her tighter into the hardness behind his fly. When his tongue brushed hers, she sucked delicately. His whole body hardened and his fingers dug into her backside, holding her tight as he rocked her against his aroused flesh.

Oh, why be coy? She had known what she wanted in Milan, and she knew it just as clearly tonight. She dragged her head back.

"Let's go inside."

His nostrils flared. "For?"

"You need me to spell it out? I want to continue the affair we started. See where it might have gone."

His gaze was flinty, his caress on her jaw light. "An affair is something you can walk away from. We're beyond that."

She couldn't argue, not with his baby growing inside her, but lust had its talons dug into her. "You don't want to see what our hormones can accomplish?"

He snorted and said in a graveled voice, "I'm quite sure they can level a city." His mouth tightened. "You realize this is all I think about? I don't have much room left in my head for being noble. Be sure, Oriel."

"I am." From a physical standpoint, at least. She led him into a side entrance up to her rooms.

Her suite was a pair of bedrooms off a shared sitting room, all with tall windows overlooking the pond. The curtains were already drawn, the only light a stained-glass lamp casting red and blue streaks across the walls and ceiling.

"Have I told you that you are the most beautiful woman I have ever seen?" He leaned against the door as he locked it.

"Have I told you that you are the sexiest man I have ever seen?" With slow deliberation, she bit one finger of her glove and began to draw it off, making a show if it.

"Is that how we're playing?" He loosened his bow tie and opened one collar button. "Strip tease?"

"It seems a shame to waste the costumes. I was barely going to undress at all." She sent him her most beguiling look and came across to press the hand that was still gloved against his fly.

He looked down at her diamond bracelet, which flashed and sparkled. His breath hissed in, and his whole body went taut.

"I can definitely work with that," he said with a slow, wicked smile.

His gloved hand cupped her neck, and he ran his hot mouth into her throat. His other hand worked a finger beneath the neckline of her gown. The cool silk of his glove scraped erotically across her nipple, making tight golden wires shoot heat into her loins.

She fumbled at his fly and got her gloved hand into his pants. As she caressed and fondled, his teeth took hold of her bottom lip, and they stared into one another's eyes. His pupils were huge and glazed with feral passion right before he slid his arms around her and plundered her mouth with his own.

This was what she had wanted to feel again— *alive*. Connected. She was still angry at his subterfuge, but this incredible desire had pulled her toward him from the first, and it was still here. *He* was. Kissing her as though he would consume her. Wrapping his arms around her as though she was everything he needed in life.

She was so lost to the passion of their kiss, she didn't realize he had backed her to the bed until he tilted her onto it. She gasped and braced her hands on the mattress, but he was already lifting her gown, caressing her legs.

"The number of times I have thought about doing this again…" He went to his knees, and the heat of his mouth scorched the inside of her knee. He took soft, playful bites of her inner thigh, swirling his tongue against her skin until her legs trembled. Then the warmth of his mouth settled against the silk covering her most tender flesh. He began to lick around the edges of lace.

"Vijay," she moaned helplessly and sank onto her back in surrender.

He shifted the silk aside to anoint her until she was molten with need. She dove her fingers into his hair and arched, abandoning herself to the pleasure he bestowed, but he didn't take her over the edge.

When she was sobbing and tense and lifting into his caress, he rose and said, "Do you mind?" as he gently rolled her onto her stomach. "I just want to see how you look with the shoes and this icicle dress up around your waist—"

His voice faded into a guttural curse as she accepted the challenge and owned it. She planted her feet apart and braced her elbows on the bed, then arched her back to lift her bottom. She cast him a provocative look over her shoulder.

Did he think she didn't know how to use her sex appeal to achieve a desired result?

His breath was rattling unevenly as his hands moved over her buttocks and thighs, caressing everywhere but the place she ached most. He told her how sexy she was. How much he wanted her as he slowly, slowly drew her panties down her legs.

When he crouched to draw them free of her ankles, his teeth scraped the tendon at the back of her thigh where her leg met her cheek.

She shook in reaction, hands fisting in the blankets as she waited in agony while he caressed her calves and kissed the back of one knee, then stood. She heard the rustle of his pants as he freed himself.

"Do you want to roll over?" His voice was deep and far away, buried in layers of carnal hunger.

"No. Like this…"

"Naked?"

"Yes." She could hardly speak as his hot tip began to trace and slide, seeking, then pressing for entrance.

She was so wet and aroused, he entered her in one smooth, steady thrust that made them both groan with abandon. His hands splayed to brace her hips before he slid his palms up to her waist, exposing more of her.

"You're exquisite." His powerful thighs shifted hers apart a little more, feet planting firmly between hers. He took hold of her hip and shoulder and began to thrust with lazy power.

She pressed her face into the mattress, moaning unreservedly. It was base and hot and no one else had ever broken her down this way, pushing her past inhibition into a state of pure animalistic pleasure. No one could hold her on this pinnacle of acute near-climax for what felt like hours, so she was lost to all but the exquisite sensations rolling through her in waves.

Only him. Only him.

Then, just as she thought she would break from the agony of resisting satisfaction, his hand roamed to where they were joined. His long finger caressed across the swollen bud of her clitoris, strumming and sending her shooting past the limits of her control. She exploded, crying out at the sudden power of it.

He gave a final deep thrust and joined her with a ragged shout.

"We may not have thought this through." Vijay could hardly speak, let alone find the strength to shift his weight off her back. He grunted with profound loss as he pulled free of her and collapsed on the bed beside her, legs dangling off the mattress.

It had taken everything in him not to hammer into her the way he'd longed to. Somehow, that controlled, exquisite lovemaking had been even more intense and left him utterly shredded.

"I have nothing left to get undressed." Speaking was an effort.

"Same." She turned her head on the mattress to blink at him. Her eyelids were heavy with gratification, adding a layer of smugness to his satisfaction.

"Was I too rough?" He had managed to hold back until the very end, but he'd lost some control as they'd hit their peak. This woman completely dismantled him every single time. He'd known it in Milan and had known it when they stood outside, necking in the hedges. He'd known coming in here that she would pull him apart in ways that weren't comfortable, but he'd done it anyway.

That bothered him, yet here he was.

"I liked it." Her smile kept the erotic memory glowing between them like a golden light of promise. "But you're right. This won't be my most graceful moment."

She stole his pocket square and asked, "Can you get my zip?"

He did, stealing a caress of her spine before she pushed up from the mattress. As she straightened, she let the gown fall to the floor in what was actually a very supple, unselfconscious display of glorious nudity before she disappeared into the bathroom.

With superhuman strength, he tucked himself back into his fly and rose to pick up her gown. He was still looking for the hanger when she appeared in a pink silk robe.

"That poor gown." She tutted. "*Never* tell my mother what it's been through."

"You think I'm going to tell your mother that I bent you over the bed and made love to you in it?"

She found the hanger and came across with it, offering him a lingering kiss as she took the gown. Her hair was still up, her jewelry on, her makeup smudged in the most libidinous way.

He could get used to this, he decided as he began to undress. The fog of sexual satisfaction was particularly delicious while watching her move around her personal space, seeing her in a way that very few others were allowed to.

She slid a knowing smile at him when she caught him admiring her. A hunger that wasn't purely sexual nestled in the pit of his gut. It was desire for all of her. Her thoughts, her laughter, her moments of doubt. He imagined her belly swelling and being at liberty to press his hand there anytime so he could feel their baby kick.

At some point she would go into labor, and that thought was enough to send a cold rush of protectiveness through him, one that propelled him across to still her hands from fiddling with the gown. He gathered her in and kissed her, holding her close, trying to convey the myriad emotions gripping him.

Her arms came up around his neck, and for long moments they were lost to lazy, sexy kisses. When they broke to catch their breath, her hands slid down to his vest.

"Careful," she said with an unsteady smile. Her gaze skittered from his as though she was as unsettled by the intensity of the moment as he was. "We'll wind up forgetting to get undressed again."

He stole a last fondle of her bottom through the silk of her robe and released her.

"Who do I return this to and how do I pay for borrowing it?" He unbuttoned his vest. "Max wouldn't say."

"Because I bought it for you."

Vijay bristled.

"Oh, don't look at me like that." Oriel began to remove her jewelry and set it in a crystal bowl on the dresser. "You didn't expect or particularly *want* to attend this party."

He'd managed to put aside their different backgrounds and enjoy the evening, but it came around hard enough to slap him now.

"I can afford my own tuxedo, Oriel." Aside from tonight, he had no use for one and had no doubt this one was priced at a premium, given this had been a last-minute alteration, but he wasn't a pauper. He'd recently inked his name onto a deal that gave him a lot more disposable income than he'd had when he had bought her a gourmet dinner in Milan.

"My father can afford his own Maserati and rarely drives," she said, "but my mother still bought him one for his birthday. Don't worry about it."

"They're married," he pointed out. "If you're buying me clothes, does that mean you intend to marry me?"

"You haven't asked, have you?" she shot back. "But consider this before you do." She held up a finger like a scolding schoolteacher. "The reason my parents chose to adopt me was that my mother values her career. She has always had to work very hard to balance her personal aspirations with being a wife and a parent. Papa has a decent income from his books and papers, but Maman is the one who can afford a custom-built house like this. Yet she is constantly judged for not being maternal enough. For emasculating her husband by earning more and holding the spotlight while he takes a supporting role and arranges his life around her touring schedule. If the shoe were on the other foot, no one would bat an eye."

"You're warning me I will have to play second fiddle to you and the riches you stand to inherit? I'm well aware, Oriel." His voice hardened along with every muscle in his body. All his sexual afterglow was gone.

"I'm saying that if you're already threatened by it, you should definitely save your breath on proposing, because I won't marry you if you expect me to apologize for who I am or what I have." She waved at their surroundings. "I'm proud of my mother for all she has accomplished. I won't reject this or her to appease your ego."

Vijay removed his cuff links and dropped them into the dish with her own jewelry. The sound was very loud inside their thick silence.

"Those were a gift, too," she said frostily. "I thought it would be a nice keepsake from a special night. Most people were very honored to be included, but apparently this evening isn't something you consider worth

remembering. Good to know. Sleep in the other room."
She turned her back and started into her bathroom.

"My father was corrupt," he bit out, loath to talk
about it, but it had to be addressed. This fight wasn't
about whether their lovemaking was memorable—it
was imprinted on his soul never to be forgotten—or
whether he would keep a pair of cuff links. He probably should have mentioned this blight in his history
before he started talking about marriage. "I was com-
plicit in his crimes."

"What?" Her jaw went slack.

"Unknowingly." He ran his hand into his hair. "But
it went on way too long. I'm deeply ashamed, but it's
something you should know about me, whether or not
we marry, given we share a child."

She moved to lower herself onto a velvet stool and
blinked somber eyes at him. "What happened?"

"I told you my parents died when I was in my teens."

"And that you raised Kiran, yes."

He nodded abruptly. "She was in the car when they
died. She uses a wheelchair now, which I only tell you to
help you understand how I could have been so oblivious
to what was going on beneath my nose. After we lost
our grandmother, we still had possession of the house
we grew up in. Technically our aunt had care of us, but
she had a family and a busy medical practice in Delhi.
We stayed in our home with some staff. I was Kiran's
de facto guardian. She still required surgeries and other
therapies. We were grieving and trying to move forward
with our lives, going to school and making what felt like
a normal life. My father's construction business continued to run under his top managers. I met with them
once or twice a year, but I didn't involve myself in it.

I was grateful I didn't have to worry about money on top of everything else."

"You were a child," she said, as if that might excuse his ignorance.

"I was fifteen when I started meeting with them. I was twenty-two before I took a proper interest in how the company turned such a healthy profit." He still hated himself for trusting so blindly. "When I did, I realized our success was built on bribery and backroom deals. Intimidation, in some cases."

"Are you sure those weren't the tactics of the people who were left in charge after your father passed?"

"I'm sure. They were following the playbook he had created when he took over a handful of broken-down machines from his own father. He had been bribing officials to win contracts for roads and bridges from day one. Sometimes he failed to meet the building requirements. At one point, a bridge had collapsed and they'd paid to cover up their deliberate watering down of material. Thankfully, no one was injured or killed, but it was only a matter of time. The level of corruption was astonishing."

"What did you do?" Her eyes were wide with muted horror.

"I took the evidence to the police. Records and assets were seized, arrests made. They were lenient with me because I cooperated, but we lost the house, the business. Everything of value. It was social and financial suicide. All of my friends were connected to the relationships my father had built. To avoid going down with the ship, many turned on us and tried to smear our name. When that happened, even our family turned their backs on us, especially my father's side."

"Because you were trying to make reparations for

a wrong that wasn't even your crime? Since when is integrity worse than living off ill-gotten gains?" Oriel asked crossly.

"Since it affected their own social standing and ability to keep their jobs. But thank you for that." He pushed his hands into his pants pockets. "Kiran was the only one who stood by my decision to come clean. Everyone else said I should have kept my mouth shut and wound it down quietly if I didn't like it. Instead we had death threats. That's why Kiran started our security system, to protect us. Many people tried to undermine our success with it, retaliating by suggesting I employed my father's methods to win the few installations we were hired to make. Our success has been achieved honestly," he stressed. "Killian, the owner of TecSec wouldn't have touched us with a ten-foot pole otherwise. So it's not ego that makes me reluctant to accept your gift, Oriel. It's my conscience. I need to earn what I have."

What a terrible betrayal. She couldn't fathom how hurtful it would have been for him and his sister to lose everything, including their friends and family, after suffering so much loss already.

"I'll have Max invoice you if it's important to you."

"It is."

She nodded, compulsively running the silky tail of her robe's belt between her fingers. "I won't take that money from Jalil. It's not mine—"

"Don't let my feelings color yours." Vijay moved to crouch before her. His big hand stilled her fidgeting fingers. "Whether you accept that fortune or not is between you and him. Just as what you do with this…" he lifted his gaze to the ceiling of the chateau "…and the rest of what you inherit from your parents is completely up to you. I don't expect you to renounce any of it. Just know that if we marry, people are going to suggest I came after you for your money. That will get under my skin sometimes, and now you know why. But I know what I'm worth. And it's not insubstantial."

Nothing about him was insubstantial. He would be a lot more easy to dismiss if he was.

"Okay, but I hope you won't think what you just told me, or the fact I will inherit all of this, has anything to do with my concerns about whether or not we marry. We barely know each other, Vijay. I always imagined that if I married, it would be because..." Why did it make her feel so gauche to admit it? "That I would be in love."

He didn't laugh. He accepted that with a nod of understanding and stood.

"Did you know that something like ninety percent of marriages in India are still arranged?" he asked. "The couples aren't usually strangers anymore, but they don't always know each other well. Even so, our divorce rate is really low. People wind up very content. Why don't we approach it that way? Tell me what you're looking for in marriage beyond love."

What else was there?

"I always thought love was the key," she said. "My parents have very different personalities, but they're in love, and that seems to be what makes their marriage work."

"I'm not going to promise you a life of love, or even that I'm capable of falling in love. But looking at your parents as an outsider, I see a couple who seem to have friendship, respect, affection. Loyalty. We could have those things."

It was a fair offer, but seemed like a pale knockoff version of the connection she really yearned for.

"What do you want?" she asked, playing her fingers into the space between his shirt buttons. "Don't say 'someone who cooks.' I promise you, I will disappoint."

His mouth twitched. "I like that you make me laugh. I want that." He ran his hands over her waist and hips. "Passion is a 'nice to have.'" He nodded at the wrinkled impression they'd left in the blankets on the edge of her bed.

"Not a deal breaker?"

"It's not." He sounded surprised by his own admission. "Don't get me wrong, I definitely want it. My mouth is watering thinking about all the ways I want to make love with you." His mouth twisted with self-deprecation while his hand drifted down to fondle her bottom. "But if that was all we had, if I thought I couldn't trust you, then no. *That* would be the deal-breaker. Trust is hard for me. It's going to take time."

She could understand that, given what he'd just told her, but she drew a slow breath that felt as though it spread powdered glass all through her chest.

"Given the way we started this relationship, I have to question how much I can trust you, too."

He acknowledged that with a stiff nod and moved his hands to her hips.

"Where does that leave us, then? With me sleeping in the other room?"

"No." The word escaped her as a barb of loss caught at her heart. She flashed her thick lashes up at him. "We're not going to learn to trust each other if we put walls between us."

"Or oceans," he said pointedly and started to draw her closer.

"No," she said, pressing away. "We have such different ideas of what a marriage means. I don't want to think about it anymore. I am washing off my makeup before you distract me again."

"Fine. I'll go brush my teeth. But Oriel." He caught her wrist. "If you want to sleep, tell me to stay in the other room."

She gave him her smokiest smile. "We'll sleep. Eventually."

Oriel had a rough start to her morning. They had slept, but not much. They might still be tentative about trusting one another, but between the sheets, she felt completely safe with Vijay. When she was with him like that, she felt, well, *loved*. It was kind of addictive.

When she woke and rose, however, she was tired and a bit achy and had to face the reality that sex hadn't solved anything. She was still pregnant by a man who was a bit of a mystery. Her life had still been cracked wide open by her birth family.

She barely swallowed her breakfast and was worried about it staying down by the time Vijay was placing the call to India.

"Do you want me to put it off?" he asked, frowning with concern.

"I think it's nerves." She had never felt so many caterpillars spinning cocoons in her middle.

His sister Kiran answered with a cheerful hello that immediately put Oriel at ease.

Thankfully, she had the excuse of a late night at her parents' party to explain any colorlessness on her part. It was also such an emotional call for both her and Jalil, bringing sharp tears to her eyes when she heard the break in his voice, that they could both hardly speak.

They kept it short, and she promised to be in touch soon to let him know when she might book a trip to meet him in person.

Afterward, she had a reactive cry in Vijay's arms, then pulled herself together and asked him to drive her to her childhood physician, where she was pronounced healthy and definitely pregnant. If her morning sickness became debilitating, she was advised to seek further medical attention. Otherwise, she should take her prescribed vitamins and consider scaling back her workload.

Oriel already knew she would have to do that, and it was eating at her.

"I know I don't *have* to work, but I've put in so much effort to get this far. Now my entire life is a row of dominoes that are falling over, one after another," she complained as Vijay drove her home. "I'll have to tell Payton to break my contracts. He'll want to tell the clients why, because some will say it's okay if I'm pregnant. Sometimes that works for their show or campaign. But I can't leak my pregnancy to the whole industry without telling my mother first. If I tell her, she'll want to know who the father is." She rolled her head on the headrest. "And what our plans are. Then there's your sister. I don't expect you to keep this from her, but will she tell Jalil? How will *he* react?"

"There is one more domino to consider."

"*No*," she said petulantly and turned her face away. "I don't want to hear it."

He pulled the car off the road to a spot that gave them a view of the river. The fronds of a willow dangled to play with the lily pads at the edge of the water.

"At some point your connection to Lakshmi will become public. You can put that off, but I doubt you can keep it hidden indefinitely, especially once you're in India. Her face is very well known. I recommend staying in front of the story to control how it rolls out. Once it's known, much will be made of the fact that Lakshmi was an unwed mother. Do you want to be judged for being the same?"

"That shouldn't matter! Not in this day and age."

"I agree." He held up a hand. "And to many it won't. To some it will be an affront. Unfortunately, those are the voices the media will amplify because that's what gains them clicks and revenue. I wouldn't want our child to suffer because we wished to make a point about free will."

"Ugh. What kind of a world are we bringing this baby into?" she muttered, bracing her elbow on the door and covering her eyes with her hand.

"Come. Let's walk a minute. Clear our heads. Is this the park your cousin teased you about last night?"

"Yes." She couldn't help a small laugh. She had forgotten about their childhood game in the pavilion of pretending to be a princess locked in a tower, taking turns rescuing the other.

"Show me." Vijay left the car and came around to open her door.

"I will not re-enact it," she warned, but enjoyed the short walk along the river's edge to the structure that overlooked the river. A family of tourists left it as they arrived.

"I don't know what I thought a knight in shining armor was supposed to save me from. My life was very simple and happy back then." She moved to the spot with the best view and curled her arm around the post. "Honestly, my life is not that difficult right now, just very unclear. I wish I knew what to do first."

"Oriel."

She looked over her shoulder.

Vijay was on one knee. He opened a ring box and offered it. "Will you marry me?"

She slapped her hand over her mouth, but a muffled squeak of shock came out. Inexplicably, tears came into her eyes. She wouldn't have expected to be so moved by a proposal from a man she had really only known a few days, but she was.

"How did you…?" She came closer. The ring was lovely. Modest, but eye-catching with its center diamond surrounded by smaller ones in a daisy pattern, all set in yellow gold. It looked like an antique. "Is that a family ring?"

"I went shopping while you were with the doctor. The jeweler said it came to him through an estate sale. It was likely made in the middle eighteen hundreds, but its provenance is mostly unknown."

As she had been for much of her life.

Her throat closed and her eyes grew hot. She could hardly speak.

"You're a romantic," she chided.

"I am not," he said with indignation. Then, with gentle affection, he added, "But I think you are, given your games here. I don't know what sort of white horse or dream castle I can offer you that you can't buy or make or achieve for yourself, but we're going to be a family. I think we can make a strong one if we go all in. I think we can make it work, even though it won't be ideal."

That was really what a family was—wholehearted, unconditional commitment. She knew that. It was how she already felt toward their child, and she believed he felt the same. It only made sense that they would close that final link between them.

The hollow pang that had sat in her heart all her life said, *But he doesn't love you, and he's said he won't be able to love you too.* It hurt quite a lot to acknowledge that, especially when that same ache made her fear she would never be loved, that there was some flaw in her that made it impossible for her to be cherished the way she longed to be.

That was something she had to resolve within herself, though. She had to believe she was worth being loved and not put it on others to prove it. Besides, maybe Lakshmi hadn't been given a choice about giving her up. By revealing that, Vijay had already gone a long way to helping her heal all those old insecurities inside her. She was grateful to him for that.

The even starker truth was, even if he never loved her, she knew she could love him. She was already halfway there. Maybe he hadn't been completely honest when they first met, but in the time since, he'd been considerate and protective and open in a way that must have been difficult for him. She admired the man he'd made of himself and knew she wasn't done learning who that man was.

It was terrifying to let her heart make such a huge decision for her, but she moved to perch on his bent leg and cupped his stubbled jaw. Her voice shook with unsteady emotion.

"Yes, I will marry you, Vijay."

He closed his arms tightly around her. His hot mouth captured hers. It was sweet and so intense it would have been frightening if he hadn't been so tender about it.

As tears of joy and trepidation burned behind her closed eyelids, she heard a faint cheer go up.

They broke away to see the family of tourists had been watching from a distance.

She and Vijay tipped their heads together in embarrassed laughter. Then he grasped her close to balance her while he got them both upright on their feet.

As he slipped the ring onto her finger, he said, "I'd prefer to marry as soon as possible."

"I have a few days of vacation left." She wrinkled her nose. "How do you feel about eloping?"

"Done."

CHAPTER EIGHT

THEY MARRIED IN a brief civil ceremony in Gibraltar. Oriel wore a cream-colored skirt with a pale rose top that set off the golden tones in her skin. Vijay was in a gray suit and tie. Their wedding was short, solemn and profound. Vijay hadn't approached his marriage lightly, but he hadn't expected such a depth of pride and satisfaction once their rings were on their fingers, either.

It felt like a beginning, a fresh one that held more promise than he'd allowed himself to believe in for a long time.

They returned to the chateau, where they called Kiran. She happened to be with Jalil, so they told them their news at the same time they told Oriel's parents. Everyone was ecstatic to hear a baby was on the way.

"I'm going to be an auntie." Kiran clapped with delight. "I can't wait to hug my very own sister!"

"I'm excited for that, too, but I have commitments in New York," Oriel said with an apologetic glance at Vijay. She had told him that as they'd been on their way to the registry office. "I have to meet with my agent, tell him everything that's happened. Figure out what my career will look like moving forward."

"Oh, but... Vijay, I thought you were coming home?" Kiran asked.

"I am." He had barely finagled this week in France as it was. The building up of the Asian division was fully underway, and he'd been paid to ensure it went smoothly.

He didn't like starting their marriage apart, though. It felt like they were getting off on the wrong foot, and his worst niggling doubts had resurfaced. He was trying to tell himself this was the sort of test that would be good for them in the long run—provided they passed it—but the separation still annoyed him.

"Vijay is bringing copies of everything my parents have on my adoption," Oriel said. "Perhaps you and Jalil can find something that ties back to Gouresh Bakshi. My parents are happy to make inquiries on this end, but we don't want to misstep and tip him off that you're investigating how he might have behaved with Lakshmi."

Jalil was pleased with that lead, and they soon signed off.

The rest of the day was relaxed, and Vijay tried not to think about the fact that they were flying in different directions the next morning, but when they made love that night, they were both more aggressive than usual. Oriel laid claim to him with her mouth and hands. He did everything he could to imprint on her that they were one.

They were both sweaty and near comatose after, but she woke him in the night, kissing him with a frantic urgency that lit his fire all over again.

He pried her nails out of his hair and pressed her hand to the mattress, pinning her with his weight. "What's wrong?"

"I'm afraid something will happen and I won't see you again."

"This won't be like last time." He sucked flagrantly

on her earlobe and settled himself with proprietary ease between her soft thighs. "You're my wife."

He was an absolute Neanderthal because he loved saying that. *My wife. Mine.* "I would travel the world to come after you now. Don't you know that?"

"I've always been fine traveling on my own. I *like* not answering to anyone, but it suddenly seems very lonely."

"You're not alone, *priyatama.*" He shifted so he could roam his hand across her stomach. He circled her navel with his thumb, then caressed up to her breast, cupping the warm swell. They kissed long and slow.

When she reached between them and guided him, he pressed into her heat.

They stayed locked like that a long time, shifting here and there, mostly kissing and caressing and re-inforcing their bond. When he heard the sweet moan reverberate in her throat and her sheath clenched hungrily around his erection, he gave them both what they were aching for. He began to thrust with tender power.

As the storm brewed, he felt her growing tense beneath him.

"Wait," he commanded raggedly, wanting them to hit the peak together. His lower back tingled, and a feral noise gathered in his throat. *"Now."*

Her voice broke on a scream of agonized pleasure. They seemed caught in the stasis of orgasm for eternity. Wave after wave rolled through him while her body milked at his. He lost track of which one of them convulsed or moaned, which sobbed or made wordless noises of bliss. He knew only that they were in this singular place together.

And when they parted the next day, he went home with an empty ache inside him far bigger than the one she'd left in him last time.

* * *

A morose cloud descended on Oriel the minute she left Vijay. By the time she was in New York, she was struggling harder than she ever had in her life to find a smile.

Her priorities had completely shifted. Her mind was around the other side of the planet, wondering what her husband was doing. Her most important goal had become a need to put down roots so her baby would have a home when they arrived. All of her work commitments became obstacles to what she really wanted.

She sat down with Payton two days after arriving and told him everything.

His jaw went slack, but he was very understanding.

"I wouldn't be doing my job if I didn't point out that you could capitalize on the connection," he said in the middle of their discussion.

"No," Oriel said firmly. "I know how many doors a famous mother opens, but I don't want to do that to Lakshmi. I have a feeling she's been exploited enough. No, the baby will be my priority for the next year, at least. I want to scale back. Cancel everything you can. If that means I have to start from scratch when I'm ready to work again, so be it."

"You will never have to worry about that, but I hear what you're saying." He promised to begin making calls.

She phoned Vijay from the car afterward.

"You sound upset," he noted. "I thought you were going to try to work while you were pregnant, not choose the nuclear option."

"Yes, but as I sat there, I knew this was what I wanted. I'm teary because it was a big step, but it feels right. This way I can come to India and properly settle in. I haven't stayed in one place for years."

"You can get to know this part of yourself before India knows who you are," he teased.

"Exactly. Has Jalil made any progress?"

"My sister, the frighteningly brilliant strategist, suggested Jalil send out letters to people who worked on Lakshmi's films, claiming he wants to make a biopic and request interviews. It's been a slow process tracking them down. A lot have retired or moved on to other things, but as word gets out in that community, Jalil expects more people will come forward."

"That's actually a great idea even if he didn't have an ulterior motive. I would love to watch something like that. Could her estate fund it?"

"I'll call him tomorrow and mention it."

"Okay— Oh. I'm having lunch with an old friend, and I've just arrived at the restaurant." The car pulled up to the curb. "He wants me to—"

"Tell me you're making my dreams come true." The silver-haired man who had been formulating exclusive skin care products for four decades opened her door.

"I'll text you later," she hurried to say to Vijay and ended her call.

She let Yosef help her from the car and kiss both her checks. He had hired her for her first magazine ad five years ago, and she wanted to tell him herself. "I'm sorry, but I'm going to break your heart. I'm going on hiatus from modeling. If you want me to pay for lunch, I completely understand."

Six days later, Oriel was exhausted. She had one more shoot tomorrow before she could finalize things with Payton and leave New York. She was in the middle of modeling skiwear, trying not to sweat makeup onto the furred hood, when one of the hovering assistants said, "There's an urgent call for Ms. Cuvier."

Her mind immediately went to her parents. Oriel unwound from awkwardly grasping a pair of skis while standing in fake snow and took the phone.

"Bonjour?"

"It's me," Vijay said in a hard, flat tone. "Payton is on his way with someone from TecSec. Don't leave until they get there. The news is out that Lakshmi was pregnant when she left for Europe."

"What? *How?*"

"A cameraman from one of Bakshi's film crews received Jalil's letter about a biopic. He decided to cash in and sold the story that she was pregnant in *My Heart Sings for You*. It was her last film before she went to Europe, and it came out when she got back. He said she was sick on set, and everyone suspected. He assumed Bakshi was the father."

They had already debunked that. Oriel's DNA test had said she had forty percent Scandinavian heritage. "Has Gouresh made a statement?"

"No one can find him, but Kiran has set up a bunch of alerts, and your photo is already turning up in sub-threads remarking on the resemblance."

"No." She looked for somewhere to sit and sank onto a closed trunk that held equipment. "How is Jalil?"

"Worried about them finding you before we have a chance to put protections around you. So am I. Payton said he can get you out of your last shoot if you want to. I'd like you here where I can see to your fences and firewalls myself. The alternative is the chateau, but…"

"Maman is starting a new tour. I'd rather be with you."

"Good. I'll start making your travel arrangements. Watch for a text."

She ended the call and handed the phone to the assistant.

"Is everything all right?"

"Not really," she said in a daze. "Let's get what we can before I have to leave."

Vijay's new partner and the founder of TecSec, Roman Killian, arrived with Payton. Payton finalized the cancellation of her last contracts, and Killian escorted Oriel to her mother's apartment, where she hurriedly packed. Then he brought her to the TecSec jet. His wife, Melodie, and their two children were already aboard.

Melodie was excellent company, and the toddlers provided a lovely distraction on the flight to Paris, where the family disembarked. Each of the children gave her a big hug that jump-started all of Oriel's maternal instincts.

From there, she traveled with only a security detail and slept most of the way to Mumbai. By the time she was asked to sit up because the plane was descending, she had almost forgotten why she'd left New York in such a scampering hurry. She hadn't found much online about Lakshmi's possible pregnancy except a few sensationalized posts on gossip sites.

Oriel had been reading up on her biological mother every spare moment, absorbing the details of Lakshmi's life with greedy fascination, and had watched a few films with subtitles. Everything reinforced that Lakshmi had been very popular and treasured as well as a talented singer and performer, but she seemed mostly a South Asian phenomenon, not known well internationally.

Watching her was a surreal experience. She seemed familiar, yet everything about her was completely different from the life Oriel had lived or the person she had believed herself to be.

Now Oriel was landing in a country that, under different circumstances, would have been her nation of birth. Her identity. She was eager to discover if it felt like home, but a greater uncertainty confronted her.

It was hitting her that she had completely overturned her life to be with a man who was still very much a stranger. As an only child, and one who had begun traveling for her career when she'd still been in school, she had a very independent spirit. It would be one thing to reshape her future around the love of her life. It was quite another to do it for passion. What if she'd made a horrible mistake?

Landing under low, soggy clouds that looked cold and unwelcoming did not reassure her. Where was the undo button for life? She had a sudden urge to backspace all the way to Milan and make different choices.

Not true, she assured the baby, patting where apprehensive butterflies were taking flight in her belly. She peeked out the window and saw Vijay on the tarmac below, stepping from an SUV with a practiced pop of a wide black umbrella.

The air hostess pressed a button to lower the hatch that formed the stairs, and a dozen impressions hit her at once.

The temperature wasn't cold, merely rain-fresh cool. A gust brought in the fragrance of washed tarmac and wet earth. The patter of the rain was steady and musical, the humidity so tangible, her deep inhale rehydrated her, filling her with buoyant excitement.

And here was Vijay, taking the stairs in an easy

stride, arriving in the opening with the umbrella so he provided a shelter to step into. Masculine scents radiated off him with the warmth of his body—spice and coffee and the damp cotton of his shirt as she stepped out of the plane.

She paused there, drinking in everything about this moment so she could remember it forever. She memorized the lights in the puddles and the green in the distance and the way her husband looked down at her, face filled with intriguing angles.

He took her breath away when he looked at her in that hooded way, holding his sensual mouth so tense and serious. His dark lashes flickered as he stole a very swift, proprietary glance to her toes and back, revealing nothing about his thoughts.

Even so, as she stood close to him, spatters of rain pelting them with the changeable wind, she felt as though she had arrived home—not because this country was in her blood, but because he was.

She had missed him. This was the place she *had* to be. It was a profound realization and yet one more way she was losing a piece of herself to the unknown.

If he had kissed her then, she would have laughed with joy, but a gust caught the umbrella and tipped it, sending a cold drizzle down her bare arm, startling her.

"Monsoon," he said. "Welcome to India."

She was so wrapped up in wanting him to show some sort of affection, she briefly thought the word was an endearment. As she realized her mistake, she ducked her head and wiped the trickle from her arm, embarrassed that she was behaving like a pubescent child wishing for a paper valentine.

The truth was, she wanted a lot more. She was falling in love with him, she realized with a catch of alarm.

It was too soon, too spontaneous, too *new*. It made her terrifyingly vulnerable when she had already sacrificed everything, but her heart had opened itself to him of its own accord. She had quit her old life because she wanted to be here, with him.

And his reception to all of that seemed very lukewarm.

Why don't you want me? Why don't you love me?

She tried not to be crestfallen, but she was.

"You are a true Mumbaikar if you're willing to stand in the rain instead of running to where it's dry." He nodded an invitation for her to move ahead of him down the narrow steps.

She dredged up an uncertain smile to cover her disappointment. "I am ruining an expensive pair of shoes."

Rain hit her ankles beneath the cuffs of her snapping wide-legged pants as she descended. Her sleeveless, light-knit mock turtleneck left her arms bare to the spits and spats that whipped off the breeze and stung her skin.

"Jalil has arranged a press conference at a hotel near here," Vijay said as they settled in the SUV. "You're up for it?"

No. She wanted to go somewhere private to reevaluate all her life choices, but she didn't think she had the option to refuse.

"Of course." She had already approved the press release and memorized the statement she would make. "I warned my parents what was happening, but do you really think people will care that much? I mean, beyond reporters."

He looked at her as if she was very naive. "I do. Yes."

He didn't say anything else, but it wasn't far to the hotel. Their car was met in the parking garage by four burly, expressionless men. *Four.* Plus two people wearing hotel security badges.

They were shown through a private corridor and past an open door to a kitchen, where a curious silence fell as they walked by. An excited babble rose in their wake.

She looked to Vijay and noted that his whole demeanor was on alert.

"Kiran wanted to be here, but I asked her to stay at the office so I can give my full attention to you and your safety."

She began to realize he was actually *working*, wearing the role of protector in the most basic way. It was sweet, but she grew intimidated as they approached what sounded like a thousand voices beyond a wall. She unconsciously tightened her hand on the crook of his elbow.

As they reached a pair of doors where a handful of people were waiting, one looked up and made a noise of surprise.

Jalil turned and did a double take. He covered his mouth, and his dark eyes filled with tears. *"Beti,"* he breathed as he held out his hand to her. "You look just like her."

"Please don't make me cry." She caught his hand in both of hers. "Not yet."

They both laughed emotively, and he squeezed her hand so hard her rings dug into her fingers, but the pain helped her keep hold of her composure.

Someone offered to touch up her makeup while Jalil went into the room. The babble of voices nearly knocked her over, but they abruptly went silent as he was introduced.

Jalil began to speak in Hindi.

"He's explaining that he had suspicions Lakshmi had

a child," Vijay translated for her. "And that she gave up the baby to protect her career, that she feared she and her baby wouldn't be accepted if she kept it."

"I can only speak English or French," Oriel whispered in belated panic.

"English is fine. When Jalil called this, he said most of it would be conducted in English. Now he's saying he's confident Bakshi was not the father."

"Has Bakshi been found?"

"No, he's still in hiding." He cocked his head. "He says he has confirmed that Lakshmi had a daughter because he has found her. You're up."

Oriel's knees wanted to give out. She swallowed the worst stage fright of her life. *It's just a runway.*

Walking for an audience had never bothered her beyond a few twinges of nerves, but her entire body became encased in ice. Her limbs felt disjointed as she allowed Vijay to escort her into the ballroom.

A collective gasp rippled over the hundred or so assembled reporters. Cameras flashed in a violent strobe. A babble of incomprehensible questions assaulted her ears.

She wore a resemblance, she told herself, in the same way she often wore an haute couture gown. That was what people were looking at, not her.

Her training came to her rescue, and she managed an aloof confidence as she joined Jalil at the podium and flashed her warmest smile.

"Good afternoon," she said as Vijay's men stepped in front of the microphone.

The room fell silent again.

"If you were surprised to learn that Lakshmi Dalal gave birth to me, you know exactly how I feel."

It was exactly the right note of humor and humanity

to win them over. The flashes continued, but she felt the shift in the room. The acceptance.

She read her statement and took a few questions. Then Jalil's people ended the conference by providing contact information for further questions. As she walked out, someone was asking the reporters to please respect their privacy.

Jalil came with them in their car so they could have a few more minutes to chat. He knew she had been traveling for nearly a full day and needed time to take all of this in, so they made a date to have dinner with him and Kiran in a few days' time.

As she and Vijay were dropped off, Jalil said he would continue on to "make a report to Kiran."

"Make a report," Vijay scoffed as they entered the elevator with the doorman who brought her luggage.

"Does it still bother you that they're involved?" she asked.

"No," he allowed. "Jalil is insisting they take their time because he worries about the age difference."

"So did you," she reminded him.

"True, but I've since seen that their personalities are well-suited. If they wished to marry, I would support their decision."

He was speaking very objectively, reminding her of the night he'd asked her what her expectations of marriage were. Passion wasn't a deal-breaker, he had said, but she had hoped it was still alive between them. So far, desire seemed the furthest thing from motivating his urgency in bringing her here.

Doubts were digging claws ever deeper into her as he opened the door into a penthouse and thanked the doorman, instructing him to leave the luggage in the entranceway.

"Oh. Wow."

Vijay had told her over their daily video chats that he had found an apartment they could live in right away, with the option to buy. From the outside, the building had looked unremarkable, but this was a tasteful, modern oasis with endless views of the sea.

"It was renovated last year by one of our clients. It was actually two units and he combined them." Vijay pointed at the loft to indicate it had two floors. "I made him an offer on condition you approve."

If she hadn't been feeling as though there was an invisible wall between them, she would have thrown her arms around him and squealed with delight.

The decor was understated, the furniture chic but comfortable. Sliding walls of glass were the only separation between indoors and the wide terrace that overlooked the Arabian sea. The dining, living and kitchen area were all one airy space with plenty of room for Kiran's wheelchair if she decided to come live with them.

Oriel and Vijay had discussed it, and Oriel had no problem with sharing their home with Vijay's sister. She had often roomed with complete strangers at different times and always made it work. Once the baby came, she would probably be very glad for an extra pair of hands. Besides, judging from the way things were going with Jalil, Kiran wouldn't be with them for long.

For now, Kiran had chosen to stay in the lower level of a duplex that she and Vijay had called home for several years. The neighbors all treated her like family, and the home itself was fitted for her chair. Plus, Kiran said she wanted to give the newlyweds their privacy.

For what? Oriel had to wonder uneasily.

There was an elevator to the upper floor, but they walked up the floating staircase to a loft with a small sitting area beneath a skylight. They passed two spare bedrooms and a home gym before entering a master suite fronted by a wall of glass. It opened onto a private terrace that had a small landscaped garden as well as another stunning view of the sea.

Oriel moved to the part of the rail that was protected by an overhang and instantly imagined walking out here every single morning, drinking coffee, tasting the day.

"You're not saying anything." He was still wearing that watchfulness. She was beginning to think it had less to do with his security persona and more to do with whatever was going on in his own head. But what was *that*?

"It's incredible," she said with a reluctant smile. "You know it is."

"The security system is first class," he said dryly as he joined her at the rail. "The location is excellent. One of the best maternity hospitals in the city is nearby."

"That's good," she murmured.

They both stood there watching the rain.

"Oriel—"

"Do you want me here?" she asked over him.

"What?" He angled to look down his nose at her. "Of course." His voice was brisk, though, and his gaze went out to the gray horizon, where low clouds hung against chopping waves. "Why do you ask?" His demeanor was as cool and colorless as the rain.

She felt callow admitting it. Defenseless because she couldn't hide the fact she was hurt. "You didn't…kiss me when I arrived."

Thankfully, he didn't laugh at her. She might have gone straight back to the airport if he had. Even so, as he looked at her with vague bewilderment, a scorched self-consciousness rose behind her breastbone.

"We're not like Europe. Public affection isn't customary here."

"Oh." She hadn't even thought of the cultural differences she would face with this move. She might look like she had been born here, but she was French. Being demonstrative in public was very natural to her. "I have a lot to learn."

"We're a nation of people who live in multigenerational homes, so it's kept behind closed doors out of respect for our elders. I honestly don't recall ever seeing my parents kiss, not because their marriage was arranged. It just wasn't done."

"Oh." She started to relax, but realized, "You still haven't, though." Fresh shyness struck, and her cheeks stung with a painful blush. "Kissed me, I mean."

"I know." His voice had returned to being clipped. He moved back to the door into the bedroom.

Her heart lurched at the way he was putting that distance between them.

He lightly tapped his loose fist on the frame. "I hate myself for asking, but I have to." He pinned her with his steady gaze. "Who was he?"

She was taken aback. "Who?"

"The man whose dreams you were making come true."

She shook her head. "I honestly don't know—"

"Lunch. You left Payton's office and you were going to meet an old friend for lunch."

"Yosef!" she recalled, then stood tall with instant outrage. "He's nearly seventy, Vijay. He gave me my first magazine shoot, and yes, I wore a negligee back then, but he never once made me feel cheap about it. Unlike *you*. Do you really think I was stepping out on you days after we married? *Mon Dieu*, when you said you didn't trust easily, you should have explained you meant there was none at all."

She tried to brush past him into the bedroom. He put out a hand to stop her, and she thrust his arm away. She glared at him, daring him to touch her again.

"I don't want to be like this," he said through his teeth.

"Then don't," she threw back at him and stalked toward the bed. "Should I feel the sheets?" She patted the blankets. "See if they're still warm from whoever *you've* been with?"

His mouth tightened. "I haven't been with anyone since you. There was no one between meeting you in Milan and finding you in Cannes, either," he clarified.

"Same." She flipped her hair over her shoulder. "Do you believe me?" Let him try and say he didn't.

"Damn it, Oriel, I had someone cheat on me. I know it's weak of me to be suspicious, but I can't stand the idea that I might not be seeing what's right under my nose." He rubbed his stubbled jaw before dropping his hands onto his hips. He stared out the open doors as though seeing a past he couldn't change.

She was still angry, but an even more insidious sense of threat crept into her.

"Who? How long were you together?"

"Her name is Wisa. We met at university and wanted to finish our degrees before we married."

"So you were…" She had assumed he would have a romantic history, but, "You were *engaged*?" She covered the sick knot that arrived in her middle.

"Yes. The wedding was days away when we called it off. She was sleeping with my best friend. I found out as the rest of my life fell apart over my father's crimes. The worst part is—"

That wasn't the worst part? She dragged her gaze up to his shuttered expression.

"I realized later that she had likely been steered toward me in an attempt to have influence over me when I took control of my father's business."

"Oh." She touched the night table for balance. "That is awful."

"I don't think she knew what was going on any more than I did." He brushed a tired hand through the air. "On the surface, we seemed very compatible, nothing to raise my suspicion. I was the heir to a successful company, and she was the daughter of a local politician. I took my degree in business with a minor in electronical engineering. She thought I should plan to go into politics. That was our only bone of contention."

Oriel was still reeling. He'd been days away from a wedding. Relationships didn't get that far unless hearts were involved.

Vijay shrugged out of his jacket and threw it onto a chair in the corner.

"After Kiran, Wisa was the first person I told about my father's business dealings. Initially she supported my going to the police, but as our friends began to distance themselves, and she realized her uncle might be implicated, I caught her on a call with Madin. It was obvious they were involved. She said it was my fault, that I had ruined our future. *Everyone's* future. That I *drove* her to Madin. We canceled the wedding, and she stuck me with the bills as a final slap in the face."

"Were you in love with her?" The question came out before she had fully braced herself for the answer.

He met her gaze unflinchingly. "I was."

Her heart plummeted like a shot bird. "Are you still?"

"No," he dismissed firmly. "But I'm suspicious of

that emotion, as you saw with my reaction to Jalil's interest in Kiran." He pushed his hands into his pants pockets. "I can't help thinking it's a smoke screen that people use to get whatever it is they really want."

That's why he had asked her what she wanted from marriage. He didn't intend to give her his heart. It was a surprising blow. He didn't want to love her. Wouldn't.

She pressed a hand over the spot where she felt as though a knife was lodged in her chest. When she tried to speak, she had to gulp in air first.

"Love can be used like that," she acknowledged, hugging herself. "My first boyfriend was only using me to get close to my mother's theater connections." It still made her feel like the worst naive fool for not seeing it. "I fell for it because..." She worked to keep her mouth from turning down. "Because I wanted that *big* love. You know? *The one.*"

He flinched and looked away guiltily.

"Don't. This isn't about you and your limitations. This is something I want you to understand about me." She hunched up her shoulders defensively. "I've always struggled with not feeling that I was loved enough. Otherwise she would have kept me. Right?" Tears rose in her eyes.

"That's not true." His shoulders sank, and he came toward her, reaching to cup her elbows.

She pressed her hand to his chest, holding him off.

"Even if it was, you've seen how much my parents love me. They would do anything for me, which makes me feel even worse for having these fears. But it's a normal thing a lot of adopted children struggle with. We worry that we were at fault somehow. It's irrational and complex and confusing, but that's how I realized I was susceptible to letting that feeling take over. Ever since that boyfriend treated me that way, I've been cautious about giving up too much of myself. I don't like getting hurt, either."

He pulled his head back slightly as if her words had shaken him at some level. Then he gave a jerky nod of understanding. His hands tightened on her elbows.

"I was only asking a question. It wasn't an accusation. I don't think you're cheating on me. I just needed to hear from you that it was nothing."

"It was nothing."

"Thank you." His hands twitched as though he wanted to pull her close while still trying to give her space. "But Oriel, look at the lengths Jalil has gone to find you. He wouldn't have done that if his sister hadn't seemed tortured by losing you. You were wanted. You were loved."

Her composure crumpled, and she went into his arms.

He held her secure, stroking her and saying, "I wanted to kiss you the second I saw you today. I want you all the damned time. Never doubt that."

She gave a small sob and looked up at him. "Even like this? All weepy and messy?"

He framed her face in his warm, broad hands. "All the damned time," he repeated.

"Then kiss me." She lifted on tiptoe and offered her tear-dampened lips.

He closed his arms around her and opened his mouth across hers. As his flavor seeped into her senses, all her reservations eased.

Then, as their kiss deepened, sharp need twisted inside her. Vijay slanted his mouth for a deeper seal, and between one breath and the next, their kiss yanked her into a maelstrom of want.

For one moment, he let her feel the ferocity of his desire as he plundered her mouth, arms tight as he crushed her hips into the aroused shape behind his fly.

He seemed to exert all his will as he made himself ease his hold and lift his head.

"You should get some rest. You must be tired."

"What happencd to 'all the damned time'?"

With an agile twist, he had them both on the bed.

"Oh!"

"Yes, oh." He tucked her beneath him. "If you are too tired, now would be a good time to say so."

"I'm a little bit tired. You might have to do all the work."

"That, my beautiful wife, would be my pleasure."

A few nights later, Vijay took Oriel to meet Kiran and Jalil at one of Mumbai's most exclusive restaurants. The pair had been over to visit twice already, and Vijay had been going to work, but Oriel had been staying in the penthouse while she acclimatized.

They'd also been making love nonstop because they couldn't seem to help themselves. He had no complaints about that, but he did suspect they were expressing themselves physically because they didn't know how to do it verbally.

He was still disturbed by what she'd said about wanting the "big" love. *The one.* He had known there was a romantic hidden deep inside her, but he hadn't appreciated how fragile her heart was. Her amazing front of confidence hid any hint of insecurities. He was glad she had spelled out for him where she struggled, but he was also—very hypocritically—frustrated that she had developed her own inner guards to protect herself. It made it that much harder for them to be sure of one another.

It would all come with time, he assured himself. For now, she was feeling cooped up, and he was eager to show her his city and show the world his wife.

Of course, she caused a stir the minute they hit the street.

It was more annoying than anything. They had a security detail. He wasn't concerned about her safety to any serious degree, but he suspected this would wear on her long-term.

At least the restaurant was used to catering to Bollywood celebrities and other high-profile clientele. It was candlelit with glinting reflections dancing off glossy floors and mirrored tiles in the wall mosaic. Partial walls of wooden slats absorbed sound and formed partitions that created pockets of privacy.

Heads turned as they were shown to their table, but Oriel seemed unfazed.

"You're taking this in stride," Vijay remarked as they settled at their table.

"The attention? I forgot it was for me," she said with a blink of bemusement. "The same thing happens when I go anywhere with Maman. I've learned to ignore it."

They all chuckled, and it turned into a pleasant, relaxing meal. They were finishing dessert when Kiran's smile stiffened.

"Someone must have posted that we were here. Why else would *she* show up?"

"Who?" Oriel asked.

Vijay knew without looking and stiffened, watching for Oriel's reaction as his past literally caught up to him.

"Vijay, Kiran." Wisa's voice was a smug purr. "What are you two doing in this part of the city?"

"Wisa. Madin." Vijay rose to greet his ex-fiancée and his ex-best friend, determined to be nothing but polite. "Please meet my wife, Oriel. And our good friend, Jalil Dalal."

"Ah, yes. Such a colorful story. It's everywhere." Wisa's gaze widened on Oriel as though she was an exotic animal, a curiosity, but something to be dismissed. "You do have a way of making headlines, don't you?" she said pithily to Vijay.

It was exactly the sort of sly, denigrating remark she and everyone else had made when he had refused to look the other way over his father's transgressions. Anything to put him down.

He was about to set her in her place once and for all when Oriel spoke up.

"Would you like a photo?" She sent a friendly nod to someone beyond Wisa.

They all glanced to see that an elderly woman in a saree was watching Oriel with a delighted smile of recognition.

"I'll come there." Oriel rose and brushed past Wisa, saying, "I don't want to offend her." She paused and set a delightfully possessive hand on Vijay's shoulder. "This would be a good time to make an escape, or I'll be here all night. You should buy their dinner, though." She nodded at Wisa and Madin. "Make it up to them that we can't stay."

"I'd love to."

The look on Wisa's face was worth whatever they charged to his credit card.

"That was savagely brilliant," he said when he and Oriel were in the back of his car on their way home.

"It's from my mother's bag of tricks. I felt petty resorting to it."

"You shouldn't. The family at the other table was happy." They'd been over the moon that their grandmother had been singled out and fussed over by a ce-lebrity. "Wisa will think twice before driving across the city to make things awkward for us ever again."

"Holding on to a grudge like that suggests she still has feelings for you." She glanced across at him, eyes wary and watchful.

"Her uncle had to pay a fine and narrowly missed going to jail. I imagine she believes I still deserve pun-ishment for that."

"Why? Her uncle was the one who broke the law," she muttered impatiently.

"Thank you." He reached across to squeeze her hand, so moved that his chest felt tight and he had to swallow a lump from his throat. "Anytime I have to revisit that episode in my life, I feel sick. I thought I was a law-abiding, principled sort of man and had to decide if I re-ally was. It was sobering to be put to the test, and when I stood by what I thought was right, I was vilified and abandoned. It means everything to me that you didn't give her a chance to spit poison in your ear."

"I should have thanked her," she mused. "If she hadn't been so self-interested, you'd be married to her, and I wouldn't have you or our baby or know any of this about myself."

Neither would he, Vijay realized with a catch of fierce possessiveness for her, their baby, and the life they were starting.

Recognizing that flashed a fresh light on all he'd been through, searing away much of his resentment and anguish. His ever-present shame died a final death, be-coming cold, flaky ashes. From now on, it would be a bitter and sooty memory, but not one that still had the ability to scorch and burn him.

"But honestly?" Oriel said with annoyance. "She

was kind of a bitch. 'What are you two doing in this part of the city?' Like she owns it. I don't actually feel bad for snubbing her."

He chuckled and tugged her across the seat, into his arms. "I felt great about it." In fact, he felt as though he was falling in love, and he wasn't that unsettled by the prospect.

CHAPTER NINE

As THE DAYS turned into weeks, Oriel had to concede that she and Vijay were very well-matched. Sexually, their compatibility continued to be an A-plus, ten out of ten. They could hardly keep their hands off each other.

They also complemented each other in broader ways. They began adding personal touches to their home by way of art and sculptures and were always in agreement. They hired a housekeeper and cook with minimal discussion and already knew what they wanted in a nanny.

She and Kiran got on as if they'd known each other all their lives, laughing and enjoying each other's company whether Vijay was in the room or not. He even brought her into the office to introduce her around. Everything was in disarray due to merging with TecSec, but she was fascinated and enjoyed seeing that side of his world.

In the hours when the rain let up, Vijay drove her to different parts of the city to help her get her bearings, and into the mountains, where everything was lush and green. They took a day trip to see the caves with rock carvings on Elephanta Island, and because it was mostly tourists there, they enjoyed one of their most relaxing, incognito days ever.

He worked a lot, which made her conscious of the

fact she didn't, but he chided, "Your job is to build our baby. That's work."

So far being pregnant wasn't that hard. Her nausea had passed once she'd caught up on her sleep. Today they were having a scan, but it was purely routine.

"I have to go to Delhi for a few days," he said, reading his phone while they waited.

"When?" She instantly felt a pang of separation anxiety. It wasn't that she was emotionally dependent on him. She was genuinely falling in love with him and hated to be apart from him.

"Tomorrow."

"Can you tell me why? Or is it something confidential?" She was getting used to the fact that he sometimes couldn't talk about certain things.

"Dangerously boring reasons. There's a problem with wiring in the building we've leased and some HR issues that need massaging. I'd ask you to come, but I won't have time to show you around. You'd be stuck in a hotel room."

"And I would miss my language class." She was going three times a week and practiced diligently with Kiran and their housekeeper. The classes were more than a determination to explore her roots, though. It was a nice reason to get out of the house, something she did for herself that wasn't wrapped up in her husband, and she was making some pleasant friendships with the eclectic expats she was meeting.

The ultrasound technician arrived, greeting them cheerfully. As Oriel stood, the young woman made a noise of amused surprise, then consulted her notes.

"Eighteen weeks? Is that a typo?" She made a perplexed face at Oriel's still flat middle.

"I'm very tall," Oriel pointed out defensively.

She had already had a small lecture from one of Kiran's well-meaning friends about ensuring her calorie intake was high enough. No one seemed to realize how thin she'd been when she'd gotten pregnant. The amount of weight she'd gained was right on target, and she was actually thickening around the waist and showing fullness in her breasts and face.

Plus, "My waist is long. There's lots of room for a baby to hide in here."

For one second, Vijay's expression seemed arrested, but he shook it off so quickly, Oriel wasn't sure if that had really been a moment of suspicion coming into his head.

"We'll confirm your dates," the woman assured her.

I know when I conceived. Oriel bit back the words.

A short while later, her affront was forgotten as the blurry image of their baby appeared with its heart pitter-patting.

Her eyes filled with tears, and so did Vijay's. As they touched their trembling smiles together, she was so happy at having this little miracle inside her, she almost told him she loved him. Because she did. And she didn't know which made her heart overflow more, their baby or him.

New Bride with an Old Flame?

Vijay stared at his screen, annoyed by the unsavory headline, but more bothered that his team was taking this seriously enough they'd forwarded it.

They had a team who filtered through all the false sightings, many of them easy enough to disprove when they claimed Oriel was in New York and she was clearly here, but this one was from the days shortly after Vijay had met her in Milan.

It was a photo of Oriel at a restaurant table with a man who had a healthy head of dark hair and the shoulders of a thirty-year-old.

The shot was actually a screengrab from a selfie video posted by someone visiting New York and dining at an upscale restaurant. As Oriel's notoriety had risen, this tourist had realized she had inadvertently caught a celebrity in the background of her vacation vlog. Now the woman was claiming her ten minutes of adjacent fame by circulating the shot on the gossip sites.

In it, Oriel was leaning in, smiling playfully while delivering a flirty look through her long, thick lashes. It was unmistakably her. Vijay knew that curve of her cheek, the ripple in her hair that caught the light. He knew that adoring expression and had started to believe she only ever showed it to him.

He checked the date stamp and was further irritated to see it had been taken in the days after they'd been together in Milan. He told himself he had no right to the soul-eating jealousy that was trying to consume him, but he had a right to the truth. She had told him she hadn't been with anyone except him since Milan. And that the "old friend" she had lunched with had been a man in his seventies.

There was also that niggling moment at the ultrasound the other day, when the technician had remarked on Oriel not looking pregnant *enough*.

Back in Cannes, Oriel had been offended when Vijay had suggested the baby might not be his. *Of course it would be yours. Don't be rude!*

But she had gone back to New York after Milan. Had

she seen—he read the caption—Reve Weston, New York billionaire, while she was there?

"Sir—"

"I need a few minutes." He abruptly closed the door of the empty office he stood in, cutting off the babble of voices down the hall.

He wanted to jump on a plane back to Mumbai, but things were still in disarray here in Delhi. He couldn't wait and wonder, though. He called Oriel for a video chat.

"Hi!" She was in her yoga clothes, hair bundled messily atop her head. "How's it going there?"

"Terrible. I'm sending you a photo."

"Of?"

"You. Having lunch with a man. In New York."

She frowned. The screen briefly went black. "What? *Mon Dieu*, that's not me." She came back onscreen. "Or it's been altered to make it look like it's me." She was frowning with concern, but not guilt, as far as he could tell.

"You don't know him?"

"I know who Reve Weston is. Every straight woman or gay man in New York does. He's one of those wealthy tycoons everyone dreams of catching. Is that what I'm up against now?" Her mouth twisted with annoyance. "People putting my image into photos to manufacture clickbait?"

"I ran it through Kiran's program, Oriel. It hasn't been edited. It was taken a few days after we met in Milan."

"Vijay." There was enough shock and hurt in her tone to cause him a trickle of compunction. "I thought we were past this."

"I'm not angry." He was trying not to be. He was trying to give her the benefit of the doubt. "I just want you to be honest about it. Tell me if you had a relationship with him and saw him again when you went back. Either time."

"Either...? Are you asking if I went on a date with an old boyfriend after you and I were married? No, I did not. I have never had lunch with Reve Weston. Ever. Or dinner. Or breakfast the morning after a night before. Please tell me you are not accusing me of getting pregnant by another man and passing it off as yours!"

"I'm just trying to get to the bottom of this."

"We are definitely hitting rock bottom if we're here," she snapped. "I'm sitting here eating my heart out, missing you because I love you so much, and you call to accuse me of *that*?"

His heart lurched. *I love you.* They were words he had told himself he didn't want or need to hear. His scorned self from years past warned him she might only be saying it to throw him off her affair, but his gut told him that was wrong. She meant it.

"You're punishing me for Wisa's infidelity," she accused, expression contorted with hurt.

The last thing he ever wanted was to hurt her, but he said, "I'm simply asking for an explanation for what is right in front of my eyes."

"I can't explain it," she cried with frustration. "But the fact you jump to the worst possible explanation tells me what you think of me, doesn't it?" She ended the call.

It was as though she'd stabbed clean through the screen and jabbed a hole in his chest. Vijay swore and pocketed his phone.

Oriel hadn't spent much time looking herself up online. She knew that way lay madness, and Vijay had people screening all of that, but in her hurt and fury, she began going down rabbit holes on Lakshmi fan forums. She found threads by dozens of people claiming to also be the product of Lakshmi's illicit liaison and therefore entitled to her fortune. Some of the posts were clear fakes, others credible look-alikes.

Some of it was very unsavory, but so was being accused of infidelity by her husband. She kept searching and came across another photo that claimed to be of her, this one more recent. It showed three frames in which she supposedly had an altercation with a photographer that ended with the man clutching his bleeding nose.

Cuvier Clocks Cub Reporter for Catching Her Canoodling

"With who?" she cried.

The woman in the photo was a really good double. She had a streak of pink in her hair, but her face and body were uncannily similar. The shocked, fear-filled look on her face was what really got to Oriel. She felt that other woman's emotions as if she was staring at her own reflection in a mirror.

Disturbed, she went back to the photo of the woman with Reve Weston and started searching for more of the couple together. She didn't have much luck until she stumbled across a list of guests from a gala that said Reve's plus-one had been someone called Nina Menendez.

When Oriel searched Nina's name, she discovered the woman's social profiles had been locked down. The only thing she was able to turn up was—weirdly—from a fashion degree program at a college in New Mexico. Nina appeared in a video from four years ago.

Oriel's skin broke out in goose bumps as she listened to Nina speak. She sounded just like her!

"I go for my first job interview on my twenty-first birthday next Thursday. No matter how that goes, I plan to have my first legal drink after. Wish me luck."

Oriel glanced at the date, and her heart nearly came out of her mouth. Nina's birthday was the day after Oriel's, but Oriel had been born a few minutes before midnight. She knew because she'd been going through all the paperwork on her adoption with Jalil.

She and Nina were essentially the same age.

"Mon Dieu, mon Dieu..." she heard herself muttering, her skin going hot and cold as she hurriedly read the rest of Nina's bio on the college website.

She was barely able to make sense of it. Nina mentioned her father's military career as inspiration for some of her designs, adding that her father had been stationed at one of the bases in Germany when she had been born.

Oriel shakily opened another tab on her browser and punched in the distance between the air force base and the small village in Luxembourg where she'd been born.

One hour and seven minutes by car.

Impossible.

For a long time, she sat without any coherent thought in her head. The words *I should call Vijay* drifted into her head, but faded before she could act on them. She had the sense that Kiran could do some intensive digging, but Kiran would feel compelled to tell Jalil. Oriel didn't want to cause the older man any further upheavals if she was being delusional.

Was she? The truth seemed as plain as the identical nose on Nina's face. She didn't know if she wanted to laugh or cry or check herself into a hospital for possible hallucinations.

When Oriel realized it was the middle of the afternoon in France, she called Max, barely stammering out, "Do you have access to any sort of database that would give you background information on a designer in New York?"

"It's called gossip, *chou*. Give me a name and I'll have all the dirt within the hour."

She told him, and he called back forty-eight minutes later.

"Well, that was interesting," Max said cheerfully. "Mademoiselle Nina is an upstart who began working for Kelly Bex a year ago. The party line is that she showed promise, but was ultimately a disappointment. The truth is, she stole a hunky billionaire, Monsieur Reve Weston, from the maven Bex herself. *That's* why she was fired, thrown onto the street, told never to darken their doorway again."

"Not so much a lack of talent, then."

"*Oui*. Because she does have talent. This was much harder to pry from one of my nearest and dearest, but he claims to have seen some of her work. He expects it to be, and I quote, 'priceless when the designer is revealed.' I've looked her up. She looks just like you. Beware, *chou*. She may try to trade on that."

"She's still in New York?"

"No. Apparently, she flew to Paris on Weston's supersonic jet yesterday. He has a pied-à-terre—which is a monstrous two-story penthouse—on Avenue Montaigne."

"*Merci, Maximus. Tu es mon héros.*" She hung up

and, with her heart racing out of her chest, called her mother's assistant. If anyone could charter a flight to Paris within the hour, she could.

Every time Vijay reached for his phone, he became infuriated by their fight, by his vacillating trust, by the seesaw of wanting to believe her and not wanting to be a fool.

He set aside his phone and closed his eyes, but all he saw was Oriel looking at that other man with the love she had claimed to have for *him*.

Jealousy was such a lowering emotion. So insecure.

That photograph wouldn't bother him so much—that was a lie, but he told himself it wouldn't bother him this badly—if Oriel had owned up to the affair and assured him the relationship was over. Instead, she had denied the association even though she had been in New York after Milan and again after they'd married.

He wanted to ask Kiran to search the online archives for more photos of this bastard billionaire, to see if Oriel had been photographed elsewhere with him, but he was too ashamed. Ashamed of his suspicions, ashamed of what might turn out to be true.

Ashamed that he might have allowed himself to be taken in. Again.

He was trying to believe Oriel's word—another lie, but not entirely. He wanted to believe her. He did. But there was a piece of himself that couldn't let go of the past. He had failed to see reality when it had been deliberately obscured from him, so he had learned to keep his eyes open. There was *photographic evidence* to refute what she claimed.

What else could he think but that she had feelings for someone else? Feelings she wouldn't admit to?

The mere idea of it scraped out his chest far worse than Wisa's betrayal. He didn't want to believe Oriel would do that to him. They were far too close, closer than any relationship he'd ever had.

He *loved* her. He wouldn't be this tortured if he didn't. He loved her and he was anguished at the thought of her with a stranger, but he was being a fool. She was here in India, making a life with him, wearing his ring and having his baby.

What did he care what she had done in the past if she was here with him now? If she wanted another man, she would be with that other man. He shouldn't push her away with his rotten suspicions. Instead, he should be looking for another explanation.

He glanced at the clock, unwilling to wake Kiran to help him, but in the morning he would ask her to come to Delhi and take over for him. He would go home, make up with his wife, and figure out what the hell was going on.

His phone pinged, and he picked it up to see a text from Oriel.

Her name is Nina Menendez. She's in Paris. I'm going to see her.

CHAPTER TEN

ORIEL HAD SLEPT a little on the flight. Mostly her mind had been cracked in half by a thought that was even more outlandish than her being the secret daughter of a Bollywood star—that she might be the twin of one.

Vijay had texted her back, asking her to wait for him, saying he would go with her.

I'm in the air. I have my guards. I'm not leaving you, but I have to meet her. She might be my twin. Please trust me to come back. I love you.

There was no response to that, but she really hoped he would trust her. She was devastated by his accusations and didn't know how they would move forward if she was forever trying to prove herself to him.

Was she running away from him as impetuously as she had married him? A little. She'd been trying so hard to become a part of his world, which was her own world too, she supposed. But she had constructed a life with him because everything she had known about herself had been shattered. Now she might have yet another layer to unpeel, and she didn't know how to deal with it.

She entered her old flat with a desperate need for a sense of homecoming, the way it had always felt when she had returned from breaks between modeling gigs. Her parents had helped her buy this place when she had begun traveling for modeling, and she had been making the payments since. She had rarely spent more than a few weeks at a time here, but it was hers, and it was where she had always been able to relax and feel like herself.

It was also in a nice, secure building in the same arrondissement as Reve Weston's. She was only a short distance from him, she realized. A half-dozen blocks from Nina.

Oriel was so worked up, she only spent five minutes in her flat, just long enough to freshen up before she had her security detail drive her to Avenue Montaigne.

The paparazzi had posted photos of the building where "Oriel" was supposedly staying with Reve, so her driver found it very easily. She had one of her men escort her past the photographers, who snapped to attention as she left her car.

In the lobby, the doorman greeted her in English. "Mademoiselle Menendez. I understood you were away with Monsieur Weston."

For a moment, her heart pounded so hard she thought she might faint. Blood rushed in her ears and she recalled that she hadn't eaten since before she had landed.

I want Vijay, she thought.

"Elle n'est pas là?" She didn't realize she was speaking in French until the man grew alert with confusion at her native accent. "I'm Oriel Cuvier. When will they be back?"

He blinked with astonishment. "I'm sorry, but I couldn't say. Would you like to leave a message?"

She left all her contact details, and the paparazzi followed her home. She ignored them. She crawled into bed and noted that Kiran had texted.

I spoke with Vijay. I'm here if you want to talk.

Oriel thanked her and said she needed time to think. Then she called her mother, who was going on stage in Vienna shortly. Estelle was flabbergasted to hear there might have been two babies.

"I don't know why anyone would do something so hurtful as to separate a pair of twins. Our application would have said we wanted a single baby, but if they had told us you had a sister, we would have taken you both."

"I knew you would say that, but I needed to hear it."

"Can Vijay not help you learn the truth? He seems resourceful. He found *you*."

"We had a fight." She didn't get into the painful details of his accusations.

"A disagreement or a fight?" Her mother's tone grew serious.

"We're having trouble trusting one another. I'm worried we rushed into things."

"Of course you did, *chou*. It's always been your way to move quickly. You walk away just as quickly if something isn't right. Is that what happened? You've discovered he's not right for you?"

"Marriage isn't piano lessons," she said grumpily.

"This is true. But you know yourself, and if you have realized these piano lessons do not make you happy, then leave him. I'll support you."

Oriel laughed, but it was more an anguished sob, because her stomach clenched hard with rejection of that suggestion.

"No," she murmured. "He's the father of my child."

He was *the one*. For her, at least. She didn't know how he felt. "We'll have to make it work." She only wished that she knew *how*.

"And that is also your way," her mother chided gently. "When you do find what feels right, you *commit*."

Oriel's heart swerved. Her mother was right. She had locked herself into a life with Vijay that would be nearly impossible to unravel. She didn't want to! But he didn't love her. Didn't trust her. She didn't know how to fix that.

"I'm about to go on, *chou*. Would you like me to sing for you?"

"It's been a long time since we've done that. Yes, please, Maman. I love you. Break a leg."

Estelle hadn't done this since Oriel was very young and missing her when she was away on tour, but she had her assistant keep the line open and prop the phone in a suitable place so Oriel could hear her while she performed.

Oriel fell asleep with her phone on the pillow and tears on her cheeks.

She awoke with a melancholy knowledge that Paris was no longer her home. She belonged in that other place, the one with a spicy fragrance in the air and sheets of rain falling from the sky. The place where a man stretched naked beside her in the morning and played with her hair when they watched TV in the evening.

Could they have that again? She didn't know, but not if she was here and he was there.

She texted Vijay.

I'm going to stay and list the flat.

It seemed a neutral enough means to open communication, but he didn't respond. It was the middle of his workday, though. He had a lot to get done in Delhi.

She called a property agent, then had boxes delivered and began sorting through her personal things. One of her guards was helping her take down a box of keepsakes from the closet shelf when her door buzzer rang, indicating someone was waiting outside.

The paparazzi had been pestering her periodically, so she asked him to leave the box on the kitchen table while he ran down to tell them to shove off.

She absently filled the kettle as she acknowledged that all this culling of her possessions was a time-filler while she contemplated the bigger unknowns in her life. How would she mend her marriage? What would happen when she returned to India?

The knock on the door sent her heart leaping.

It was probably the guard returning, she cautioned herself, but she hurried across the room. Had Vijay come? She didn't actually want him to come after her. She wanted him to trust her to return to him so they would have a foundation to build on.

She flung open the door with anticipation anyway and confronted a mirror.

Her reflection wore a different outfit, something in denim. Oriel wasn't taking in superficial details when there was so much else that was exactly *her*. The wave in her dark hair, her arched eyebrows, the shape of her nose and the flecks of greenish gold in her eyes. The way her jaw hung slack and her mouth worked to find words.

Oriel's mouth was doing the same. No coherent thoughts were coming to her. Her throat had closed, her chest was tight, and her whole body began to tremble.

There was a rushing sound in her ears, so a man's voice in the distance barely made sense. "I thought I should bring her up since you went looking for her yesterday. She was going to be mobbed downstairs."

She and Nina stared at one another for twenty-five years and nineteen weeks and three days and however many hours and minutes and seconds had passed since they had exited the womb they had shared.

Oriel didn't know how she knew that to be fact, but it was. This was her sister.

They took a step at the same time, hugging themselves back together again.

A whistling kettle broke them apart.

A different man's voice said, "I'll get that. You two sit down."

He nudged them inside and closed the door, then snagged a box of tissues from a table and held it between them.

That's when Oriel realized fat tears were dripping off her cheeks. She took a few of the tissues and sniffled, beginning to mop up. She watched her sister—*her twin*—do the same. They were both gasping and shaking in the same way.

They both smiled through all of it as they moved to the couch and sat. Still neither spoke. Each time one of them tried, each time they looked at the other, they welled up again. Oriel knew exactly how Nina felt. Her heart was too big for her chest. Her emotions were so expansive, her shoulders ached. There was a lump in her throat too sharp to swallow.

After a few minutes, Reve came back with two cups and set them on the table. Oriel couldn't have said what was in them, but Nina looked at him with naked love that she blinked away when he raised his gaze.

Oriel felt that agony of unrequited love inside herself, too. Amid this upheaval, her heart throbbed with want for Vijay. He wouldn't be able to do anything, but she wanted him here anyway, sharing this monumental moment with her.

She wanted him to squeeze her shoulder the way Reve did Nina's as he asked, "Do we need introductions? I'm Reve. This is Nina. I presume you're Oriel unless there's a third one?"

"*Mon Dieu*, can you imagine?" Oriel laughed into her handful of damp tissues.

"There's not," Nina said. "There are only two of us." She looked around, and Reve came from the door, where she had dropped her bag. She smiled her thanks at him again with that same glimmer of adoring love. "Reve and I were in Luxembourg, trying to find some answers about... Well, everything. Me. I didn't actually know my parents weren't my birth parents until you were making headlines and people started calling me by your name. I thought you'd think I was a crackpot if I didn't have some proof that we could be... It's weird to say it. Twins," she said with a teary laugh. "We raced back here when Reve's doorman sent the message that you were here in Paris and had come looking for me."

"Did you find the clinic? What did you learn?"

"We found some records from the doctor who delivered us." She sent Reve a look that held a scold, but started digging into her bag. "And we met a woman who was a maid at the house where Lakshmi stayed. I showed her a photo of Lakshmi's manager. She said it was him, that they claimed to be married, but she said they fought all the time. They spoke in Hindi, but she could tell he wanted her to give up the baby. Lakshmi didn't want to. She said Lakshmi wrote letters whenever he went out and threw them in the fire when he came home. The maid pulled this out of the grate one day. She wanted to know what was going on, but she didn't know what to do once she'd read it. Then Lakshmi delivered and they were gone."

"And she kept it all this time?" Oriel carefully unfolded the paper. It had been folded in four and was scorched where the corners had come together. Only the middle of the page remained, but she'd written in English.

...know we promised we wouldn't write. I hope your boy is improving...
...never wish to separate you from him, but want you to know...
...could marry him, but he says the baby will be white...
...midwife assures me all is well, but I sense she's hiding...
...and when it's time insists I must give it up...
...know what else to do. I wish you were here to...

"To our father?" Oriel bit her lips to keep them from trembling. It meant so much to know there had been love between them, even if it had been an impossible one. "This is so sad. My heart is absolutely broken for her."

"Me, too." Fat tears sat in Nina's eyes, and her voice cracked. "I don't think she got to see us or hold us or even know there were two of us."

They searched each other's eyes, anguished for the mother they hadn't known and the memories they had missed making as a family.

"My parents would have taken both of us if they'd been told. They're actually really excited to meet you," Oriel said with a small, quavering smile.

"Oh, my gosh, when I tell you how I came to be with my family…" Nina sent the heel of her hand across her cheekbone and glanced at Reve, seemingly at a loss. "We're going to need something stronger than coffee."

"We have more paperwork that we want to give to Lakshmi's family, too," Reve said.

"It's okay," Oriel said, waving Nina off from reaching into her bag again. "That can wait a few minutes. I want to know everything about you. I already know you're a fashion designer."

"And you're a model. It's like we're twins."

They laughed in a way that was eerily similar and that might have made them dissolve into fresh tears, but an abrupt knock on the door had them both twisting to look at it.

Reve ambled over.

"Ah," he said as he saw who was behind it. "The husband."

CHAPTER ELEVEN

IT WASN'T VIJAY'S worst nightmare, precisely, but he really wasn't thrilled when a man—*the* man—opened the door of his wife's flat.

Reve Weston was handsome, rich. At home. Smug.

"Vijay!" Oriel leaped to her feet.

Reve stepped aside, and Vijay saw Oriel's double stand and smile in a tentative greeting.

The resemblance was eerie and an easy mistake in a photo. In person he knew immediately which one was his wife. There were small, obvious differences. Nina's teeth were not quite perfect, and was that a streak of pink in her hair? She was a tiny bit shorter, but she was every bit as beautiful as Oriel.

Even so, rather than inciting a spark of sexual attraction in him, he only felt endeared toward her for her close resemblance to someone he loved. He didn't feel a gut-deep hunger and overwhelming need to connect or a stark, protective urgency to touch and reclaim intimate space the way he did toward Oriel.

"This is a plot twist, isn't it?" He moved into the sitting area and greeted Oriel with a light kiss on her cheek.

When in France, he conveyed when her lashes flicked up at him.

He hovered close enough to inhale her scent and absorb the light brush of her body against his.

She dipped her chin and rolled her lips together, indicating their conflicts were not resolved, but she stayed in the arm he looped around her waist. Her gaze up at him was not hostile, merely vulnerable and deeply uncertain.

He had hurt her. The knowledge squeezed his guts in a cruel fist.

"Vijay, this is Reve Weston and Nina Menendez." He heard the catch in her voice. Her joy was so visceral, it cracked something open in him. "My twin."

"That's what the birth records would suggest, at least," Nina said with shaken laughter as she took his hand.

"And anyone with eyes," Reve drawled.

"Still." Nina glanced back at him. "I imagine Lakshmi's family has been inundated with people claiming to be her daughter. I'm happy to do a DNA test."

"It looks like it will be redundant, but I've already connected with the lab we use here," Vijay said. "They have someone who can take the samples and rush the results. I'll make that call shortly, but…" He looked at Oriel, and whatever was in his face made her pupils expand and her lips tremble. "I need to speak with my wife."

"You should speak to your family, Nina. Things are going to get very chaotic when the jackals at the door downstairs realize there are two of you." Reve sounded grim enough that Vijay was put on high alert to threats he couldn't see.

Nina bit her lip and nodded with agreement, maybe remorse, but she smiled as she reached for Oriel. "I didn't mean to impersonate you. I've been trying to stay under the radar, but they're relentless."

"Vijay, you should arrange protection for her," Oriel said, looking to him.

"Already in the works," he assured her.

Reve shot him a glare that warned him to stay in his lane.

Vijay didn't flinch, and only said, "Do you think I'm going to let anything happen to my wife's sister?" He reached for his phone. "I'll have one of my guys lead you out through the maintenance entrance that I used to come in. Tell your car to meet you on the south side."

While he and Reve exchanged information, Nina asked, "Will you come for dinner? Now that I've found you, I don't want to miss another minute."

"Me, either," Oriel said emotively, but she looked to Vijay as if she knew they had things to talk out, too. "I'll text you in a little bit?"

"Perfect." They hugged each other so tightly, it added another layer of ignominy to Vijay's guilt over suspecting she'd lied to him.

The pair left, and Oriel stayed at the closed door, chewing her bottom lip as she regarded him. The space between them was a cavern of vipers and land mines, and the valentines of love she had sent him, which he had crumpled and stepped on.

"I apologize," he said sincerely. "I should have trusted you. I knew you wouldn't hurt me like that. In here I knew it." He tapped his chest. "Up here…" He tapped his temple. "But I won't let that happen again. I love you, Oriel."

He saw her jerk and heard her breath hiss in, but her expression only grew more anguished. His heart lurched as he realized he might have done irreparable damage to something that was becoming increasingly precious to him.

He took a step toward her, and she put up a hand.

"I'll give you a pass because there's no way you could have known I had a twin, but the fact is, you *don't* trust me, Vijay. And I can't fix that." She shrugged with despair. "And I can't spend my life worried about how you'll interpret everything I do, especially when there are people out there who will use my image and cast doubts and—"

"Shh. Stop."

He came forward a few more steps, but she kept her hand up to hold him off.

"I promised to come back and I *will*. Look around. I'm packing!" She waved at the full boxes on the floor, and at the bare walls. "I'm selling this flat. I'm going to live with the father of my child. I hope we can repair this marriage of ours, but you didn't even trust me to come back. Instead you've chased me here, and what did you think when Reve opened the door? That he'd just left my bed?"

"I thought I should have been here," he said fervently. "Because I made a promise to you when we learned you were pregnant that I would be here for you through all of this. I meant *all* of it. Not just the baby, but this. Learning who you are. You told me once that you always wished for a sibling. The minute I realized that's who she was, I knew you would be so excited, but also rocked to the core. *I* have questions, Oriel. You must be…"

His heart hurt for her, for all the anger and confusion she must feel at having been torn from the woman who gave birth to her *and* the sibling she should have had in her life all this time.

"Somewhere in there, you're wondering if you should have known that Nina was out there, aren't you? You think you should have found her long ago, on instinct or something."

"I think she knew before I did, but she didn't reach out. She said it was because she thought I wouldn't believe her, but…"

"I know." He came close enough to gather her in. "You feel cheated. And also guilty for wishing you'd had that other life where you grew up with her and Lakshmi."

She nodded while tears tracked down her cheeks.

"See? I know you, Oriel. More importantly, I *love* you. It kills me that I hurt you so badly, you felt you had to come here and face this alone."

Her eyes were leaking more tears. "I'm used to doing things on my own. I've told myself it was the way I liked it, but from the moment I left Mumbai, I've been thinking that I want you here with me, even though you can't do anything."

"I can do this." He folded his arms around her and held her, just held her and rubbed her back as she trembled.

Slowly she wound her arms around his waist and leaned on him, sighing out a lifetime of pent-up grief. He closed his eyes in gratitude.

"I love you, Oriel. I should have said it the first time you did. I've been sick with myself that I didn't. I know my heart is safe with you. *I know that*. It wasn't you I didn't trust. It was love. It hurts to love. It bloody *hurts* to love someone this hard. But I forgot that it heals, too. It gives a reason to hope and to push on when the rest of life is too bleak to face."

* * *

Vijay's hand stroked her hair, and his stubbled jaw rested against her cheekbone. A bubble of hope was trying to crack open her breastbone.

"Can I also say," his voice rumbled next to her ear, "that even though I understand your sense of urgency to meet Nina, and that you were hurt and angry with me, if you had trusted me just a tiny little bit more, you might have held the plane and let me come with you?"

She sniffled back her tears and looked up at him, chagrined. "Guilty."

"You probably would have had more faith in me if I'd told you I love you." He slid her hair behind her ear. "I do. So much." He looked at her as though he was beholding something magical. "I've had to beat and claw my way into the life I have. It didn't seem like being this happy should be this easy, but I won't give you a reason to doubt my feelings again."

"Me, either."

He touched her chin, and their mouths flowed together in the simple, inevitable way they had between them. Perfect and tender and now an expression of that wider, deeper, heart-expanding emotion.

He took great care as he tightened his arms and swept his mouth across hers, but his love was so tangible in that kiss, she shook under the force of it.

"Come," she invited him, taking his hand and drawing him into her bedroom.

They settled on the bed fully clothed, sharing soft, soothing kisses that held no urgency because this was love in its purest form. It was touch and acceptance of their human flaws and celebration of their perfection. Of their divine connection.

They were a special combination, though. One that

couldn't help but create passion when they were together. Soon it was snapping like flames around them, burning away a fold of collar so kisses could extend down a throat. Demanding layers be removed so they could rub their bodies together in the exquisite friction of animal desire.

But even when he slid into her with a carnal groan and her body responded with a sensual clench, their coupling was imbued with the intense love that emanated from their pores. She petted his spine and he sucked on her earlobe, but sweet light shone behind her eyes. His voice was hoarse with joy as he moved, telling her raggedly, "I love you. We belong like this. Always. Together."

That was how they crested the final peak. Together. Shattering in unison. Destroyed, yet rebuilt with pieces of the other embedded within their souls.

EPILOGUE

"I LOVE THAT she thinks I'm you, but she's hungry, so…" Nina spoke ruefully as she handed Lakshmi, whom they all called "Lucky," to Oriel.

The six-month-old began to nuzzle and root at Oriel's cheek. Thankfully, Oriel's sister, the genius designer, had been immersing herself in their roots by studying the construction of traditional Indian clothing. She had sewn Oriel's celebratory saree and included nursing snaps in the blouse. Oriel adjusted her *pallu* and settled her squirming daughter to latch on.

"Also, I have somewhere to be."

"Oh?" Oriel was teasing her, and Nina knew it. Her sister was an open book at the best of times, but they had a wonderful ability to read each other very well.

"Don't ask me," Nina pleaded with exasperation and beckoned someone from across the marquee tent.

Oriel chuckled. "Don't worry. I don't know what Maman has planned, only that it will be spectacular."

For anyone else, the bringing together of all these people for Oriel and Vijay's wedding reception would have been enough, but Madam Estelle was determined to outdo herself and make it a memory that would be talked about for years. Nina's family were here, along with Jalil and Kiran and other treasured connections from around the globe, all dressed in a mix of Western and Indian garb.

The courses of French and Indian cuisine had been amazing, and the tribute to Lakshmi had been heart-wrenchingly sweet. The marquee was draped in silk and strings of flowers. Everywhere there were tropical plants, a wild abundance of color, and spices lending fragrance to the air. There had been speeches, a song from Estelle, and a toast from Oriel's father that would live in Oriel's heart forever.

It was already a night of pure enchantment.

"Did you need me?" Vijay asked, his warm hand descending on her shoulder.

"No, I—"

"Yes," Nina corrected her. "Sit." She nodded at the spot on the love seat that had been Vijay's for most of the evening. Nina had stolen it when he had moved to the bar with Reve.

"She's more and more like my sister every day," Vijay remarked to Oriel as he retook his seat and brushed a light greeting across their daughter's curled fist.

Nina laughed, then poked her tongue out at him before she disappeared.

"What's happening?" Vijay asked.

"I have no idea, but I suspect we'll need…"

He was already fishing into the diaper pack for the baby earmuffs. He slipped them onto Lucky's head as the lights began to swerve all over the tent, gathering everyone's attention.

A firm thump-thump sounded on a *tabla* drum. A flute and sitar strings drew people in colorful sarees from all sides of the tent.

As Madam Estelle began to sing in Hindi, the dancers settled into a precise formation on the dance floor, beginning a slow, undulating walk. They were Oriel's cousins and Nina with her sisters, and there was Kiran among them, spinning her chair and raising her arms in a graceful ballet, giving her shoulders a shimmy before clapping her hands to pick up the tempo.

Vijay's arm closed around Oriel's shoulders, and he drew her tight into his side. She felt his chest expanding with laughing emotion, but they both had tears in their eyes.

"I could not feel more loved," he told her sincerely.

"Me, either," she admitted, deeply touched that her mother would go to all this trouble to celebrate this side of her daughter's life.

The energy picked up, and the dancers moved into more of a hip-hop style until the music abruptly cut off with a group clap.

A dozen people in suits abruptly stood. They wore serious expressions as they popped their collars, then pretended to spit on their palms before they smoothed their hair back on both sides. The music resumed in plucked strings as they sidled onto the dance floor.

"Will there be a rain machine?" Vijay asked.

"Don't put it past her."

It was a dance-off between gowns and suits, full of push and pull, defiant head tosses and waved scarves, straight out of a Bollywood musical.

Dying with delight, Oriel fell into her husband. "This is too much, but I never want it to end."

"It won't," he promised her. "The credits will roll, but we'll continue to live happily ever after."

"Promise?"

"I do."

She believed him.

* * * * *

COMING SOON!

We really hope you enjoyed reading this book.
If you're looking for more romance, be sure to
head to the shops when new books are
available on

Thursday 19th August

To see which titles are coming soon, please visit
millsandboon.co.uk/nextmonth

MILLS & BOON

MILLS & BOON

THE HEART OF ROMANCE

A ROMANCE FOR EVERY READER

MODERN

Prepare to be swept off your feet by sophisticated, sexy and seductive heroes, in some of the world's most glamourous and romantic locations, where power and passion collide.

HISTORICAL

Escape with historical heroes from time gone by. Whether your passion is for wicked Regency Rakes, muscled Vikings or rugged Highlanders, and the romance of the past.

MEDICAL

Set your pulse racing with dedicated, delectable doctors in the high-pressure world of medicine, where emotions run high and passion, comfort and love are the best medicine.

True Love

Celebrate true love with tender stories of heartfelt romance, from the first rush of falling in love to the joy a new baby can bring, and a focus on the emotional heart of a relationship.

Desire

Indulge in secrets and scandal, intense drama and plenty of sizzling hot action with powerful and passionate heroes who have it all: wealth, status, good looks...everything but the right woman.

HEROES

Experience all the excitement of a gripping thriller, with an intense romance at its heart. Resourceful, true-to-life women and strong, fearless men face danger and desire - a killer combination!

To see which titles are coming soon, please visit

millsandboon.co.uk/nextmonth

MILLS & BOON

Coming next month

THE SICILIAN'S FORGOTTEN WIFE
Caitlin Crews

"I wish only to kiss my wife," Cenzo growled. "On this, the first day of the rest of our life together."

"You don't want to kiss me," she threw at him, and he thought the way she trembled now was her temper taking hold. "You want to start what you think will be my downward spiral, until all I can do is fling myself prostrate before you and cringe about at your feet. Guess what? I would rather die."

"Let us test that theory," he suggested, and kissed her.

And this time, it had nothing at all to do with punishment. Though it was no less a claiming.

This time, it was a seduction.

Pleasure and dark promise.

He took her face in his hands, and he tasted her as he wanted at last. He teased her lips until she sighed, melting against him, and opened to let him in.

He kissed her and he kissed her, until all that fury, all that need, hummed there between them. He kissed her, losing himself in the sheer wonder of her taste and the way that sweet sea scent of hers teased at him, as if she was bewitching him despite his best efforts to seize control.

Cenzo kissed her like a man drowning and she met each thrust of his tongue, then moved closer as if she was as greedy as he was.

As if she knew how much he wanted her and wanted him, too, with that very same intensity.

And there were so many things he wanted to do with her. But kissing her felt like a gift, like sheer magic, and for once in his life, Cenzo lost track of his own ulterior motives. His own grand plan.

There was only her taste. Her heat.

Her hair that he gripped in his hands, and the way she pressed against him.

There was only Josselyn. His wife.

He kissed her again and again, and then he shifted, meaning to lift her in his arms—

But she pushed away from him, enough to brace herself against his chest. He found his hands on her upper arms.

"I agreed to marry you," she managed to pant out at him, her lips faintly swollen and her brown eyes wild. "I refuse to be a pawn in your game."

"You can be any piece on the board that you like," he replied, trying to gather himself. "But it will still be my board, Josselyn."

He let her go, lifting up his hands theatrically. "By all means, little wife. Run and hide if that makes you feel more powerful."

He kept his hands in the air, his mock surrender, and laughed at her as he stepped back.

Because he'd forgotten, entirely, that they stood on those narrow stairs.

It was his own mocking laughter that stayed with him as he fell, a seeming slow-motion slide backward when his foot encountered only air. He saw her face as the world fell out from beneath him.

Continue reading
THE SICILIAN'S FORGOTTEN WIFE
Caitlin Crews

Available next month
www.millsandboon.co.uk

LET'S TALK
Romance

For exclusive extracts, competitions
and special offers, find us online: